LYCAN

THE AFFLICTED
BOOK ONE

D.L. PROHASKA

Copyright © 2023 by D.L. Prohaska
All rights reserved.

Cover Design by Prohaska Studios

DLProhaska.com

Thank you for purchasing an authorized edition. Please do not participate in or encourage piracy of copyrighted material including: reproducing, scanning, uploading, or distributing this book without permission from the author.

The Library of Congress has catalogued the hardcover edition as follows:

ISBN 978-1-962248-00-6 (hardcover)
ISBN 978-1-962248-01-3 (paperback)
ISBN 978-1-962248-02-0 (e-book)

First hardcover edition: September 2023
First paperback edition: September 2023

Printed in the United States of America

This is a work of fiction. Names, characters, places, and incidents either are the product of the author's imagination or are used fictitiously, and any resemblance to actual persons, living or dead, businesses, companies, events, or locales is entirely coincidental.

*To my father from whom
I inherited my love of monsters*

STAUNTON PRISON

JUNE, 1758

I used to count the days. Now I number my nights.

How changed my circumstances have become in a matter of moons. The waning crescent, peeking through iron bars, mocks me as I await its banishment from the sky—and my banishment from this world. How did I come to this fate? The story may be too fantastic to believe. I hardly believe it myself, yet I have lived it. As have others. Others who may still be out there. Others who may have answers. Oh Lord, how I long for answers, but I will never know.

Whatever profit there is in sharing this tale will be measured by the outcome. I leave that to better men. In any case, the hours are long. Rather than allow my mind to melt with the wax of the candle, I will write.

1

The leaves had just begun to turn; the maples hinted at the brilliance of the coming scarlet that would envelop them when I approached the Calvert estate on the evening of the 29th of September, 1757. I had traveled to Chestertown to celebrate the feast of Michaelmas. The two-day journey by carriage from Philadelphia, where my ancestral home resided, to the port town in Maryland was a pleasant one, for I always anticipated the welcoming embrace of my betrothed, and that trip was no different.

Beatrice stunned the crowd with her elegant robe of crimson damask, lace trim framing the delicate curve of her neck. Her pale blue, deep-set eyes were inviting like secret woodland pools on a hot day, at times icy, but limitless and freeing. I had been swimming in them since the moment I met her.

"Much obliged you've condescended to join us, sir." She winked and kissed my cheek. Her forward ways were a shame to her father, but as my face flushed, I felt as if she had won me all over again.

"As you are well aware, madam, I am enthralled, and so am not at liberty to decline." I took her hand and kissed it before offering my arm.

At the fire stood our good friend, the tawny, burly, properly clad trapper, Gregory. He could not contain the discomfort he felt in the formal English attire, and I laughed to myself when I thought what a spectacle he would make were he dressed in the backcountry garb he would have preferred.

"How now, Gregory? You look rather stuffed!"

"I feel it, sure enough! This waistcoat's rather restrictin'."

"You make a handsome gentleman when so inclined, sir." Mary, Beatrice's sister, strode up to our party of three and took Gregory's arm. He smiled, color rising to his cheeks.

"It is a wonder you have graced us with your presence at all. It has been, what, six months since we have been so blessed?" Beatrice asked, a twinkle of mirth in her eye.

"I apologize. I've been . . . detained. But I found my way here today. That should count for somethin', right?"

"Truly." Mary gave Gregory a knowing smile, and I fought the urge to give a questioning look at Beatrice. I had not noticed that love was brewing between them before that night. Mary directed Gregory to join her in the dining room, and Beatrice and I followed close behind.

The goose was laid out in splendor. In fact, the entire table was a treat to all eyes present. I looked forward to Cathleen's blackberry pie. The Calvert's cook had carried the recipe with her from Ireland and, as a devout catholic, many of the traditions of the holy calendar as well. Mr. Calvert was never particular about keeping religion, but the girls loved any excuse for a party and he loved any excuse to please his girls. Since the death of their mother, he had showered them with every indulgence, never questioning what it would cost him. A seat remained empty in honor of Elizabeth, and Cathleen did not neglect to acknowledge her beloved mistress by serving the empty chair to the same feast the party enjoyed.

Other friends and acquaintances had made a special stop at the Calvert estate for the banquet, and lively conversation ensued.

"Mr. Bancroft, I hear you are leaving for the Virginia colony? Another one of your attempts at self-reliance, I presume? Even so, what a loss for us. I wonder what could entice you to go, considering whom you will leave behind?" Gertrude, the plump cousin of Beatrice, was always rather liberal with her opinions as well as her plate. I looked at Beatrice, who encouraged me with a smile.

"Yes, well, I am terribly sorry if my plans disappoint. In truth, it is for the one whom I leave behind that I go to Virginia."

"And why Virginia?" Gertrude's skepticism slithered over the table in my direction.

"Land. The future lies west, madam, and I intend to make a life for myself. And my future bride." I kept from meeting Beatrice's gaze, but I could see out of the corner of my eye the blush that came to her cheeks.

"I shouldn't be surprised if Mr. Bancroft is dining here again in some months, when he has had his fill of this endeavor." Gertrude spoke aside to her neighbor as if in confidence, yet loud enough for all at the table to hear. Gertrude's amiable husband, Mr. Ainsley, gave his boisterous approval, ignoring his wife's whispers.

"Of course! I hear they are practically paying settlers to fill in the backcountry! This war threatens all the colonies and the more red-blooded Englishmen on the frontiers, the better." He had risen to the rank of officer in the royal army only a fortnight hence. It was no secret, nor was he ashamed, that the title was purchased rather than merited.

"I wonder you have not enlisted, Mr. Bancroft. A young, able-bodied man like yourself would make a fine soldier," Gertrude said before she shoveled another helping of squash into her dangling maw.

"My dear Mrs. Ainsley, you would not wish to lose my company for the backcountry, yet you admonish me for not removing myself to join the army. Which is it, madam? Would you have me stay or go?"

After wiping her mouth with the crisp, white tablecloth that draped over her lap, Mrs. Ainsley rested her plump hands near her plate and looked at me with her piercing glare. "I would have you serve your country, sir."

Mr. Ainsley shifted nervously in his seat. "Yes, well, perhaps it may be served just as well by posting himself like a fence keeping the savages at bay, as by posting himself in the army to shoot them there, my dear."

"I hardly see the comparison, my love." Mrs. Ainsley reached for her wine glass and, as if she just noticed that others were present at the table, turned her attention to Gregory, who sat across from her. The glass hovered over her plate as she resumed her interrogation.

"And what about you, Mr. Marshall? Why are you here tonight instead of training to fight the French? It seems you would prefer to barter with them for pelts."

Gregory, whom I observed had been enjoying his meal and conversation with Mary, paused a moment as if to comprehend the question presented to him. "Well, Mrs. Ainsley, ma'am, you see, my father passed away this last May and my mother's already sent three sons to battle for the crown. I'm the last in line, and it seems to me it'd better serve my country to keep my family in food and bare necessities than to leave 'em with nothin' but what my sweet old mother can knit with her gouty hands."

The glass never reached Mrs. Ainsley's lips. Instead, she set it back down, a look of begrudging resignation on her face, and kept her peace about the war for the rest of the evening. As Gertrude directed her attention elsewhere, I sighed in relief and smirked at Beatrice. Unlike Mr. Ainsley, I had no desire for glory. The thought of war, of being forced to live without and suffer the fear and anxieties of battle, not to mention the wounds, drove me to choose any endeavor that would take me as far away from the fight as possible, as long as it drew Beatrice closer. The backcountry would serve to do both.

As the table was cleared and the pie brought out for dessert, the conversation grew livelier, yet coarser by default of the steady flow of wine. Beatrice and I, huddled in the corner, listened to Gregory tell stories of near death encounters with French trappers. After one particularly gruesome account, I watched as Mrs. Ainsley grimaced and covered her face, but not before glaring at me.

"I do believe Gertrude desires a similar fate for me," I noted out of the side of my mouth to Beatrice as she recovered from Gregory's tale.

"Hush! You know that ever since Mr. Ainsley's promotion, she has become the loudest proponent of this war."

"She is so quick to send every eligible man to battle. I do hope she will not end up regretting it," I muttered as I lifted my glass in a toast to Gregory the bard while Beatrice poked me in the rib.

I remained with my love for just over a week. We spent our days meandering along the river on her father's lavish property or hosting impromptu luncheons and dinner parties. Near the end of my week, we took a carriage ride into town.

The bustling port of Chestertown was an amiable diversion at first. Merchants and tradesmen milled about, registering their goods and hawking their wares. The red brick houses and shops lined the shore, their many windows like eyes gazing out over the bay. Those eyes watched the schooners, laden with the burden of commerce, being loaded with flour, tobacco and salted pork headed for trade in the West Indies. They were witness to sloops bringing the colonies wine, salt and human chattel.

Beatrice and I stood alongside those windows, watching the auction that blighted the otherwise virtuous wharf. A small group of criminals, damned to servitude, were unloaded alongside a hogshead of Madeira wine. The auctioneer belted out the physical attributes that made each mortal a valuable commodity. Beatrice walked on, unfazed by the spectacle she had been witness to since her infancy. But I found it harder to turn away as the creatures stood, void of dignity, stripped of humanity. Another load of human goods shuffled to the auction block; this time the sickly, battered bodies of those stolen from African soil. Their chestnut skin glistened as the sun reflected off the beads of sweat and blood, the only adornment for their naked bodies.

We carried on to the horse race that promised a distraction from the sorrow spilling over the docks. I found Beatrice's company still more diverting as we spent the carriage ride discussing our future in the most modest and proper terms. But underneath the decorum of our unpresuming conversation were the hints of passion and longing that we both felt but suppressed for the sake of propriety.

All the while, Gregory had been courting Mary's favors, and the girl returned his advances with even less discretion than Beatrice had returned mine. They joined us as we found an advantageous view of the sport. I observed the two and was convinced—more than a temporary affair was afoot. I could not help but frown as I considered that a match with a trapper would be, though not impossible, less than ideal for Mary. The girl's father was a man of wealth, but his descent came from the working class of old England. He was not too proud to shun a hardworking, industrious man. However, he would require proof of the man's long-suffering and assiduity. I wondered, considering how sparse his presence had been of late, if Gregory had it in him to persevere for his prize.

Gregory, originally from Virginia but at home in just about any colony that had a wilderness nearby, was thrilling company. He was jovial, honest, and fair. He was no one's better, but he would also be bettered by no one else. His height and girth were intimidating, but his kind smile put all at ease. Mary looked like a china doll that would break at his touch, but he was always gentle when he took her arm.

At the horserace we discussed our plans for the fall, and I discovered his path led him to the Virginia colony as well. Although he hesitated at first—which surprised me considering the bond we had rekindled in our time at Chestertown—he eventually agreed to travel with me to Williamsburg. The formidable stature of my friend promised a certain level of protection that I could not muster myself. After all, I was ill-equipped for life in the wilderness, for I had spent all my time in the larger towns and cities where conveniences were readily at hand. All I had to offer was my companionship, and he assured me he would appreciate it, seeing as he had been alone for "too long." He consented on the condition that I leave with him the following day. My sweet Beatrice, patient soul, obliged to wait for me in Maryland. I was going to prepare a place for us.

"Come back to me, my love." Beatrice stood a step above me as I took leave of her.

"Is that an order? For you know I cannot disobey."

"It is a command! Though I know I must yield should a power greater than myself require else of you."

"God forbid it!" I winked, and she laughed.

I took her hand and admired the ring while she bent for a kiss. The bard's words rang true to me that day; parting from my beloved was such sweet sorrow.

Beatrice nodded toward our friends. We watched as Mary slipped a small token, wrapped in an embroidered handkerchief, into Gregory's hand as he took hers to bid adieu. He was not a born gentleman and nearly missed her hand when he leaned for the kiss, too enraptured was he in her visage. My darling and I could not help but share in the mirth as we beheld the awkward lovers bid farewell. Beatrice waved with all the enthusiasm that befit her station as our wagon, loaded with furs and hopes of future and fortune, rumbled away.

The dirt road was littered with muddy ruts and protruding

roots, but Gregory navigated his cart as if the path was laid with brick. We passed empty fields that once boasted stalks of wheat which had since been scythed into sheaves. In some places, shocks remained on the field, waiting for their time of threshing. A thriving grist mill stood on the banks of a creek and a recent rainfall threatened to overflow the sluice gate. I could hear the grinding of the millstones even over the rushing water. The October air was fresh and crisp, and the leaves began to put on their golden death shroud.

I had the world before me and all its splendor, and I was happy.

"Do you remember the day we met?" I asked Gregory, as the sight of a scarecrow reminded me of the fateful day five years prior. He began laughing when he noticed it as well.

"I'll never forget the look on your face and the way you threw your hat on the ground at my feet!" He roared.

"You nearly shot me!"

"I was off by a mile! In fact, I'm ashamed to admit I had such bad aim then."

"A mile! I would venture to guess it was an inch, at most."

"Well, in any case, don't go standin' around in corn fields lookin' like a scarecrow, and no one will use you for target practice." We both laughed, though on the day of our meeting I nearly soiled myself, and Gregory, not quite a man yet, thought he was about to hang for almost killing a gentleman. To show him I bore no hard feelings, I invited him to join me on my visit to the Calvert's plantation. I had made Mr. Calvert's acquaintance in Philadelphia while he was there on business, and he offered his hospitality should I ever be in Chestertown. I was on my way to take him up on the offer, having yet to meet his charming daughters. Neither of us could have foreseen the friendship and fraternity which that chance meeting would afford us.

It was a friendship that had saved me, more than once, from my foolishness. For I had not the worldly wisdom that Gregory seemed to possess instinctually, and in my attempt to discover what life I truly desired to lead, Gregory was there to pull me out of dangerous paths that were indiscernible to me. Perhaps if Mrs. Ainsley had known what Gregory had done for me, she would have shown him more respect. Certainly more than she ever showed me.

Shortly after our musings, we arrived at the docks of the Rock Hall Ferry that would take us across the Chesapeake Bay to Annapolis. The flat, rectangular boat, with just enough room for a wagon, horse and two men, was ferried by a man Gregory knew well from his frequent visits to the Chestertown tavern. I was not much of a traveler and spent very little time conversing with those outside my station. But Gregory was more at home with a ferryman than a room full of gentlemen. I envied his ease. While I worried about the water sloshing onto my boots, Gregory rolled up his sleeves and took a pole, assisting the ferryman in his task.

"How's the fur business these days?" The ferryman looked over the wagon piled with pelts.

"Trappin' ain't a problem, but tradin' is gettin' to be. Those French bastards were the only thing in the way of makin' a name for myself. They called me 'coureur de bois,' whatever that means, and threatened to confiscate my pelts. Say the land is theirs, but it ain't. King claimed all the land as far west as it goes, so I had every right to trap in the lakes. The Injun federation's on our side too, though some tribes up north'll only trade with those French dogs." Gregory took his frustration out on a log that barred the way of our crossing, heaving it to the side with his pole. "I traded most of what I had in Albany. What I got here is all the fortune I have in the world, and I'm takin' it south to see what I can do with it there. Might just finish the fur business altogether once I find another viable trade. I bought a hogshead of coffee beans a while back and couldn't barely give 'em away. Thought for sure coffee could rival tea, but I guess it didn't catch. I like it though. It's got a kick to it, right?"

I agreed. Coffee did have a rather potent appeal, and I understood how the rough and sturdy tradesman preferred the black pungency in a tin bowl to pale tea in a delicate porcelain cup.

We spent the night at a tavern near the harbor and made merry with other travelers present. After a late bed and an early rise that left my brain addled, we made our way to the dock to board a merchant vessel for the next leg of our journey. Our intention had been to take the ship south on the bay to Williamsburg, and all would have gone according to plan but for the lack of a suitable ship that could carry our wagon. What they offered was a tobacco boat. It could hold ourselves and the furs, but Gregory insisted we transport the wagon to Williamsburg, no exceptions. Our choice was to wait for another ship or start out on the road. There was increased risk from native attacks, which gave me some apprehension, yet Gregory repeated that we must make Williamsburg by the next Lord's Day. I wondered at the urgency, for I saw no reason that a few days' time would hinder my friend's plans, but his countenance proved to me he would not yield. Waiting on another ship was impossible.

We made ready to leave as soon as we acquired a second horse. One steed could only pull the farm wagon for short distances. The road we were forced upon would require two. Gregory attempted to bargain, but settled for an overpriced palfrey. The trade seemed rather prohibitive to me, but I was not as accustomed to barter as Gregory was. For a moment, I considered returning to Chestertown and putting off my venture for another time. Something foreboding brewed in my gut, and I felt as though this slight inconvenience was an omen of worse troubles in our future. How I wish I had listened to that premonition! Instead, I was duty bound to remain with my friend, come what may. After all, I had persuaded him to make the journey together.

For three days, we traveled on the King's Highway without incident. Gregory was rather fond of ale houses, of this I well knew, and each conversation began something like "While having a drink at the Inn at Hartford," or "I can't be sure I remember right, since I'd imbibed a pint or two with fellows in New York," and the like. Yet no matter the road we passed that promised victuals and spirits, Gregory adamantly refused respite from our travels, reminding me of his Lord's Day appointment with Williamsburg.

"Surely no business is conducted on the Lord's Day. Why the haste to arrive on a day of rest for your fellow tradesmen?" I was weary already and longed to sleep in a bed rather than on the hard ground. Gregory bristled at my inquiry and may have lapsed into a fit of anger, but corrected himself and took a deep breath before responding.

"Mysterious, right," he said with a smirk. "Have an appointment to keep, and I'll not be late for it. I'd like to have you in my confidence, but it's between the Lord and I." At this he crossed himself, to my surprise, for I knew he was not a papist.

His response satisfied me. After all, I only saw Gregory at random times throughout the year, the fur trade taking him on long expeditions into the wilds of the Great Lakes and its surroundings. A man of his virile nature may have sins to atone for that did not concern me. Considering his ardent fondness for Mary, I concluded he may be wiping his slate clean, so to speak. Only, there were plenty of churches in Maryland. In any case, I was determined to drop the matter and aid my friend, as far as it depended on me, to our destination on time, even if that meant sleeping in the woods.

The evening of the aforementioned conversation brought about a rather pleasing diversion, for myself at least, as we made acquaintance with other travelers headed in the same direction. They had camped on the road, just as we ourselves prepared to do, and as they were rather congenial souls, we decided to continue on our way together. Gregory made certain our new friends were destined for Williamsburg, or thereabouts, within his timeline and, as they seemed eager to reach civilization as well, no one objected.

I felt safer still with greater numbers in our train; four additional healthy men and two ladies, well worn by travel, but amiable and well bred. In one carriage rode the two couples: Mr. and Mrs. Moore and Mr. and Mrs. Wright. Theirs was a lifelong friendship, as both couples hailed from the same small settlement in Maryland. The newlyweds meant to start their lives together, taking advantage of the same promise the west made to me. Thus, we bonded over our shared dreams of life at the foot of the great mountains.

The pair of men, bound for Norfolk, had joined the newlyweds the day before. They were less inclined to be hasty in their travels and seemed to hint at taking their leave whenever it pleased them. Jeb and Amos were their names and, while friendly, were less verbose compared to the happy couples. Our small caravan traveled another three days and nights together, uneventful but for one conversation which means more to me now than it did when I first experienced it.

It took place on the third evening we spent with our companions, when a challenge was made by the young and giddy Mrs. Wright for all to share a ghost story round the campfire. The ladies began, at the insistence of their husbands, with the story of a specter with whom they were acquainted, who lived in an abandoned cottage on the outskirts of their small village. Mrs. Moore pulled out a lace shawl and danced around the fire as she imagined the ghost would, adding a visual component to the narration. The story was amusing, though rather silly, and the ladies laughed like schoolgirls as they told it until Mr. Moore, a clear pedant as I assessed him from prior conversations, divulged the scientific explanations for the specter, the story losing all of its ghostliness and the ladies spirits dulled. Jeb, quiet but observant, interrupted Mr. Moore upon his conclusive proof and began the story that I will attempt to relate verbatim.

"I seen me a wolf-man once." Mr. Moore feigned annoyance

at being interrupted, but yielded when he noticed the party's attention turned to the formerly mute companion. Gregory got up and excused himself. I asked if he was well, for his face had a sickly pale to it, but he assured me he was overtired from our travels and could benefit from turning in early. We all wished him goodnight and restored our attention to Jeb. It seemed a full minute passed before he elaborated on his exclamation.

"I done some long-huntin' in Injun territory. Amos here was with me then too, though he can't attest to my story as he didn't see nothin' himself. But he can attest that I ain't one to lie, unless it's to get me outta the stocks, and this here tale would sure put me in 'em. So I got nothin' to gain by it." His arguments as to the validity of his tale were convincing enough to all gathered round that open air hearth, as evinced by heads nodding of their own volition, encouraging the speaker to continue in his truth.

"I took me to a spring we was campin' near on a night when the moon was full. Moonlight can feel like daylight a'times; when it bounces off water 'specially. I meant to bathe in the company o'myself and that full moon, and no offense to the ladies present, I got as clothed as Adam in the garden and dove in. Water was a fresher'n bath than I had in a long time. But I had no time to relax afore I heard a rustle in the bushes. This weren't too large a spring to see clearly, 'specially in that full moonlight. If things weren't hid in the shadows, they was clear as day. I 'spect the creature ran full to the bank o'that spring as he was heaving out of breath when he bent to cup water in his hands. I say hands, but for I don't know what else to call 'em. They was paw-like, but each toe longer than any dogs toe I ever seen. And the way he held 'em, scooping the water, twas uncanny, like a man. Full snout like a wolf and pointy ears, but the way his head sat on his neck, 'twas not like no wolf I yet seen nor since. He was standing on his back legs, bent like a dog's, but spindly like a man. And mangey lookin' too, like his skin was sick and his fur rubbed off in spots. He took another handful o'spring afore he caught sight of me. Got back on his four legs, hackles raised, and snarled. Looked ready to dive in after me. I don't go nowhere without my rifle, not with Injuns huntin' for scalps. I was closer to that gun than the beast was to me, and I tell you, he looked at it and knew it too. He backed into the shadows and alls I heard was some rustlin' and then a low howl a far ways off. Waited in that spring till dawn, not chancin' nothin'."

A moment passed before we realized the story was over. All remained silent as our minds left the spring and the wolf-man Jeb encountered there. Amos finally spoke.

"I told Jeb was just a sick bear. Seen one afore; wasn't worth the shot was so scrawny and the fur in patches, like Jeb says."

"That reminds me of a rabid coon I had to shoot on our farm. You know, rabid animals exhibit aggressive behaviors . . ." Mr. Moore continued to educate the crowd on rabies. I, sitting closest to Jeb, was the only one to hear him sigh with conviction.

"Tweren't no bear."

2

The morning after our ghost tales, we hit a literal bump in the road. Traveling over a rocky stretch did not bode well for our wagon and one wheel broke loose, leaving us stranded in the wilderness. Our new friends were obliging and offered to remain with us until we settled upon how to proceed. Though Mr. Moore was ready with a slew of suggestions, our options were few. The heavy load of furs and skins could not be carried by merely one horse, which left us both walking aside our beasts for the remainder of our journey. This was unacceptable, as Gregory again insisted he must have his wagon. We could wait until our companions, graciously offering to obtain the supplies needed for our repairs, returned. Gregory quickly declined the offer. He must be in Williamsburg; there was no time to wait. The consternation this dilemma brought to my friend was immense. He brooded and paced, asking himself repeatedly "what to do," and even now and then striking himself on the head, apparently trying to beat forth the answer.

Our companions, who were themselves eager to resume their journey, did not miss his heightened agitations. Provisions were running low all around, and it was less than desirable to barter with natives when their loyalties may lie with the enemy.

Gregory stopped short in his pacing, stood tall while fixing his coat, and walked toward our small group of onlookers with his usual wide smile and hearty resolve.

"I've got it now, sure enough. Just had to mull it over a bit. I do believe I forgot where I was for a minute there! I'm well acquainted with some long hunters who've got a stop hereabouts where they store goods on their way out west. I believe I can locate it and feel almost certain it will have what I need to get this wagon rolling again!"

"Wonderful news, Gregory! We will wait here with your wagon while you seek out this post," said the obliging Mrs. Wright.

A flash of anger, ever so slight, crossed Gregory's countenance, but he quickly recovered. I must have been the only one to notice, as our companions did not flinch as they awaited his answer.

"No, thank you, ma'am! I would have you and . . . all my friends here carry on without me. I know these woods, sure as day, and have had dealin's with these Injuns enough to know they won't hinder me. It'd make me happy knowing you all will be sleepin' in real beds sooner than later!"

The parties seemed rather relieved at hearing this and did not insist on their offer to wait any longer. The ladies turned off to collect their belongings from our makeshift camp when Gregory drew me and Amos aside.

"I'd be much obliged to you, Amos, if you could take my friend here to Williamsburg. He would be safer with folk such as yourselves than traipsing through these woods with me."

Amos assented. He would be honored to have me join him, but I declined to be offered up in that manner.

"I appreciate your concern, my good friend, but I wish to remain with you and finish out our journey together."

It was apparent to me that Gregory was distressed. I worried that his fretful frame of mind would be a hindrance in obtaining the help he sought. And it was not in his character to pass his charge off to a stranger. There must have been something behind his agitations that I meant to uncover; at the very least, provide succor for. Gregory appeared to think on the prospect of me remaining with him, but looking at the determination in my eyes, gave up his idea and acquiesced with a simple nod of his head.

We watched the caravan proceed without us and, as the sun was hovering near its zenith, we determined to carry out our plan immediately so as not to be lost in the woods as night fell. After pushing the wagon off the road and into a natural alcove where it would not be noticed by the casual passerby, we turned west and began our digression on horseback. Gregory led the way through brush and bramble. There was no beaten path to follow, but only the position of the sun and Gregory's knowledge of this forest that to my untrained eye looked rather like all the same trees multiplied and placed sporadically through the landscape before us.

Gregory spoke little. He was not his jovial self and sat rather apprehensively on his horse. Soon I came to realize why.

Out of a crowd of tight-knit trees, I saw three natives, fully frocked in what I assumed to be their hunting garb, emerge. They approached warily, and I could not help but notice the strange way they honed their sights on Gregory, while seeming to ignore my horse and me completely. They would not draw near but remained where, I gathered, they could retreat if the need arose. I watched the interaction between these men and Gregory with great interest. I have seen natives converse with white men before and found their stature and demeanor to be noble and self composed. They stood erect and firm, clearly prepared to fight, but not supposing the need to assume a posture for battle. These natives, on the other hand, held their bodies in an attitude of defense. They kept their legs apart, hands at the ready to grasp the bow or tomahawk fastened at their backs, and their eyes would not leave Gregory's, though my horse cantered in fright. The encounter was surreal. No words were spoken. Gregory was the first to break the standoff by clicking his tongue and directing his horse to move on. The natives retreated into the forest, refraining from turning their backs on us, or their eyes off Gregory.

"They followed us quite a way there. I wondered when they would show their faces." Gregory said, once again in his casual and disarming manner. But I saw the corner of his mouth twitch as he spoke.

We arrived at the outpost soon after this encounter and found the proper tools and supplies needed to repair the wagon. Gregory's spirits lightened considerably, and he spoke in his congenial manner on our return ride to the road where we had left our belongings. As he instinctively forged our path, I was again in wonder at the skill with which he could navigate the wood. If left to fate, I would have been lost twice over.

We repaired the wagon, this taking much of the rest of our evening, and found that it would not be prudent to break camp and move on with dark swiftly approaching and the road being fairly overgrown with arching trees. We made our fire and remained for the night.

The trouble with our wagon only began the string of interruptions which now plagued our journey. It rained excessively most days; the nights becoming almost bitter cold, such was the pattern of weather that October. I made an observation to Gregory about how dreary and blustery had been the past several weeks. His response was a distracted grunt. With each new trial, my friend became more sullen. I rarely experienced the energetic companion I had departed with.

We continued along the King's Highway, which was kept by the individual towns and counties it passed through. The further south we traveled, the poorer the road became. The rain resulted in the flooding of creeks and lowland areas, such that we were forced to ford a stream Gregory had assumed would be nearly dry. No bridges had yet been erected. The distance was short and our wagon was sturdy, so we were able to cross to our satisfaction, however the delay, along with countless others, cost us precious time. Neither of us was comfortable traveling by night, though the waxing moon enabled us to see well in the clearer places of the wood. At the pace we were going, we would just make Williamsburg by Lord's Day.

The day after our passage across the stream, we were waylaid by a pair of men seeking aid. They claimed to be having trouble with their carriage and sought assistance with one of the wheels. Gregory pulled me aside while still keeping himself between the vagrants and his livelihood.

"They don't need our help, you can be sure. These men are thieves and they mean to rob me." He continued to smile at the men as he spoke. I fought the temptation to look back at the strangers, or to express my surprise, but instead reached into a bag affixed to the side of our wagon as if I was searching for a tool with which to help the poor travelers. "How can you be certain?" I asked under my breath. Gregory pushed me aside and commenced to rummage through the bag himself as he answered.

"Mrs. Moore's lace shawl is hangin' in the window there. And I can see other items I remember from their carriage. Oh, no doubt they stopped, trying to do someone a bit o'good, and were taken out by these thieves. I need you to do as I say, and we can be on our way soon enough."

"Of course," I answered. My heart throbbed as I imagined the poor couple's fate. It would have been my own had I not been with Gregory, for I never would have noticed the shawl. I was wary to think I could do anything to aid my friend against two large and presumably armed villains.

"Go back over and tell 'em we have a tool in the wagon, but we gotta pull it around closer so's not to have to carry it far." The direction was simple enough, and I approached the men with as much confidence and apathy as I could muster. They seemed obliging enough and leaned against the carriage, enjoying something hot in their cups. Gregory checked the hitch and climbed into the driver's seat, clicking the horses on. At first the wagon moved toward the broken down carriage, but I watched in dismay as Gregory pulled hard on the reins and sped off down the road.

He looked back at me, and his eyes said run! I stood frozen for a time, dumbstruck that my friend would leave me vulnerable before these villains, but my feet soon hastened to obey and took off toward the fleeing vehicle. I was no athlete, and the villain, who was apparently prepared for deception, was upon me before I could make it to the road. Before he was within reach, he tossed the scalding contents of his cup at the back of my head. Instinct made me stop and clutch my neck, giving my attacker's accomplice time to disable me with the butt of his gun. I was aware long enough to see Gregory stop the wagon, pull out his hunting rifle, and take aim at my attacker before I lost consciousness.

I awoke to Gregory shouting and a gunshot. I was unable to sit up or look around and could only pray that the shot did not dispatch my companion. All was soon silent. I could sense a body lying next to mine and, with great pains, I turned my head to see the open, lifeless eyes of my attacker.

I reached for my scalp and felt the sticky blood produced from my wound. As I attempted to rise, my heart pumped faster and the flow of pressure and pain was more than I could bear, so I remained prostrate. I would not allow myself to drift off again. I knew I had not lost consciousness for long and my eyes were heavy with sleep, but my survival depended on maintaining my wits.

I laid for what felt like hours, and in reality may have been mere minutes, before I heard footsteps approaching. They were not threatening steps. They sounded cautious and apprehensive. I remained still, hoping to appear dead should it be the other thief who came to claim the spoils. Suddenly, a man dropped to his knees by my head and held a handkerchief hard at my temple.

"Oh, Fenn! What have I done? Tell me you aren't hurt too bad and all." Hearing Gregory's voice gave me courage, and I opened my eyes and attempted to rise. I was dizzy at first, but I felt I could at least stand and perhaps make it to the wagon to sit and gain my bearings. Gregory pulled me to my feet and, as if sensing my desire, helped me sit with my back against a tree while he retrieved our vehicle. From its contents, he produced some spirits in a flask to revive me.

"I chased the other one, but he sure could run. I lost him, I'm sorry to say. Don't like to think he might come back to avenge his friend. I'll have to search the carriage for guns and such." Gregory lost no time and descended upon the property. My head throbbed, and I felt I could lose consciousness at any moment. I kept myself still while Gregory loaded our wagon with a fowling piece, two pistols, and the rifle my assailant had grabbed before Gregory's sharp shooting brought him down. He tied their horse to follow our wagon, preventing the survivor's ability to overtake us should he, in fact, seek revenge. I was in no condition to travel erect, so Gregory fitted out a bed for me. It was then I realized the pile of furs was not all that made up the bulk of our cargo. Underneath was an iron cage affixed to the inside of the wagon with bolts. I could feel the cold metal through the thin fabric of my shirt as it peeked through places where the furs had been rearranged. The front of the cage had a lock; the key attached to a chain. I wondered why the furs were not kept inside, why the cage was apparently kept hidden, and why the key was attached if the assumed purpose was to keep valuables out of the hands of villains? I pondered these things for a moment as the wagon rambled along the road before I finally allowed myself to sleep with abandon.

A jolt awakened me as we halted. Though it was dusk and my head was cloudy, I could see Gregory was frantic as he looked in all directions. I attempted to sit up, but as I did, my wound smarted and I fell back in repose. I felt my scalp and could perceive that a scab had formed and the blood, that had been wet and sticky when first it flowed, was now hard and caked onto the side of my face and neck. The chill of night overtook me, and I shivered, attempting again to rise, this time successfully. Once my vision cleared from the grogginess of sleep, I looked around to see that there was no perceivable road. Trees, bush, and undergrowth seemed to choke us on all sides. I wondered how Gregory had maneuvered the wagon and why we had left the road to begin with. Gregory noticed I had come to myself and, as if he could hear my thoughts, he answered them:

"I would have bet my hide this was a shortcut. I thought I knew these woods, but they look to me now like an alien land and I feel as if I'm dreaming."

"It is alright, Gregory. What if we turn around and head back the way we came? Surely we will find the road again soon enough."

Gregory's countenance suddenly changed, and the confusion and panic gave way to rage.

"It's too late! Don't you understand? All's lost if I don't make it to Williamsburg before night!"

I was apprehensive about suggesting anything to remediate the situation. Gregory seemed beyond his wits, and I feared what he might do if pushed any further. However, I thought it was an undue panic on his part when it must only be Saturday, and surely we were close enough to Williamsburg to arrive by Sunday morning. I ventured to say so. Gregory's eyes flamed. He bared his teeth at me and raised his hand as if to strike. It is frightful and amazing to see what man is capable of, and I believe Gregory's good nature and love for me were all that kept him from smiting me that very instant. He appeared to come to himself again and swallowed back his fury. He took a breath, not overly deep, but it was enough to settle him before he spoke again, this time controlled and with more civility.

"The Lord's Day's past. There's no hope." The sun was no longer visible on the horizon and, but for the coronal glow and a diminishing red lining in the clouds, the sky was swiftly passing to night. Gregory started at the natural order of the heavens and reverted to panic. "Get up! You must get up! Surely you can. You've been asleep for two days!"

Two days! I could not imagine I had been dumb to the world for so many hours. And my companion had only his thoughts to keep him company on a lonely road.

I attempted to appease Gregory's nerves, though I knew not why I must depart from the wagon. As I carefully and haltingly made my way off of my bed of furs and out of the wagon, Gregory quickly unloaded our supplies to make camp. The moon was rising and, as it appeared to be full, I felt such haste was unnecessary; it would supply enough light even in this dense wood to manage our way with a tent and fire. Prior experience prohibited me from making any suggestions to my companion, no matter how helpful, in his duress, and so I silently did what I could to aid him.

I made the campfire while Gregory pitched the tent. He lined it with furs, leaving only one or two, presumably as a cover for the cage he had not wanted me to learn of. I noticed he had stealthily opened the door and kept the key in the lock as if at the ready. This confused me ever more, as I assumed the cage was meant for the furs. But if they were in the tent, they were not handy. What could it all mean?

Gregory looked about him—at the tent, the fire, the wagon—and finally sighed with as much relief as he could muster. He was still apprehensive. The furrow in his brow was deep and his eyes reminded me of a dog who has been startled by the shout of his master. I found a flask and helped myself to a draught of spirits, hoping they would ease my own rattled nerves. Finally, Gregory took a seat across from me by the fire, looking up at the moon, muttering to himself. He looked back and jumped as if startled to remember he was not alone, as he had clearly wanted to be. He took out his handkerchief and wiped his forehead.

"You must think me a crazy fool." He chuckled, though with no mirth. "I don't rightly know what's become of me." His eyes seemed to focus on me clearly, as if until then they had been clouded over, and I thought I could see tears brimming, waiting to fall. "Please, forgive me! I . . . I shouldn't've taken off like that! Don't know why I thought you could catch up, but I didn't know what else to do." He wiped his cheek and sniffed, adding another log to the fire.

"I know how ardently you wished to arrive in Williamsburg on time, and I am sorry if I was the cause of our delay." Surely that was why Gregory had wanted to travel alone in the first place, and I had been nothing but dead weight. He waved me off.

"It couldn't be helped."

We sat in silence for some time. Occasionally, Gregory looked at the sky in apprehension. His knee bounced and his hand shook while holding a cup of coffee. He looked as if he was waiting for something. The night grew achingly colder and my teeth chattered. The fire was dwindling, and I felt the warm embrace of sleep beckoning me to bed. I rose and took my leave of Gregory, at which a sense of relief came over his countenance, and I perceived it was my lack of presence that he wanted. I would not miss the hint this time, and removed myself without another word.

I had imbibed in more spirits than was my habit and felt the heaviness of head that came with intoxication. I was easily lulled into a deep slumber that would have happily consumed me till morning had it not been for the howl of a wolf and its sharp, piercing fangs.

It was the howl that forced my eyes to open. The sound was but an arm's length away through the thin layer of canvas that acted as my shelter. I told myself to remain still, though my muscles spasmed with the desire to rise and run. Gregory was nowhere to be seen from my vantage point, and I hoped it meant that he was standing guard, his gun at the ready. I heard a clanking sound, like a chain being pulled through a grate, and then a growl I had never heard before. It began low, and then rose with a pitch that sounded almost human, like a man screaming with a guttural gurgle in his throat. I had heard stories of catamounts who shrieked like a woman and coyote cackles that reminded one of children's laughter, so I took the noise to be the sound of some sort of predator, perhaps one who had found its prey.

The wolf outside my tent whimpered as the growl began again, and this time I sensed a creature stalking beside me, only the piece of cloth between us. Then, the animal leaped at the wolf. I heard a squeal and scrambling feet as the wolf fled into the woods before silence reigned once more. I held my breath to avoid signaling the animal to my presence. The creature moved to the entrance of the tent and, in the dubitable glow of the moonlight, I could not tell if it was a wolf or a bear or a lion, but I could hear its hissing breath and felt its rage radiating like hot coals in an oven. One clawed hand reached in and pulled the fabric aside as the shadowed form of the creature stood in the curve of the moon. In an instant it was on top of me, and I felt its fangs sink into my shoulder, so close to my throat that I believe if it had shifted its weight it would have torn into the vein in my neck. I heard a gunshot, and the monster, so I believed it must have been, shrieked. I felt a slash in my side as if the talons of an eagle tore into my ribs, and then the creature was gone. The shock of the attack and my wasted nerves clouded my head until all went black, and I was awoken again by a cry, this time from a man.

All was silent for some time before I ventured out of the tent. My shoulder was bleeding steadily, and I staunched the wound with a rag I tore from my shirt. My belt lay beside me, and I wrapped it tightly around the rag and under my armpit, hoping to stop the flood of life that ebbed from me. The gash on my side flapped open when I stood, and the shock of the sight and the pain forced me to vomit. The violence of that action caused more blood to gush, so that I stumbled, almost losing consciousness. I was able to crawl out and in the moonlight could see a man lying lifeless near the wagon, his rifle by his side. I could not be sure if the man was Gregory, and before I could check if he was deceased, the loss of my blood proved fatal and I felt myself let go of life, drifting into eternity.

Oh, how I wish I had seen heaven that night and passed through St. Peter's gate to my eternal reward! Instead, to my great surprise, I awoke with the dawn.

3

The body was not Gregory.

    I struggled to even look upon it at first. The mangled corpse was far from the neatly presented bodies of the dead I had witnessed. I would have avoided the scene altogether if his identity had been apparent. But as I could not know for sure who the body belonged to, I had to approach it; doing so with all trepidation, holding my breath, until I was sure it was not my friend.

    The face was unrecognizable as the fiend had mutilated its victim before retreating into the night. Still, I knew enough of Gregory's apparel and stature to know that the man lying before me was not him. I recognized the gun he held as one that we had confiscated from the villains who attempted to rob us, and I assumed, therefore, the man had followed us bent on revenge, however in vain. The horses were missing, and I surmised they fled and likely became fodder for the wolves I had heard the night before. But I could not know for sure what creature was responsible for the carnage I surveyed that morning. What should have been the bodies of two men left a bloody scene for any passerby to behold. Fortunately, or unfortunately as it may be, Gregory had brought us far from any road and no one but the wild men of the woods could chance upon the scene and charge me as the villain.

I took stock of my injuries and found that the wound in my shoulder and the gash across my side were both already mending, having closed and scabbed over completely. Though a pool of blood surrounded where I had collapsed, I felt refreshed, as if I had rested for weeks. I knew I had not slept long, for the man's body was not yet rigid or bloated, as I had seen the bodies of wild animals become while decomposing. Once I realized I was no longer in mortal danger from my wounds or from any enemy, man or beast, I commenced to search for Gregory.

A trail of blood ran from the tent to the body of the man, and then on into the thick underbrush of the dense wood. I assumed this blood issued from the injured beast who attacked me, as I remembered the gunshot and the recoiling of the monster which resulted in the gash in my side. The creature must have turned on the man with the gun and dispatched him before retreating. Perhaps Gregory had hunted it down and was somewhere in this vast wood dressing his prize. I had every reason to be terrified into a stupor, yet I called out for my friend and followed the blood trail as far as it would take me.

I faced much difficulty with this attempt, as the terrain was not what I was accustomed to. There were portions of the wood where the trees seemed to grow on top of each other. I met with fallen logs the width of several men, and what to me was a great deal of struggle to overtake seemed but a leap for the creature as the blood trail continued over and under and through.

Finally, I came to a bog that extended from a swampy part of a creek. I lost the trail in the bog and, so that I would not also become lost, I gave up my search and returned in the direction I had come. Just then, I noticed something white caught in a thicket. I snatched it up to discover it was a ladies' handkerchief, no doubt the one which held the token pressed into Gregory's hand by Mary. So Gregory had pursued the beast!

I yelled his name and stood silent, waiting for a reply, but heard nothing. Not even the humblest creatures of the wood returned my call. Gregory! Where was Gregory? I feared that he, unable to see the danger before entering it, succumbed to the bog's entrapment. I tucked the cloth into the only pocket that had not been torn and commenced to return to the wagon, following the trail of blood once more.

Whatever creature could sustain the loss of so much of its vital fluid and continue across such terrain must have been a terrible one indeed. This thought occurred to me, and I wondered what had possessed me to pursue the trail with no protection apart from my bare hands. I prayed God would watch over my journey back to the wagon and thanked Him I had not met with the mark I pursued.

I returned to the camp after much exertion and found the grisly scene undisturbed. The body lay exposed to the elements, and I worried it would draw the attention of the wolves, or worse still, the creature that had attacked me. I swallowed back my revulsion of the deed that must be done and set to work to give the man a Christian burial, though I knew not whether he warranted one. Without proper tools, I could only scrape up a shallow grave for the victim and resorted to leaf litter and rocks to top it off.

What a shame it would be to abandon the furs to decay, especially if by miracle Gregory should be alive and return for them, so I remained with the wagon for as long as my victuals would allow. I was out of practice as a hunter, yet I had no other choice but to try my hand at acquiring some fresh meat to add to the store of grains and coffee that made up my pantry. It was not the season for berries, but I came by some nuts that I roasted along with the rabbit meat that I was fortunate enough to get with the help of the fowling piece.

I managed three nights alone in the woods, though I could not sleep deeply for fear that the creature would return to finish the work it had begun. Two guns remained loaded by my side and I kept the fire blazing each night to deter the wolves. All hope I had that Gregory would return vanished, and I resolved to prepare myself to find civilization in whatever way possible.

By providence, I discovered one horse grazing in a small clearing while I hunted for rabbits, and I was able to coax it to return to me. To my delight, the lead rope remained around its neck, which was fortunate, for when we came upon the campsite where so much violence had occurred, the horse reared and attempted to flee. Keeping hold with all my strength, knowing that this poor beast was my best hope of returning to the land of men, I hushed him and petted him into a calm resignation, and he was soon bridled and hitched. After breaking camp, I began to load the wagon with the furs and supplies when I noticed the door to the cage was open and the key was broken from its chain. I could not account for how this occurred other than to conclude that Gregory had taken refuge in the cage before pursuing the beast. I fastened the door, locked it, and dropped the key into a saddlebag. The goods loaded, I departed the lonely graveyard.

Though I could not decipher one path as favorable over another, somehow I knew which way I ought to direct the horse. Before nightfall, I arrived at a road that I felt sure must lead into Williamsburg, and so I turned my wagon southeast and followed the path. I understood now that Gregory had attempted to bypass a wide loop that went around the marshlands, hoping to save us half a day's ride. As night was approaching quickly, I rode as long as I could. I slept that night with my gun at my side on the pile of furs in the wagon. Not a soul passed my way for the rest of my journey to Williamsburg.

The rain and bitter cold elapsed and my last day's ride was mild, the blue sky and autumn sunshine a stark contrast to the dreariness of my mind as I mulled over the events that had robbed me of my companion. The lonely road was a persistent reminder of my loss. I vacillated between hopeful confidence in Gregory's talents and the dreadful fear that he had succumbed to an attack no less violent than mine. The agitation these conflicting emotions caused me left my nerves raw to every shadow, and I jumped at every strange sound. What would I do without Gregory? He was not just my guide and companion; he was my dear friend. I felt the weight of his absence as I sat heavily on the wagon seat.

I arrived in Williamsburg on the 29th of October, a bustling Saturday. The capitol was a veritable hive of activity. Before I even stepped foot on the principal thoroughfare of Duke of Gloucester Street, I noticed the poor black workers toiling about hither and thither under the direction of task masters. Houses and shops were being built by black carpenters in the surrounding landscape of the town center. I recoiled at the sight of so much human bondage, unaccustomed as I was to the prevalence of slave labor in the southern colonies. I remembered the auction in Chestertown only weeks before and wondered if any of these poor souls were among those sold that day. The northern colonies had their share in the atrocity, yet a maid or servant here or there could not prepare me for the shock of hundreds laboring away in service of the fairer flesh.

I walked Gloucester Street toward the new Capitol building, replacing the first, which had burned in '47, and passed the market square where temporary booths were erected offering goods produced all over the colony. I tipped my hat to a lady who passed by carrying a basket over her arm. A slight scowl crossed her mouth as she neglected to return my gesture. I looked down at the ragged attire I had put together after my old suit had been torn and stained with blood. Compared to the well-dressed gentry of Virginia on market day, I was certainly a sight to behold! I slipped into an ordinary and inquired about a vacancy. The man working at the bar would not meet my eye but assured me it was fortunate I had found any lodging at all, what with the House of Burgesses in session and the politicians swarming.

"Thank you. One thing more. Can you direct me to where the mail is posted?" I asked, before finding my room.

"Yes, sir. The post runs through here, sir."

"Very good. Are there any letters for me?" The man seemed put out by my added inquiry, but obligated to serve.

"Mr. Bancroft, you said?" I nodded. "I will check for you, sir."

"Thank you."

As I waited, I glanced around and noticed the men loitering about the tavern in their expensive silk waistcoats, white powdered wigs, and neatly tied cravats, likely debating the points of policy they wished to advocate when they returned to the floor of the House. Once again, I was reminded of my haggard appearance and looked forward to completing my toilette and beating the dust out of my travel worn suit.

"Here is a letter for you, sir."

The man handed me the paper, and by the seal I knew it to be from Beatrice. It afforded me my first taste of happiness in days as I hid away the letter from my beloved to read later.

Thankfully, it was not too late in the day to inquire about town if there was any knowledge of Gregory or what had become of him. I asked at every ordinary and all the shops that I could find, but none knew a man of his description. One shopkeeper remembered him from prior trades but had not seen him in several months.

Finally, I inquired at a tavern that sat on the farthest end of town from where I had begun my search and met with the same answer. I seemed to be beyond recourse when I remembered Gregory had been anxious to arrive on the Lord's Day for what I presumed to be a meeting with a minister. How foolish I had been not to ask at places of worship as well! I turned back to the bar-keep, asking if he knew of any ministers likely to take an interest in helping a man like Gregory. He directed me to try my luck at Bruton Parish Church, which, fortunately, was located just across the street. If my friend meant to meet with a reverend, it would likely be there, the man said. Again, I was disappointed as they did not know him at the church either.

I wondered if my task was impossible as I returned to the tavern and sat at the bar, hovered over a pint of ale. A young woman approached, and I was struck by her uncommon beauty. Her skin was a creamy tan color, and silky, jet black hair framed her face and provided a stark contrast for her icy blue eyes. Her jacket and petticoat were of a brown, woolen material that was plain, but her stomacher had an intricate pattern of bead work that reminded me of those worn by the tribesman in their counsels. She was common, but carried herself like a wellborn lady. I was stunned as she sat next to me, knowing a tavern was not ordinarily a suitable place for a proper woman to frequent. The bar-keep approached and, without a pause, took the coin she placed on the counter and poured her a pint of the same ale I was enjoying.

"Did you find your reverend?" The barman asked as he refilled my mug.

"No, unfortunately, there is no minister in Williamsburg who was expecting nor knows my friend."

The bar-keep stood to the side, away from the woman, while he cleaned out the inside of a mug. He stopped and pointed at me as a memory came back to him.

"You know, I might remember the man you described, now that I think on it more. But it's been months since he passed through here, if I'm correct. I never saw him talkin' with any minister, though. Did see him with an older gentleman who he called 'preacher', but I don't rightly know the man was one. I know that don't leave you much to go on."

"No, but thank you." He nodded and went back to cleaning his mug.

I returned to mine, prepared to finish my pint, when I noticed the young lady had gone. On the bar where she left her drink, with scarce a sip missing as the liquid danced about the rim, was a pamphlet for the college of William and Mary's school of divinity.

"The college here . . . do the students frequent this tavern?" I asked.

"Course they do! Almost daily. There's a table of scholars just there now."

In a corner of the room sat a handful of young men, boisterous, but generally controlled, likely mulling over the thoughts of the day as they sloshed back cider. I approached confidently and inquired if they knew of an older gentleman, perhaps a professor, who may frequent the tavern and may have been acquainted with a trapper who sometimes traded in Williamsburg. It was improbable, but I took a chance.

"Oh, you mean 'preacher'? He isn't a professor, he's a student." I must have looked confused. "Yeah, I know, he's a bit older, but he doesn't lord it over us." The men were already in high spirits and they laughed as their spokesman told me about the preacher.

"Do you know where he is? I must speak with him. It is urgent."

"He's in Staunton? Right?" He looked at another gent at the table, who confirmed with a nod. "He left a few days ago. Said his sister had a sick 'bairn,' as he called it, and asked him to come home."

I bought a round in gratitude for the students, who in turn sang my praises as I left the tavern and returned to my room at the ordinary.

I had planned to travel west for my future, and now I knew I must travel west for Gregory's. If I could find this 'preacher' and learn from him, if possible, what drove Gregory to those woods and his supposed demise, I believed, perhaps, I could kill two birds: help my friend and accomplish what I had set out from Chestertown to do. Yet all could wait for daylight, and I commenced to delight in the lines from my Beatrice.

My dearest Fenn,

I pray my tidings find you in good health and safety in Williamsburg. I am writing this as the warmth of our last embrace lingers still in my arms. It is bittersweet to watch you leave as I know you go to begin a new life for us, yet your parting robs me of home.

Mary sends her love to Gregory. Father has admonished her to be the pursued, not the pursuer, and so she will not write until she is written to.

Do you remember those days before we were betrothed? Oh, the lengths you went to, the lengths you are still going to, all to please Father. It is fortunate for you that my heart was won much easier, otherwise, imagine the obstacles I could have erected for you? Could you have endured a double gauntlet?

Return to me, my love, and I will follow you to the ends of this known world, and the one hereafter.

Yours truly and always,

Beatrice

Oh, my love! If I could have but forgotten my mission and returned to my heart's joy, I would have been content. What are the riches of this world compared to love? Yet I could not abandon the task at hand.

As I composed a letter in return, I thought of Beatrice's blue eyes and I remembered the woman from the tavern. Her mysterious vanishing and leaving behind the clue that would lead me in the right direction . . . it seemed far from coincidental. I shook it off. What did it matter who the woman was, or why she was there?

I put pen to paper, thought only of Beatrice, and forgot the stranger.

My dear Beatrice,

You have found me in good health this day, though my travels have not been without tragedy. All was well until Gregory and I fell in with thieves, and then some mysterious creature attacked us in the wilds. I have been injured twice over. Fear not for me, my love, I have recovered. But Gregory, he has disappeared, and I believe he may be lost to the Sheol of the woods. I do not mean to leave you with so brief an explanation, but I am afraid I do not understand what has happened myself.

My dear, I would leave all plans for our future and return to you now to comfort and be comforted, but I believe I must seek a man who may know something that vexed Gregory to his soul. There is no more I can relate about my conviction other than that I feel bound to complete Gregory's mission and, fortunately, it will take me on my intended path west. I will settle our future, and perhaps Gregory's, and we shall be together again, my heart! You know I would run any gauntlet, overcome any obstacle, to ensure that I will spend the rest of my life as yours.

I am enclosing a token of affection which Gregory held always by his heart and which he lost only in pursuit of the demon who nearly stole my life from me. I pray it will bring Mary comfort.

Forever yours,

Fenn

The next day, I befriended a group of homesteaders setting out from Williamsburg. Though my new companions were ordinarily distrustful of men from the northern colonies, my less than genteel appearance afforded me wary friendship and a caravan to ride west with.

"Land! Land as far as the eye can see is for the taking if a man has the bile and brawn to claim it for himself," was the invitation from the farmers leading the caravan.

I spoke to a surveyor staying at the tavern who assured me that as long as I had enough to trade with the natives or bargain with a rich landowner, I could secure myself enough property to make my great-grandchildren "wealthier than Solomon." Before departing with my new friends, who consisted not only of the men but their wives and children as well, I found a merchant to purchase Gregory's furs. My companions confirmed I had received a fair sum, and I determined to keep a separate purse for Gregory, should I ever find him alive again. They also encouraged me to keep the wagon and horse as my means of transport, as a hearty farm wagon would pass over the rough backcountry terrain easier than a carriage. In a few days, we would depart.

In the meantime, I took advantage of the local diversions, namely the theater where the play *Cato*, by Joseph Addison, was performed. It was not my first partaking of the play and, in fact, I had memorized some lines while it was delivered nightly in Philadelphia. I found this time the irony of sitting amongst slave owners listening to the hero speak of freedom struck me.

> "Meanwhile, we'll sacrifice to liberty.
> Remember, O my friends, the laws, the rights,
> The generous plan of power delivered down,
> From age to age, by your renowned forefathers,
> (So dearly bought, the price of so much blood,)
> Oh let it never perish in your hands!
> But piously transmit it to your children."

To their children, yes, but what of the poor souls from

whose backs, and at the price of so much blood, had their wealth been gleaned? I shook my head. Perhaps I would benefit from a thicker skin, as Beatrice had developed, for I was in the south now and was to become a member of a slave owning society. Who was I to question the fiber of which an entire economy and way of life is woven?

I could not yet imagine what it was like to be a slave.

It was then early November and the leaves in the lower latitudes were entering their autumnal glory. Our caravan departed from Williamsburg on a river road headed for Richmond. The company I traveled with was pleasant and lively. I had not been in the presence of children for some time and it was refreshing hearing their laughter drowning out the squeals of the wagon wheels.

One may wonder why I sought land in the backcountry to begin with. I was born into a family of considerable wealth, as was my beloved. Her father had fought for the British and earned his bread with his blood. My father, on the other hand, descended from Lords and Ladies, tracing their lineage to the Plantagenets. Both our fathers came to the new world having acquired land grants from King George II.

In the spirit of this new world, Mr. Calvert required that any man who married one of his daughters must generate wealth by his own hands. I could easily purchase an estate anywhere in New England where Beatrice and I would live comfortably, yet her father deemed an inheritance insufficient. "A man must work to eat" and so I considered what I might do to win my beloved. I admit, I had not applied myself to any one occupation and squandered my education on society and entertainment. Truth be told, I had no clear direction as to what career would satisfy me. But I knew I must have Beatrice.

I was willing to become a tradesman if need be to win her father's blessing. My father suggested I start a farm, or more to the point, a plantation, in the less-inhabited backcountry. I had the means to purchase land and establish myself without years of apprenticeship. I would only need the hired hands to work the land; and I could not assume that hard labor would be disagreeable to me. Perhaps it was what my aimless soul needed. In any case, I had already sworn off owning slaves and so I would, quite literally, work to eat. Beatrice surprised me when she wholeheartedly encouraged the plan and even delighted in the idea of her own kitchen garden. We were like children dreaming of the day we would play house and it all suited us immensely.

I had almost forgotten why I was on a dusty road in Virginia in the first place as I daydreamed of my future happiness with Beatrice. The company I was with planned to meet with a surveyor who worked on behalf of the Virginia colony, settling a land dispute between Virginia, North Carolina, and the Cherokee. Their hopes were like mine: a life on the frontier of the new world. But their frontier would not end with the foothills of Appalachia.

"We mean to cross those mountains, soon as a way opens up. Long hunters have made some headway in that direction, as I heard tell, and it's just a matter of time afore homesteaders lay claim to that land the King says he owns. All the way to the Pacific, wherever that be."

"Do you not fear the Indian tribes, or the French, for that matter? I understand the French have claimed the land over the mountains as well." I asked, truly curious about the threats brought on by the war which I had yet to feel.

"Bah, I ain't got time to be afraid of the French. And the Injuns is all fightin' amongst themselves to pay no mind to a few families. Plenty of land for all, the way I see it."

I did not share the enthusiasm or careless nature of my new friend. I had seen enough of the wild and encountered ill natured beings, human and naught, to be wary of the uncivilized lands. As our caravan rambled over hills and valleys, newly worn by hoof and wheel, I grew anxious about the choice I had made to move my entire existence west. Those plans made in the safety of the tidewater could never prepare me for the untamed wilds of the piedmont.

We reached a community outside Richmond and found an ordinary with vacancy. Like Williamsburg, the land around the fall line of the James River was abustle with growth. I watched as a flatboat loaded with hogsheads of tobacco floated past the tavern, landing near a warehouse where it would be stored before being distributed elsewhere. Though the population was smaller than the cities of the coast, I found the hum of industry and progress no less melodious.

My company was determined to spend only one night by the James River and to proceed onto the Three Notch'd Road the next morning at dawn. I took the opportunity afforded me that night to write again to my heart.

> *My beloved Beatrice,*
>
> *I write to you from Richmond where my caravan has stopped before departing on the Three Notch'd Road in the morning. We are made up of farmers and merchants whose hope for future prosperity lies in the fertile land that meets the mountains. Tomorrow we take our leave and continue on to Staunton, where I may then travel southwest with the multitudes on the Great Wagon Road to Big Lick. These names mean nothing to you now, my love, but if my plans, and the Lord's will, prevail, these places will sound like home erelong. I hope to find a bit of land that will promise mountain views to rival those of Chambery.*
>
> *I have now a glimpse of the rolling hills in the distance each time we emerge from a wood and overlook the valley. I am told the mountains are a sight to behold and wreathed in a blue mist as if the clouds of heaven hover to kiss the peaks of the earth.*
>
> *Yet, try as I might to think only of our future, I am daily*

reminded of the road that brought me here. A hazardous road, full of villains and nightmares. What drove Gregory into those woods? I am consumed with the mystery of it. I cannot describe in words the torment that I witnessed in his visage on our last days together. Is it right that I should pry into his past? Am I held responsible for whatever caused him to abandon reason for the senseless wilds? I do not know, Beatrice, but I feel as though his fate is somehow tied to mine and I must find out why.

I long to hear from you, my love. I pray there is a letter waiting for me in Staunton, for it will greatly ease the burden I carry.

Simply,

your Fenn

4

Days passed on our monotonous journey over hills, through woods, across streams, always bumping about so that my tailbone became sore from the vibration. I noticed the trees we passed at intervals were cut with three horizontal lines, and I understood then why the road was named thus. There were no shortage of taverns and ordinaries along the way, which afforded us rest and libations. We left one such ordinary, which we hoped to be our last, anticipating arriving in Staunton by nightfall that day. The sunrise illuminated the clouds with red and gold behind us, while ahead, the outline of the mountains was dimly visible.

I felt excitement and yet apprehension at what lay before me, should I finally speak to the 'preacher'. I rehearsed how I would approach him with such a sensitive topic and how I may navigate his responses, were they unfavorable. My mind wandered into the possibilities for Gregory's angst, some of which were villainous and did not bode well for the memory of my friend. I shook my head as if to shake the thoughts away. Instead of speculating, I would let the scholar share what was prudent, and if I was not to know the details, I must be content.

We had difficulty passing through the Woods Gap. The ruts

that paved our way were deep, and the mud sucked at the horses' hooves and the spokes of the wheels. One wagon broke an axle. We were prepared for such an event and the men were quickly underway repairing the damage. However, we would not reach Staunton before nightfall as hoped, and so someone suggested that we remain and complete the journey the next day. This was agreeable to all, so we made camp. I felt more agitated than usual and resolved to retire early and regain some of the control of my nerves that I had lost over my weary and tumultuous journey. As I reposed, waiting for sleep to take me, I overheard chatter around the fire that roused my attention.

"There's been another killing, so I heard at the tavern. They found a highwayman shot off the road north of Williamsburg."

"Well, that ain't news. Them thieves get what's comin' to them and no one bats an eye."

"Surely I hope it is not left to citizens to mete out justice?" A woman's voice questioned the nonchalance of the gruff men.

"If we left it up to the law on these trails, the thieves would ransack us all and be halfway 'cross the empire before anyone caught 'em."

"Too true, but that ain't all I heard. A hunting party found another man in the woods. He was buried, but whoever done it was in a hurry cause the hounds found him easy enough. He weren't shot though. Mauled as I heard it. Missing near half his face." Gasps and scoldings from the women reminded the men that there were sensitive ears listening in. I could hear shuffling and concluded that the women had taken the children off to their respective beds. The men continued in hushed tones.

"Just like the one found up in New York some weeks before."

"I heard it that one in New York was devoured almost completely. Only knew it was a man cause the fiend left hands and feet intact. May not be the same thing as got this one."

"Mayn't 'cept it do seem awful strange to be a coincidence."

"I seen what catamounts can do to a man. I lay my bets on a hungry female or a male staking his territory."

"Sure, sure, could be."

"How do they know it ain't Injuns? Those red devils take scalps. Who's to say there ain't cannibals among them beasts?"

"Not unless they're ripping men apart with their bare hands. Wounds weren't from no weapon from what I heard. Also said there was another man who musta got away . . . a trail o' blood into the woods."

"Just as likely the poor fellow shot one off afore he was killed. Beast probably bled to death somewheres."

"Could be. 'Cept the hunters followed the trail. It stopped at a swamp and one of 'em found a necklace hangin' from a branch like it was ripped off. Said it was a pretty thing belongin' to a lady, no doubt. I don't know no catamount wearing ladies' jewelry."

"Hmm," grunted one of the men, contemplating the possibilities.

'The necklace was Mary's! And must have been what was concealed in the handkerchief she had placed in Gregory's hand,' I thought.

"Well, someone's got to know what happened there in those woods, cause someone was there to bury that body."

It had never occurred to me I would have to answer for the death of the villain. But surely now someone would look for whoever was involved in the grizzly event. I was free of all guilt, yet I knew I must not be found out. There were too many strange circumstances surrounding my experience that I could not explain. Poor Gregory! He must have succumbed to the beast. I thought perhaps in his struggle with it he lost Mary's necklace, though it seemed odd that his body had not also been recovered. The animal may have dragged him to its lair in the marshy bog. A hollowness carved out a place in my gut as I concluded Gregory must be dead.

"Anyhow, I bought the necklace off the hunter for my wife.

It's her birthday next week, and the hunter had no use for a trinket as such. He gladly took my old rifle in exchange."

At this I was agitated beyond reason. Why should it bother me so that the man had possession of Mary's necklace? Gregory had no need of it anymore. Still, it seemed disgraceful that it should be bartered away and line the throat of a seasoned woman when it was a token of affection between young lovers. I thought perhaps I could trade him for it, but how could I reveal myself to have been eavesdropping when all the men thought me asleep? And how could I divulge my desire for it without betraying my knowledge of the murder in the woods? I could steal it, but if I were caught, well, I already heard the conviction of duty the men had toward thieves. My only hope was in some design of providence that would enable me to obtain the necklace on Gregory's behalf before it adorned the neck of the farmer's wife. I allowed myself to sleep, though it was a fitful rest full of dreadful dreams.

Staunton bore the evidence of the flood of population that I had witnessed in other parts of the Virginia colony. Most farms were small, single-family homesteads with skilled laborers spread throughout the countryside, trading their talents and wares as currency. But the threat from the native tribes and the French was pushing many families to seek protection in numbers, so small towns grew to accommodate growing fears.

We found the tavern that seemed central to the comings and goings of travelers on the Valley Road. Our caravan planned to rest there for a day or two before continuing south. Before any other task, I approached the tavern-keep to inquire if he held any letters for me. I was overjoyed to be handed an envelope with the seal of my Beatrice. I did not even wait to be alone, but opened the letter as I sat at the bar.

Dearest Fenn,

Surely there is still hope for Gregory! What greater foe for that creature than our mighty friend? He has likely pursued the beast relentlessly and will carry its hide as a trophy when he finds you again. Still, Mary and I have been in fervent prayer since we received your letter, and we will not leave off praying until we hear he is safe! Mary carries the kerchief with her always, longing for the day she will return it to the hand of her beloved.

What a comfort it is to have a sister to share my hopes and fears with; who knows what it is to love, be loved, and long for that love when it is away. I know it is a comfort to Mary as well, to have me to sympathize with her. Father urges us daily to resume our frivolous pleasures. He longs to see us happy again, so he says, but I assure him I could not be happier than knowing my Fenn is well. So I wait for your letters daily.

Oh, but we are not wholly without distractions! Gertrude, your favorite cousin-to-be, visits almost daily now that Mr. Ainsley has departed for his military duty. She believes he will continue to rise in the ranks and covet the title of captain, no doubt hoping to benefit from the privileges associated with such a station. Can you imagine our dear Gertrude living in a soldier's tent? Neither can I, yet she has promised more than once to follow her husband into the front lines, should the opportunity arise. She sends her greetings and assures me you will return sooner than later. I assured her she will be disappointed, but she will not heed me.

When you are reunited with Gregory, and I believe in my heart you will be, urge him to write to Mary. A single line from him would soothe her restless soul in ways that no amount of words from you or I could ever accomplish.

All my love . . . and longing,

Beatrice

I smiled like a fool and laughed aloud as I imagined Gertrude hiking up her skirts as she cooked a meal, heaven forbid, over a poor man's hearth! The letter refreshed my spirits and convinced me to renew my hopes concerning Gregory. The found necklace was not irrefutable evidence of his death. I had no reason to assume he was gone. I added the letter to the others that I carried, close to my heart, and left the bar to seek the 'preacher'.

It was difficult at first to find a body who spoke English, as many of the settlers in the area were of German origin and kept their language. However, I soon spoke to an Irishman who informed me he knew of whom I described and directed me to a homestead in the country outside town.

Night was closing in, and I decided it would be best for me to rest and refresh myself before pursuing the man in the morning. I walked back to the ordinary, taking in the mountain's sight at dusk, which I had neglected to pay much mind to previously with my thoughts befuddled as they were. My eyes were attempting to adjust to the dimming light, so I could not be sure of what I saw, but when I turned to pursue my path, a man resembling Gregory entered the tavern. Hastening to follow the specter to ascertain if it was truly my friend, I entered a minute or two behind him. I nearly fell back from the noise and plumes of smoke, and it took me a moment to collect my bearings before I approached the tavern-keep to inquire the whereabouts of the man I thought to be Gregory. A person of his description was staying in a room on the second floor and I was welcome to 'discover if he be present.' The directions to the room were provided, and I hurried to be reunited with my friend, whose unknown fate had caused me so much grief.

I rapped on the door, but there was no reply. I waited and knocked again before trying the handle and discovered the door was unlocked. Upon entering, I found the room empty. Someone had been staying there, as was evident by the disheveled quilt on the cot, a basin of water at the vanity, and smoke trickling from the wick of a candle that had been snuffed out. However, no belongings remained that would suggest a lodger planned to return. I thought perhaps he had removed himself, yet I did not pass him on entering the room or on the stair that led to the guest lodgings. My only recourse was to search the tavern floor. Perhaps he was having a drink by the fire and I had not noticed him in my haste.

I rushed down the stairs, back into the haze and bustle of the lively tavern. I searched, expecting to find my friend telling one of his tall tales to a group of lodgers while toasting to backcountry living. There was no Gregory to be found. I felt like a fool. Beatrice's words must have caused my mind to fabricate a likeness, that or my eyes deceived me, and yet, someone who resembled him had been at the tavern, a fact acknowledged by the tavern-keep. I resigned to return to my room at the ordinary and hoped that whoever wore the frame of my lost friend would show himself on the morrow.

It was just after dawn when I set out on the path leading to the homestead said to house the scholar. The extensive farm was bustling in the early morning light. I observed several children milling about, feeding livestock, pitching hay, milking a cow, and sweeping the porches. The fields were strewn with autumn crops, waiting to be harvested. A large building was being erected to the right of the main house, and I noticed it was taking on the style of those in Williamsburg and Richmond. I gathered that the family farming there had been successful, certainly owing to the growth in exportation to the mother country, and improvements to their living arrangements were inevitable. The main abode was a simpler structure of hewn logs and plaster that made up most of the buildings in the remoter parts of the backcountry. When I knocked at the door to the house, a woman welcomed me, introduced herself as Mrs. Arnot, and I noted at once her ruddy hair and Scottish accent. Her husband, David, she said, was in the field bringing in the sheaves. Mrs. Arnot showed me to a chair by the fire, the area acting as a parlor, and offered me tea, which I declined.

"Thank you, Mrs. Arnot, for your hospitality. I am come, however, to speak to the student from William and Mary's, whom I presume to be kin of yours. Is he indisposed for a visit?"

"I dunna ken bu yer welcome t'wait while I check wi' Elias, that is, Maister Baird."

"Thank you, kindly."

It was fortunate that I had some experience speaking with the Highland Scots, or I may not have understood the thick drawl with which Mrs. Arnot spoke. One of her wee ones was playing with marbles by the old stone hearth. I guessed the lad to be around three or four and when he spoke to me, his accent and his childish lisp made it impossible to decipher what he meant. I nodded and smiled and tossed a stray marble his way. He smiled back and went on with his solitary enjoyment.

The scholar, Mr. Baird, entered the home shortly after my exchange with the boy. I rose and shook the man's hand, introducing myself, before he joined me by the fire. He beckoned affectionately to the young lad and whispered in his ear. The boy gathered up his marbles and trotted happily out to the yard where his siblings had, after the completion of their labors, begun flying kites.

"I gave the lad a promise o'sweets would he give us the room."

"I see."

"He's me nephew, William. Clara, Mrs. Arnot, is me sis."

He leaned in as if to make me privy to a secret. "Truth be told, we're a family o'Jacobite rebels." He smirked and sat back in his chair, as if satisfied that the air was clear between us and there would be nothing to hinder our conversation. I wondered what I should say to such a confession. All were aware of Bonnie Prince Charlie's rebellion, but as the fallout of the scandal occurred several years hence, those who were exiled in the colonies were treated none the worse for their failed attempt at usurpation. I nodded, unsure how to begin the conversation until I remembered why Mr. Baird was in Staunton.

"I hear your sister has an ill child? How fares it?"

"Oh, I am sorry to say, the wee bairn has passed. We buried her yesterday."

"I am terribly sorry, sir. I can come another time. I should not intrude on your family's mourning." As I rose to leave, he waved his hand for me to stay and assured me he was glad for the distraction. He was clearly uncomfortable with the freshness of the wound and returned to the subject at hand.

"So then, what can I do for ye, lad?"

"Well, perhaps I should tell you my story and you may understand why I am here." This seemed agreeable to my host, and so I took a deep breath and began with Gregory and me leaving Chestertown to travel to Williamsburg together; Gregory's insistence on arriving in town by October 23rd, noting that it was the Lord's Day and Gregory implied he had an appointment to make. I paused, waiting to see confirmation in the man's countenance, but he continued to listen, unmoved by the account. I then described our encounter with the thieves, Gregory fleeing into the marshland, and the attack on our persons, including the death of the second thief, by the creature in the wood. The scholar did not betray any alarm or concern and simply waited for me to finish my story. I concluded by relating why I assumed Gregory must have been planning to meet with a preacher and the evidence I had for believing the said minister was he.

"And that is why I am here today. I have pursued you on this trail hoping you may be able to illuminate the areas of my story which remain dark to me."

The man's piercing eyes studied mine. It seemed as if he were searching for the answer to my question and would pluck it from my mind. His brow screwed up, and he leaned forward in his chair, the way he had done when he confessed to being a Jacobite. He rose and crossed the room to the front door, which had been left open by the little urchin, and closed it carefully. He returned to his chair, made himself comfortable, and finally spoke.

"I have a tale of me own for ye, lad. I dunna ken ye'll believe me. I dunna ken I believe it meself. Ye can do what ye please with it."

And he related a history which, at the time, I took for a mockery. I do not remember every detail of what he said, but I will do my best to relate the spirit of his story as follows.

The seminarian met a man a little over a year hence. The man was a fur trader who had spent a season with hunters in French territory and had a full wagon with furs to trade in the colonies. He was drinking in the tavern one night and stumbled upon Mr. Baird, who had just finished a long day of lessons. The man began speaking nonsense about a demon in the woods near Lake Ontario. He and his company of hunters had camped for the night on the shore of the Great Lake, attempting to avoid detection by the French who claimed the area. As it was a full moon and the weather was mild, they neglected to build a fire. From what Mr. Baird could glean from the man that night, a beast fell upon the men and dispatched each one before devouring them in turn. In his description, the beast looked like a sickly wolf or bear with the gestures and mannerisms of a man. He described its snarls and screams like that of a catamount. The fur trader was severely wounded and awaited his gruesome fate when a small band of natives happened by the shore in their canoe. They took aim and shot at the beast, deterring it from finishing its ghastly feast, and it retreated into the night. The natives found the fur trader alive, though just barely. Taking compassion on him, and confusing him with a French trapper, they carried him to Fort Niagara and left him at its gates, fearing lest they should be accused of his demise. The fur trader felt the sleep of death sweep over him and succumbed to it. A Frenchman awakened him, pointing a rifle in his face.

"I guessed the lad was a bit mad in the head, till he showed me summat I couldna answer for."

Mr. Baird described the mangled scars on the fur trader's shoulder and neck. My hand unconsciously went to my own shoulder, which now bore a wretched scar of its own. The scholar noticed the gesture and nodded, assuring me his story was not over.

Months later, he was invited to a social gathering at a homestead north of Williamsburg when a man stumbled through the door, soaked with sweat and out of breath, claiming a monster was hunting him and had killed his companion. The men grabbed their guns, ready to kill a bear or wolf, such as the stranger described the creature to be. Mr. Baird remembered the tale and followed the hunters on their mission. It was a full moon, he said, wet and frigid, the type of night that would have blanketed the land in a white sheet in New York. But there, in Virginia, the ground was simply sparse. The men entered a clearing where the remains of the harvest left bits of corn stalks and squash vines scattered about.

Mr. Baird drew in closer to me, as if the walls were listening in. His voice was hushed, and I found it hard to understand, so I leaned in closer as well, absorbing the story and concentrating on each word he spoke. In the center of the clearing, a creature stood. He repeated it stood, on two legs, and howled at the moon. But the howl was "like the scream of a dyin' man." It saw the men and darted into the woods before any of them could get a shot. The next morning, a woman was found half devoured near the homestead where the beast had been spotted. The people believed it to be the work of a wild animal, though they could not account for what exactly they saw in the field the night before. Most agreed it was a sickly bear. Mr. Baird was not convinced.

Several months later, he was reunited with the fur trader and the man was overcome with agitation and vexation. Mr. Baird attempted to minister to the man, encouraging him to confide in him his sins and be rid of guilt. The man insisted he could not; he did not know what he had done, only that he was sure he was possessed and entreated the 'preacher' to cast out the demon. At this, Mr. Baird assured me he was not one to believe in superstition, even if there were "fairies living in the hills of Scotland," and he told the man it was not likely he was possessed, but merely in need of a hot meal and a good night's rest, offering to buy both for him. The fur trader obliged and expressed his gratitude, but assured the scholar he had figured out a way to keep his demon under control, in any case, and would have no more need of his assistance.

"I didna see the man afore last night. I dunna ken if it was him for sure, but I thought I saw him lurkin' about the farm."

"As did I, but by the tavern, if it is the same man. Was your man my friend Gregory? You have not told me his name."

"George was the name he gave me."

"But it could be the same man!"

"S'pose it could."

I wanted to spring up that second and flee to find Gregory, but Mr. Baird, noticing my agitation, put his hand on mine and assured me he had one thing more to convey.

He left the fireside to rummage in the kitchen, returning moments later with a tray of tea and bread. The hours had passed since we began our strange tales, and I recognized my hunger pains with the arrival of sustenance. We commenced to tea in silence as I waited with as much patience as I could muster for the man to complete his story and release me to seek my friend.

This was the remainder of the scholar's admonitions which, in the moment of hearing, I rejected with abhorrence and resolved to abolish from my mind completely. Now I know it was the forebodings of a conscientious seeker of the good of mankind.

"What do ye ken about werewolves?" he asked me. His gaze

was piercing in that moment, as if he thought I held a secret and refused to bring him into my confidence.

"I know very little, unless you speak of the myth of King Lycaon."

"Aye, that's one tale. I dunna ken much meself but I've been larnin'."

I asked to what purpose a student of divinity would devote time to learning about werewolf lore. Thus, Mr. Baird unraveled the cause and regaled his bizarre suspicions. He claimed that a story had been passed down in the backcountry of a creature that sought to devour humans on nights of the full moon. I obviously saw the connection he was attempting to make and remarked that just as likely it was a rabid beast who was seen most clearly on the brightest nights. The scholar acknowledged he had considered the same explanation, and would have rested his mind on the ordeal, until he heard my tale. He did not believe in coincidence, being a servant of the sovereign God. I was sent as a sign and he was to speak a word of prophecy to me. I became agitated as I had not anticipated receiving any message for myself but merely clues into the behavior of my friend.

Mr. Baird could not claim to know for sure if Gregory was the fur trader under a different name, but he believed that 'George' had been attacked by a werewolf. I showed my disbelief at the minister's superstitions, and he nodded to acknowledge he understood and was not inclined to wish to believe it himself, but that stranger things have happened and he was not above believing in the supernatural. Supernatural, yes, but a monster such as a werewolf seemed beyond the realm of possibility to me.

He then leaned forward once more and whispered. His eyes portrayed an almost pleading gaze as he related the conclusion of his prophecy. He believed that I had also been attacked by a werewolf. I laughed and scoffed as I unconsciously fingered the scar on my shoulder. Mr. Baird did not laugh. He noticed the scar that slid up my collarbone to my neck, peeping over my cravat. A scar that should still have been an ugly wound. He looked compassionate as he spoke with gentleness. Not only was 'George' bitten by a werewolf, but Mr. Baird believed he also became one. The trapper committed crimes, he was sure, but he could not remember them, and believed himself to be possessed. People have since been murdered in similar circumstances too striking to be coincidental. And Mr. Baird believed—oh, heaven's mercy on me—he believed I was to become a werewolf as well!

The smile that lingered on my face turned to a tight-lipped frown as anger swelled in me. I would not be made a fool of. This man was a charlatan and surely there was some remedy he would offer that would empty my pockets. He assured me that was not the case, and he only warned me to beware and stay away from society on the night of a full moon. I would not let him finish his ravings, and I arose and stormed out of the farmhouse with all the pride and civility I could muster.

I returned to the tavern I had sought Gregory in the night before. The tavern-keep had not seen the man I described since my last interrogation, and his room had been cleaned and lent out to a new boarder. The friends whom I traveled with sought me to relate their plans that they were to leave at dawn the following morning for Big Lick. I was disappointed to be going before finding Gregory, but decided I had only seen a fancy of my imagination. A hope made manifest. Most likely Gregory was dead and I, wanting to believe the contrary, saw his likeness in another brawny man of the backwoods. I assured my friends I would join them and returned to the ordinary to sup and retire to my room for the rest of the evening. I sought pleasure in the only mode possible and sat to write another letter to my dear one.

> *Beatrice, my love,*
>
> *I have found the person I have been seeking, but all in vain. The man is a lunatic, and I will not even dignify his*

ravings by repeating them to you. I wish only to say that I am bound for Big Lick on the morrow and will pursue our future goals with all fervor, now that my second task has been accomplished, no matter how unfruitful.

I hope, I pray, you are right about Gregory. In fact, I fancied I saw him here, in Staunton, though it must have been my imagination, for I never found him, though I searched and searched.

In any case, my eyes have, at last, beheld the glory of the mountains that will be our home. They rise like a fortress, barring the way west. I imagine God's fingers tore into the flesh of the earth and rent it asunder until all that remained were hills and valleys; a magnificent wound down the whole of this new world. And the leaves! Vermillion, like blood

I stopped writing as the image of torn flesh leaped back into my mind and I saw the gaping wound in my side again as if it were the night I received it. My memory brought back to me the picture of the creature's face. Its horrid jaws dripping with my blood and the angry look in its eyes when the bullet tore into its flesh. Eyes like a man's. Gregory's eyes?

No! I shut out the vision and forced my thoughts back to the mountains. I scratched out the words "like blood" on the page and from my mind and continued my description.

Vermillion, ~~like blood~~, gold, and rich evergreen, blanket the landscape in waves. The autumnal brilliance is outdone only by the blue haze which crowns the peaks. This evening I sat on the porch of the ordinary watching the sun set over the mountains and into the unknown west. I have never before dreamed of crossing these brilliant hills, but today, I feel drawn to discover what lies beyond.

My future is incomplete without you, my love, and I long for the day I can come and take you to be with me where I am.

> *Yours, most ardently,*
>
> *Fenn*

I cannot find words to describe the visions that haunted my dreams that night. In fact, my voice was shut off as I awoke from a nightmare and found I could not scream. I could not move. My eyes flitted to and fro about me, looking whence my doom would come until I was convinced I was awake in a rented room and not in a hazy wood under a full moon with a monster's fierce eyes piercing mine as he tore into my chest . . . stealing my very heart.

Those dreams have been my constant ever since.

5

The morning of our departure, it was discovered that Gregory's wagon was missing. My horse had not been touched. The saddle bag was unmolested, but the wagon that I had left in the stable yard of the ordinary was nowhere in sight. I reasoned, with hope, that the only person who would confiscate the wagon would be its owner, as the thing itself was not worth the trouble. The horse would fetch a higher price and would be easier to lead off unnoticed, yet the horse remained. Could it be that Gregory was not only alive but had returned in the night for his wagon, leaving me the horse to resume my journey?

I only wondered why he would not reveal himself to me. Surely I would not refuse him his property; in fact, I would be overjoyed to find him alive and could supply him with more than just the wagon, but also a purse of money from the sale of his furs. But perhaps Gregory assumed me dead and believed his wagon had been carried off by passersby who found the scene of carnage. As I was ruminating over the potential scenarios, all of which assumed a live Gregory had repossessed his property, my fellow traveler pointed out the soft glow that meant the sun would rise and the train would leave on the Wagon Road.

I was fortunate to have traveled with a light load so I could store all of my possessions in the saddlebags of my mount. Quitting my room and collecting my horse in time to join the procession, I expected to find myself amongst a sea of carts, wagons, and carriages. Instead, we were waylaid by a herd of cattle being driven north.

It was now mid-November, and the days were growing colder, especially in the parts of our trek where the road climbed higher into the hills. We would reach the Big Lick in three days, barring any delays. No one in our caravan could have imagined what would eventually befall us.

The first two days were uneventful. In fact, it was so dull at times that, for amusement, I challenged myself to identify the passing trees and wildlife to the best of my ability. Some children that walked nearby heard me mumbling about leaves and bark and joined me in my game. I could tell the sycamores by the nuts that hung from the naked branches, but I doubted I could differentiate them from maples when in leaf. The magnolias, with their glossy leaves that defied winter, were easy to spot. The redbuds held onto their heart-shaped foliage longer than most of the other flora and so I could put a name to them as well. Apart from these, I only saw brown trunks and branches, but the children could name them without hesitation. As for fauna, the usual squirrels and chipmunks, rabbit and groundhog, occasionally crossed our path. A fox peeked out of a thicket, and then quickly about-faced to return to the shelter of the woods. A young black bear scurried up a tree, and a small herd of elk grazed as the males, still in rut, sparred nearby. These beasts I knew, but the birds were far more numerous and less familiar to me. When a hawk swooped down and snatched up a bird almost as large as itself and carried it off to feast, I was the winner, for I knew the prey to be a mourning dove, though neither I nor the children knew what to call the capped hawk with gray wings and a russet belly.

That game could only hold my attention for so long as most of the creatures were shy and many of the trees we passed repeated themselves. I imagined the ancestors of those trees had thrived in that wood for hundreds of years, dropping their seed and bending, when necessary, to allow the next generation to benefit from the life-giving rays of the sun.

I then imagined the life I wanted to cultivate for the future generation that would spawn from the union of Beatrice and I. I understood the benefit of raising our own in this wilderness as I watched the healthy and hearty children of these farming families. Their concern was primarily what they could learn from their elders, and how they could be of assistance, or so it seemed to me as I observed their interactions. Recalling my own childhood and the care with which I was brought up, I could not deny I had been protected from much of the toil of life that comprised the lot of the mass of humanity. I was grateful for my intellectual education; I merely lamented that the same care was not given to my natural education. Beatrice would also see the beauty in this frontier life for the sake of our progeny. This was a way we could bend and allow the sun's rays to enrich the lives of the future generation.

Perhaps these moments of romanticism were naïve; no doubt in many ways they were. Life in the larger towns and settlements, where numbers protected from the threats of the wild, was far easier on the whole. One jaunt on a wagon road next to babbling children could not possibly afford me a well-rounded view of life on the frontier. Still, I was looking forward to the acquisition of my own bit of heaven, as I now imagined it.

On our second night, we camped along a river. We would have to ford the waters to continue, and so waited until morning when we were fresh and our strength renewed from a good night's sleep. There was much milling about the campsite, laughter, scolding as the young ones entered the witching hour and grew restless, and the droning sound of men making plans for their families. I sat with a group of such as they discussed how they would go about crossing the river. As the water level was low—it had ceased to rain since the downpours that plagued Gregory's and my trip to Williamsburg—the wagons would be wheeled, floated, and pulled by the horses, who could cross by swimming. The current was not swift, so the men agreed. I cringed at the certainty that I would cross on the back of my horse and not inside a dry wagon as the women and children would. I quickly bucked up, remembering the many trials I had already faced, noting that wet stockings would be uncomfortable, but I was unlikely to experience any real hardship. The conversation moved from river crossings to news of the war with France the men had collected while in Staunton.

"We're heading to the front lines, so they say, though I heard no talk of war in these parts."

"Ah, I ain't concerned. I got a peace treaty right here they can sign their name to." The men laughed as the farmer patted the rifle that lay across his lap.

It had been quiet in the southern colonies, considering the conflicts raging in the north. I felt safe on this busy road with this relatively large caravan. It was quite easy to let one's guard down when surrounded by allies.

I retired to my tent and decided not to eavesdrop this time. I would get a peaceful night's sleep and be ready for our passage across the river.

The ruffling of the tent flap woke me. In the moonlight, which I noticed to be full and bright, I made out the form of a man rummaging through my bags. He was frantic and seemed unaware that he was alarming me to his presence. I did not know whether I should reveal myself to him and ask what it was he wanted or remain still and pretend to sleep, hoping he would leave me in peace. My purse was not worth the price of my life. But as he turned his head, I saw his profile and could not mistake the identity of my intruder.

"Gregory!" I whispered, though I felt I could have said his name aloud, as the whisper was not very discreet.

He turned to me; his eyes wide with terror. "The key! Where is the key?!"

I was shocked that after weeks of separation and supposing he had died a gruesome death, my friend had naught for me but a request for a key. I saw his angst and racked my brain to think of what he could be after. Then I remembered the key to the lock of his wagon. I recalled I had picked it up and dropped it in the saddlebag the day I left the woods and the scene of Gregory's supposed demise. Rising, I motioned for Gregory to accompany me to the horses, and he followed like a dog waiting to be fed, pacing as I searched the bags for the trinket. Handing it to Gregory, he nearly ran me over; he was in such haste to tear off into the woods.

"Gregory! Please friend! What is the meaning of this?" He stopped and looked at me. He was desperate to leave, but I could tell his affections for me stayed him to hear me out. "I thought you were dead!"

"Yes. Yes, I woulda done, too. I'm sorry, friend, but I gotta go. Now!"

"Stop, Gregory!" I remembered one thing that might keep him in my presence and blurted without thought to consequence. "Stop! A man here has Mary's necklace."

Gregory turned. "I looked. I didn't find it."

"It is here. I heard him say he bought it off a hunter who found it when he followed the trail of the beast into the woods. I thought it was the sign of your demise."

He looked up to the moon and seemed to attempt to judge the minutes based on its position. He turned back to me and spoke, his tone frantic with impatience. "Where? Please, there's no time. I need to know where to find it!"

"Stay. I can arrange for you to recover it in the morning. I am sure the man will hand it over at a small price if we explain it is yours."

"No! I need it now or never. I gotta leave. Please!"

I glanced toward the carriage I knew to be the one in possession of the jewelry. Gregory noticed and ran with haste, but attempted this time to show more stealth. As far as I could perceive, no one in the camp stirred as Gregory quietly searched, but I could tell he was becoming more frantic as the relic did not reveal itself.

As I watched Gregory, a great illness swept over me. My stomach lurched and my head felt as it did when it met the end of the rifle. I was overcome and stumbled to a large tree to brace myself. The horses began snorting and pawing in agitation, and I feared the camp would startle at the commotion and find a thief amongst them. I cried out to Gregory, but my voice was faint and barely a whisper left my lips before I fell to the ground, gripping my head in excruciating pain.

How many times will I awake to a scene like the one I beheld that morning?

I was curled in a ball by the river, nearly naked and shaking. As I rose, the few rags of my nightshirt that still hung about my frame slipped off my shoulder, yet I was too befuddled to notice. It was difficult to arouse myself completely, so I splashed water on my face, only to find my hands covered in blood. I thought I must have hit my head during my fit. The water was bitterly cold, and I feared sickness, but I washed my face and hands before rising. My tent lay at the edge of the woods and as it was still dark, but for the first rays of dawn on the horizon, I resolved to reach my tent and clothe myself before anyone in the camp noticed my indiscretion. I wondered what had happened to my shirt and tried to remember why I was out of my tent.

Hearing a commotion from the direction of the caravan, I could not understand such liveliness in the early morning. I also feared that the more people milled about, the greater the chance my nakedness would be discovered, but I was exceedingly relieved to arrive at my tent unnoticed. I dressed quickly as I perceived that the sounds of the camp were of lament. Upon walking into the center of the ring of wagons and tents where I had sat with the men the night before, I beheld a scene of horror matched only by my night in the woods—when the carnage left by the fiend left me scarred. Bodies were torn asunder and sprawled about. Whatever monster attacked did not discriminate by gender or age as a child lay motionless, clinging to its mother in a final grasp for sanctuary. The mother had attempted to shield the child and paid for it with her arm. Both were quickly covered with a canvas, as were the bodies of several other victims. I was aghast and approached a man who stood motionless as he surveyed the scene.

"What has happened here?" I asked as a lump filled my throat and I feared I would be ill.

"Monsters," was all the man could say. A wolf pack, most likely. A wolf like the one who attacked me and killed the thief.

A wolf with human eyes.

I hesitated. The scene was gruesome and tragic. I wanted to escape the discomfort I felt, not knowing what to do or how to react; but to stand by and watch, or worse, flee from those in need, would be cowardice beyond what even I could stomach. So I took a deep breath to steel myself and began helping the men transfer the victims onto boards and canvas mats and carry them to their respective family wagons. Some women had lost consciousness at the sight of the carnage and were being tended by others who held smelling salts to their own noses so as not to succumb themselves. The children had been banished to their wagons and told to remain inside no matter what. They were likely too terrified to disobey. All around me was terror and chaos, and I felt small and powerless.

I heard commotion coming from the direction of the woods and the women screamed, likely expecting another round of attacks to commence. I heard him before I saw him and the pitiful sounds of his cries for mercy tore at my already mangled senses.

"No! Please! You don't understand. I'm sick! Please!"

I came around the corner of a wagon to see two men dragging Gregory. He was naked, but for a shirt one man had covered him with for the sake of the women. He was smeared in blood, and it was clear he had been wounded in the leg. Oh, Gregory! Had he been caught stealing from the farmer and chased into the woods? I expected the men to be dumbfounded by the sight they returned to.

"Oh, he'll vouch for me! Please, Fenn! Tell 'em it wasn't me." He took in the scene before him with a look of terror and shook his head. A groan of despair escaped him. "I couldn't do this in my right mind. I wouldn't do this!" He dropped to his knees and sobbed. The men threw him down; one of them tied his hands behind his back and the other end of the rope to a wagon.

"We got 'im! The savage beast! The unholy monster!" cried the man in triumph. Gregory continued to sob.

"What is the meaning of this? Why is he being treated like an animal simply for taking back property that was his?" I questioned the men as they walked into the camp.

"Are you mad? This man's a murderer!"

"Impossible! I know him to be a good and honest fur trader. He is not capable of this slaughter. One man alone could not have done this!"

"Aye, you're right. One man didn't do this! There were two. Both dressed in wolf skins and howling at the moon while they ripped these poor souls to bits. I know not what they used, but it was a fearsome weapon, to be sure."

The absurdity of men tearing human beings limb from limb tempted me to scoff at the assertions being made. I asked where the evidence of wolf skins was, but the men could not produce any. Gregory, even with all his girth, looked weak as he lay on the ground, half naked and utterly dejected. I then asked what the men planned to do with him.

"The magistrate will deal with him. We won't add any more blood to that already shed this day."

They planned to deliver Gregory to whatever law there may be in Big Lick. We would wait another day to cross the river as the families wanted time to bury their dead. A night watch ensured that the other murderer did not return to increase the death toll.

That night I dreamed. I was in my body, but it did not resemble a man. I looked down to see long, wiry hair trailing from my arms and down the back of my hand. My fingers were elongated, claw shaped and topped with nails that curved and came to a sharp point. I looked ahead of me to see a person screaming and shielding her face with her outstretched arm. In my dream, I felt rage. I felt hunger. I felt desire. And as I leaped onto the woman, I awoke screaming and sweat streamed from my brow. A man came to my tent to find out if I was being attacked. He saw I had awoken distraught and nodded his head in kind acknowledgement.

"Ye aren't the only one as can't sleep tonight. I expect the monster will meet us all again in our dreams." He handed me a flask, and I drank a draught and settled myself back into my cot.

Yes, I suppose the monster would visit those who had seen it. They would replay the image of its attack and the fear of being next.

But I dreamt as if the monster was me.

6

As the caravan continued on its way to Big Lick, I sought a way to talk to Gregory in private. The men had chained him to walk behind one of the wagons and he trotted to keep pace with his lead. He nearly drowned when we crossed the river. He had on only the shirt he was given after being caught and a pair of breeches. Someone had tied a strap around his wound, though it did not seem to bother him in the least. The cold, however, was biting and his breath shot out in cloudy sobs, his frame shivering so that he looked to be shocked by the cold as if struck by lightning. I had only pity for my friend, as I still believed him to be wholly innocent and a victim of coincidence.

An opportunity presented itself when I noticed the man tasked with keeping watch over the prisoner was exhausted and drifting in and out of sleep. I offered to guard him in his stead, but he was hesitant to allow me, as he knew I was sympathetic and likely feared I would free Gregory. I reminded the gaoler that I did not have the key to his chain, so the man could not escape. He accepted my argument as fair and of sound logic and was soon asleep. I walked beside the unfortunate, so our conversation ran almost no risk of being overheard.

"Gregory! Oh poor soul! I have already explained to the men

that you came to retrieve your key. I did not mention our attack by the same beast for fear that they would appoint us the murderers of the thief. Still, the men will not listen. What more can I do?"

"Oh, don't you see? Are you blind, man?"

I knew my face betrayed my confusion. He lowered his voice, though it was clear he found all futile and might as well shout it to the entire caravan than keep it in confidence.

"I am the monster. I did murder the thief."

"That was in defense. You were defending me."

"Not just that thief, but the other as well."

"But that is impossible, Gregory. I saw the beast. It was a wolf or lion of some kind. I heard wolves that night. The man's face was ripped off. My shoulder . . ." I did not go on. Gregory's countenance was one of deep shame and remorse at the mention of my injury. I could not accept that my friend had attacked me with such violence. I remembered the monster, but at that moment I saw the eyes—Gregory's eyes—and I finally understood.

"It cannot be. There is no such thing."

"Aye, but there is. It walks beside you as we speak."

"The preacher, the man you sought after . . . he said that I . . . Gregory, was I the other?" He looked forward and would not meet my gaze.

"I'm sorry. I'm so sorry." He sobbed and fell to the ground. He would have allowed himself to be dragged by the wagon had I not yelled for the driver to stop and pulled him to his feet.

"Please! He cannot walk in this condition."

The man driving the wagon looked at Gregory as if he were a lame mule; he would have put him out of his misery had he not promised the women to deliver him over to be tried and executed.

"He will walk or he will drag, but he ain't riding."

Gregory recovered and, knowing I would continue to intercede for him, composed himself to the best of his ability.

"Don't bother yourself on my behalf. I can walk." He took a deep breath and carried on with the wagon. I allowed the knowledge of his confession to permeate my understanding. The dream was not a nightmare; it was a memory. I was naked. I was covered in blood . . . it was not mine.

"How?"

"I don't know. I tried to learn what I could, but I never knew the one that done this to me. And I couldn't exactly hunt him down seein' as the change only occurs on full moons, and I can't account for what I do when the change comes over me. But I've been followed, more than once. Seems I'm being hunted. I think I lost its trail, but I can't be sure."

"Another . . . one like you?"

"Maybe. I don't know. Someone small, petite, I mean, maybe a woman? I just know I was bein' followed before I came to Chestertown. Thought all those people would keep me safe, and it was just after the full moon, so I knew I had time 'fore the next one. On the road, when we saw those Injuns, I thought it was the one following me, till they showed themselves. Then I thought it might find me in those woods. That's why I was so scared. Anyway, I meant to head to the mountains for good with the wagon when I realized I didn't have the key and I had to find you."

"The cage in your wagon. That is to keep you restrained?"

"Yeah. Once I knew what I was, I built it myself. I heard about murders. I couldn't explain what I'd done, but only that I had blood on my hands and didn't know where it came from. The next full moon came and the same thing happened. I talked to a man in New York who heard some old stories brought over on the boats to this new world; some superstitions of a man becomin' a wolf and murderin' people. I asked him for more, but he said that's all he heard. Only said so since others had claimed to see a man-wolf on the nights of the full moon . . . when the people were killed.

"Then I went to the library company in Philadelphia,

searchin' for a book that might explain what was happenin' to me. You know I ain't a learned man and can't read well, but I found only one mention of what I was lookin' for. Just a story of a man who got turned into a wolf, or maybe it was his sons. Anyhow, it didn't answer how I ended up like this other than he got his from a pagan god. Pagan gods are equal to demons in my book, so I knew, sure enough, that I had been possessed.

"I went to the preacher in Williamsburg. Well, I thought he was a preacher 'cause he carried around a Bible and had it with him when I met him in the tavern, so I just thought of him as one. Anyway, I begged him to cast the demon out that was working its evil with my hands, but he refused. Said I was just in need of rest. I hoped he was right and went on my way. Had my cage by then, and it worked alright, so I decided to be content till I could figure out how to get rid of it. Thought I had an idea, but I needed help and Baird was the only one who knew."

"And so we had to get to Williamsburg by Lord's Day? So you could be cured before the full moon?"

"Sure enough."

"What was your idea?"

"I thought maybe I had to die again so it would let go its hold on me and then Baird could bring me back to life . . . somehow."

"Oh, friend."

"He likely woulda said no anyhow."

I allowed the tale to linger. How could I accept this story? How could I believe I was a monster? A demon possessed man? It was incomprehensible. Gregory took a deep, painful breath and went on.

"That night, in the woods, I waited for you to go to bed. I didn't want you wondering why I was locking myself up in a cage. I had used it afore and it worked. Those times I woke up bruised, my tattered clothes all around me, but the beast never made it out to murder. It musta wised up that night somehow. The cage had no damage, so the beast musta unlocked it and climbed out. I woke up in the swamp, sunk to my chest in mire, and I knew. I couldn't go back to the campsite and see what I'd done." We both remained silent. I remembered the feel of his teeth in my shoulder, the way the flesh looked when it was flayed from my ribs. He could only imagine.

"I made my way to Williamsburg. Baird wasn't there; I thought maybe he would be back, so I waited. But after a few days, I saw you! You were alive! I couldn't believe it. I listened for stories at the taverns, but they were only of a highwayman found dead. I believed I had spared you somehow. Maybe the monster in me just run off into the woods after a deer or somethin'. I thought of revealing myself, but I saw you had my wagon and must have pegged me for a goner, so I let you believe it. I left then, on the Notch'd Road, to find Baird."

"I saw you in Staunton?"

"Yes. I learned on the way what I'd done in the woods that night. One body was found. I was torn between grief and feelin' relieved . . . If you'd walked out of those woods . . . well, I feared what that would mean. The monster knew where you were, in that tent, sure enough. You would have been his meal. So when I saw you again in Staunton . . . I knew you were just like me." Again a sob rose in him, but he swallowed it down and composed himself.

"I fought with myself over whether to continue on. But you had my wagon. I had to get it if I was goin' to spare more lives. Time was runnin' out, but I believed I could overtake your caravan and get my wagon before it was too late."

"But why did you not speak to me? I looked for you, but you had vanished."

"I couldn't come to terms with what I'd done to you. I was sore ashamed."

"You could have spared me this!" I said, waving my hands around the caravan at the wagons filled with grieving families.

"I know." Gregory would not lift his eyes, but looking was unnecessary. One could hear in the silence the sorrow that filled each wagon. The mournful creaking of the wheels and the worn and weary huffs of the horses and oxen were the only sounds that interrupted the procession that once held hope, but carried now despair.

"I'm sorry, Fenn. I tried. Finally got the nerve when I saw you headin' to that homestead. I followed you. I saw Baird come to the door and close it after you been there for a bit. I didn't know why you'd gone to see him, but I decided I'd tell you after. Then I saw how you left that house, and I knew he had told you what I woulda." His head raised and his eyes traveled slowly to mine. "Did you believe him?"

"No. No, I did not." Still, I wished Gregory had raved at me like a madman preaching that the sky is falling and the world is ending. I would not have believed him, either. But at least he would have tried.

"I wouldn've either," he said, looking back at the chain that bound his hands ever before him. "Not till I saw my hands covered in blood would I have thought I had a monster in me."

I had blood on my hands and I was foolish enough to believe it had been my own. I could blame Gregory and feel myself absolved, but all men are blind when they choose to be. Looking around at the caravan once more and seeing the grief and terror that consumed every countenance, I held up my hands as Gregory stared listlessly at his own, and I could not deny it. I was a werewolf.

My fate was tied to Gregory. Now I understood why I felt compelled to find answers. If he was capable, so was I. What he had become, it was my future. No, it was my present and my future. And his fate, awaiting death in the name of justice, would eventually be mine . . .

Oh, Lord, it is mine!

I had to believe it was possible to save him.

"I must get you away from these men, Gregory."

"No!" Gregory shouted at me and drew the attention of the

other wagons nearby. One man motioned to me, asking if I needed help. I assured him I was alright.

"No," Gregory repeated quietly. "This is just. This is what I deserve." He hung his head. "I'm tired, Fenn. If the demon in me has learned how to unlock the door, how am I supposed to keep it under control any longer?"

"I could help you! We are the same. We could do this together. We could survive."

"How? How can we help each other when we will both turn into wolves together? Like last night . . ." He shook his head and sighed, "I don't want to survive anymore. If I can't really live, what's the point in breathin'?"

"What do you mean, Gregory? No one here knows who you really are. We can escape and go back home."

"Don't you see? There's no home for me. There's no future."

"Mary."

"I wouldn't have her wed a monster! What sorta child comes from a demon and a human?"

"But what about Mr. Baird? Could he not cast out the monster, if it is a demon?"

"I went to him. I talked to Baird after you left his homestead. He's not ordained, but he tried. For hours, he tried. He tried to the point of sweatin' blood. I couldn't let him die for me. I killed too many already."

Gregory may have failed at ridding himself of this scourge, but I did not want to believe there was no redemption, no hope, left for us. Gregory and I were victims of evil. Why should the victims suffer consequences for works which they had no knowledge of; no will to commit?

We walked in silence for some time. I fought all doubt and defeat in an attempt to conjure a saving grace for my friend, for myself. Perhaps in the night I could free him from his shackles, and we two could escape together. We could find a way over the mountains; the natives might know a way. We could recuse ourselves from humanity and survive on the flesh of animals when the change overtakes us, until we discover a way to be delivered from this affliction. Gregory consented to try, and we hatched a plan, waiting for the cloak of nightfall.

I waited until the waning moon was high in the sky to afford some light with which to execute our escape. Mary's necklace was secured from the farmer, not entirely honestly, except that I left him a small sum of money for a replacement. I hid my belongings in Gregory's wagon, which had been confiscated by one of the men, a merchant, who had secured Gregory's capture. The farm wagon was hitched to the back of the man's Conestoga and, thankfully, the horses were nearby enough that I could have the wagon hitched in minutes.

I planned to put flame to my tent to create a diversion. There was a breeze that night and I hoped the flame would spread, requiring the attention of the entire camp. While the fire was being extinguished, I would release Gregory from his chain and we would escape. Before undertaking our plan, I found out whether Gregory was fit for the exertion that would be required of him. He was in high spirits, though not entirely himself, which was excusable considering his dire circumstances. I produced Mary's necklace, at which his eyes alighted, and he motioned for me to put the charm round his neck. It was a small, silver thing, in the shape of a cross with a dove on top. A token of faith and the spirit of God who descended like a dove, and yet was greater than any evil that might dwell on earth. I wanted to believe it was not only a reminder for Gregory of his love's affections but also of the power of heaven to overcome hell.

I looked around to be sure no one saw me leave his side, for at least one man was pacing the campsite, keeping a watch over the prisoner and ready to give a cry should there be danger. I was able to return to my tent unnoticed and, with quivering hands, I reached for the torch I would use to light my tent.

At that moment, I heard a guttural cry of lament. The moaning continued for less than a minute before a gunshot cracked, and the sound reverberated between the treetops. I dropped the torch and peered through the flap of my tent to see what had happened. The night watch ran to the wagon whence came the sound, while others in the caravan became animated and scurried to discover the meaning of the commotion. I could see Gregory sitting by the wagon wheel with a look of worry on his face. Our plan was foiled. We would have to wait another night. I emerged from my tent and shook my head at Gregory. Too many eyes were looking about the wagons and not in the opposite direction where we needed them.

Just then, I heard a growl of anger, and the farmer stormed from the wagon.

"Where is that murderer? I'm going to end this now!"

The man was heading directly for Gregory. I wanted to interject, but Gregory looked at me; his eyes told me to stay where I was.

"Josiah! You stop that now! I'll not have blood on your hands on account of this beast!"

"Be still, woman! You don't know what yer talkin' about. He's just killed Marcus."

"You're speaking nonsense now, husband! This rogue has been chained and remains so!"

"He brought death on Marcus when he killed his wife and daughter."

The men argued about what to do with Gregory. The farmer was in a blind rage and would not listen to reason. He was determined to execute the prisoner and not wait for the law to do it. The children who had come to see what the noise was about were whisked away by their mothers to the wagons. Others were shouting, encouraging Josiah to take revenge on behalf of their loved ones. One man quieted the throng and spoke up.

"What's to stop the other beast from seeking revenge on us? We know this man weren't the only one did attack us. He sees we kill his friend and he'll be after us! I say we keep on and take the man to Big Lick. Let them deal with him."

"Oh, we don't have to worry about that! We got the other murderer here in the camp. Truth be told, we brought him here, and he be the one that led his beastly friend to us."

"What are you saying, Josiah?"

He looked toward my tent, believing I was still inside asleep, as I remained hidden, having revealed myself to no one but Gregory. He lowered his voice. "I'm saying that rich city boy. He brought this calamity upon us."

"Don't be ridiculous! He was here with us that night."

"Was he? Who saw him? Did anyone see him when the attack happened or just that morning when he came out of his tent pretending not to know what went on here? How can anyone sleep through those howls, screeches, screams? It's not possible!"

Some of the men's eyes lit up with revelation. Others shook their heads, as though believing it to be nonsense.

"I say we bring him here and ask him to explain himself. See if we can trust what he says. Either way, this man dies!" He pointed to Gregory, whose terror was turning to rage.

"There was no one else! It was just me. Do it! End my misery. But leave other innocent souls outta this!" Gregory was pleading while commanding.

Josiah stared at him in suspicion and then spoke to the group. "You see, he's trying to save his foul partner."

The arguing began again concerning my guilt, and I knew if I was to live I must act immediately. I lit the torch and fired my tent, along with every tent I passed on my way to the wagon. There was much arguing and yelling before someone noticed the fire spreading in the breeze. The camp forgot their feud and sprang to put out the flames before they lighted the wagons. I saw the merchant leave his property and run to help with the fire, and so I immediately began unhitching Gregory's wagon from his. I retrieved my horse, and as I returned to the wagon, a young boy stood staring at me, the fire of the tents, and now one wagon, framing him in a halo of inferno. The flames crept ever closer to him while he stared as if trying to determine if he should call out to stop me or watch me leave. I quickly hitched the horse and mounted. The boy was near to being consumed by flame. The human in me wanted to leap to his rescue, but the animal in me wanted to survive. I did not have to choose, for a woman swooped in to snatch up the child, not looking into the darkness where the boy watched a monster slip away.

I looked back at Gregory, his face illuminated by the firelight. He looked in my direction and saw me in the glow of moonlight. He was kneeling, and I looked around for any way I might rescue him, but the fire was spreading, consuming the wagons despite the efforts of the men. One man, however, was not rushing to save the wagons. He was standing with his shotgun pointed at Gregory. Gregory was smiling, holding Mary's necklace to his lips, when the barrel released its lead into his skull.

I turned the horse and, as quickly as I believed the poor beast could manage, I raced down the Great Valley road back to Staunton, leaving the caravan of blazing wagons behind me.

7

Dreams of fire and blood haunted me, and I awoke to find myself in another strange bed, in another strange place. At least for the moment, I was safe.

I had ridden through the night and did not stop, crossing the river and accomplishing in hours a trip that had taken the caravan days. When I felt secure enough to let my horse rest and graze, I paused but neglected food and sleep for myself. I would not allow my mind to replay the scene of Gregory's execution, for I feared it would rob me of my will to flee. I would not mourn until I reached the only place I knew I could hide.

Arriving at the homestead the following night, I prayed Mr. Baird had not already returned to Williamsburg. He did not appear surprised to find me knocking at his sister's door. In fact, his face showed compassionate concern as he led me to a snug loft in the barn. Overcome with weariness, I ignored the ache in my stomach, sleep being the greater need.

The next morning I found Mr. Baird on the threshing floor with Mr. Arnot, shirt sleeves rolled up and sweat already lining his brow, as they lashed the wheat with a flail. No one spoke as I rolled my own sleeves, took a flail, and joined the men in their task. I had never known labor like that. I had never worked until my body cried out. But it was what I needed. I worked that long day in silence, the monotonous motion allowing my mind to drift and scenes I had suppressed to pass before my memory. The work was cathartic, and I cried, sweat, and toiled until my body and mind were spent with remembering.

That evening, after filling our stomachs, Mr. Baird and I walked the perimeter of the property, watching the sunset. I had not the heart to regale him with the details of what had befallen myself, even less to share with him the fate of our mutual friend, but Mr. Baird seemed to know, no doubt had predicted what would happen, and he did not require an accounting from me. Instead, he asked me about my plans, considering my circumstances. It seemed ridiculous to my reasonable senses that I should continue in my foolish endeavor to start a farm, and I acknowledged so to my confidant. But he thought on the idea and decided it was likely the best course to take. I could find seclusion on a large tract of land and secure myself, or be near enough to the mountains to take the trek over when the time for my transformation was upon me. I mentioned Beatrice and the many promises I had made, promises I now had no hope to keep, but felt bound to try, come what may. He looked at me again with compassion and promised to aid me in whatever way he could.

"But are you not expected in Williamsburg?" I asked. He stopped walking and looked at me with a smile in his eyes.

"I study to help those in need. When there is a need before me, the studying will keep, lad. This," he pointed a finger to my heart, "canna wait."

Before long, Mr. Baird was made privy to a large swath of land to the west of Staunton that was being parceled out to prospective farmers by the wealthy merchant William Beverley. Much of the land Beverley had been granted in '36 was already spoken for, but there was some acreage that had been overlooked because of its less desirable situation. I could not hope for better. Signing for the land using my mother's maiden name of Pole, I hoped I would avoid detection should Josiah and his caravan return to Staunton to seek me out. I could not hold it against them if they came looking for me. If it were not Gregory and I who had unwittingly and unwillingly committed the heinous crimes, I would have offered to accompany the farmer on his hunt for the second villain.

I was now the owner of a fifty acre lot at the foot of the mountain range with the stipulation that I must clear and plant crops in the next three years. This was not a difficult commitment, as I intended to begin work on the land immediately and only wanted help.

The families that settled the backcountry were not slave owners, by and large. This I found to be intentional, as the profiteers who scooped up available land and then dished it out advertised heavily among the Germans, Scots, and Scots-Irish who were not of the slave-owning persuasion. The wealthy plantation owners of the tidewater relied on a barrier protecting their interests, not only from the French and Indians but also from the threat of runaway slaves organizing themselves in mountain communities and initiating a revolt. A line of non-slave family farms would act as a living fortress.

Even so, slaves could be rented. I found that to be an abhorrent idea when a neighbor, a talented smithy, suggested it. I chose instead to seek hired hands and asked Mr. Baird to advertise for me in Staunton on his way to Williamsburg. As we were entering winter, for it was now early December, and harvest was over, I found many willing hands eager for work through the cold, desolate months.

Through some of my workers, I learned that a farmer, whose wagon had been burned on the Great Valley Road along with several others, had spun a yarn about wolf-men in one of Staunton's taverns. The more he imbibed, the more he talked, and the more he talked, the more fantastical his tale became before his listeners waved him off as a lunatic. He told them everything about the night of the attack—my attack—and about

Gregory and me, but no one believed him. I was relieved to hear that just a few days later, what was left of the caravan had rolled out of town the way it had rolled in.

The next full moon drew nearer as I planned how I was to avoid shedding more innocent blood. I had the wagon and the key, but I would not trust the contraption alone. In order to put distance between my possessed-self and the innocent souls that surrounded me to the north, south, and east, I resolved to travel as far west by whatever path I could find that would suffer a horse and wagon to forge on. The surveyor gave me a rude map of the county indicating where the inhabitants had marked their territories, allowing me to move in the most opposite direction of civilized life possible. I knew I would trespass on tribal territory and could only hope I would remain unmolested and that the natives had moved on to their winter lodgings, wherever they may be. I would allow myself a week or more for the entirety of my travels, and so I paused the work of clearing my land in order to protect the people of the backcountry.

The night before I was to leave on my solitary journey west, I wrote to Beatrice. I had neglected to write to her since settling in Staunton. I knew not how to convey to her what had happened to Gregory, nor I for that matter. My intense guilt and shame, and the adaptation of a new identity amongst my neighbors, left me unsure how to begin a correspondence once again with my love. I swallowed all my apprehension to give her news, for news I was sure she wanted, and I worried that my silence would cause undue strain.

Beatrice, darling,

I apologize. This letter is long overdue. I never succeeded in my journey to Big Lick. Instead, I returned to Staunton over a fortnight ago, and yet I did not write to you immediately for reasons I cannot divulge completely, but I will attempt to share what I can.

I told you I would be joining a caravan through the backcountry to my intended destination, and so I did. Yet during my excursion, the most unusual and disastrous event occurred, which I am disinclined to relate in detail. However, know this, Gregory returned, only to be accused of a monstrous deed and sentenced by civilians to execution. Oh, Beatrice, the same fate was to be meted out on me had I not escaped!

It is now beyond doubt Gregory is gone from this world. I know not how you may comfort your dear sister, for I am sure her heart aches for his loss. Yet, she must know that he died kissing the memory of her, for the necklace she bestowed on him became his rosary in the time of his greatest need.

I fled from my accusers by traveling north on the Valley Road and returned to Staunton. I believed my former friends might follow me, should they discover which way I went, so I resolved to waste no time in securing our land, which would take me away from the town and into the wilds where I hope to avoid detection. In any case, intelligence leads me to believe I am no longer at risk.

I have, however, in abundance of caution, taken my mother's maiden name, which you will remember, and ask that in your future correspondence you address me as such.

Enough talk of misery and woe!

We have land, my love! I need only cultivate it, and I will send for you, my joy, to join me here in this fairyland.

Yours always,

Fenn

I was struck by the ability I displayed to forget the affliction of my soul; the delusion leaving me capable of making such a promise to my beloved. Marriage to me would mean certain death come the first full moon. However, my arrogance forced me to believe myself capable of overcoming such an obstacle, and I would not abandon hope. In my naïvety, I had every intention of being cured from my scourge and living happily ever after with my bride.

I returned from my sojourn into the mountains shortly after Christmas. I was invited to celebrate the New Year at the festive hearth of an acquaintance I had made during my infrequent sojourns into Staunton. It could have been the court of a king, and it would not have been more pleasant. I was warmed by the invitation and the company of such amiable people, a stark contrast to my lonely trip which left me frostbitten and nearly frozen to death.

It was Christmas day when I had stopped the wagon in a crag, knowing I could not travel further into the mountains, and the full moon was upon me that night. I supped on frozen, dried meat and a flask of spirits which warmed my body but not my soul. I was sorrowful to spend an otherwise holy day awaiting the emergence of the unholy in human flesh. My flesh. I was disgusted but thankful to be alone and have no witness, no victim, to add to my shame. The key was wedged securely in a crack between two boards of the wagon just within reach after locking myself in. I hoped the beast would not be wise enough to look in all the nooks and crannies for a means of release; but I had not accounted for the thrashings of the monster which dislodged the key and dropped it under the wagon. Not only that, but the wagon had rolled a few feet, though I had secured it to a tree, and so the key sat maddeningly just out of reach.

I spent much of the frigid day following the transformation tying what I could spare of my clothing into a noose which I used to drag the key to the wagon. My clothes had been shredded into rags, and the short walls of the wagon were my only protection from the cold. I thanked providence that I had brought a net, among other useful supplies, that was secured to a pole and could fish the key out of the dust. Even so, I had been exposed to the cold for far too long and only the penetrating rays of the sun on a cloudless day had given me respite. Once I freed myself from the cage, I spent a while pressed against the body of my horse, drawing his warmth into myself before I hitched the wagon and made the weary trek to my homestead and the fire of the hearth.

But that ordeal seemed a distant memory as I listened to the tales of those whose company cheered me and reignited my hope. I had preserved life, those of others and my own. Perhaps I could repeat the feat indefinitely, I thought, while soaking in the fire's warmth. I had not considered that winter had just begun. My thoughts were interrupted by a hand on my shoulder.

"Mr. Pole! I hear you have been looking for laborers to clear your land? How have you fared?" asked my host, a Mr. Miller, whose name suited him as he owned a mill on Middle River. He was of German descent, though his family lived long enough in the colonies and depended heavily on trade that his English was nearly perfect.

"Well! I have more hands than I know what to do with, but I know this will not be the case come spring, so I mean to take advantage of it." Mr. Miller motioned for a lad who I judged to be not yet twenty to join our conversation.

"I hope you may find use for two more hands, Mr. Pole. My young friend Matthew here is a hardworking, able man who has a talent for toiling in the earth. His father is a smith in town, so he does not have an opportunity to develop his skills at home. Perhaps he may join you as an apprentice?"

"Mr. Miller, I hardly believe I have anything to teach this young man. In fact, it will probably be quite the opposite. But since I will be sorely in need of farming expertise, I see no reason why Mr. . . ."

"Howe, sir," answered the tall, dark-haired young man as he tipped his head to me in introduction.

"Why Mr. Howe should not assist me in planning and planting when the time comes."

"Thank you, sir," Matthew nodded again. He seemed disinclined to carry on the conversation until Mr. Miller thanked me for my consideration of the boy and walked away to mingle with his other guests. "Thank you again, sir, for allowing me the opportunity to work with you on your farm."

"No, I am the one who should be doing the thanking, Mr. Howe."

"Please, it's Matthew."

"Matthew," I conceded. "I confess, I know nothing of the life I have traveled all this way to lead. Now I will not have to bear the jests of the men in town when I ask my stupid questions."

"Where are you from, sir?"

"Please, call me Fenn." He nodded and smiled. "Philadelphia, originally."

"My family is from the northern colonies as well—Massachusetts, but we have been here in the backcountry for about ten years now, since before the twins were born."

"The twins?"

"My brothers, sir, I mean . . . Fenn, sir." I laughed as he stammered over formalities.

"How many are you?"

"Six total. Only four children. My mother had trouble having more after the twins and we buried my three other siblings. They were born asleep."

"I am sorry to hear that, Matthew. So your father is a smith? What kind?"

"Well, he mostly works with iron around here. There aren't many families needing silver work, though he is skilled in that as well. But he believes that will change soon enough."

"Yes, well, it seems Mr. Miller is on his way to finer things. I have noticed quite a few homesteads are improving their estates." After all, we stood in a parlor that was separate from the rest of the house; with doors, no less. The walls were lined with wainscoting and embroidered fabric covered the cushioned chairs that sat in the corners of the room. Mr. Miller's new home was built on the hill overlooking the river and could be seen by every passing boat. Its grand pillared entrance and many windowed façade reminded me of the homes in Williamsburg that were hammered into being by slaves. I wondered if Mr. Miller had rented slaves to build this house or if he had managed to do it with paid labor.

Matthew explained the situation with his father and why Mr. Miller had suggested petitioning for my aid. Mr. Howe was intent on Matthew taking up his trade. Matthew had apprenticed under his father for the seven years that was customary. He expected his son to take on more responsibility at his growing kiln.

Matthew, however, had no love for ironwork. Instead, he spent his free time watching things grow. He loved plants. He had already taken over most of the work in his family's kitchen garden and had requested of his father to clear more of their land and begin raising a crop for trade. The man was against the idea and did not want to fracture his business into two endeavors. Smithing was enough, he said, and Matthew would make a fine living from it.

"I don't mean to dishonor my father. I have even found him a very good apprentice who will take my place. But I don't expect he will take my decision lightly."

"Yes, I can understand the concern. I wish I had known the details before I promised to take you on. I do not wish to incur any ill will from my neighbors."

"Oh, sir, I mean, Fenn, I wouldn't wish that either. Mr. Miller has offered to speak to my father, and he has already said he will make it clear you had nothing to do with my decision. He and my father are good friends, both serving as deacons under Reverend Craig at Augusta church."

"Why is your father not here tonight?"

"He is not comfortable with frivolity. He doesn't like to celebrate with drinking and games at Christmastime. He came from Puritans and still holds on to some of their ways."

"I see. Well, I will hold to my promise, but if working for me is in any way seen as a slight against your father, I hope you will let me know."

"Of course, Mr. Pole." We both smiled and ended our meeting with directions to my homestead. He knew the way, and in fact, his father's property, though not bordering mine, was directly east, and he knew a path which followed the property lines of my neighbors, ending at the eastern border of my acreage.

In the weeks that followed the new year, I had developed a strong bond with the young man, Matthew. He was bright and affectionate and yet struggled under the weight of his father's expectations. The news of his choice to leave the family trade behind came, not as a shock, but with great disappointment to his father. He believed strongly in duty, yet he acknowledged his son was a man and must make his own way. However, once he accepted the new apprentice, he would have no room to reinstate his son should he decide to return to the kiln. Matthew acknowledged the situation was fair and assured his father he was ready to embark on his new endeavor wholeheartedly. We spent the first days of his apprenticeship by my fire, laying out the plan for my kitchen garden and the few acres of land that were cleared for spring planting. We were still discussing the merits of the crops that carried the most success in trade, i.e. wheat, corn, and the ever-growing demand for tobacco, when the urgency of the full moon led me to depend on Matthew still more.

The days were now freezing, as well as the nights, and as I neared the time I must leave for the mountains again, I wondered how I would survive. What if something happened to the key?

I had already removed the cage from the wagon and studied its design. It was a piecemeal of traps and other miscellaneous ironworks, shoddily soldered, but sound and that was all that mattered. It reminded me of a gibbet and was fitted with an iron padlock and the chain which previously held the key. I did not trust the monster not to figure out how to unlock the cage, as Gregory's had done, and so I had to discover a way to restrain and free myself in the same contraption without leaving the key so precariously lying about. I secured the cage with bolts into the masonry work of the cellar of my abode, which had just recently been completed.

My house, at that point, had four walls of log, plastered and weather-boarded, a fireplace with a chimney, and a door cut out of one wall. I was grateful that I had dug a cellar, though the rocky terrain made it difficult to dig far, and reinforced it with stone. A heavy door was set into the entrance to the cellar and fastened with a lock. I did not believe the door would be enough to thwart the beast, who had shown itself to have unnatural strength, yet it afforded me some peace of mind to think myself doubly secure.

"Matthew, I wish to discuss something with you that is very private. But first, I must ask whether you are inclined to be of assistance beyond the state of my soil?"

Matthew considered for a moment and assured me he was willing to help in any way I needed, so valuable was my friendship to him.

I explained to him that an ailment came upon me once a month and it caused me great mental anguish. He did not press me for further evidence because I did not elaborate on the illness. He trusted me, I knew, so I told him of my contraption, refraining from referring to it as my gibbet—the name I called it when alone in my thoughts—which would secure me through the night and keep me unharmed and peaceful until morning. I knew this to be a lie, assuming that a monster in a cage would remain neither unharmed nor peaceful, yet I wanted to reassure my new friend that containing me in my contraption would be the greatest kindness he could bestow on me. He was at first reluctant to oblige, concerned that it did my dignity an injustice to be treated like an animal. But, after much entreaty, he agreed to the task. And not a moment too soon, for the following evening brought the full moon.

    I will not deceive myself; I felt great unease concerning this plan. I knew I had not divulged the danger this request would put my young friend in. So desperate was I for the possibility of a real future, I was willing to put another soul in harm's way in order to achieve it. I see that now. Yet, at the time, I believed success could be achieved if all precaution was taken, and so I carried on with my scheme.

    I showed him the contraption and explained to him what must be done. He must lock the cage and keep the key upon his person. He must then lock the cellar door and retreat to his own home, not returning until dawn to release me. I warned him I may look disheveled, but not to fear, for it was only the ailment and all would be well.

    Matthew returned the following evening at dusk, and I recused myself into the cage. I fought to control my nerves as I knew any mistake may cost lives, perhaps even Matthew's, and the sweat beaded my brow though the temperature plummeted below the point of freezing. Matthew's hand shook as he locked the bolt, and he looked at me with trepidation, as if expecting something unnatural to occur. In my mind only did I acknowledge something unnatural would surely occur, but not for hours yet.

    I listened while Matthew locked the bolt to the cellar door and heard the jingle of the keys clanging together in his pocket. I held my breath in anticipation of the sound of his retreat and was satisfied when the horse's hooves became a distant tapping sound and then silence.

    Matthew's face was the first thing I beheld when I awoke. My cage had withstood the sound beating the monster had given it. One bar was warped, and I marveled it remained intact. I noted to myself that I would reinforce the bar before the next full moon. Matthew pretended not to notice the crooked iron bar and unlocked the cage quickly to set me free. My clothes hung from my frame in rags, slashed apart and unsalvageable. Matthew, in his kindness, looked away and handed me a shirt, which I had, in forethought, hung on a peg near the cage.

"I didn't expect you to look so. . ." said Matthew in a quavering voice. He had attempted to remain stoic but failed, though I allowed him to think he did not.

"Oh, it is nothing, really lad! I am in your eternal debt for aiding me."

"I'm afraid I have only made you suffer."

"Heaven's no! I am overjoyed that my contraption has served its intended purpose. Thank you, friend."

The boy, I call him such though he was but ten years my younger, turned and smiled. He was grateful to be of service to someone who appreciated it, I reasoned, and so I knew I could count on him to remain faithful.

"I must ask you one thing, Matthew."

"Yes, sir?"

"Please, allow my contraption and the night of my confinement to remain a secret. I fear that those with superstitions will assume evil out of something benign. I trust you know what I mean." Matthew had shared stories of his family heritage. His grandfather was a child in Salem village during the hysteria of 1692 and 3, and his father had grown up with the superstition somehow soaked into his being. He saw demons hiding behind every ill wind. I feared his sensitivity to monsters would bring him sniffing at my door, but Matthew assured me he would speak not a word of our arrangement to anyone, most especially his father.

8

I was beside myself with the prospect of a real future with my love. I knew it would be months before I could send for her in all confidence that her father would give her his blessing, but I believed those months to be what was needed to ensure that my contraption would hold my secret and I could dream without nightmares.

I will not go into detail about the monotonous months of winter and early spring. Much was still to be done on my homestead to prepare for planting after the last thaw, and so I was absorbed in clearing acreage, acquiring farm implements, and gleaning knowledge from my generous neighbors, all with the confident direction of Matthew. The question of what crop to trade was still one we wrestled with. Others were planting tobacco, and becoming quite wealthy, but I was disinclined to use slaves, and so was not interested in crops which required excessive land and excessive hands to tend. I decided first to establish my farm to produce all I would need to sustain my family. And then, because corn and wheat grew well in the region, I would devote a part of my field to each.

A homestead required not only crops, but livestock as well. So once my house was built and sufficiently furbished, I looked to install fences for a paddock and a barn to house the flock I intended to purchase. A dairy cow, chickens, sheep, a pair of horses, and a pig would suffice to start. I found I enjoyed hunting and had time to practice, so I could supplement my meals with deer and turkey, which were plentiful.

Matthew spent many evenings at my hearth where we shared stories. Some nights he read aloud from a worn copy of *The Pilgrim's Progress*. It was, at the time, a special story for him, as it was one his father had read aloud when he was a child. Yet, as Matthew read, he would often become serious or saddened, and he would share more about his family.

Over the course of our friendship, I gathered that not only was his father superstitious, he could also be a harsh man, given to over imbibing, and so becoming increasingly heavy-handed against those who upset him overmuch. The rift between him and his father was growing, and I encouraged him to mend the relationship, if possible. The new apprentice did not live up to his father's standards, and so he was increasingly scornful towards his son, whom he had perceived left him high and dry. Still, Matthew was delighted at this opportunity to wet his feet in the puddle that was my small estate before leaping into the ocean of possibilities for a young man of his abilities in the southern colonies. He meant to own his own plantation someday, and I believed he would be brilliant.

I still required Matthew to leave the property at night and return home to his father for fear of setting a precedent of presence that would heighten his curiosities on the night he locked me in my cage. Instead, he was accustomed to riding home in the evenings and returning in the mornings, a ride that cost him about a half hour each way. My scheme of restraining the beast was successful for two months, and I entered the planting season with high hopes that I would soon be afforded the right to petition for my bride to accompany me.

In April, as we approached the full moon, Matthew was determined we should put in the corn crop on the 23rd without fail. He had learned from the Saponi how to plant corn and believed it must be planted on the day of a full moon to ensure a successful crop. I was not averse to the idea and only wanted that we should finish our planting in time for seclusion in my cage. We worked from dawn to dusk, it seemed, stopping only to refresh ourselves before returning to the work of planting. I was sorely in need of rest by nightfall, but knew my body would be in a fitful passion and would not have the luxury until the following day. All went according to plan as I entered my cage, and Matthew locked me in as usual. I could see that his energy waned quickly, and I hurried him off to return home as soon as possible. I heard him lock the outside door, but as I was exhausted from the day's work, I slipped quickly to sleep, neglecting to listen for the horse as it galloped off to safety.

I awoke in my newly planted cornfield.

I cannot express the anguish I felt when I looked up and perceived that the colorful morning sky, and not the gray stone walls of my cellar, greeted me. There was a chill in the air, and I immediately felt the cold pass over every part of me laid bare. I slowly raised my hands for inspection and recoiled at the sight of blood.

Dear God! What had I done? I scrambled quickly to my feet and ran for my house, noticing my leg stung with each step, and looked down to discover a wound in my calf. I would not give myself the benefit of closer inspection and continued to sprint to the small building that should have been my sanctuary, yet betrayed me. The door was standing open as I ran in, searching for any sign of the crime the beast had committed. The cellar door was thrown, the hinges torn completely from the stone. I had enough mind to notice the lock was sound. I looked into the cellar to see my cage bars were intact, save for the one faulty piece that had warped. Fool! I had neglected to repair it, so focused was I on setting up my unattainable future.

I quickly threw on a shirt, breeches, and boots when I

noticed a satchel by the fireplace that I knew belonged to Matthew. He had not left!

I ran from the house, calling his name, searching left and right for any sign of life. His horse, normally hitched to the beam of my porch, was missing, and I prayed Matthew had heard the hellish racket from the cellar and fled for his life. I ran toward the Howe's homestead, which was roughly two miles away through the woods. Matthew's daily rides had carved out a path, creating a road the spring growth had not yet overcome. As I ran as fast as my smarting calf would allow, my hope grew. I traveled a mile or more without sign of mischief until I turned a corner and saw before me the mangled body of a horse. The intestines were spilled and trailed a few feet away from the carcass. The throat and flank exhibited deep gashes, at least six inches long and clear through the muscle. I searched the area for any sign of Matthew, crying his name. Could he have survived? Had he shot me and fled for his life?

I heard a grunt in answer to my call. Scrambling down a bank, I discovered Matthew, badly wounded, clinging to his rifle with one arm and holding his stomach with the other. I could see the blood streaming over his hand and knew he did not have long before he would be gone. I approached him, and when his eyes focused on my face, he recoiled and lifted his rifle with his free hand, shooting and just missing my other leg. The exertion increased the trickle of blood to a stream. I could hear the gurgling sound as the last of his life flowed out of him and he perished before my eyes.

"No! Matthew, come back!" I slapped his cheek as one slaps a drunk, but he did not stir.

I tried what I could to revive him, but all was in vain.

My stomach lurched, and I moved away from the body so as not to defile it with my purge. I returned to the still form of my friend and searched one last time for any sign of life. But Matthew was gone. I had murdered him. My eyes clouded with tears and the knot in my throat forced me to cry out in anguish.

I hushed myself, remembering the peril I was in, should someone hear and follow the sound.

I wanted time to mourn at his side, but I could not spare it. Though the road was only known to Matthew, I feared any number of circumstances that could bring another soul across our path, and so I hastened. I had considered leaving him in the wood and allowing another to find him. It would be assumed a wild beast had attacked, an occurrence that riddled the colonies with fear of the dark. Yet my care for Matthew, and my responsibility, forbade me from abandoning his body. I took great care not to mangle it further as I heaved him up the bank to the path. I remembered I did not have a horse with which to carry him back to my homestead and his was, as I already stated, another victim of the monster. The road was only ever used by Matthew, and so I decided I could leave his body next to his mount and return home to retrieve my wagon and horse. I would be gone for the space of over half an hour and so, fearing the carrion birds may find him before I returned, I covered him with all I could find that might protect the body until I could retrieve it.

I ran home, not with the same speed or abandon as I had run to find Matthew, but I kept what pace I could with a wounded leg. My mind ran all the while with plots and schemes of how I might present Matthew's death to his father. Would he believe it was a wild beast? Would he suspect foul play? Would there be an inquisition into my history and home? I could not afford to be connected with the attacks of the caravan I had traveled with, especially when the locals remembered the fantastical tale they heard in the tavern about a wolf-man living among them. My only recourse was to hide the body and wait for an inquiry that would surely come when his horse was discovered and he was missing from the scene. I would tell the truth as far as I understood it from when I fell asleep: Matthew left my home shortly after dusk, and as every other night, returned home on the road he had paved through the wood. One would likely assume he was attacked and dragged off to feed a pack of wolves or a lion's brood of cubs.

When I finally returned to my home, I hitched my horse to the wagon and tied a strip of cloth around my leg, which had stopped bleeding, though the hole had not yet fully closed. I did not have time to discover if the bullet remained lodged in my flesh or if it had passed through. I mounted my horse and took off with all haste, only keeping a pace that the poor beast could bear while pulling the wagon. The road was not fit for wheels and I had much difficulty maneuvering to avoid tangled roots, stumps, and stones that threatened to disable my wagon and ruin my claim of ignorance should someone find Matthew's body. I somehow made it to where the body of the horse lay across the road, and to my horror, the horse was the only carrion I discovered.

The coverings I had placed over Matthew were thrown aside and the gun, which I had propped up against the horse, was missing as well. It could not have been a beast that found the body and dragged it off. What use had a dumb animal for a gun? A man had found him! For a moment, the memory of awakening alive when I had no right to be sucked the breath from my lungs. No! I physically shook my head. Matthew would not become what I had become. It was unfathomable. I refused to believe it.

I would not stay to inspect the scene any longer. If a person had happened upon Matthew, that person may still be in the area and, though I could likely claim ignorance, I did not want to have to account for why I was in the woods. I returned home.

The bullet had passed through my leg, and so I had only to properly bandage myself. I noticed, however, that the wound had, by then, closed completely and a scab encased the hole the ball had made. I changed my clothes and busied myself with repairing my gibbet. The work was inadequate and I would need help from a smithy to return the device to its necessary strength.

However, Matthew was gone, and I could not ask his father. I did the best I could with the resources at hand and waited.

I expected to hear horses' hooves and a knock at my door at any moment, yet the sun set, the moon rose, and no one came. Those I had hired through the winter months had their own gardens and farms to attend to now that the planting season was in full swing; no one was likely to come to my abode. I was deeply vexed, for I sorely missed my companion, and now felt the pang of loneliness more acutely than ever before. My trappings had failed, and though I may have been able to reinforce my prison, I could never trust it. My future with Beatrice died with Matthew.

I remained on my homestead for a fortnight before want of necessities drove me to town. In all that time, not a single soul visited me looking for answers. The anxiety of such an excursion made me ill, and I wretched more than once on the road. The town was alive with the spring weather. I avoided the blacksmith shop for fear I would be confronted by Matthew's father. The general store was on the other end of town, and so I quickly gathered my needs, paid with a buckskin I cured over the winter, and returned home. I was relieved to not make contact with any soul I knew well, only the shopkeeper whom I had dealt with in the past, and I kept the chatter from evolving into gossip by asking questions about planting root vegetables, though mine were already in the ground.

A letter from my beloved awaited me at the tavern, and I read as my horse sauntered along Matthew's road.

Fenn, my love,

Mary received the news of Gregory's shocking death with stoic dignity. I know she suffers, and her manner does not become the bright and joyful girl we both know. I fear her mind has fractured along with her heart. But each day I sense she remains with us inside her mortal shell, and I pray ardently she will recover.

When not in the presence of my dear sister, I cried deeply over the loss of our dear friend, but also tears of joy and sighs of relief escaped me, knowing that you are safe and in one piece. But I admit, I was confused to read, in the brief narrative of our friend's demise, that you might have shared his fate. I cannot help but speculate why. How can anyone think so very ill of you, my love, when I know you to be otherwise well respected? There must be an explanation to satisfy my curiosity, and so I will not worry over questions and simply wait for your reply.

I am overjoyed at the news of a bit of land to call our own. And yet, a wilderness lays at its doorstep full of terrors and threats. I wonder, have we made a mistake? Have we been hasty overmuch to start a life that we have abandoned sense and looked to a country that is not suitable to our upbringing and station?

But, I am a silly girl. Pay no mind to me. I can be brave and weather the storms, if only my love is by my side. And we mustn't give Gertrude reason to be smug, must we?

Send word, my heart. I long to hear more of this wonderland that is our small piece of Eden. I dream of it as I watch the ship's load cargo from the backcountry, destined for Europe and the West Indies. I say to myself, "one day, it will be the product of our hands on these boats."

Patiently yours,

Beatrice

My hand trembled as I held the letter. I had been careless with my words in sharing with Beatrice details that were unnecessary. Gregory was, in fact, dead. That was all I had to tell her. But now, if news spread concerning the caravan massacre, and it likely would, she would wonder all the more. Yet, what did it matter? The life I had hoped to build with Beatrice, however impractical it had been in the first place, was impossible. I could only hope she would never know it was I who had killed those people alongside Gregory. In any case, I held the letter to my breast, christened it with my tears, and returned it to the saddlebag.

As I neared my homestead, I passed the place where my future had been lost, poured out in blood. Nothing remained but the weather worn and scavenger torn bits of a horse's carcass. It had been dragged to a thicket, and the vegetation was quickly consuming it as, in turn, it fed the vines and grasses that grew thereabouts.

Back home, with another full moon approaching, I contrived a plan for how I might protect my neighbors henceforth. Now that my cage was unreliable and I had no one to lock me in, I decided on a scheme of avoidance. I would do as before: travel as far into the mountains as I could, this time on horseback only, and I would hope the beast would not stray too far from my mount . . . or eat it. It was all I could think to do.

On a bright morning in May, I loaded my horse with a small saddlebag equipped with rations and a change of clothing. The weather was warm and muggy that day, and I sensed a shower may greet me in the afternoon. As I finished arranging my cargo and checking the tack, I heard the faint clop of horses' hooves. I froze and my heart thumped so that I felt it could be seen vibrating in my chest. I had become so accustomed to the silent stillness of my property that the sound of another living soul ushered in a panic. I could not tell who the rider was as he, or she, was still far off, but the sound came from the direction of Matthew's road.

"Oh, Lord," I mumbled aloud, "it is the lad's father come to question me at last."

I took a deep breath and collected myself. 'I must remain calm,' I thought, 'and show not a hint of guilt lest I draw from him unsolicited suspicion.' I continued checking my tack, smoothing the saddle bag flaps, and brushing my horse, determined not to seem startled or apprehensive of someone's approach. The rider did not dismount, nor did he speak, so I was forced to look up from my work to address him. I nearly stumbled backward when I beheld what was most assuredly a specter. The likeness of Matthew sat atop the horse before me, and not merely the likeness, but the very man himself.

Once again, I had set aside what I knew to be true in exchange for what I wanted to believe. I knew before that day that Matthew was alive, and I knew why. I did not need to see the holes in his hands, or rather, the scars on his throat and stomach, to know that he was a werewolf. And yet, my mind was so deluded by the falsehood I had planted there and allowed to grow that I was genuinely dumbfounded when what was true stood before me.

"I suppose you would be shocked to see me alive, seeing as you left me for dead." Matthew spoke with unveiled bitterness.

"Is it possible?" I asked, barely audible as I approached as though to touch the form before me and so be sure it really existed.

"Oh, I would say it's more than possible. It happened."

"No. No, you were dead. I watched you die."

"You did more than watch."

"Oh, Matthew, please, allow me to explain."

"I didn't come for answers. I came because I saw why you cage yourself and the monster you become, and I won't have you killing anyone else. I came to tell you I'll be locking you up this full moon, but after that I want you to get out of here and go somewhere you can't hurt anyone or I'll turn you in. I will!"

"I do not doubt that, Matthew. Only, please, I'll tell you what I know of this affliction and what I plan to do to protect the innocent souls it preys on."

I could tell Matthew did not want to listen to me, but curiosity won over his indignation.

"Ten minutes."

I was grateful to have the opportunity to unload the burden I had carried exclusively since the death of Gregory. I invited Matthew in to sit and have some refreshment, but he was wary of going anywhere near my abode and I did not press him. He dismounted and stood, arms crossed, waiting for my story.

"First, I cannot begin to convey to you the depths of my shame and despair over what I did to you. I know it is beyond a mortal man to forgive such injustice, by a friend nonetheless, that I do not ask you to absolve me. Only know, I would have sooner gouged out my own eyes than allowed the monster in me to destroy one of my only friends in the world."

Matthew was unmoved by my penitence, but he waited quietly for me to continue.

"It will not be news to you when I say that I have come under the scourge of a demon, and it wields its power over humanity on the night of the full moon. The cage was the work of a friend, another sufferer of my affliction, and when he perished, I inherited it. The first full moon I was alone. I took the wagon to the mountains, but it was an unreliable plan, as I could not know whether the monster would learn to unlock the cage, and I risked losing the key in its fitful rages. So I enlisted your help. I knew I could trust you and you would be discreet. I never intended for any of this to happen."

"So you entangled me in your ill-fated plan? Stupid fool that I am. My father always said I trusted too easily."

"I would not have asked you, but for the fact that I found you to be an exemplary young man! Faithful and dependable. None of those qualities makes you a fool."

"Just easier to use."

"I was not using you, Matthew. I believe in your talents and I sincerely wanted to better your situation and see you establish yourself on your own land. Our arrangement was meant to be temporary until I could send for my love to join me here. But now I see that can never be. I can never trust even the trappings of iron against the enemy." I would have kicked the cage that had failed me if it were present. Instead, I felt my knees quiver, threatening to give way. The death of my future settled in as another truth that would not be shaken, even by my most fervently held hopes. I shuffled to the stool I kept near my doorstep and leaned upon it to steady myself. I took a deep breath and continued.

"I will not need you to lock me up as I am going over the mountain again; as far away from man as possible. I will just have to pray that the monster does not find another soul. I suggest you do the same."

"Why on earth would I flee over the mountains with you? So you can finish the job?"

I knew the outcome would most likely be the same as when Mr. Baird attempted to break the hateful news to me. However, I had to warn Matthew what I feared was the truth of the matter.

"I must tell you now how I became a werewolf."

Matthew rolled his eyes. I knew he did not want to suffer to listen to my story, but I sensed he was also intrigued. He sighed and waited for me to continue. I told him briefly about Gregory and our travels together before we were attacked.

"A man was killed, but I was wounded and did not immediately succumb to my injuries. I collapsed outside my tent and felt the life ebb out of me. I believed I would meet my maker. Then in the morning, I awoke and found my wounds nearly healed."

Matthew's countenance changed as I described the violence to my body and pointed to the scars he had seen before, but never inquired about. I could see, just above Matthew's collar, the evidence of claws and teeth. I did not ask to see the scars across his stomach, the site of the mortal wound.

"I later discovered that the monster had been my friend. He used the contraption to imprison himself, but the werewolf had somehow learned to use a key and had unlocked the cage. He had been infected with the demon when he was likewise attacked and survived. He was rescued by some tribesmen who dropped him off at a French fort in the north. Believing himself to have perished as well, he awoke and was tended by the French."

I could see the horror in Matthew's eyes that he desperately tried to contain. He understood my insinuation and was, as I expected, appalled.

"I am not a monster!" Matthew stated as he rose to return to his horse.

"And neither am I. It is not me that has murdered. It is my flesh, but it is not me."

He turned around and looked into my eyes with the confidence one musters when correcting a child and wants to be understood. He even raised his finger to my face as he spoke.

"I will not become what you have become!"

"But Matthew, how are you alive? When you awoke, when you assessed your wounds and saw they were already healing, what did you make of it? How can you account for it?"

"By the grace of God, I am alive today, and no thanks to you! I remember you found me. I remember shooting at you, and I remember losing consciousness. You left me for dead! A native in the woods came to help me."

"Someone found you?" This time my knees failed me entirely, and I trusted the stool to carry my weight. What if this native had witnessed the attack?

"Yes, a woman. She took me to her tent, dressed my wound, and I could return home that evening. My wounds were not nearly so bad."

"Did she see me? I mean, the monster?" He considered for a moment and shook his head.

"I don't think so." He frowned and his voice grew angrier. "Is that all you care about? That you aren't caught for trying to kill someone? What matters is you abandoned me and she didn't."

"You were dead, Matthew! I tried to bring you back. It was

impossible. You had no heartbeat. I only left you to get my horse and wagon so I could bring you back here."

"And what would you have done then? Eaten me?"

"Good Heavens, no! I told you, I am not the monster. The monster is in me, I admit, but it is not me."

"Well, I wasn't dead. I'm not dead, and I'm not a werewolf or whatever you claim to be." He forced out the words, but I could tell he was less convinced of their truth.

"What did you see that night?"

"Do you think I ever want to relive, even in my vaguest memory, that night? I can't control the demon I see in my dreams, but I can control whether I conjure him in my mind while I'm awake."

"You are right, I apologize. I will not ask you to remember."

Matthew took a deep breath and seemed to remember why he had come.

"So you'll be going over the mountains?"

"I would be on my way already, but for your visit."

"Then I won't delay you any longer." He stepped in his stirrup and mounted his horse. I rose from the stool that was supporting me to plead with my friend.

"Please, Matthew! Come with me. Or go your own way. Whatever you do, please risk not the regret I live with by leaving another's warning unheeded."

"Good day. I wish you success, and I expect to hear how you will prevent further bloodshed when you return." With that, Matthew rode off at a gallop to his road and disappeared into the trees.

I mourned for him and prayed God would spare him from my curse. But if not, I hoped the Almighty would convict him to secure himself for the sake of those around him. I could not attempt to persuade him any longer. I had already lost an hour of travel and I desired to be as far into the wilderness as possible.

9

It was shortly after my return from the wilds that I heard a horse approach my property. I feared whom it may be, what news the messenger might bring. I looked out of my eastern window to find that the rider fit the gait and stature of Matthew.

"Thank God!" I sighed as I stepped outside to meet him. I believed he had come to carry through with the promise he had made before I left for the mountains. However, once I beheld his countenance and saw the fear and anguish it held, I realized that admonishing me to leave civilization was not the reason for his visit. He nearly crumpled to the ground when he dismounted and may have fainted had I not raised him up and quickly deposited him onto the stool that had served me in the same purpose just days before.

"Matthew, good heavens! What is it?" I did not have to ask. I knew what plagued him, yet I had attempted to bury the truth once again with my foolish hopes. His face was as pale as freshly starched linens and his eyes were wild, darting in every direction, as if he expected to be overcome by an enemy at any moment. Burying his head in his hands, he began to sob, heaving and gagging, so that I ran inside to bring him a cup of cider to calm his nerves. He recovered himself and, as a storm was rolling in and it began to rain, he entered my home with more eagerness than I expected. He seemed reluctant to talk, so we sat for some time, listening to the thunder rumble as the fire crackled.

"I had nowhere else to go," he finally spoke.

I waited for him to elaborate, fearing that any questions would drive him to anger or grief.

"You were right. I should have heeded your warning." A sob rose in his chest, and he caught it by breathing in quickly, not allowing himself to lose his composure again. "They're all gone. Every one of them. It killed them all." His eyes were transfixed by the blaze before him. I believed he was transported somewhere in his mind, for he was no longer present with me. I gently pulled him back.

"Matthew. Do you mean to say that your entire family has perished?" I asked in as compassionate a tone as possible given the circumstances, and hoped it would not cause him to retreat. He seemed to snap out of his revery and turned his eyes to look in mine, the first time since he had arrived that day.

"Yes." The word caught in his throat and came out as a whisper. After a single cough, he repeated his confirmation forcefully, as if trying to convince me. "Yes. I just don't know how to believe it." I knew well the feeling and was overcome with empathy. I moaned with grief for my friend, but I would not allow myself to cry, so I rose to prepare a meal. Matthew returned to staring at the fire. He spoke, not to me, not to anyone, but painfully put his thoughts to words, and I was able to peer into the panorama that was playing across his mind.

"I said good night to Mother and Father. They were sitting at the fireplace. Mother was sewing, Father was reading the Bible. He always read the Bible out loud to Mother while she sewed. Constance was sewing as well. A sampler, I believe. Peter and Paul, the twins, they were already in bed in the loft where I was heading. I climbed the ladder and undressed to my shirt. Then I got under the covers and saw the moon outside the window. It was full, and the light was so bright I thought I would never fall asleep, but I was sore tired that day and I . . . I don't remember falling asleep . . ." His voice trailed off for a moment, and I observed his hand shaking upon a knee that bounced of its own will.

"I woke up. I woke up naked by the fire. The floor was sticky . . . why was the floor so sticky? I pulled up my hand. It came up like it was dipped in molasses, and all I could smell was wet iron. When I stood up is when I saw him. Father had pulled down his gun, but it got him before he could shoot. It was his blood sticking to my hands and knees." Matthew lifted his hands, inspecting them as if he would find the blood there still. "The door was open, so I went outside. It was hard to see since the sun wasn't all the way up yet, but I could tell there were two people lying on the ground near the stable. I went back inside. I just had to know for sure. They were there, in the bed, when I went up the ladder. They looked peaceful, and I would have thought they were just sleeping if the blood hadn't run off their cot onto the floor. I can still hear it dripping through a crack in the floorboards." I imagined the scene myself and nearly left off cooking to weep, but I could see Matthew was not finished, so I stifled my cry and waited. He opened his eyes to the fire once again and went on.

"I put them all in bed. Their bodies were cold, but they were still soft. I had to drag Father. I hated to do it, but he was so heavy. I carried in Mother and Sister. Their faces were spared, and I kissed them all and prayed the Lord's prayer over them. I don't know if that was the right prayer . . . it's been so long since the babies were buried." He choked a sob back before his face went blank as his mind retreated, likely to some place where his family was alive.

The meal was ready. I dished up a plate for Matthew, though I doubted he would eat much of it, and one for myself, and I sat with him again at the fire, placing the plate on a table beside him. My presence brought him back to his story.

"I burned it to the ground. Their funeral pyre. I should have buried them, but something told me to burn it. I watched it burn till I heard horses. I jumped on Bess and took off on my road, but I couldn't leave yet. I found a spot to hide and watched. The men who came, they would have tried to go in, but it was already too late. I stayed there, in my hiding place, for two days watching over them until they found what was left. The men buried them beside the babies who had never breathed. The town came to pay its respects, and when they all left, I ran back to the little cemetery and saw six new grave markers. I am dead to the world. I killed myself when I killed them, and I won't escape the unquenchable flames that will be my funeral pyre in hell."

I calmly put a comforting hand on Matthew's, but he recoiled at the touch and looked at me sharply. I took my hand away, not wanting to anger him further. His fierce eyes cooled, anger melted into despair, and he picked up his plate, took a small bite, and then put it back on the table.

"I wish I had died that day. Why did I live to become this, this thing? Why did you let me?" His eyes searched mine, and I pictured the moment he died. Would it have mattered if I had killed him seconds before he was about to expire? I do not think so. And I do not believe I could have done anything differently; I was not a murderer.

I put down my plate and thought for a moment how to give him an answer that would satisfy.

"Just as you have no memory of what happened to your family, I have no memory of what happened to you. By the time I reached you that morning, it was likely already too late. It appears that if the monster is interrupted in its kill, the scourge carries on in the victim, like a sickness having time to take over the body."

Matthew looked as if he would be ill. "What is it?"

"I do not know exactly." I stood up and paced the small room, collecting my thoughts, for how does one explain the inexplicable? Returning to my seat, I offered what I could. "I call it a demon, and yet it cannot be cast out. It is an affliction, but only displays symptoms on the full moon. In my right mind I have no desire for human flesh, no passion for bloodlust, yet if the monster takes over I become a murderer of the foulest kind."

I looked at the food waiting on the table and regretted fixing it. Matthew remained present in the conversation and had not drifted back to scenes of horror, so I continued. "Have you heard the myth of King Lycaon?"

Matthew let escape a derisive chuckle. "My father didn't believe it was right to read myths. He didn't want the names of pagan gods to cross our lips and blaspheme the Lord."

"Of course, he was a devout man." Matthew scoffed and nodded in a gesture of sarcastic agreement. I ignored it, assuming in his grief he was expressing an array of emotions. "Well, in any case, I feel it is necessary to tell you this one." I recalled the details of a story I had read many years ago in Plato's *Republic* before I continued. "Lycaon was the King of Arcadia. He attempted to deceive the god, Zeus, into eating human flesh, an act which, if successful, would have ruined the god. Zeus caught the scheme immediately and turned Lycaon into a wolf, presumably to feast on human flesh and be thus defiled."

"So he was cursed by Zeus. Then we have been cursed by God?"

"I do not think so, yet I cannot understand why He allowed this scourge, either." I stood and paced again as I pondered the possibilities. "Perhaps our souls departed. Perhaps we died and our bodies were reanimated to house the demon until it can feed. I want to believe that is not the case and I am still a human being with a soul that can be redeemed." I had never articulated such, even in my thoughts, until I spoke the words to Matthew. Was I beyond redemption already? I could not bear the thought, and yet I wondered if the reason Gregory could not be healed by Mr. Baird was because he had no soul to be saved? What was I, then? "It must not be too late for us! I cannot believe there is no soul, no conscience at work, if

Gregory and I both sought ways to cage the beast in order to save the innocent."

"To save the innocent?" He scoffed. "Perhaps it was only to save yourselves."

"From man's judgment? Yes, perhaps that is a primal fear and force that drives me to restrain the monster from his meal. But eternal? That is a far greater fear, and I do not want to be like the fallen angels who look to heaven from the abyss, longing for repentance but not permitted it."

"What if we are already damned? Would it not be better, would God not prefer it, if both of us ended this now, before another soul is sent to eternity by our hands? Caging it didn't work for you, not completely. I am here now and my family is dead because you persisted with living when . . . maybe, you should have removed yourself from this world completely." There was a sting in his words. At first I wanted to defend myself, but I understood. For the first time, I felt sick with bitterness towards Gregory. He had risked and forfeited my life when, maybe, he should have removed the risk. I hung my head for a moment before answering honestly.

"To kill myself? No. But to turn myself in and be killed? I have thought it. When I rode away from a flaming caravan after watching Gregory's execution—for what I am and what I did—I hesitated for a moment, and I nearly turned back. I would have faced my accuser then, repented, and endured the just punishment for my sin. But I rode on."

"Why?"

I sat down in defeat. "I was afraid," I said, as my eyes moved to the fire and I felt myself become entranced as Matthew had. I saw before me the flames of the caravan. The caravan gave way to a massive kiln. Hell fire? No. The refiner's fire. If we had the fortitude to endure hell on earth, could we escape hellfire for eternity? But I realized I had jeopardized Matthew's soul in order to save mine. Perhaps I was, indeed, destined for destruction. I considered why I had really wanted to live, and I knew it had nothing to do with my soul.

"Yes, I was afraid. To die. To no longer exist. But if I am honest, I wanted to continue on, even with the scourge, if I could only have Beatrice. I ran for her. For her, I stayed alive. I fear I would do it all again, for her." I gathered up our plates and dumped our suppers into the slop pail for the pig. "But, perhaps it is possible to be rid of it for the sake of the innocent, for the sake of our souls. Perhaps, together, we can find the way, and free not only ourselves, but the others of our kind as well."

"You believe there are more?"

"There must be. Gregory was attacked by one. There is at least one other, then, here in the colonies, if he has not already perished."

"Or crossed the ocean by now."

"I do not think so. He would be weeks, possibly months, on board a ship with no way to conceal his identity when he turned . . . and no one left to man the ship."

Matthew gave a hearty sigh and ran his hands through his hair before standing. I could see the days of angst had worn through him and he was spent.

"This . . . I can't do this anymore today. I would humbly ask for a place to sleep tonight, for I feel I am entitled to that much and more from you."

"Of course. You may have my bed."

"That won't be necessary. I'll sleep in your hay loft. It will be just as comfortable as any backcountry bed I've slept in."

"Good night, Matthew." He was already opening the door to leave. I stood, and he turned back.

"In time, I may be able to forgive you. I see you would not have done this to me on purpose. Just as I . . ." Overcome once more with grief, Matthew's words stuck in his throat, and he left the house without another word.

He did, eventually, forgive me. He could not, however, forgive himself.

. . .

As I will my hand to write this narrative, it seems impossible to fathom performing any act without consciousness. Could a puppeteer be at work, moving the strings of our bodies while our heads are empty wooden spheres? We believe when we have the faculties of our minds under our own control that we are the ones moving the strings, yet how much of our lives are the involuntary acts of a brain that does not need us to tell it what to do? I breathe without thinking. My food brings nourishment to my body without my instructing it how to. My heart keeps beating, even when I long to die. It is not so impossible, then, to wonder what other acts the body is capable of while the mind seems not to be in control. Or when it is in the control of something else.

Over the remainder of the month, I attempted to help Matthew see reason in his struggle against the flesh, the part of him he could no longer control. It could not be strictly physical, as if it were an illness that must be fought with medicine or suffered through until it had run its course. It was not a common outworking of human nature, either. We did not murder in anger, hatred, self-defense, or from the pleasure of it. It was an act wholly involuntary to our conscious minds. To what extent is our person held accountable for the act of a body not under our control? How can the body be punished without suffering injustice to the conscious mind of an otherwise innocent person?

A small stack of letters from Beatrice grew in the drawer of the hall chest. In between talks with Matthew and the basic needs for our survival, I read over her words, wondering how I was ever going to respond. She was, and rightly so, beginning to believe something terrible had happened to me.

My heart!

I say my heart, for you have it and will have it, whether you remain in this world or have already passed on to the next. My thoughts spin and tumble through a labyrinth of horrors as

I imagine the countless dangers that may have stolen you from me. But how can I say such a thing? If you are gone, it is because God wills it. Who am I to accuse Him of the theft of his own? But I pray He has not taken you home.

We have read strange things in the papers about a caravan massacre. Father and Mary know nothing of the scant details you shared with me in your letter concerning the circumstances of Gregory's death. But I have read the stories, and I must wonder if it is the same "monstrous deed" of which Gregory was accused. But how could that be? And if it is . . .

Fenn, what has happened to you?

I tell myself you have not received my letters. That some mischance has kept them from you and you are alive and well, waiting to hear from me. Only, you are silent, and I wonder, would you remain silent even if I was?

Please, my love, do not permit me to suffer any longer if it is in your power to comfort me. Send me word you are alive. It will be sufficient.

Yours, irrevocably

Beatrice

How could I reply when what I must write would tear out my very heart while stabbing hers? I could not lie to her, and so I could not answer her.

Forgive me, my love.

The only soul alive that I knew to have compassion for the plight Matthew and I now shared was Mr. Baird. He had spent the winter in Williamsburg at the college of William and Mary, but I believed he would be returned to his sister's plantation to help with the spring planting. I broached the idea to Matthew of traveling to Mr. Baird's. We had both been holed up on my land for weeks, not beholding another human form, and I grew restless for news of the world. Though I did not mention it to Matthew, I also hoped Mr. Baird would have more information for us about our condition. Matthew consented, though he noted the need for discretion, and I heartily agreed. We would have to forge a way through the woods and avoid the beaten paths where possible. As we saddled our horses, Matthew gazed at me with a keen look I well knew.

"What do you hope we will accomplish at Mr. Baird's?" I should have known better than to think I could conceal my design from Matthew.

"I do not deny that I expect Mr. Baird may have more information that could lead to a cure. He was completely unperturbed by the idea of the werewolf, and so that makes him our greatest friend on earth. Even though he knew I was one, he did not shun me or cower from me. He tried to help Gregory. If he could, he would continue to help me. In any case, we have nowhere else to turn, and unless we wish to be each other's sole companion into old age . . ." I did not finish the sentence. We were both young and the idea of decades of marching back and forth over the mountains was a daunting one. I wondered if it would not be best for us to bid adieu to civilization altogether and turn nomads in the western wilds. No, we must be free of our affliction, and I did not believe the answer to how lay west.

Matthew seemed to consent to my plans simply for lack of having anything better to offer himself. He would have ended his suffering by his own hand were it not for my admonition that all was not lost. I had reminded him that recusing ourselves from society during a full moon was an act of mercy and love for our fellow man, and if we would endure hardships for the sake of others, we must have nothing in common with the monster that breaks free from the shackles of our minds.

"But my hands!" It was the one thought Matthew continually returned to. His hands had done evil. Whether he willed it, he insisted he was responsible, for it was his body that acted. And he did not want to exist knowing he could kill again.

"'I do what I do not want to do'—we are in good company," I reminded him of the apostle Paul's words.

"You can't compare the struggle against the flesh with a demon who kills with abandon," he had argued.

"Exactly! Do you not see? That is what I am trying to help you understand. It is not us. It is not our flesh we are at war against. It is something that has dethroned our conscious, defiled our bodies, and . . . "

"Damned our souls."

Oh, Matthew. I feared he had descended beyond where I could reach.

"Please, friend, listen to me. As long as we are alive, there is hope."

"Hope for what?" Matthew was not angry. He was despairing.

"Hope that while this evil has overcome our bodies, it has not, it will not, overcome our souls. We can choose to be people, not monsters. And as long as we still have that choice, there is hope."

That conversation was days before the beautiful morning of the first of June when we led our horses through untrodden territory, on our way to the Arnot's.

As I remembered my admonitions to my friend, I prayed I was right.

I pray I am right.

As I await judgment in this cell, as death reaches out its hand to me, I fear most of all what lies beyond. The undiscovered country. Without hope, what other option is there but despair? And if I succumb? If I allow my mind to entertain the idea that I have already lost what should be most precious to me, even more so than my dear sweet Beatrice, what right then has this body to exist?

We sat atop our mounts in silence that day, both of us lost in our own thoughts, so much so that we did not notice the rider passing us on the only part of our journey we chanced to travel on a known road. It was too late to quit the way and take refuge in thick foliage. The man had already spied us. I whispered to Matthew to turn his head, as if noticing an animal as we passed the stranger. The rider's eyes met mine. I smiled and nodded. His gaze passed to greet Matthew, and he noticed the lad looking away. For a moment I thought I saw recognition in his eyes, his brow furrowed, but he looked at me once more, said good day, and carried on his way without a backward glance.

"Did he recognize me? Who was it?"

"It was the farrier. I do not know for sure, but I do not believe he recognized you." I hoped the change in the man's visage was simply a response to being slighted at not receiving a greeting from my companion.

The sickening feeling of danger remained with us until the forest gave way to the open fields of the Arnot farm. Men were hard at work, harrowing the kitchen garden and sowing the last of the summer vegetables. I noticed Mr. Baird standing in the hot southern sun, wiping the sweat from his brow before returning to his work. The clop of the horse's hooves alerted him to visitors, and he looked up, shielding the rays with his arm. A smile of recognition came over his face, and he stood and welcomed me heartily.

"It's about time I took a wee break. Come, lad, ye and yer friend, for tea."

I introduced Matthew, neglecting to use his last name, to Mr. Baird, sharing with him only my desire for a visit. Mrs. Arnot was working about the house and I was not aware how much Mr. Baird may or may not have shared with her about my affliction. It seemed Mr. Baird understood the hesitation in my speech, and he offered for us to walk with him to a spot near the river that offered a cool respite from the heat of midday.

It was at that spot I brought Mr. Baird into our confidence, explaining briefly how Matthew had come to be one of the afflicted. Matthew remained silent through the shortened summation of my attack and kept his face downcast when I told of the tragic death of his family. The "preacher" put a hand on Matthew's warmly and told him grace was sufficient, even for such things. I watched Matthew for any sign of comfort from Mr. Baird's words, and while I saw polite reception, his eyes remained despondent and his hand slipped out from Mr. Bairds. When the old man, older by at least a generation, was aware of our current state and our plan to use the mountain barrier as the means of protecting our fellow man, he shared a story about a recent experience he had at the tavern in Staunton.

"While waiting on a friend who was to meet me, I overheard a conversation being had at a nearby table. Most of the talk was useless prattle, but I caught the hint of somethin' possibly pertaining to yer situation. I'll do me best to tell it as I heard it:

'I heard there was one up north last fall. Blamed it on the French and Injuns, but I ain't heard no French tears apart a man like that.'

'What was the situation?'

'You know how the army's been quiet about the attacks. They don't warn't no one to desert on account of a monster on the loose. Well, this time, nearly all the men in the fort saw the thing. Say that's how the French was able to win the fort, the men was too scared to fight proper. Not to mention the red devils swarmin' all over the place.'

'What'd they say they saw?'

'No right animal, as they could tell. Weren't a catamount, nor a regular wolf. Says this one stood on its hind legs and had long fingers like a mans, though they was covered in fur. I don't like to give heed to old wives' tales, but some say it's what they call over in Germany a werewolf.'

'Hogwarsh. Ain't no such thing. Rabid wolf, be my guess. Or like you said, it was just them Injuns.'

'Well, we can guess what we want, but we weren't there to see it.'

'True enough. But just say it were a monster as such. What if it be the French is sending 'em out? Like a weapon?'

'You know, I can't believe I didn't think on that. Suppose it could be. Can't trust the French, no matter how genteel they be.'

'What fort you say it were?'

'Henry, on Lake George.'

Mr. Baird said his friend arrived at that point, and he heard no more of the conversation.

"They used the word werewolf?" I asked.

"Aye, they did. Seems the one that made Gregory a wolf is still alive."

"And not trying to protect anyone else," Matthew said in a low voice. I felt condemnation in my heart toward the man in the Great Lakes. Yes, it was clear he was not preventing the monster inside of him from having its fill. And yet, I justified my continued existence while judging this man for his. How easy it is to make accommodations for one's own sins while finding others to be reprehensible.

"Is there anything more you can tell us about this affliction? Anything that might help us find a cure?"

"I canna say I ken more than I did afore. Even at William and Mary's, there ain't much to be found about werewolves. But, I have not been idle an' I dunna plan to give up now."

"Why would you concern yourself with this? Haven't you more worthwhile pursuits?" Matthew's tone was skeptical, but not ungrateful.

"I'm called to concern myself with any way I can relieve suffering and help a soul overcome sin and the devil. 'Love thy neighbor as thyself,' an' I mean to."

10

"I wonder if it makes any difference if we flee to the mountains or not," Matthew said that evening by the fire. I could not mask the look of amazement I gave him. It seemed an obvious answer to me.

"Of course it does. Can you imagine what we would do if we stayed?"

"I thought it wasn't we who killed."

"You know what I mean, Matthew. We must get away from here if we are to protect our neighbors."

"Right. I mean . . ." It was clear he wanted to say more but stopped himself, considering my expression. "Never-mind. You're right."

I looked at him for a moment to judge if his countenance agreed with his words. He seemed sincere. I was certain the news of the man killing in the Great Lakes, seemingly without remorse, had weighed on Matthew's thoughts as it had mine.

The following morning, we were on our way to the west side of the property and the tree line that separated my homestead from the wilds when we heard horses' hooves barreling down the only road leading to my property: Matthew's road.

"Does anyone else know of that way?" I asked Matthew.

"Only my family."

In haste, I dismounted and instructed Matthew to ride the horses, quietly, as far as he could into the densest part of the wood. He objected, but I reminded him he was presumed dead and must not be seen. I ran to an area of my property where I had planted beans and squash, which was already putting out leaves, and began pulling up the weeds that threatened to choke the sprouts. The team of horses, three in all, entered the clearing, and one man dismounted to knock on my door. I rose from the posture of plucking and walked back toward home. Another rider saw me approaching and yelled to his acquaintance that I was in the field. They waited for me to reach my home before introducing themselves.

"What can I do for you, gentlemen?" I asked after names were exchanged.

"Mr. Pole, I am the deputy magistrate. We have received word that a man we believed to be dead may, in fact, be alive, and he is wanted for inquisition into the deaths of the members of his family, five souls in all."

"Oh, that is awful. Yes, I think I heard something about a family perishing. A fire, was it?"

"Yes, most tragic. It was presumed the eldest son was also in the home when it burned to the ground, but we have a witness who claims to have seen the boy on the road heading toward town just yesterday."

"Well, gentlemen, I admit I am confused as to why you have come here, if the lad was seen heading to Staunton?"

"We learned from some townsfolk that the boy, Matthew Howe was his name, had been working for you, extensively, over the winter months."

"Yes! Matthew was very helpful in getting my property in order for spring planting. The boy has a talent for agriculture."

"Yes, well, when was the last time you saw Mr. Howe?"

"It must have been when I planted my corn. April, was it? I believe it was April, sometime late in the month."

"You don't know the exact date you planted your corn crop?"

"Well, I know it was the full moon that night, as Matthew said the natives taught him to plant on the full moon, though I do not believe it matters much, but I left it to Matthew to decide. It was his last day working for me as I had no other need of planting help, and he was wanted at home for the season."

"And you have not seen him since that day, sir? Are you certain?"

"Absolutely. As I said, I had no further need of his assistance, and I rarely travel into town if I can help it."

"That is interesting, sir. You see, the man who told us he saw Matthew said the young man was traveling with another. You, sir."

I forced my face to hide my mounting trepidation. One lie after another crossed my lips, yet I had no choice. If I was to protect Matthew and myself, I had to convince these men that they were wasting their time on me.

"I admit, I traveled to visit a friend yesterday, but I was not with Matthew."

"Who were you with, then, Mr. Pole, if you were not riding alone?"

No one came to mind. I had no one else in the world but Matthew.

"A son of the friend I was visiting."

"Does he have a name?"

What were the Arnot children's names? I could not recall them as the eyes of inquisition were staring me down. David was the father, and I believed his eldest was his name's sake.

"David Arnot, junior, sir."

"Thank you, Mr. Pole. We will check in to confirm with the Arnot's. Until then, I am inclined to take you into town and hold you at the tavern while we verify whether he was the lad with you."

"Surely that is not legal!" I had no recourse if the men wanted to take me by force. My guns were inside and the only one we had brought with us was in the saddle of my mount, which Matthew had. I could run, but where would I run to? The woods were too far. They would catch me or shoot before I could make it. I could only object, and in that moment, I wished I was the wolf.

"By order of the King, we can hold you for less, I assure you. Sam, take him on your horse; Levi, help me look around this place. I have a feeling we may find evidence that someone other than Mr. Pole has been here . . . and recently."

I protested, struggling against the arms that grabbed me, but to no avail. The other men were stronger and tied my hands so that I was without recourse to fight or flee. I prayed Matthew had heeded my words and rode on into the woods.

The men would find evidence of the young man; his possessions were scattered about the property as if they were my own. Whether they could attribute them to Matthew was another thing altogether, but I hardly believed it would matter. They would find the gibbet in the cellar; a discovery that would pique their interest. I remained quiet, awaiting the result of their search. Eventually, I was thrown onto Sam's horse with whatever property the men decided was evidence, and we drove back on Matthew's road to town. To my great relief, my friend remained undiscovered.

My room in the tavern acted as a jail cell while I awaited more questioning. I was required to remain in the tavern until either Matthew was found or until I provided information leading to his discovery. Another deputy was placed at the door to my room to prevent my escape. Though I knew that a crime had been committed, and Matthew was in fact alive, I did not appreciate being held against my will simply for being an acquaintance of the man. I considered changing my approach and admitting to having been with Matthew on the road that day, yet having no knowledge that he was supposed to be dead. But I knew that an admission of such would only implicate me, as I would have had no reason to lie in the first place if I had not known Matthew was attempting to avoid discovery.

They questioned me on two occasions. The first: what my business with Matthew was, what I knew of his family, and the like. I attempted to relate as little as possible to answer the question without incriminating myself or my friend any further. The second round of questions was about my gibbet.

"What's the cage for? Seems strange a homesteader would be in need of such a contraption, and in a cellar no less."

"Indeed. I . . . I" I scrambled for an answer. What need could a man like me have for an iron cage? Not for livestock; I barely had any, let alone a need to contain them in such a rude contraption indoors. I could not pretend to use it for my wife or children, as I did not have any, and I would abhor the idea of such a thing even if it were a plausible excuse. I played it off as a trap I fashioned for catching the wild beasts that terrorized the woods. It would be the truth in spirit.

"It is a trap. I designed it myself. After hearing much talk of the man-eating wolf or lion, whatever may be, that has been murdering up and down the colonies, I thought perhaps I could catch the beast before it makes prey out of anyone else." The men thought on my answer for a moment and seemed to consider it plausible—a good idea, even. I believed myself to be out of danger when the men rose to leave.

"Is that all? May I leave?"

"We are still looking for the lad, and we don't want you helping him."

"I can assure you, I will not be helping him. I do not even know where he is, if he is still alive. I have nothing to gain by harboring him on my property."

"Perhaps not, but we have reason to believe that he is a dangerous sort and want him taken to the jail where he can await trial and execution, if need be. We aren't prepared to take any chances."

"Please, I cannot stay here any longer. I have much to attend to at home."

"Then tell us where we can find the lad, and we can let you go."

"I have already told you, I do not know."

They walked out of the room while I pleaded with them to allow me to leave. I had only one day to remove myself from civilization before the monster emerged, and I feared I would never make it far enough. I would have to escape somehow, but in so doing, I would forfeit my life in Virginia and in the colonies, for I would be a wanted man, along with Matthew. Neither of us could remain in the land of law.

I had no friend to call on, no leverage but money, so I attempted to persuade my gaoler to neglect the lock when he brought in my meal. The man seemed sensible enough and inclined to acquiesce, seeing as I was not wanted for committing any violent crime. Yet he had been warned to keep a close watch over me and, under no circumstances, allow me to leave my room. He did not want to share my fate, so he forwent my offer of compensation to look the other way. I acknowledged his position and thanked him for his kindness in that he made sure my meal was pleasant and the beer was not watered down, as would be expected for a lodger of my circumstances.

I paced the room, insensible as to what other recourse I had. The room did not have a window. It was used for storage, but a small pallet had been erected for my stay. There was no escape but through the door, which led into the tavern, past a guard. Should I break the door open without alarm, I could not pass unnoticed through the throngs of men on the other side. My only attempt could come in the middle hours of the night, when my guard would likely be asleep and long before the inn-keepers began their early morning labors of drudgery.

The storage closet contained a forgotten collection of old rusty carving knives that once awaited refurbishment, but were now lost in a heap of discarded wares that apparently the owner was remiss to part with. One such knife could pry off the hinges of the door, and I noticed the wooden frame, though not old, was already exhibiting signs of decay. It was well into the night when I heard the noise in the tavern die down to a murmur. I began my work then so as not to draw attention to myself should the hinges prove creaky or require more force to draw out. The nails pulled free from the wood with less effort than I expected, and I wanted only to lift the door and pull it out at an angle to remove it from the frame.

Eventually, presumably close to midnight, the tavern fell silent, and I was able to extract the door with considerable ease. My guard was slumbering in a heap on his side, a bottle of spirits his only companion. I slipped past and he stirred, murmuring and grabbing the bottle to nuzzle it in his chest. He remained asleep while I moved as noiselessly as possible through the rest of the tavern. I wondered if the front door would require a key to unlock, a thought which had not occurred to me in all my dealings with the door to my cell. But when I approached it, I saw that it was kept locked by a bolt that could be drawn without a key. I quietly unbolted the door and pulled. It squealed and I stopped, waiting to hear my gaoler rise and charge into the tavern, rifle drawn, but the building remained silent, all boarders tucked away for the night and the inn-keep turned in as well.

I slipped into the night and closed the door behind me. It would not be long before the guard discovered I had escaped. And by escaping I was a villain on the run. There would be no safe place for me from Staunton to as far as Richmond. In any case, I would need to fly to the wilderness and gain as much distance as possible before my affliction emerged. I was about to steal a horse from the stable when I looked up and saw that the moon was full and approaching its zenith. In my confusion and distress over the prior days, I had miscalculated the night on which the moon would be full. I had lost a day!

There was no time to run to the mountains. I resolved to

quit town on the back of a borrowed horse and return to my homestead. My only hope was the broken gibbet and a heavy cellar door. I raced against the moon's rising, but realized rather quickly that all would be in vain. My homestead was miles from town, and I could not overrun the cosmic dance. The moon was at its height when I felt my mind overtaken with lethargy as if I had imbibed for hours and finally succumbed to the spirits' stupor. I feared I would fall from my mount, and so I clumsily slid from its back, reeled it round to face town and slapped the rump, sending it galloping home. I stumbled into the thick underbrush of the woods and failed to struggle against unconsciousness, for the last image I have of that night is the moon laughing at me through the quivering branches that hung over my head.

To some, waking is a pleasant sensation. A night of restfulness brings a morning of clarity and refreshment. The day springs upon one with all of its hidden chance and promise and one steps into the morning light with a surety and grace that cannot be found when one's head crashes on the pillow in the evening.

I have come to detest the morning.

I cannot know what it will reveal for me, for several of my mornings have brought me only confusion, pain, shame . . . and blood. That morning was one such, and I woke shivering, naked, and terrified. I was lying in an alleyway next to the tavern, the morning light barely penetrating the trees, though the glow of the sun's rays could be seen lighting up the mountain on the horizon. Screams and commotion throughout the town met my ears, and I believed my presence had been overlooked merely because I had tucked myself away behind some kegs and a cart that obstructed the view of me from the road. I crouched behind the barrels and looked about for anything with which to cover myself. A man ran past the alleyway with red streaks across the front of his nightshirt. I looked down at my hands and saw the sticky brownish-red of hours old blood.

I heard the men talking just at the end of the alleyway I hid in. I made myself as small as possible and held my breath.

"It was that werewolf! I'm telling you now, it was him. Or the lad what done the same thing to his family."

"That was fire, not this."

"Fires just the way he covered up what he done."

"You're mad, man. This was clearly wolves or a rogue catamount. No man could have done this."

"A man who acts like a wolf could."

I knew the voice. The farmer, Josiah, was there, in Staunton, and if he saw me, it would be the end of me. He was the only witness to my demon, aside from Matthew, and though no one may have listened before, surely someone would now. My only recourse was the woods behind the tavern, but I had no clothing, no horse, no means whatsoever, for my entire fortune was in my homestead. I hastened to the back of the tavern building and, by a gift of mercy, there hung laundry that a poor servant must have neglected to bring in the night before. It was damp with dew, but better cover than merely the skin the good Lord gave me. I dressed and slipped quietly into the woods, following a stream that ran around the town and through my property. I chanced passing by my home and, if able, acquiring some of my personal effects, which I wished not to be discovered or taken. Perhaps my horse was still present as well, and I would have a means of travel. I walked a mile before I came parallel to Matthew's road. I dared not take it, for it was the easiest path to my homestead, and I knew now that others were aware of its existence. While approaching my home from the rear, taking a roundabout way through the woods, I saw nothing amiss on my property. There was no sign of horses, no men snooping around my effects. It looked deserted. The minuscule amount of livestock I owned were free roaming and likely by the creek. I left the safety and cover of the woods and crossed the field to my house. I entered and decided no one had been about since my abduction, so I moved quickly, gathering up what I could fit in a saddlebag. A step on the creaky floor behind me brought me to a halt, and I felt the cold muzzle of a rifle pressed into my back between the shoulder blades. I slowly turned around, and there stood the farmer with a crooked smile on his face, now holding the piece to my chest, his finger poised on the trigger.

"Hello, Mr. Bancroft." He pronounced the name with an odd sort of pleasure, as if he had tasted a well-roasted slab of beef and planned to savor it with relish.

"Please put that down, Josiah."

"I warned them 'bout you, but no one would listen. Called me a mad drunk. I ain't no drunk and I know what I saw. You killed all them people today, and you and that other wolf-man, you killed my friends."

"I do not know what you think you saw. I had nothing to do with any of it." At least, my conscious self had nothing to do with it. I could not account for the demon within.

Josiah's smirk turned to an angry frown, and he motioned me with his gun to exit the house. I complied, knowing he was not above meting out justice by his own hand. I watched him execute Gregory, and I believed his intention was to do the same to me. The sun was bright as I stepped outside, and the glint off of the barrel was blinding. When I could focus again, I saw the farmer was not alone. Two other men, one dark haired and slight, the other large and fair, had accompanied him. I now saw their horses, hidden in the thicket just beside Matthew's road.

The farmer instructed the men to tie my hands to a post, and I gathered that was to be the chopping block for me.

"I ain't gonna let you get away this time. A deputy said a man had escaped from the tavern. Said he thought the man might have been another victim of the monster. But I knew better. So I asked what the man was called, and he said a Mr. Pole. Now, I don't know no one named Pole, but when he said your first name was Fenn, I knew there weren't two men with that same queer name about here. I asked where this Mr. Pole lived, and here I am. I'm not messin' around with the idea of magistrates and such this time. The only way we're safe is when you're dead."

I attempted to plead for my life, but Josiah's anger and sense of justice made him cold to all entreaties for mercy. He would not hear of my innocence. I attempted a different approach and admitted to my affliction.

"It is not me doing this! There is a demon within me I cannot control on the full moon. All would have been well. I would have been far from civilization over the mountain, had it not been for the men who kept me prisoner to question me about the doings of a boy I have not seen in months. Please! I am seeking a way to be rid of this affliction. If it were you, you would hope for the same mercy, I assure you."

The farmer was resolute, but the other men's countenances changed to confusion and wonder. I presumed they did not actually believe there was such a thing as werewolves, but they must have a murderer to unleash their revenge upon and Josiah had convinced them it was me. Now I had confessed, but I could perceive they were inclined to take me alive rather than dead. Josiah pulled his rifle up and aimed at my forehead.

"Quit yer lying! That's the same story your friend made when we caught him red-handed." He put his finger on the trigger. The dark-haired accomplice asked him to wait a moment so they could talk it over.

"Nothing to talk about! He just confessed. Punishment for murder is death. Bible says so."

"But he says it weren't him. His body, but not him. I don't rightly know what that means, but I am inclined to take him to the reverend and have him sort it out."

"So he can put on his wolf suit and kill some more?"

"Wolf suit? You think a man in a suit could do all that?" questioned the larger man. The farmers' accomplices were losing their resolve. I took the opportunity to further my case.

"No, no man could do that! That is what I am saying. It is not me, but an evil that lives within me. I want rid of it! I am willing to die for my sins, but I do not want to lose my soul in the process. Please, take me to the reverend." Josiah would have no more talk and pressed the rifle into my head. I could feel the shape of the muzzle leaving an impression on my skin. I closed my eyes, waiting for the blast that would be the last thing I would ever hear.

I heard the bang, but it sounded far away. I waited for the sting of death, but instead heard a groan and the dark-haired man yelling at his accomplice to take cover.

Another bang, this time from Josiah's gun. The shot was fired, not at me, but at a man standing off to my right on the side of the house.

"It's the lad! It's that boy they was looking for that killed his family!"

Josiah was reloading. I yelled for Matthew to run, but he would not listen. He raised his rifle and shot before Josiah could finish ramming the ball. That time, the shot hit its mark, and Josiah hit the ground. The smaller accomplice snapped out of his shock and took aim with his rifle. Matthew had not noticed, surprised for a moment at what he had done, and then scrambled to reload. I yelled again for him to get away, but it was too late. Another shot was fired, and this time it struck Matthew in the chest. He fell back and clutched the wound. In the confusion of shots, I did not notice that an arrow was lodged in the large man's stomach. An arrow! I searched the tree line and the woods, but saw no sign of a bow-wielding accomplice.

The fair-haired man was on his side, bleeding profusely. His companion surveyed the situation. He could not save his friend and apprehend us both. He seemed to consider the ghost with the bow before he ran to his horse, returned to his friend, and, with surprising strength for his stature, flung the large man over the beast's shoulder. As the blood from his wound ran down the dapple gray's leg, the dark-haired man came to me and hastily undid the knot that tethered me to the pole, keeping my wrists tied. He meant to have me walk alongside the horse back to town. I tried to reason with him that his friend would not survive, especially if they could not ride unhindered, but he would not mind me. I entreated him to let me tend to the wound of Matthew, but he ignored that as well. While being dragged, half running, half stumbling, behind the horse, I looked back and saw Matthew lying motionless on the ground.

11

I was taken to the magistrate in Staunton. Court was not in session, so I was brought to his estate just outside of town. His was a house following the style of the wealthy merchants and planters. A brick façade with columns leading to the door, and large windows, eight, evenly placed on both sides of the house. The second-story windows were accented with gables, and chimneys jutted out of the roof on both ends. A beautiful house that I would have appreciated under better circumstances. We waited in the parlor for him. I stood, held by two men-at-arms, for lack of a better term. I do not know if they were in the paid service of the crown or just laymen volunteering to uphold the law, but they performed their duty vigorously. The magistrate entered the room with a look of consternation, holding the warrant filed against me.

"Your name, sir?" asked the man as he stood before me.

"Fenn Pole." No, that name was no longer my safeguard. Josiah was behind my capture, so my real name was likely on that warrant. "I mean, Bancroft, sir."

He looked at me with a questioning frown before returning to the paper in his hand.

"It says here you are accused of murdering . . . four people in and around the town of Staunton early this morning. A farmer, Josiah Bell, from Big Lick, accuses you of the deaths of six souls and the suicide of a seventh on the Great Wagon Road. The details of the murders are . . . quite horrendous. How do you plead?"

"Not guilty, sir. If I may explain myself, sir, you will understand . . ."

"Unnecessary, Mr. Bancroft. You will stand trial and you, or your lawyer, should you acquire one, may explain then. Take him to the jail at the courthouse."

"Wait! Please, sir! It was my flesh, but not me, sir!"

"So you confess?"

"Yes, but no, sir. It is an illness. I cannot be held accountable for an act I did when not in my right mind!"

He paused for a moment. His eyes left mine, and he looked at the ceiling as if he could see through it to someone or something. I could not see what might draw his attention away, but after a moment he sighed and reviewed again the warrant for my arrest. He looked back at me and answered. Though I was weary and in pain, I believe I heard a hint of compassion in his voice.

"That will be decided at your trial." He nodded to his men and promptly exited the room. They shoved me down the porch steps, and tethered me once again to follow a horse as it trotted to the courthouse, another mile away. By the time we reached my new home, my feet were considerably blistered and open wounds festered. I had not the energy, nor the means, to care for them. Instead, I slumped onto the flea infested straw that made my bed, and welcomed the numbness that came over me as I drifted to sleep.

The gaoler was as kind a man as they come, and he offered me alcohol and an old rag when he discovered the state of my feet the following morning. He said he was 'not want to kick a man when he was down,' and answered to God for how he treated a creature, even if it was a villain. I was grateful for his compassion, but could tell by his demeanor he was not one to be crossed. He could surely adjust his treatment of a creature following an offense. I was cordial, but did not ask him for any favors, save only if I was permitted to hire an attorney, and if a letter could be sent to a minister to visit me. These requests were ordinary and easily permitted, he answered, and he soon brought me paper, pen, and ink, of which I was much obliged. He reassured me that the expense would be added to my debt, along with 'room and board.' I set about to beseech Mr. Baird, who I considered my minister, ordained or not, to come to my aid.

Mr. Baird arrived at my cold and comfort-less domicile shortly after. I was rather surprised my message reached him so quickly. He was loath to inform me, however, that he had never received my message, but heard of the attack in town and that someone had apprehended the murderer. It must be me or Matthew, he knew. He was sympathetic to my plight, yet honest in his speech. It was only a matter of time before I would have to face the law for the evil works the monster did with my flesh, and though I may not have been conscious of my acts, my body had committed atrocities. The court would not find it easy to separate one from the other. I admitted to the complications. Perhaps I would gain sympathy if I claimed I had been temporarily insane. Mr. Baird thought it was the only honest argument I could make.

In any case, Mr. Baird knew of a lawyer from Williamsburg who had just recently set up an office. They had become friends over the winter college session, and he felt the man would take the case. He would send a letter immediately and hope his friend would arrive before the trial, set for a fortnight hence.

For days, my only visitor was Mr. Baird and the gaoler who brought me my rations. I learned from the scholar that the news of my incarceration was traveling quickly throughout the colonies, and my trial was expected to bring visitors to Staunton. It had even been suggested I be transferred to a larger city where the court could seat more spectators, but the Staunton magistrate fought to keep it in town. Mr. Baird believed it was to support the local tradesmen who would benefit by the influx of humanity for the spectacle.

But all I could think of was Beatrice, who would find out what I had become, and why I had not written. The first word she would hear of my well being would be from newspapers advertising my trial. When I was left alone, I could not contain the tears that flowed and the sobs that heaved as I considered the grief this would cause her. I could endure what might await me; after all, the choices I had made spawned the sequence of events. But Beatrice had no choice, and now she must bear a heavy burden because of me.

The lawyer arrived a week from the day Mr. Baird's letter was sent. He must have ridden with all haste to reach Staunton so quickly. The man introduced himself as John Andrews and shook my hand without apprehension. I felt immediately more at ease than I had in weeks.

"I am sorry to make your acquaintance under these circumstances, Mr. Bancroft, but I would be honored to offer you my services."

"Thank you, Mr. Andrews. I sorely need them."

We discussed the angle of defense, and he agreed that insanity was the only reasonable claim that could be made. He would argue that a human being could not be held liable for the sin of a demon, or the work of a sickness, which one was afflicted by. That it must either be cast out, cured, or contained to insure the public health while not putting into jeopardy the immortal soul of its victim host.

"What can I hope for, in your opinion, Mr. Andrews?"

"At best, exile from the colonies, I am sorry to say. At worst . . . you will hang."

I could not dwell on the latter—how can one comprehend no longer existing? As to the former, life did not seem worth living if it meant I would never see Beatrice again. I would lose, no matter the verdict.

As the day of the trial drew closer, Mr. Baird and Mr.

Andrews advised me to prepare myself for an arduous battle as the sensibilities of the day, and the war with France, would likely bring about a prosecution that lacked compassion or imagination. The masses would wish to see me hanged, quartered, and burned to rid society of one more threat to its welfare and peace.

In my honest and darker moments, I could not blame the populace for wanting to destroy me. Had I heard of the atrocities committed by my transformed hand, I would have felt the same. I prayed for reason to win the day. I prayed they would give me the time necessary to discover the cure for my malady and rid my body of the invader who threatened to mark my soul irrevocably for hell. For now that I faced judgment from the law, I could think of nothing but eternal judgment. I had not been devout, as others would define it, but I always considered myself on the right side of the eternal divide.

Now that it is possible I will die with a demon in my body, I cannot imagine any other recourse, but that I will be sent to hell along with it.

Mr. Andrews came to see me the day before my trial, and his face seemed less grim and set than it had in our prior meetings.

"I have what may be hopeful news for you. The magistrate's wife is said to be suffering from an illness of the mind."

"I hardly see why a poor woman's illness should be good news for me."

"It means he may be more compassionate than I had thought. He knows what insanity does to a person. He may be more inclined to have mercy should the jury find you guilty."

"When they find me guilty," I said, simply matter-of-fact. "I hope you are right. I have all but given up, listening to the throngs outside these walls demanding my damnation."

My trial brought hundreds of visitors to Staunton, as predicted. I was the center of a new hysteria, not far removed from that of Salem when witchcraft was the evil of the day. Those who claimed themselves to be beyond the superstitions of their grandfathers were the first in line to get a glimpse of the monster that tore babies from their mothers' wombs and decapitated horses before ripping out the organs of their riders, for such were the stories circulating about the werewolves that had wreaked havoc in the colonies. The majority spread the idea that this affliction was catching, like a horrific case of smallpox, and there would only be more werewolves were I released. I, of course, knew that my release was impossible. Without a viable option for further restraint, I was bound by moral and ethical obligation to remain as I was, in a cage, to bar the monster from his vile appetite.

The hour came for my trial. I felt apprehension, naturally, considering the circumstances, and quivered in the barred box that housed the accused, while my defense, a jury of my peers, and spectators, filling every available square inch, filed into the courtroom. Soon after, the magistrate entered wearing a powdered wig. It changed his visage from the one I had seen on the day of my arrest, and he looked more serious and scornful. I worried I would not have a favorable sentence after all. The court waited only for the prosecution, which was not yet late, but nearly so. Long minutes passed, and the magistrate betrayed his impatience by retrieving from his pocket a golden watch with which he mouthed the time inaudibly to himself on half a dozen occasions, before the prosecutor finally took his seat.

The magistrate brought the court to order and called on the prosecution to begin.

"Gentleman of the jury."

The jury, I noticed, was a group of tradesmen and farmers, some I knew and some I had never seen before. Not one of these men could truly be called my peer, for no one from the tidewater region that was familiar with genteel living was present. These men, I judged, would be more inclined to believe in ghost stories than the reasoned men I had grown up around in New England. I decided that was not a bad thing, after all.

"You see before you today a criminal of the most loathsome persuasion. The prosecution seeks to prove to you fine, hardworking folk, that this man here, Fenn Bancroft, has, with malicious intent, murdered and consumed ten victims of which we can account for. You have heard stories coming out of the Great Lakes of the monster who has been attacking and devouring victims in that region. We cannot know for sure this man was not responsible for some, if not all, of those deaths as well. We will seek to provide eyewitness and tangible evidence to prove to you, beyond a reasonable doubt, that this man is a murderous cannibal who deserves nothing less than death and dismemberment, as is fitting under English law."

Some from the crowd cheered, looking forward, no doubt, to the spectacle of my death. The magistrate called for order and invited the defense to make his opening statement.

Mr. Andrews stood before the jury and the crowd.

"You have heard from my honorable opponent here that the defendant, Mr. Bancroft, has, with intent, murdered and devoured ten poor souls. We wish to argue that this man is innocent, not of the act of murder, but of the intent."

A murmur arose among the audience and the jurymen fidgeted in their seats, clearly not expecting to hear the defense admit that the man on trial was guilty. I wondered if this was the best way to open, but I had to trust that Mr. Andrews knew what he was about.

"Mr. Bancroft has been suffering under an affliction of the mind and body that can be defined as none other than a form of lunacy, which, under certain circumstances, causes a fracture from his humane self and turns the law-abiding gentleman you see before you today into a ruthless, animalistic killer. We will not waste the court's time arguing, falsely, that Mr. Bancroft had nothing to do with the murders. We will, however, strive to prove that Mr. Bancroft was not the murderer. He was the shell with which the actual murderer committed these heinous crimes."

More and louder chatter spread through the crowd, to where the magistrate slammed his gavel repeatedly until silence was achieved. The prosecutor, a German lawyer named Wilhelm Schultz, called his first witness.

I recognized the farmer at once, though he walked with a considerable limp from the bullet wound he had sustained weeks before. My initial feeling was relief that he was alive, but then I felt I was being too generous considering he wanted nothing more than for me to die. So I feigned indifference. He, however, did not hide his disdain and derision as he surveyed my poor self locked in a cage.

"That's the only place the likes of you are fit to be alive, that's for certain!" the farmer sneered. The magistrate called for silence from the witness until he had been sworn in.

"Mr. Bell, how do you know the defendant?" Mr. Schultz began.

"We was in a caravan together from Williamsburg to the backcountry here. He was with us on the wagon road about halfway to Big Lick before him and his evil friend attacked."

"What exactly did you witness when the caravan was attacked?"

The events of that night were a black cloud to me, but I recalled overhearing the chatter during the aftermath and knew that no one believed, at least out loud, that a monster out of myth had ravaged the caravan. The moment Gregory was dragged from the woods, naked with a bullet hole in his leg, the accepted assumption was that he had donned a costume with which to hide his identity in order to perform the butchery. They also assumed that Gregory had an accomplice and that I, especially after my disappearance following the fire, was him. However, Josiah seemed hesitant to declare with any certainty what it was he actually saw.

"I can't say as I know for sure. There were screaming women and children, which got in the way of a clear view of the fiend. Alls I could tell for certain, after hearing from the other witnesses in my company, was that the thing walked on its legs like a man, it was sickly looking, but sore strong, and its head had the shape of a dog or some such creature. Once we found the man responsible and he confessed, we didn't care overmuch what the thing looked like and just figured he was a murdering mummer."

"What was the nature of the wounds which dispatched the victims?"

"They was eaten on the inside, sir."

There was a gasp from the crowd and grimaces on the faces of the jury.

"Eaten?"

"Yes, sir. They was missing some of their organs. The last one which we saw him tearing into . . ." At this point in his story, the farmer seemed to become nauseated and took a moment to compose himself. "The last one was whole when we got to him, but the wounds was so bad he was pleading for someone to put him down."

"And did you?"

"Not me, sir, but a friend of mine. Yes, we put him out of his misery."

I was relieved, and yet saddened as well, for the man whose life was cut off. He may have survived the wounds and lived, so to speak, but only to become like me.

"Tell me about the man you caught and held accountable."

"He was friends with him." Josiah pointed without looking at me. "Declared so themselves, and he was tryin' to help the criminal. Cared more about him than what the monster done to us. The monster's name was Gregory, so he told us, and he was big and strong. Wasn't hard to believe that he could have done the damage to the bodies we saw. Soon as we caught him, he confessed. We had bound him and intended to bring him on to face the law in Big Lick, but when one of ours took his own life cause of what these two done, we couldn't travel with him no longer and brought justice ourselves."

"So you are saying you killed Mr. Bancroft's friend? This Gregory?"

"We was forced to take the law in our own hands, or so's we thought. It wasn't murder, it was an execution."

The crowd murmured again, and I saw some faces show disdain for what the farmer had confessed. But he was not the one on trial.

"Why do you believe Mr. Bancroft here was involved in the attack?"

"Most of us saw two attackers. They was clearly friends, and when he heard we suspected he was the other killer, he fled. Didn't stay to help anyone when the caravan caught on fire. Just saved his own skin."

"Thank you, sir."

The prosecutor sat down, and Mr. Andrews rose to question Josiah.

"You say most of you saw two men attacking the caravan that night. Can you describe the other attacker, the one who was not apprehended?"

"Well, like I said, there was a lot of bodies running to and fro, and even though there was a full moon, it was still night, so hard to tell for sure. But both men was wearing disguises, so I can't rightly say for sure what the other one looked like. Only, he was smaller than that Gregory."

"So no one saw the defendant kill anyone that night?"

"Not directly, sir, but we had reason to believe he was the other one, judging by the way he acted and how he ran away."

"You said he ran after you and the other men were discussing his potential involvement in the murders?"

"Yes, sir, the night the caravan burned."

"The night you executed Gregory?"

"Yes, sir."

"Is it not possible, Mr. Bell, that Mr. Bancroft overheard your discussion as you held a gun to the head of his friend and feared for his own life, so he ran?"

"No reason to run if you are innocent."

"Would you have believed him innocent if he had stayed?"

"Well . . ."

"Thank you, sir." Mr. Andrews returned to his seat. Josiah was clearly agitated and could not refrain from blurting out.

"Clearly he is the killer, since he done it again in Staunton! So I would have been right to execute him then and there, along with his friend. Would have saved more lives had I done." The crowd shared their approval with shouts and claps of affirmation.

"Mr. Bell, please refrain from speaking until you have been addressed. Are there any further questions for this witness?" The magistrate looked to the prosecution and defense in turn. Both Mr. Schultz and Mr. Andrews declined to question Josiah further, and he left the stand.

Mr. Schultz called for his next witness, the owner of the tavern where I had been kept for questioning.

"Mr. Thomas, tell me about the circumstances under which Mr. Bancroft was a guest at your tavern."

"Oh, Mr. Bancroft was being kept under guard for questioning, sir."

"Questioning? Concerning what?"

"They was looking for a young man who killed his family. They thought Mr. Bancroft knew where the lad was, but he wasn't telling, so they were keeping him till he talked."

"And that was the night of the attack?"

"Yes, sir. I remember cause it was a full moon, and the first thing I noticed when I heard the screaming was how bright it seemed though it was still night."

"Tell the court what you witnessed that night."

"I woke up when I heard a scream. It was coming from somewhere across the street, but I wasn't sure exactly where. I put on a robe over my shirt and went out to see what the fuss was about. Like I said, the moon was so bright I could see all around, but didn't hear nothin' else. I waited a minute or two, listening, until somebody slammed into the door of the apothecary's and fell into the road. When the, I don't know, man I guess, got up he looked in my direction, I thought for sure he was going to come for me. He was scrawny looking but covered in hair, and his head didn't look like a person's head—it was like a dog walking on its hind legs. His teeth were bared, and he had claws for hands. I just about fainted, but someone stumbled out of the door he had just busted from, and when he noticed, he went back, I think, to finish the job. I ran inside and locked the doors and grabbed my gun. I wouldn't go back out, but I watched from my window. About an hour or so later, I saw the thing again, lurking about the woods, sniffing the air and listening before running off toward whatever sound he heard. I stayed in that window with my gun till the sun rose. It was just about dawn when I noticed a man running round back of the tavern, naked as the day he was born. I went to the room Mr. Bancroft was locked in the night before and found he was gone. I thought maybe he had been one of the victims, but Mr. Bell was sure he was the killer when he came to the tavern lookin' for him. It was then that I realized the naked man looked like Mr. Bancroft."

"So Mr. Bancroft had been questioned in connection with a man who killed his family, and he escaped on the same night that an attack similar to that of the caravan took place. And you saw Mr. Bancroft still in the tavern's vicinity come morning?"

"Yes, sir."

"Would you say the stature of the disguised murderer fit that of Mr. Bancroft?"

"If I had to guess, I would say yes, close enough. The murderer was about the same height and build, but like I said, it didn't look quite like a man. More like a wolf or some such creature. But I suppose that could have been a disguise."

"Thank you, Mr. Thomas."

Mr. Andrews approached and looked over his notes before beginning his round of questioning.

"Mr. Thomas. You say you saw what looked like a 'wolf or some such creature.' That the murderer you saw had a head that 'didn't look like a person's head' and 'it was like a dog walking on its hind legs.' Now, I know it was night and the light of the moon is not the same as broad daylight, but tell me, if you can remember, what direction were the legs bent on the killer?"

"I don't understand."

"Well, a dog or a wolf, their hind legs bend in the opposite direction of a human's. I wonder, if you recall, what direction were the legs bending when the attacker you saw that night walked?"

The tavern keeper looked up to the ceiling, likely fishing through his memory for the scene he had witnessed. It was a scene I am sure he had played back over and over, just as I would were I to have seen myself standing in the street that night. A look of horror came over his face as he saw it again in his mind.

"Oh, Lord, they were backward! Like a dog! I remember exactly because it pounced on the poor soul in the doorway, and it looked just like when a dog is playing with a stick."

"When you saw Mr. Bancroft, naked, running to the back of the tavern, did he run like a man?"

"He was crouching to hide his nakedness, but, yes, he was moving like a man."

"Did he have knees that bent backwards?"

"Not that I could tell. No, sir."

"Do you know of any costume or disguise that could make a human bend their knees backwards?"

"No, sir, I don't."

"Thank you, Mr. Thomas."

Other witnesses were questioned. Similar stories were told of a wolf-like creature slashing and slaying and feasting on its kills. The prosecution relied heavily on the circumstantial evidence of my escape coinciding with the night of the attack and my likely involvement with the caravan massacre. Mr. Andrews stressed the form and gait of the murderer. The woman who laid out the bodies was also brought to the stand.

"Mrs. Price, you say the wounds were consistent with those left by a dog or cougar attack, correct?" Andrews asked.

"Yes, sir. The slashes were deep, often in rows like claws, and even left scratch marks on the bone of some of the poor bodies."

"Is it possible fingernails could inflict that sort of damage?"

The woman sniggered. "No, sir."

"Yes, it is ridiculous, is it not?"

"Certainly."

"So then, in your opinion, how would a man leave wounds of that sort on a body?"

"I don't know. Knives?"

"But none of the witnesses saw the killer holding any knives. They all described the hands as claws."

"Maybe he made claws out of knives or dog paws or something?"

"Possibly. What about the teeth marks in the flesh? Tell me about those."

"They looked to be made by canines."

"The large teeth that dogs and cats have?"

"Yes, sir."

"Do humans have canines?"

"I believe they are similar, but these teeth were large, and the bite went deep. I have seen plenty bites of that sort from mongrel dogs."

"How can you account for the bite marks if they are supposed to come from a human?"

"I don't know, sir. Maybe he fastened dog teeth to his mouth?"

"Seems like a lot of work for a man to do. Especially a man who had nothing with him but the clothes on his back while he was being held illegally in a makeshift jail cell."

"Well, they said there were knives in that storage closet, and leather straps . . ."

"But no claws or canines, I gather."

"Not that I know of, sir."

"Thank you."

It had been a long and tiring day, listening to the horrifying account of the beast's devastation, and I yearned for my cell and the festering, flea ridden bed. The hundreds of tiny bites could not compare with the onslaught of accusations against me I had suffered that day. I was grateful for Mr. Andrews and his tenacious and pragmatic approach to my case.

"Tomorrow you will take the stand," Mr. Andrews warned as he met with me that night to discuss the case and what was to come. "Get as much sleep as you can and just answer honestly. Our case relies on the jury seeing that you are under the burden of an illness you cannot control. As far as I understand it, there is nothing you can say in all honesty that could jeopardize that."

"Thank you, Mr. Andrews."

He left as Mr. Baird entered, and the door was locked behind him.

"How do ye, lad?"

"As well as can be expected, I believe."

"The people are split about ye. Some believe ye've got a demon in ye that ye can't control. Others believe ye've got a demon in ye that ye can."

"If only I could prove to them it is not me who controls the beast!"

"Maybe ye can, lad. Maybe they just need to see the beast for themselves to ken ye can't control it."

"They already have, and they still believe it was me behind it."

"Ah, not everyone, lad. And what's more important is what the magistrate thinks and, if what Mr. Andrews says is true, he may believe it more than most."

"The jury will condemn me."

"We dunna ken that. Keep yer hope."

Mr. Baird prayed for me and left me to rest. I did not sleep peacefully, but what sleep I could get would have to be enough for the trial I would endure on the morrow.

12

I took the stand. My knees trembled as I stepped into the space where a lectern stood and placed my hand on the Bible that lay there. I saw some in the crowd watching carefully as I touched the holy book, perhaps waiting for smoke or flames to rise from my hands as the devil dared to finger the word of God. But nothing of the sort happened. I swore to tell the truth and meant to keep my word.

"Mr. Bancroft, tell us about your affliction, as you call it," Mr. Schultz asked as if he were challenging me to a duel.

I explained what I knew of what I was. Human, but something else living inside me that only had access to the world on nights of the full moon.

"So you expect the court to believe that you become a, well, for lack of a better term, a werewolf?"

"I would not believe it either, but it happened to me."

"Where is the costume, Mr. Bancroft?"

"There is none."

"Is it not true that you have found a way to contort yourself into the shape and gait of a wolf, don a skin with its claws and head, like some of the Indians are known to do, and use that disguise when you rip apart your victims for your monstrous appetite?"

"Absolutely not! You will find no such evidence either. I abhor the wretched creature and I want only to be rid of it!"

"But you can't get rid of it, can you?"

"I have not found a way . . . yet."

"Can you describe for the court what happened the night of the caravan attack?"

I shared what I could remember. Gregory's arrival and frantic searching for the key to his wagon which, I explained, held the trappings that would prevent the beast from roaming free. My ignorance of my condition. Waking up with blood on my hands and no memory of what had happened to me. Gregory's capture. His execution.

"So do you admit to being Gregory's accomplice in the murders of Mr. Bell's friends?"

"I have no memory of the event. I cannot know whether I murdered anyone that night or account for the blood on my hands. Gregory knew what he was and attempted to protect those around him. He failed, and that is why I am what I am. But the attack on the caravan that night was unintentional and, had the key been with the wagon, and I locked up with Gregory, all would have been safe."

"Can you say the same concerning the people of Staunton?"

"Yes, in fact, I can. I had a plan and, had it not been for my unlawful detention in the tavern that night, I would have been far away from civilization when the change occurred."

"I will humor you for a moment and assume the beast is real. Is that the only plan or means you had of protecting civilization?"

"No, I also had Gregory's cage."

"This cage?" My gibbet was carried into the courtroom by two men. The broken and warped bars held glaringly out for the jury and audience to see.

"Yes."

"Can you tell me what happened to the cage?"

"It was damaged, sir."

"What damaged it?"

"I did."

The crowd gasped. Some scoffed, likely imagining me, slight as I am, wrenching the bars of an iron gibbet apart.

"When was the cage damaged?"

"I had successfully kept myself locked up for months when the moon was full and the beast emerged. One of those full moons, the beast broke free."

"The court will note that it was also discovered that a heavy wooden door leading into the cellar of Mr. Bancroft's house was ripped from its bolts. Mr. Bancroft, were there any victims the night you escaped from your cage?"

"Sadly, yes."

"Could it have been the family of five poor souls?"

"No."

"Which you covered up by burning down the home."

"No!"

"And then framing the only survivor you left behind?"

"Oh, God, no! I care for Matthew. I would never frame him."

"So you killed his family and burnt the home to hide the evidence?"

"I already answered you, no!"

"Then who did you kill that night, Mr. Bancroft?"

"Matthew!" I blurted out. The crowd looked at one another in disbelief. One of the jurymen bared his teeth in anger. I recognized him then as Matthew's uncle.

"How can that be, Mr. Bancroft, when a witness, just yesterday, spoke under oath that he saw you with Matthew days before the attack in Staunton? Another witness said he shot Matthew when you were apprehended."

"Because he is like me. He is afflicted now, as I am." The

crowd was hushed and some held hands over their gaping mouths.

"So you have made another demon like yourself?"

"Not intentionally."

"Do you mean to imply, Mr. Bancroft, that Matthew did, in fact, kill his family and torch the house?"

"Yes." The intake of breath sounded like a gust of wind had blown through the only window in the room. "But it was not him, it was the monster inside him."

Mr. Schultz, visibly annoyed with my defense, ignored my statement.

"Why was Matthew even there the night you emerged from your cage, Mr. Bancroft?"

"He was helping me. He was locking me in."

"Did he know what you would become?"

"No."

"So you knew it was possible that this beast you claim to be could get free and kill the boy, and yet you had him help you, anyway?"

"I knew it was possible, as all things are possible, but I always sent him home before it was even close to midnight. That day, we had worked so long and hard planting the corn crop that we were both exhausted. He failed to go home. It just happened that was the night the beast broke free. I would put no one in harm's way intentionally."

"But it is possible that you will again. Whether or not you intend to."

I did not speak. It was true.

"Mr. Bancroft, what do you remember of the attack on Staunton?"

"Nothing."

"You remember nothing of that night?"

"I remember nothing of the attack. Before the change took over, I knew I had little time to get to safety. I thought I had another day, but once I emerged from the tavern, I realized it was the night of the full moon and I had only minutes. I rode out of town, hoping I could make it to my home in time, praying the distance would be enough to keep the monster from humanity, but I could feel the change coming over me and I knew it was too late. I slipped off the horse and sent it back towards town. When I awoke, I was lying outside the tavern, naked, blood on my hands, and I could hear people yelling. I knew what had happened. I tried to get home so I could run away. Josiah, Mr. Bell, came to kill me. That is when the shootout happened, and I was brought back to face trial."

"Do you deny you killed those people, Mr. Bancroft?"

"No, I do not deny that it was my body. But it was not me."

Mr. Andrews looked on with compassion when he stood before me for his round of questioning.

"Mr. Bancroft. Let us first establish the validity of your claim. You are a werewolf, correct?"

"I do not want to align myself with the monster. I have a werewolf inside me. It is a parasite. It is not me."

"Of course. No conscientious soul would embrace such a thing. When the wolf takes over, are you aware of what it is doing?"

"Not at all."

"Do you have any control over it whatsoever?"

"Absolutely not. It is like a black cloud comes over me. I feel myself fading and the beast taking over, and I am shut out of my mind."

"To what lengths have you gone to preserve the welfare of your fellow man once you knew you were under this awful affliction?"

"I spent the first month in the mountains with Gregory's cage. It was not ideal, so I built my cellar and had the cage affixed to the walls with a large, heavy door as a last line of defense. When that also failed, I spent the next month once again over the mountains. Matthew and I planned to do the same the month that I was arrested. That full moon was the night of the attack."

"So, Mr. Bancroft, is it right to suppose that, given the proper means and protocol, you could be successfully contained on the nights of the full moon and the public would be safe?"

"I believe it is possible, yes."

"Why do you want to live, Mr. Bancroft?"

The question came unexpectedly, and I sat speechless for a time. I wanted to live for the same reason any person wants to live. But that would not be the answer Mr. Andrews was looking for.

"I want to live because I believe if I die, and this demon is still inside me, I will be sent with it to hell." I could see that the idea stirred the crowd. Perhaps they had not considered that the monster who massacred their neighbors would have a human element that longed for redemption.

"So you worry for the state of your soul?"

"Yes, as all men do. My heart, my mind, my soul, none of those which make me who I am, Fenn Bancroft, were present when those poor people were slaughtered. Is my body guilty? Yes. But am I guilty? The part of me that may be redeemed from this mortal coil? No, I wholeheartedly believe I am innocent. I wish to be given the chance to be cured. I wish to be given the chance for my soul to be redeemed from the grip of the enemy."

"Thank you, Mr. Bancroft."

I stepped down from the box where I had taken my stand. My legs felt weak; my knees as if they might lock and send me tumbling to the floor. I saw all the eyes, every one in the room, watching me as I walked, and I wondered if they were waiting to see if my knees would bend backward. I should have been praying in supplication to the only one who could reach His hand down and deliver me; instead, I imagined what I had looked like to all the people present, as a man, and as a wolf. After taking my seat, I waited for the lawyers, the jury, and the judge to determine my fate.

. . .

In Mr. Andrews' closing statement, he pleaded for grace. He asked for a chance for a man, unwell and afflicted, to be given the opportunity for a cure. Should the verdict be guilty, he asked the judge to be merciful. He looked to the crowd and asked them to imagine themselves in my place and do unto others as they would have done unto themselves. I noticed a woman wipe a tear from her eye. Perhaps I could hope at least for mercy.

I returned to my cell that afternoon. The jurymen deliberating while I wrote the first letter to Beatrice that I had penned in months. It will also be the last.

> Beatrice, my love,
>
> I pray this letter finds you well. I beg you to forgive me for my silence. I have not known how to tell you all that there is to tell. I pray you have heard nothing of the rumors which are sure to reach you through the waves of public discourse so that my words may be the first you hear on the subject and the ones you will trust in the presence of all other whispers.
>
> My dear, I have been tried for murder, and I await my verdict. My heart is heavy for, to be honest with myself and with you, I must admit it was my body that performed the crimes for which I have been accused. My mind, my soul, is wholly innocent. I was not a partner to the undertaking of the demon, which has overcome my senses and made me the harbinger of doom upon my fellow mortals. You will hear stories, my dear, stories which will curdle the blood in your veins, and you will imagine all manner of heinous deeds. Put not my face to them, for I, your beloved, was not there. The beast which performed the acts bears no resemblance to the man you will remember when you close your eyes and my visage is cast before you as I was when we parted.
>
> Oh my love, if I could only blot out these past months and

return to the day I left you! I would do anything to never have gone in the first place. Now I fear I will never see your sweet face again.

Farewell, my love. Adieu.

Before we were required to return to the courtroom, Mr. Andrews asked what I wanted done with my effects should the verdict be immediate execution. My anxious stomach tightened at the idea that death might come for me that very day, but I knew it was prudent that my affairs were in order. I expressed my desire for all that is left of me to be given to Beatrice. I did not imagine that my material possessions would comfort her; I only wanted that my earthly treasures, those meant to be the start of our future together, should go to the one who was most treasured by me. He promised to carry my last letter to her as well.

This narrative of my affliction, I instructed to be given to Mr. Baird. I have spent these many days in this cold cell putting down my story in hopes that he may find a way to cure what others may remain. It is the least I can do.

We were summoned to return to the court, and I waited with bated breath as the magistrate ran his hand through the sparse patch of hair that adorned his crown before placing the wig back atop his head. He met my eyes for the first time. "I am sorry, young man. This is a loathsome calamity to befall you, but also the deeds which this . . . alteration of your person has done is also a calamity which calls for reparations to be made. Can the monster be punished, and the man preserved? I do not see a way. The court demands justice. The people demand justice. No one is safe so long as your body is alive. And though I have pity for your soul, I pray that God's mercy, which is greater than any human court, can sort out the man from the demon. I sentence you to death by hanging, to be performed tomorrow morning."

I saw the truth of it. The jeers outside the cell wall were loud and clear. I had heard the hatred and vehemence with which my fellow man deemed me unfit for life. The public outcry for blood would not be so easily assuaged, not by the tears of a few compassionate women. There was no way to persuade the masses that the creature would not get loose and kill again. And I could not promise it.

The sounds of cheering and the sense of relief that spread throughout the room were further evidence that my death could provide a small wave of peace in the wake of fearful and tumultuous times. And so, I do not hold any ill will toward those who have condemned me. I have reconciled with my mind the burden of guilt which I must bear as the vessel, though I the man may be innocent of willful wrongdoing. It is not enough. A body must pay the price for the sins of the flesh.

But my soul . . . where will it be when the body it inhabits is punished? Again, I want to believe that which may be impossible. I may go to my death as naïve as I was when I foolishly set out on the road to my castle in the sky. Even so, I choose to hope that my soul is not lost. That, as the magistrate proclaimed, God may sort the demon from the man.

I only regret to see the utter hatred displayed on the visage of those who will delight in watching me choke out the breath of life. There will be friends among the crowd, but so few compared to the many who believe me only to be a monster in the guise of a man. I could not convince them, though I tried, that I was but a man beset by a monster.

Am I not counted among the victims of this progeny of Lycaon? But that idea is vile to the crowd.

I felt as though I was already walking to my execution on the brief journey back to my cell. The sun's accusation beat down upon me. The earth below my feet shifted as I stepped, as if the ground could not suffer to hold me. Only the rough stone walls of my cell welcomed me, as would a sanctuary. I sat and lifted my pen, which shook as I added a postscript to my letter for Beatrice.

P.S. The verdict is in the favor of justice.

As the final hours of my life ebbed away, I took comfort in a visit from Mr. Andrews. He hoped to steel my courage, and offered me a bottle of spirits as a condolence, I believe. We shared a drink, and our conversation turned to reflect upon one who shared my burden. Mr. Andrews reported nothing had been heard concerning Matthew since my arrest. If he is alive, he has been quiet, and I pray he has found a way to contain his demon for the sake of mankind.

But I could not mention the werewolf of the Great Lakes. Mr. Andrews believed me long enough to defend me; I would not expect more of him. But that werewolf, the one who passed the affliction on to Gregory, and he to me, I wonder if he curses every full moon, just as I have. How long has he been carrying this burden? Where did he receive this abomination? More than stretching out this wretched life, I wish to have time to find the answers to these questions.

But, alas, my time is at an end.

Execution is upon me this morn. I feel unfit to ask a holy, righteous God to allow a monster such as me to tread his hallowed halls. Yet, as blood has been the testimony of my sin, I pray another's blood may cover me and save my wretched soul!

- Fenn Bancroft
June 1758

13

I did not die.
 I should say, I was not fortunate enough to die. But I was hanged, I was buried, and yet I live!

I awoke from what should have been eternal rest to find myself sewn into a burlap sack, awaiting my turn to be interred. Mr. Baird stood over me, praying and quoting scripture at what was to be my funeral. A sparse funeral at that, for the crowds, satisfied to watch me die, had no need for closure by watching me be buried. It was fortuitous that the sexton was busy digging my grave when I squirmed in my sack. Mr. Baird was quick to counsel me to remain quiet and immobile, to allow myself to be disposed of, and assured me he would find Mr. Andrews and they would liberate me from the earthen tomb. I had time to remember the events of the previous day as clods of dirt were tossed upon my presumably lifeless corpse, and I escaped to my memories to avoid the panic that threatened to cause me to cry out that I was being buried alive.

Mr. Baird had been at my side as the first rays of dawn stole into my dank cell early that morn. He prayed over me and delivered the news that the unlikely pardon he had sought on my behalf had been denied. My death was far too important to the illusion of safety in the colonies, especially when considering the turmoil of war with France and the native tribes threatening the future of the new world.

I felt a calm resolution overtake me to be courageous as I approached death. I had, in fact, already suffered what I suspected was death once, and that in a slow and gruesome manner, so I assured myself that this time it would be quick and, Lord willing, painless. It never occurred to me it was possible I could not die a second time.

My peace and tranquility wavered as I approached the hangman's noose, seeing before me a crowd of spectators who considered the death of a criminal as not only the outworking of justice, but also entertainment that would break up the mundanity of an otherwise monotonous day. Amid the crowd, I noticed striking blue eyes framed by black hair. Where had I seen her before? Out of all the faces of emotion in that sea of strangers, hers was stoic and unfeeling. In a way, it was comforting, for there was much fanfare surrounding the event of my demise and many were amused.

As I stood with the noose dangling in front of me, I thought of the practice of public execution and how it should be a sobering experience to behold. Yet, before me was a crowd drawn to this spectacle and among them, the virtuous and diabolical alike, were gleeful faces, come to pass judgment over a man and watch him pay for his sin with his life. Surely, some simply enjoyed meeting the reaper this way. Perhaps it reminded them it was not their turn. Another's death would satisfy Hades' quota, and they would live to see another day.

A lone tear left my eye, and I wished only for a handkerchief to relieve me of it. What an odd and out of place thought for the moment of my departure from life! But as the rope slipped over my chin, it bore away that tear that slid precariously down my cheek and hung on my chin. I could not help but smile at that simple moment of grace.

There was no ceremony or drawn out declaration of guilt,

but only a short reading of my sentence, and then a trap door was released. I remember seeing the sky, blue with wispy clouds, snap into view before the light of my eyes went black. What happened following my second death was told to me by Mr. Baird after he and my lawyer dug me out of my grave and we quietly filled in the spot where my body was supposed to remain.

While I had swayed to and fro after the jolt of my snapping neck, I was pronounced dead and flung onto a wagon that would take me to the burial ground. A guard was stationed around my corpse and the scaffold, preventing the rowdy onlookers from defiling my carcass or tearing down the hanging post. The sexton and I made up my lowly funeral procession, and while the wagon rambled away, pandemonium ensued. The crowd rushed to tear off rope, wood, nails, anything one could get one's hands on to take home as a souvenir.

"Tis a shame. The monster got off easy," Mr. Baird overheard. It was a sentiment making up the opinion of much of the crowd, no doubt. They likely would have preferred an execution more medieval for one of the most vile criminals of their day. Hangings were not bloody enough.

In time, only Mr. Baird, Mr. Andrews, and a group of children putting on their own mock execution remained about the town square where justice had been served.

Mr. Baird watched as the wagon drew near to the cemetery outside of the church grounds, for a man convicted of a crime such as mine was not given the courtesy of a Christian burial, when he caught the lively conversation of a group of the more intellectual members of the crowd discussing the benefits of public execution. Distracted from my laying to rest, they drew him into a nearby tavern.

"I couldna help overhearin'," he explained as he presented his well thought out and cited arguments against capital punishment according to the Bible and other learned men of the time.

"I woulda stayed to go on more, but I heard a voice in me

ear say, 'Your friend needs you now.' I had looked at Mr. Andrews, and he was as confused as me."

"Yes, I had wondered what this beautiful creature wanted with Mr. Baird. No offense," Mr. Andrews added.

"None taken, lad. I woulda wondered the same," he chuckled. "She musta seen me lookin' at Mr. Andrews 'cause then she said, 'Not him.' That's when I remembered ye there, alone, carted off to be buried in an unmarked grave with no one to say yer eulogy. I excused meself and left Mr. Andrews to carry on the conversation."

"Trade embargoes," was all Mr. Andrews said as he gestured with a nod of his head, as if I should know what that topic entailed.

To my good fortune, Mr. Baird had arrived in time to pray over my corpse and find it squirming. Before I knew where I was, I wondered if I would face judgment, or if my soul was already there and my body was simply an animated shell. All was darkness with flickers of shadow. I heard only the rhythmic sloshing of dirt and supposed it to be a fellow sufferer of hell, laboring away for eternity. The Sisyphus of diggers. As I contemplated what my damnation duties would entail, I began to move about to gain a sense of my surroundings. That is when I heard the familiar voice pleading with me to be still, and I realized I was not in hell. I gasped, but there was scant air to fill my lungs. My heart pounded; my hands shook with abandon. Why was I alive? In horror, I came to the truth of it: I could not die. I could not die because I was already dead, and it is appointed unto man once to die and then . . . Oh, Lord, will I never face judgment?

After my successful exhumation, I helped my friends fill in the grave that would house the memory of Fenn Bancroft. Who was I? Whoever I wanted to be, or no one at all.

"Could that woman have kenned ye wasena dead?" Mr. Baird asked as I snuck into the back of the wagon the lawyer had obtained, with remarkable forethought, from the magistrate. My gibbet was there as well as it also was the rightful property of my estate. It sheltered me from the eyes of those who would recognize the man they had just hours before beheld swinging from the town square. Before I could answer, the sexton returned to the graveyard. Mr. Baird and Mr Andrews nodded to the man and hastened, with quick nonchalance, to steer us away from the evidence, or lack, of my death.

As Mr. Andrews rambled the wagon over ruts and rocks, he shared the intelligence he received while he continued his conversation with the merchants.

"I was made privy to some fanciful tales that I would have scoffed at had it not been for the fact I am sitting next to a dead man who turns into a wolf every full moon. I mean no offense to you, of course, Mr. Bancroft."

"Just call me Fenn. I no longer have any heritage in the living." My melancholic answer disgusted even myself, but I knew not who I was any more than a child who loses its parents. "I would be a fool to be offended by such a thing, for it is the truth of the matter, however much I wish the contrary."

"In any case, I would like your opinions whether this information holds any value for our common interests. The verbose men whom you left me to converse with, Mr. Baird, soon tired over the discussion of trade laws and, in the wake of the gallows, returned the conversation to the events that had brought us thither. One of them commented on the evidence of the possibility of others of the werewolf kind, particularly the one killing in the Great Lakes. He said there were murders reported on the same night as the Staunton Slaughter—forgive me, that's what they are calling it—around the forts at Lake Ontario. That our friend Fenn here confessed that Matthew was also a werewolf was further evidence the men cited that proved the numbers are growing."

"Yes, well, that is information we have been privy to all along. For we know someone turned Gregory into the wolf, and that someone being in the Great Lakes. But until today, I believed Gregory to be dead. Now I know he is as invulnerable to death as I am. I hope the wolf they spoke of was not him, but the one who made him." As I spoke of Gregory being alive, the reality of it washed over me and I caught my breath. I had believed him to be gone. I had grieved him, and now we might be reunited. It was as if he had been dug out of a grave alongside me.

"Aye, and more than likely it was. I dunna think Gregory will ever let the beast loose again, not after what he's seen and done already."

We continued to speculate as we traveled to my modest estate, intent on collecting what valuables remained undisturbed. There was little evidence of the gunfight that had ensued on the property. According to Josiah, after being left for dead, he regained consciousness and limped to town for help. He saw the body of Matthew lay still and assumed him deceased. In fact, no living soul was there the day our wagon pulled up to the property, nor was there a body where Matthew should have been.

I entered the small house I had called home for only a few short months. Immediately, I felt the heat from the fireplace where a fire had recently been snuffed out. The bedding was disheveled on the solitary cot, and the pantry held food that I had not provided for it. Someone had been carrying on in my stead. Though I conceded it could have been a squatter, I knew it was more than likely Matthew. Upon further inspection of the cellar, I was certain. A rude contraption constructed by my friend had been erected where my metal cage had sat. It was not the ordered bars of the gibbet, but a patchwork of metal and wood that resembled a dense thicket. I peered inside the den to find spikes of wood lining the walls. I could only imagine the damage left on the man after the enraged beast thrashed about in that prickly dome.

"We must stop here for the night. My friend Matthew shall return, I presume, and we will persuade him to depart with us," I announced to my companions, who waited patiently outside.

"The farmer assured everyone that the boy was dead. It's

likely someone from the village came to inter him weeks ago," the lawyer decidedly deduced. I could not help but chuckle as I corrected him.

"I stand before you alive when you watched me hang. Matthew is alive. In any case, no one would have bothered to bury the young man who killed every one of his family and set their home alight to hide the evidence. They would take comfort in divine justice served and leave the carcass for the carrion. There is no carcass, nothing left of one, and I have evidence that there never was one."

I explained to them what I had discovered in the bowels of my lowly house. Mr. Baird was curious to see the contrivance, while Mr. Andrews mulled about the property looking for bones he would not find.

After the inspections were complete, we retired to the porch to wait for Matthew to arrive. He would recognize the wagon. Even so, he may fear it was a ruse to trap him, and so we stayed where he could see us from afar.

It was nearing dusk when a tall but gangly looking young man emerged from the tree line carrying a gun in one hand and a rabbit dangling in the other. He noticed the wagon and started, as if unsure whether he should return to the cover of the dense woods or if he had already been spotted and should raise his gun in defense. In moments it appeared he had remembered the wagon, and his eyes scanned the landscape for any sign of its owner. I was there, on the porch, along with the "preacher" he would recognize and a third man that was a stranger to him. I raised my arm in a gesture of peace, hoping Matthew would not flee. After a time, he continued to approach the house, though he kept his head low and did not raise his eyes to any one of us.

"I thought you would have been hanged by now," Matthew said as he walked past us and into the house, declining even to turn his head in recognition of his guests. Matthew had likely spent his weeks in seclusion and was out of the habit of discourse, I conceded. I shrugged and entered, following my young friend as the others remained outside, waiting for an invitation. I shut the door behind me to give us privacy before I spoke.

"I believed you to be deceased as well, but here we are."

"I thought I would die again, but no. I woke up just the same. Wounds healing too quick and just a terrible headache to show for being shot."

"It appears we cannot face death a second time. At least not by the usual means."

"Appears so."

"I discovered your apparatus. I am sorry for nosing about, yet I had to be sure you were still here before we left for the Arnot's."

"It's your home. You may have the run of it." Matthew was busy preparing his catch and had yet to look at me. I wondered at the coldness. After all, we were on amicable terms before our violent separation. I rekindled the fire in the hearth, hoping its warmth would have a parallel effect on the acrid mood that hung heavy in the room.

"Matthew, I believe I know where the man, or monster, who has spread this affliction may be. I mean to discover him and attempt to gather more information about where this wretchedness began. Perhaps he has knowledge that could aid us in discovering a cure."

"Right," Matthew said as he slammed his knife on the table.

"What is it, friend? Why are you angry?"

He laughed, a derisive, ironic sort of laugh which made me regret asking.

"Really? You don't know why I would be angry? You told everyone that I killed my family, burned down my house, and that I'm a werewolf!"

"How do you know this?"

"I know where the printer puts his stack of papers out for the boys who deliver them to subscribers. I've been taking one every night to keep up with the trial."

"Matthew . . . I am sorry. There is nothing else I can say other than I believed you to be dead or far away and it would not affect you."

"Well, it doesn't really, does it? Everyone assumed I had done it, anyway. I am a fugitive, and if they all think me dead, that's probably for the best. I just figured the werewolf part wouldn't ever have to be known by anyone but us.'

"You are right. It was not my secret to share."

Matthew was silent for some time as he slashed at his kill with a knife, shredding the pelt into several strips and chunks rather than pulling it off in one neat piece. I waited patiently, and eventually his eyes left the carnage before him to meet mine.

"I can see," he paused and held the knife to his temple as one would a pointer finger. "I can see when it takes over."

I did not at first realize what Matthew was saying. His gaze did not falter as he gave me time to work out his meaning.

"You mean you are conscious?"

"Yes. I'm not in control, but I can feel the rage and hunger, and I remember it all when I come to myself again."

"Why, that is amazing, Matthew!" I admit I was more jovial than would be prudent at such a declaration, but the implication overcame me and I could not contain it.

"How is that amazing? I don't want to know what happens when that thing has its way! I wish I could kill it, but I can't 'cause I can't die! I must live, and so I do, but I'm not happy about it. It's far from amazing to see what that beast sees and feel what it feels." He made his disgust manifest in the way he butchered the poor rabbit, leaving its carcass a mess of muscle, bone, and sinew. I took a breath and resumed a moderate tone.

"What I mean to say is, if we can see and remember, then perhaps eventually we may thwart or control the monster through the faculties of our human mind over its carnality. We may take dominion over the beast, and perhaps then we will have no need for cages anymore."

Matthew chuckled again while he held up a piece of rabbit

flesh and skewered it onto the pike that would roast over the fire. "Your undying optimism amazes me."

"Come with us. We leave this place in the morning and head for the Arnot's. Mr. Baird has arranged for us to take shelter there before we depart for New York and determine our future."

"What future?" Matthew's bitterness oozed out of him with each word, and I lost my patience.

"Oh, for heaven's sake, any future is better than sulking for eternity! You may resign yourself to your cursed state, but I . . . I'll be damned if I do! I will not rest until I discover all there is to know about what I am, what we are, and if I cannot find a cure . . . perhaps there is a way to end this."

"What about your soul?" I caught the hint of mockery in Matthew's question, but I ignored the slight and answered honestly.

"If I have lost it already, then it is lost." I threw up my hands and sat down on the stool by the fire. "I had prayed my execution would be the just payment and penance for my sin. I was at peace with my fate and walked to the gallows, hopeful that I was walking toward home. After I awoke, I admit, I felt despair." I was restless on the stool and stood to walk about the room as Matthew roasted his victuals and gazed at the fire. I stopped before the young man and put my hand on his shoulder.

"I do not know, friend, what will become of my soul. Perhaps, as long as I am a man, I can strive against the monster and, in that way, win favor in God's sight. It may be too late, but I cannot abandon hope." I prayed and longed for it to be true, that there was a way to find redemption. Matthew looked at me. Could he see the mustard sized faith in my eyes? I hoped he could take some of it for his own.

"I admit, I have lost faith that there is any such thing as God, let alone any such hope as redemption. I've seen and felt the evil that's inside. Where does it go when it's not the monster's turn? Isn't it still in me? I know how I felt about my father before the monster killed him," Matthew whispered a sigh of defeat. "Perhaps this beast is simply the manifestation of the evil we desire when we are loosed from all inhibition and restraint. Maybe it's the very root of our nature as man and yet we fight against it . . . for what? I can't be destroyed, but I can't live freely. Yet I have power within me to destroy and to be free." He paused, reflecting as drops of rendered fat sizzled on a log in the fire. "I've had many nights alone and all I can do is think, and if I'm honest, my thoughts slide more often into the Slough of Despond than on the Holy Way. I fear the Giant Despair has already gobbled me up."

I had noticed Matthew's copy of Christian's journey—it had lived on my mantle since the quiet nights of simpler times—seemed to have been discarded, lying in a corner, disheveled and forgotten. Matthew could have burned the book, but he did not. Something in him was still connected to what he was, in spite of his father.

However, I could not help wondering if I was deluding myself, believing the way could still be open for me? What was keeping me connected? Who would come along to point me to the place where I could throw off my burden? The silence may have gone on indefinitely had not Mr. Baird rapped at the door, recalling me from doubts that threatened to swallow me whole.

I welcomed Mr. Baird and Mr. Andrews inside and set to work searching the pantry for something suitable to prepare, for none of us had dined sufficiently that day. Mr. Andrews introduced himself to Matthew and was greeted with a laconic, but not wholly discourteous, "Welcome." The men found what seats they could in the small living space and joined in the silence that lingered there. Finally, Mr. Baird broke the stalemate.

"I presume ye ken ye cannae die? No' by the natural way, anyhow," Mr. Baird asked in a matter-of-fact tone that would have been appropriate if discussing the weather, but under the circumstances, seemed out of place. I expected to hear a rude or sarcastic remark from Matthew, but he was subdued.

"Yes."

Silence consumed us all once more. As I labored in the area of my home that could loosely be termed a kitchen, Matthew came out of another trance into which he was prone to sink since the massacre of his family, and elaborated.

"Yes, I understand I can't die by any hand, including my own." As my guests understood the implication, Mr. Andrews shook his head in compassion. Matthew ignored the sympathetic visages before him and inquired of Mr. Baird, "What do you mean by 'natural way'? Is there any other way to die?"

"Oh, I expect as there's a way to become a werewolf, there must be a way to un-become one."

"What way might that be?" There was hope hidden behind Matthew's attempts at remaining nonchalant. It was subtle, but I knew him well enough to recognize the slight lilt in his voice.

"I dunna ken, yet. But we mean to keep searching and there's a lead we mean to follow."

"The one you think started this?"

"Aye. Started it, or brought it here. Either way, he may ken more than we."

Matthew did not resume the conversation, but was drawn back into the numbing effect of the fire. After we ate, beds were assembled, and all were asleep before the sun had finished setting.

In the morning, Matthew consented to join us.

14

Mrs. Arnot, Mr. Baird's sister, was hospitable to those of us who arrived at the homestead that afternoon. She had five children, her home was under construction, and she had barely the room to house the members of her own family let alone guests, and yet she smiled and welcomed us in, offering us pottage before we had time to remove our coats. Had she known the delicate situation she was putting her family in by housing fugitives, she likely would have been decidedly less amiable.

We remained with the Arnot's one night while the seminarian put his affairs in order and collected what he thought would be useful for our journey ahead. That night, while Mr. Andrews and Mr. Baird rested, Matthew and I worked on our gibbets, having the use of a forge on Mr. Arnot's industrious homestead. I watched Matthew work skillfully to reinforce a cage of his own design before he moved on to repair the break I had caused in my gibbet, the one that had cost him his humanity. As the iron glowed red and melded together, I was overcome by how foolish I had been to trust in my meager, inadequate repairs. That foolishness had led to more death and my banishment from the world of the living. My mind spun and my heart raced as I was reminded of every naïve choice I had made and what it had cost those around me. I made a vow as I stared into the fire: I would not be so irresponsible again. But could I keep it?

As if in answer, I dropped the tongs I held to assist Matthew.

The metal clattered on the hard dirt floor, and Matthew turned to look at me. "Are you alright?"

"I am sorry, Matthew."

He paused for a moment before he bent down and picked up the tongs, handing them back. "It's ok. I don't need them yet. But you may want to dust these off so the dirt doesn't catch fire when I use them."

I left the fire of the forge and found a rag with which to clean the tongs. A tear dropped onto my dusty apron, and it was then that I knew I was crying.

The following morning, all agreed, aside from Matthew, who was indifferent, that any further answers would come from the source of the affliction. Finding Gregory would be an added blessing, should he be somewhere along the way.

We traveled north on the Wagon Road as far as Lancaster, stopping at taverns and ordinaries when it was safe. I attempted to grow the start of a beard, though it was especially uncomfortable and made me look decidedly less like a gentleman, but I hoped it would protect me from detection. After all, I had left behind my former self, and his clothes, and would have to learn to embrace the life of a common laborer. Matthew did not waste energy worrying about disguising himself, as he did not fret one way or the other if he was caught.

We spent our time on the road becoming better acquainted. I was interested in hearing more about Mr. Andrews, as I already knew Matthew well and Mr. Baird well enough.

"What is there to tell? I grew up in the Province of New York. My father was a lawyer, so I carried on the family business until I tried a few too many cases he didn't approve of. I left his practice to start my own. I heard the population in Williamsburg was booming, so I was determined to open an office there. I had yet to really get my feet wet in the area before Mr. Baird requested my help with your case. He knew it sounded like something I would be interested in."

"Why should my case interest you?"

"I have a particular affinity for defending persons driven to crime by poverty and those who suffer from lunacy. Your case being the latter, of course."

"And do you still think me a lunatic?"

Mr. Andrews, John was his Christian name, thought for a moment, likely considering how he should answer. He had obviously believed so in the beginning and had argued the case as such. But listening to the witnesses during the trial and speaking to a live man he watched hang was evidence of the supernatural. Yet, he had not seen the monster first hand; perhaps he was still unable to comprehend its existence.

"I don't think you're a lunatic, not in the traditional sense of the term. I can't say I believe in werewolves, though."

"Even so," I shrugged, "regrettably, they exist." John nodded as the wagon rambled on.

Matthew and Mr. Baird rode ahead, discussing farming, and their domestic conversation inspired me to inquire into John's personal life.

"Is there a Mrs. Andrews in the brewing?"

"Unfortunately, no. The law has been my mistress. I have found it difficult to pursue another."

"And yet, here you are with us."

"Yes, well, there is something about all of this that is too tempting for me to set aside. Perhaps it's research."

"I hope you never have to defend another werewolf, or anything of the kind!" I laughed, but John was thoughtful.

"I had never tried a case with a death sentence before. Truth be told, I was rather shaken over the fact that you had staked your life on me and I failed you. As I watched you swing back and forth, I wondered if I could practice law again. Seeing you climb out of your grave . . . well, I was awash with horror but also relief."

"I thought you did a fine job, Mr. Andrews. It was an impossible situation and it could have been much worse." I could see John pondering what I could mean by worse. Would parts of me have climbed, crawled, sloshed out of the grave and worked themselves back together like a puzzle while Mr. Baird and John watched? Yes, that would have been worse. I wondered how far immortality could go.

The full moon approached, yet we were still several days from where we hoped to find answers. It was more difficult there, in the tidewater, to find a large stretch of forest that was not owned or inhabited by humans. We were satisfied to find a hilly region where wagons could not easily scale; where we could hide away and transform outside of hearing, or at least far enough away to be taken for ordinary wolves. We carried the gibbets, two men each, up a steep embankment that led to a small plateau of woods before it banked again to a creek bed. The creek was a suitable place to make camp, and we were comfortably situated before sunset. Both the non-afflicted were anxious as they waited for the moon to rise. This would be the first time any mortal watched the transformation, and it seemed at once a fascinating observation as well as an intrusion. Matthew was disconnected from the event, referring to his other self as "it," and spoke as if he was going to observe the transformation as well. Admittedly, I was more interested in preserving my dignity and wished to have a change of clothes at the ready when dawn brought me back to my human self. Guns were loaded, as an added precaution, while Matthew and I crawled into our cages and waited to be secured.

The change began as I watched the moon reach its zenith. I observed Matthew as he fought to remain conscious, the monster's clawed paws grabbing the bars in front of him, wrenching and straining, trying to break free. I could see the hunger, the rage, and I knew he could not control it. He was simply a bystander for the usurper. Within seconds of Matthew's change, I was overcome by the stupor that clouded my mind until all went black.

When we awoke that dawn, the mortals described to us what they had witnessed the night before. It was the first time I would hear of my transformation from someone who was not a victim of it.

Mr. Baird and Mr. Andrews had watched "in horror" as we became beasts. Mr. Andrews did not go into detail about the transformation itself, which he described as "revolting," and I could not help but feel defensive at the words of disgust he used to describe the incident.

"Felt as if we were in a faerie story, lad," was all Mr. Baird would say, and I imagined the fairy tales I had read as a child and understood.

Aside from the obvious, yet ludicrous, morphology that happened before their eyes, the men were even more astonished to find that, while my monster writhed and raged like a cat in a trap, Matthew's eventually became calm and subdued. Mr. Baird was intrigued and made Mr. Andrews follow him to inspect the creature closely.

"I was apprehensive, to say the least, and declined the invitation more than once, but Mr. Baird was persistent, and so I followed the preacher into the midst of demons." Again, I cringed and John could see how he had offended me. "My apologies. I know it is not something you can control." In time, I suspected, John would accept the werewolves as a foregone conclusion and set aside the shock for analysis, but that day he seemed to want only to forget that the monsters had ever emerged.

"Matthew was quiet at first, but when he saw me gawking at him, the beast took over and began battering the cage in time with you, lad. Mr. Andrews here turned tail and ran back to the fire and the safety of guns while I looked hard in Matthew's eyes for any sign of the man in there. I couldna see the lad for the monster, so I went back to the fire, and we tried to rest."

Apparently, I had attacked my cage relentlessly, carrying on nearly the entire night, leaving the men little peace for sleep, while the eventual silence from Matthew's cage made the men wonder if at least one of us would rest. By dawn, all was quiet and, as if we each understood the mutual need for rejuvenation, no one stirred, but allowed the day to pass well into the noon hour before camp was packed and the journey recommenced.

We reached Lancaster in Pennsylvania and John left the wide, well-trodden path of the Wagon Road for a narrow, overgrown one leading south. His task was to deliver my estate to Beatrice. Once complete, he would return to Lancaster, and then we would all continue on to Philadelphia and take the King's Highway to New York City, followed by the Albany Post Road to Albany. From Albany, the Mohawk Trail would lead us through the disputed territories to the Great Lakes. Though I longed to follow John and see my beloved one last time, I knew it was impossible.

"I wish I could have secured you your life; your life as Mr. Bancroft, I mean," John said, my regret clearly written in the contours of my face.

"Yes, well, in any case, life as Mr. Bancroft was not really possible, anyway. I held on to a castle in the sky that could never be a reality for me. At least now that he is dead, my Beatrice can live on and be happy someday." I had resolved to let Beatrice go. It had been a torturous choice, made easier only by the certainty of my execution, but even after I discovered I could not die, I allowed that life to be buried and I would not resurrect it.

John shook hands with the others before mounting and clicking his steed into a trot. We watched him ride off before we found an out of the way ordinary to settle in till he should return.

. . .

After a day or two of mulling about the small accommodations, I wondered why we had allowed Mr. Baird to set aside the plans for his life to risk it in this scheme to find the first wolf. Matthew and I were obviously on this mission with purpose and Mr. Andrews condescended to deliver my estate as was his duty as my lawyer, but Mr. Baird had no reason to continue on our, possibly, fool's errand.

I offered Mr. Baird the opportunity to quit our mission.

"There is nothing for you here, my friend. We can manage on our own and traveling into the contested territories will only put your life in danger. I suggest you and Mr. Andrews return to Virginia after we are reunited."

"Oh, I thank ye kindly, lad, for yer concern, but dunna fash. I ken what I'm riskin' followin' ye both."

I knew him to be a man of his word and immovable once he had decided upon a thing, and so I left off trying to persuade him.

More tedious days of waiting brought no word from John and, growing restless, we ventured into a tavern that attracted travelers passing by on the Wagon Road. A table of soldiers, newly enlisted and preparing to join their regiment, were close enough to overhear. They were Colonel Abercrombie's men and were heading north to Fort George on Lake Iroquois, one of them was a talkative fellow and, once I made eye contact, he brought me into his conversation.

"You boys planning to join our little war here?" asked the young soldier, not entirely lacking experience as evidenced by his rank, but still innocent enough to call any war "little."

"The business is our own," answered Matthew, who was sour after all our dull inaction.

"Oh, I don't mean to pry. Just curious what gentlemen like yourselves are about. I can tell you aren't trappers. Those fellas look like they are about to become the animals they're hunting. No. You all look like honest folk. Though you've clearly been on the road a while." No one offered the soldier an answer, and he shrugged, returning to the meal he was grateful to have before joining Abercrombie's march. I remembered our purpose and decided the soldiers may have information that could be helpful to us in the future.

"Have there been any reports of wolf attacks in this area recently?" I asked after the soldier had taken a long quaff of ale. He wiped his mouth and soured his forehead in thought before answering.

"Wolf attacks? Oh, you mean like the ones that were happening in the forts near the lakes a few months ago? Haven't heard of any recently. There was one, same night as the attacks that happened somewhere in the backcountry. They say that Virginia killer was a man, and he was hanged. Thank God! Sounded like a vile creature from what I heard." The soldier took another sip.

I furrowed my brow and clenched my fist, but there was no use being angry with someone who did not know he was equating me with the beast that invaded my body without consent. I relaxed as another soldier at the table who had been heretofore silent and intent on finishing what remained on his plate drifted into the conversation to add his intelligence.

"I just heard of one, oh, less than a week ago. Happened on the coast somewhere, I think in the Maryland colony, if I remember right. First time a wolf attack like that was reported in the towns. If it was an animal."

"What do you mean, 'if it was an animal?' Animal or man, gotta be one or the other," retorted the first soldier.

"Maybe there's a third option," the intruder offered, and then retreated from the conversation as quickly as he had entered it. I ignored the insinuation and turned to the soldier who had begun our dialogue.

"There was an attack in Maryland?" As I said the name of the colony, I felt a tremor in my voice. An awful foreboding nearly took my breath away but, as I had yet no reason to fear, I resolved to remain calm. "What town did you say it was?"

"Oh, I don't know. This is my first time hearing about it. Hey, Tom." The man looked up from his plate, annoyance written on his face, likely for being dragged back into a conversation he was clearly finished with. "You know what town over in Maryland?" the soldier asked him. Tom took a moment to think, washing down what he had been chewing before answering.

"I believe it was Chestertown. Yeah, I have a lady friend there who writes to me. She said it was two young women. Sisters, I guess. That's all I know."

If the man continued talking, I did not hear it. I stumbled out of my chair and pushed away from the table, walking like a drunkard out of the tavern and into the muggy night air. I found a tree and sat against it, holding my head between my knees in hopes I could keep my wits about me and avoid losing the small amount of victuals I had consumed. Oh, sweet Beatrice! And Mary, too? Damn the devil!

Matthew and Mr. Baird joined me, waving off the nosey soldiers who followed them to see why I had left so abruptly.

"Cannae hold his spirits, this one!" Mr. Baird motioned to me in jest, and the soldiers shrugged and went back inside to their meal.

"Oh, God! What has happened to my Beatrice?!" I felt the vomit rising in my throat and scrambled away from the men who hovered over me in concern. I managed to keep from becoming ill.

"It might not be her. They don't know any names, just sisters. I'm sure there are many sisters in Chestertown." Matthew tried to sound confident, but I could hear him wavering in his tone and knew he believed it was Beatrice as well. I shoved out my arm towards them as they hovered over me.

"Oh, lad! Let's not get ahead of ourselves! Like Matthew said, we cannae ken for sure who the lasses are. Let's wait to hear from John. He should be back any day now."

"No. We go to Chestertown."

"I doubt the man is still there," Matthew said, watching as the soldiers left the tavern, stumbling and singing a song about Yankee Doodle.

"He's there." I gritted my teeth and rose, pushing past my well-meaning companions and forced each foot to follow the other as I made my way back to our ordinary. Matthew and Mr. Baird followed without another objection, likely knowing they would be hard-pressed to keep me at bay.

I hastily gathered my things and rushed out into the dark. I refused to wait until morning, though my companions tried to convince me that the night was no time to travel, especially under duress, but I would not heed them and saddled my horse. They would not allow me to travel alone, the wagon and horses were made ready, and we set out soon after midnight.

As the sun was rising, we noticed a traveler approach whose gait was unmistakable, as well as his expression.

So it was true. My beloved was gone! I collapsed there on the road.

I remember not how we came to an inn, but I recall sitting in a chair with a cup of something steaming while my companions stood by, waiting to be useful. I had no tears, though my head throbbed and my throat was tight, so I knew I must have sobbed with abandon. My mind felt fractured, and I could not comprehend the very great wound that threatened to destroy it. My body could heal rapidly. I had come back from the dead. But this fissure in my heart was permanent. I suppose my countenance betrayed that I had come back to some form of consciousness, for John came and knelt beside me and spoke gently.

"I wish I didn't have to tell you this. I know it will be more than you can bear, but you are not alone. We aren't going anywhere." I already knew my Beatrice was gone; it was already more than I could bear. "I found Gregory in Chestertown. He was there . . . when they died."

I wanted to believe John meant Gregory had been a witness to the girls' slaughter, but I knew that was not all. I pictured Beatrice and Mary, terrified and helpless against the massive beast that was sure to be Gregory when the monster took on his flesh. The teeth and claws profaning their angelic faces.

"No!" It came out as feigned disbelief but also a command, as if I could make it untrue by saying so. "It could not be Gregory. It could not!" But it could and I knew it. I knew what I had done to Matthew. I knew what Gregory had done to me.

"I didn't want to believe it myself. I hoped we would find evidence that it was someone else. But it appears, from all we could tell, that though Gregory tried to contain it, the beast was able to get free."

"Why was he even there?" I asked through gritted teeth.

"I will tell you everything I know."

What follows is the story, which we heard from John in an ordinary halfway between Lancaster and Chestertown that day in late July.

15

"It was nearing evening of the day I left you all, so I stopped at the first ordinary along the path and rented a room. As I sat among the other patrons, eating a hearty dinner, I finally had time to think about what I had seen and heard just hours before. I am a student of reason. Logic is my livelihood. How could I make sense of a world in which the impossible could occur? I could no longer deny that werewolves were real. I would have to call my eyes and ears liars and never trust my senses again. I took in the faces around me and wondered, 'if there are more, could they be here now?' My eyes glanced past a beautiful young woman with raven hair and shocking blue eyes. My mind had been enraptured by the possibility of other demons about me that at first her face didn't register. But then, as if the part of my brain that held memory grew a mouth and learned to speak, I heard in my mind 'the lady from Staunton!' and looked back to where I had seen her, but there was no woman there. Only an old man, travel worn yet working diligently to clear his plate. I scanned the room. I even stood to look over heads; perhaps she was sitting somewhere else? But she was gone. Or maybe she had never been there and my eyes were playing tricks on me. When I came to myself, the old man was staring at me. I averted my eyes, returned to my seat, and went back to what was left of my dinner.

"My dreams that night were a mixture of claws, fangs, and blue eyes illuminated in a sea of black.

"I went directly to the Calvert estate upon arriving in Chestertown. A servant named Cathleen greeted me and inquired about my business. When I mentioned the name Beatrice, a sound that can only be described as a yelp mixed with a groan emitted from the throat of the woman as she bid me inside to the parlor to await the master of the house. I was only mildly suspicious of the servant's behavior and imagined that a male caller may be an irregular occurrence, and for reasons of propriety, the father would inspect each one. I didn't wait long before a man dressed in a black coat, black breeches, and a black tricorn hat entered the room. He tipped his hat to me and introduced himself, motioning for me to have a seat by the hearth.

'You say you are here to speak with my daughter, Beatrice?'

'That is correct, sir. My name is John Andrews. I'm a lawyer from New York, well now Virginia. I've come from Staunton and I'm afraid I do not come under glad tidings. Your Beatrice, well, her betrothed is . . . dead, sir, and he charged me, before his unfortunate demise, that what remained of his estate would be delivered to Miss Beatrice, along with a letter.'

'I see. . . is that the same Fenn Bancroft that was all over the newspapers? The one whose murderous rampage drove my poor Beatrice sick with sorrow?' I gathered they had read of the Staunton Slaughter in the Maryland papers.

'Yes, sir. I'm sorry to say the same one.'

'I am glad to hear he's dead! Nothing unfortunate about it. When did it happen?'

'Nearly two weeks ago, sir. He was hanged.'

"Mr. Calvert made a harsh noise in his throat and I could tell he had choked back a sob. He shook his head in what I believed to be confusion and disbelief, which made no sense considering how he seemed to feel about Fenn. He stared at a portrait hanging above the mantelpiece, so I followed his gaze. It was of three beautiful women. Two were young, with girlish smiles and lace trimmed silk gowns. The third was older, more matronly, but no less charming, holding a parasol on a sunny day. When I looked back at Mr. Calvert, his eyes were listless and I wondered if he was still with me, but eventually he responded.

'I am sorry you wasted a trip, Mr. Andrews.' He took the seat across from me. 'It will be impossible to carry out your duty, for my daughter . . .' A choke stopped the words in his throat, but he coughed and excused himself before continuing, 'my daughters have been murdered.'

"Obviously, I did not expect the news. I couldn't speak. I didn't know what to say. I looked at the letter in my hand, and then back to the face of Mr. Calvert, and words, at last, stumbled out.

'I'm sorry . . . murdered? . . . how devastating! You say daughters, sir? How many have you lost?'

'Both of them. Beatrice and Mary.' He nodded to the painting. 'They were inseparable, and they died together. In that fact is the only consolation I can claim.'

'I hope the murderer has been apprehended and will face the justice of the law! I would be much obliged to be of service in this case, if it would be helpful.'

"Mr. Calvert stood and walked to the window where he looked out at the bay, which even I could see from across the room.

'I appreciate your offer, Mr. Andrews, but unfortunately it will not be necessary unless a wolf can be brought to trial.'

'A wolf, sir?' I stumbled on the words.

'Yes.' Mr. Calvert continued to stare out of the window, over the landscape. He turned around and spoke with apparent, yet controlled, grief. 'Yes, I was told the wounds were that of a beast of claws and teeth. The damage that I beheld when I found my little women . . .' He couldn't go on until he returned to his chair and stared into the empty fireplace. 'But I read what Mr. Bancroft had done to his victims . . . I could have believed it was him . . . but you say he died two weeks ago . . .'

'Sir, if I may inquire, when did this happen?'

'Only two nights hence. We had a small gathering of friends for dinner and the girls felt they had overindulged and took leave of the party to walk along the river. I had no fear for their safety. The moon was nearly as bright as day, being full that night.' I nodded and offered my condolences again. I put on the face of an attorney, not allowing my thoughts and feelings to be displayed. There was nothing left for me in that house of mourning, and I bid the father farewell, gathered my hat and coat, and turned to depart when Mr. Calvert stopped me.

'Excuse me, Mr. Andrews, are you sure Bancroft died then . . . it couldn't have been him?'

'I watched him hang, sir. I assure you, the man, Fenn Bancroft, is dead.'

'Right.' Mr. Calvert grew listless, as if he forgot he had company. But he recovered quickly and rose, picking up a folded letter from his desk. 'This is the last thing she wrote to him. Put it with whatever you have of his and burn it all, will you?'

"I tipped my hat and departed. Outside, on the street before that large riverfront estate, I felt my heart racing, and I bent over to catch my breath. I have never, even in my most difficult court cases, had the wind stolen from me the way that exchange did. When I composed myself, I rode into town.

"Dougherty's on High Street had vacancy, entertainment, and society; it seemed much of Chestertown was gathered there that evening. I settled into a room before ordering supper in the dining hall, hoping to find out more information about this wolf from the local gossips. Most of the customers were engaged in conversations around the room, but one sat huddled in a corner and appeared to be attempting to blend in with the wood grain. I noticed the man as strange among all the lively others due to his despairing manner and unkempt clothing that hung like rags from his dejected body. He was nursing a pint, and I watched as he wiped tears from his eyes at intervals, though he never turned his head to let anyone in the room see him cry. On the other side of where I sat, I overheard some chatter about the recent murder.

'Me wife is on about me now to stey awey from the river. I said, 'Woman, how else is a fisherman to make a livin' if he can't put out on the water?' She jest went on about wolves. I ain't afraid of wolves.' The fisherman took another gulp of his libations and waited for affirmation.

'I ain't heard of wolves attacking in these parts.'

'You ain't heard talk of the two girls been mauled to death on Chester River? Their father believes it was a wolf. No one saw the beast and only evidence is what it left of 'em.'

'I seen what dogs can do. No reason to believe it was a wolf.'

'True enough. Like I said, I ain't afraid of wolves.' There was a lull in the conversation while the men drank and finished what was left of their meal. The fisherman was obviously still ruminating on the possibility of a wolf attack.

'What you think's been eatin' bodies up in the Great Lakes?'

'I can't say I've heard much about it, but could be any wild creature, angry or hungry enough to attack a man.'

'I heard it was a werewolf.'

'You ain't afraid of wolves, but now you're giving credence to a crazy thing like that? Really, man?'

'Oh, it's just what I heard. I ain't said I believed it!'

'I should hope not!'

"The man in the corner grew agitated. I was far enough away to doubt the stranger could hear the conversation going on next to me, but by the man's body language, I couldn't be sure he wasn't listening in and reacting to the calloused comments of the fishermen. The unfortunate got up and slinked out of the dining area to the guest quarters. I casually left my table and pursued. I watched him retreat into a room at the end of the hall and slam the door behind himself. Approaching the door and listening, I heard nothing but some rustling. I knocked, and in a few moments the door opened slightly and an eye peered round the corner.

'What can I do for ye?' the man asked, as if he dared me to answer.

'Forgive me, sir. My name is John Andrews, and I am looking into the unfortunate deaths of two young ladies in the area. I'm asking around if anyone may have seen anything or has any information.'

"The man betrayed a grimace of anguish, but he quickly answered.

'I'm sorry, sir, I have no information for you. Good night.' He began to close the door, but I held it open with my hand.

'Please. I notice you seem affected by the information. Did you know the girls?'

'Knew 'em. Loved 'em. Yes, I did, sir. And I'll beg you to let me mourn in peace.' The door closed once more. My foot found itself being used as a doorstop.

'I am terribly sorry for your loss. Might I ask how you knew the ladies?'

"The man opened the door wider and stood to his full height. He seemed to lord over me with his strong build and, I'll admit, handsome face, but his clothes, as I had noticed in the tavern, were ripped and revealed various parts of his muscular physique, including a shoulder. That's where I noticed a rather large and mangled scar that trailed from his neck down to his armpit, the evidence of teeth marks and flayed skin. I pretended not to see, but I knew immediately who stood before me and why his behavior was so peculiar.

'We were friends,' the man said through clenched teeth to keep from crying. 'And now, I beg you, good night.' This time, he succeeded in blocking my advances and shut himself in his room.

"I didn't know what to do with what I presumed to be the truth of the matter. Gregory was alive, of course, as Fenn had already assumed was the case since death seemed to be unattainable for the werewolves, but it appeared he had returned to the object of his affection, and in doing so, had brought calamity upon not only her but her sister, Beatrice, as well. Why would he remain anywhere near those he loved, knowing what he became? I couldn't find the logic in it. Yet, Gregory was in Chestertown and the murder happened only days before. Was it possible he was not the murderer and had only heard of the loss of his love on arriving in town?

"I approached the innkeeper.

'Sir, I have a question regarding one of your patrons.'

'I'll help if I can.'

'The man in the room down the hall there—can you confirm for me when he arrived?'

'That quiet fellow with the peculiar request? He's been here for, oh, 5 days now.'

'May I ask what the peculiar request was?'

'He just wanted us to keep the room for him, but would not be staying in it one of the nights he was here. Said he had business to attend to overnight but would return in the morning. That wasn't the peculiar part. We have tenants who pay for the room and use it merely to keep their belongings till they leave town. This man, he wanted us to keep his window open the night he was gone. He was adamant. I said alright; didn't hurt anyone to have it open, though it put a bit of a chill in the air. Well, anyhow, is that all you need?'

'Yes, thank you.' I departed to my room but found it hard to sleep, my brain being unsettled by shock after shock with hardly a moment between to come up for air. Now that I was in the quiet solitude of my room, the information washed over me and I allowed the varied emotions to have their time before I pulled out a law book and began reading the requirements of the colony of Virginia for licensing ordinaries.

. . .

"I watched the comings and goings of the peculiar man I took to be Gregory. The stranger left the inn the following morning, but didn't leave Chestertown. Instead, he spent his days mulling about the various taverns and public houses before departing into the woods to spend the evening; I didn't know where. This man's countenance never wavered from anguish and sorrow, occasionally anger, and he appeared aimless and lost, as though he couldn't tell from where he had come or where he was going. I didn't want to cause the man to flee by pursuing him, so instead I kept my distance and watched. The stranger seemed not to notice anything except his own emotions and spent his time numbing the pain with ale. This went on for several days before I was approached on the street. I could smell the heavy scent of campfire before I turned to see the man. It was the stranger, and he was calm and intent.

'Don't think I haven't noticed you watchin' me. I told you all I know. Let me be.'

'I apologize if I have distressed you. But I believe you may know more than you have let on.' The stranger walked away, christening the road with saliva. 'We have a mutual friend. Fenn Bancroft,' I called after him.

"The man turned around and screwed his eye as he studied me, searching my face to discover how much I may know. The stranger's face fell into one of dejection and he nodded for me to follow him into Dougherty's, which stood across the street. I directed the man to my room and offered him a seat on a chair in the corner while I sat on the bed.

'Then you know who I am, I gather?' he started the interrogation.

'Gregory?'

'Aye, that's my name. But do you know what I am?'

'I do. I have seen the affliction in Fenn and his friend Matthew.'

'Matthew? Are you saying there's another? Oh, God, did I make another?'

'No. No, it was Mr. Bancroft, unfortunately, who passed it on to Matthew.' Gregory sighed, but it was clear this information didn't bring him any relief. 'Might as well have been me, anyhow. I'm the one who gave this awful curse to Fenn. And now . . . well, you've likely gathered that it was me that . . . killed those girls.' Gregory shuddered, and a quick but violent sob escaped him before he composed himself.

'I had hoped that was not the case, but I considered it,' I conceded.

'Part of me wishes they had lived to become like us . . . least then they would still be here and we could all be together. But then, how could I damn those perfect creatures? It's better they're gone, even if it was too soon.'

'Why did you come here, Gregory?'

'Oh, Lord, I've asked myself that every moment of every day since. Seems every choice I make is a bad one.' He sighed. 'I been followed, or hunted, since I became this monster. I thought I'd be set free when the farmer shot me in the head.' I nodded. 'Oh, you heard about that? Well, I woke up soon after, lying by the river bank. Seems they tossed me into the river, but I washed up a ways down. I put two and two together and, I'm sorry to say, I blasphemed the Lord that day when I knew I couldn't die.

'In any case, I thought maybe I had lost my stalker, but no chance. Few months later I just knew he, or she, found me. I planned to go west over the mountain and take my chances with the Injuns, but I just couldn't leave without seeing her one last time. I had my new cage, which hadn't failed me yet, and I meant just to catch sight of her, you see, and that was all. I don't rightly know how I could have done it. When I woke in the morning, I was in my cage. But then I came back to the inn, and it was all the talk—two girls been torn apart by a beast. I ran to their house and saw the blood still soaked on the ground.' Gregory took a moment as I believe the scene replayed before his eyes and then continued. 'I've been here since, trying to make sense of it. Not caring who sees me or knows me. What difference does it make anyhow?' He fidgeted with a necklace in his hand. 'But I must have done it. Right?'

"I had to agree. Who, or what, else would have been in Chestertown and killed those girls? Those particular girls. It was far too coincidental and all evidence would point to the werewolf who was within miles of them on the full moon.

'Tell me every detail you can remember of that night. I know it will be difficult, but if there's a chance you are innocent, should we not pursue it?'

"Gregory did his best to recall every moment of the night, though he had spent the last several days drowning in liquid forgetfulness. A few days prior to our meeting, he had arrived in town and rented a room at Dougherty's. He slinked about town, keeping to the shadows and alleyways, but hunting out all the places he believed Mary might be. He had seen Beatrice, on occasion, and their father, but he had yet to see the object of his affection. Determined to get what he came for, he stayed, planning to rise early and catch her leaving her home. He stole to the Calvert estate and hid in some overgrowth, waiting.

"He couldn't explain then why he had been so intent on seeing her before he departed west. It was the only errand he desired to accomplish and his sight was so bent on it he would not turn aside, even though he knew that evening was the full moon and he would be forced to flee the town and lock himself away in the woods where he had left his cage. The cage had been faithful thus far, so he took the risk. It turned out to be a necessity as he spent the day waiting for Mary and finding that she would not leave.

"As the sun was setting, carriages were arriving at the estate. They were hosting a party and, as their guests approached the grand house, Gregory finally got the glimpse of his love as she darted out of her doorway to greet her friend with an embrace. Her face was illuminated in joy, and Gregory felt he could finally be at peace, knowing she was happy.

'I wanted to jump out of the bushes and run to her. Let her

know I was alive. But I knew I couldn't. Whatever grieving she did for me, I didn't want to make her have to do it again.'

"He had spent the entire day in the thicket and knew he had to get back to the woods, so he hurried off toward his cage. It took him what he believed to be about two hours to reach his hiding place by foot and found his apparatus untouched and, likely, unnoticed. He had eaten nothing since his hasty breakfast before departing to keep watch for the girl, and so he scrambled about the moonlit woods, searching for whatever might pass for a meal.

"By the time he returned to the cage and secured himself inside, he guessed the moon was still an hour from its zenith. He had devised a new scheme for the key: hiding it under rocks and brush within arm's length. He had tested this method over several months and found that the beast, in its incoherent ravings, didn't search the ground for the key but merely scrambled at the lock, which he knew by the scratch marks it left and the bars that were warped due to its immense strength. He had spent months testing his contraption before he was satisfied it was sound. So that night he felt secure in his restraint and allowed himself to sleep before the change overtook him.

"When he woke, his clothes were torn, as usual, and the cage was locked, but the key was not under the rocks. It was on the ground, out of arm's reach, and Gregory feared he would not be able to free himself. He used a stick to drag the key closer to the cage and eventually found purchase on it.

"He noticed he didn't feel the intense pangs of hunger that he expected, but then he saw what was left of a poor rabbit who had stolen too close to the cage and met with claws and teeth. Gregory left the woods and, as it was still the quiet hours of early morning, he snuck his way back to the tavern and through the window he had requested to remain open. He put on clothing which was whole, washed the blood from his hands and face, and laid down to rest after his trek from the woods. He had an early dinner in the dining hall, half listening to the guests who were taking a break from the business of the day. It was then that Gregory caught the news that soon spread across the tavern like blood from an open wound.

'Two girls have been murdered.'

'No, not murdered, eaten!'

'Well, not fully eaten. My cousin's friend, who saw the bodies, said they was torn open and their organs ripped out.'

'But they likely died before that—I heard their faces was torn up and big claw marks, or maybe it was bite marks, was on their necks.'

'I walked by there this mornin' on my way to do some fishin' on the river. The blood!'

'Where, you say? Oh, the Calvert estate! Poor old man lost his wife not two years ago and now he's lost both his daughters, God rest their souls.'

"Gregory ran from the tavern and down the road that led to the Calvert's in time to see a carriage pass by with two bodies lying covered in the back. He kept going, refusing to believe it could be the same house where less than a day before he had seen Mary, full of life. But there was the blood on the ground, and there was Mr. Calvert, sitting in the grass where he had held their broken bodies until the servants could remove the girls. Gregory watched him stare into his empty arms.

'I don't know how I made it back to the tavern, but I remember waking up in my room, and it was that day you found me. Didn't know what day it was. I didn't care. Still don't. Damn this body, I had to eat something. I didn't want to, but it was all I could think about. So I left my room and swallowed down some bread and ale before the talk of the tavern sent me back. Then you asked me about it. And I knew I had to leave.

'I left Dougherty's the next morning, but when I tried to leave town, I couldn't. I felt like I had to do penance, but how? What could I possibly do to make up for this? I would die, oh gladly would I give my wretched life to make amends, but I can't. Damn it all, I can't die!'

"I considered the evidence while Gregory sat sullenly staring out the window. Could the beast have learned to open the cage, feast, and then return to fool its host? Was it capable of such intelligence? The monster I saw that came out of Fenn was a dumb animal capable of only rage and desire. It had no sense in its eyes. Yet, Matthew's wolf had been sullen and subdued before Mr. Baird and I disturbed him, and it even looked like it was thinking. But then, Matthew said he could see and feel what the animal felt. No, I didn't believe such a thing was possible without the interference of the host. And it was clear Gregory had no recollection of letting the monster out to murder his darling and her sister. Why would he?

"Gregory and I went over all the evidence. Though Gregory was not a client in the traditional sense of the word, I wanted to prove, one way or the other, the man's involvement in the murders. I had to know if it was Gregory or if the population of werewolves was growing. Both Gregory and I concluded he must have been the murderer. Every circumstance aligned and, on further investigation of the cage, we found that the lock was faulty. The beast didn't have to use the key; all he had to do was pull hard in a certain direction and it would dislodge.

"The sorrow overwhelmed Gregory at this evidence of the truth, and he wept all over again for his love and for the pain it would bring to you, Fenn. He would have served justice upon himself, but knew it was futile. He was doomed to hold the grief in his heart and to know that another man would feel the same; a friend he dearly loved. I felt for the man and I tried to convince him to join us, believing that the mission would help him overcome the sorrow that was drowning him.

'We should go to them. You would be a vital help for us as you know this country. We mean to seek out your creator in French territory. He might know how to help you . . . how to help all of you,' I said.

'But then I have to face Fenn. And how am I gonna tell him it was me that did this to Beatrice and . . .' Her name wouldn't come to his grieving lips. 'No, I can't. I won't burden him with that.'

'We need you, Gregory.'

'No, you all need me like you need a hole in the head. I'm just gonna mess it up like I always do. I'm goin' west and I'm not comin' back. I'm gettin' far away from people, cause alone is what I deserve to be.'

"I left Gregory there in Chestertown. I don't know where he will go or what he will do, but I'm afraid his grief and guilt will be a heavy weight for him to carry alone.

"As I made my way out of town, I passed the Calvert estate one last time. A magistrate and a handful of busybodies stood near the river as a woman, Cathleen, the same servant who answered the door, tried to speak through racking sobs. I stopped to ask what the commotion was about when I saw him on the ground. A bullet hole to the head, the gun still looped over his trigger finger, and the blood soaking into the earth, mixing with the blood of his daughters."

16

I would have been glad to have never seen Gregory again. I did not care if he lived or died, though I knew the latter was impossible, so I hoped he would be utterly alone for all time. The thoughts which crept into my mind surprised me, so I would not dwell on Gregory, for the memory of his face made my stomach turn. Instead, I forced my thoughts to remain on Beatrice, my heart reaching, pleading for her goodness to bring me back to the self I had left behind. But she was not there. She had been wrenched from this world and I could find her no longer. In her place was an endless chasm.

While my thoughts ran their course, I could not bring myself to look at Matthew, either. As we prepared to leave Lancaster and carry on with our plan of finding the Great Lakes wolf, I avoided contact with my young friend. At first, I knew not why. He seemed unaware of my aversion to him, or perhaps he took it to be the outworking of mourning. Either way, he carried on, indifferent to the bitterness that had crept into my heart. Why should I be bitter with Matthew? What had he done?

He had forgiven me.

And I wanted nothing to draw me out of the comforting mire of hate.

Anger and malice, as I felt toward Gregory, had been directed at me only months before. While Matthew had wrestled with who to blame for his family's murder, I had seen the bitterness in his eyes. I had borne it in patience, knowing it was warranted and believing Matthew when he told me he would come to forgive me someday. I knew he had. Yet I looked at Gregory as one who was beyond grace and forgiveness, forgetting I had blood on my own hands.

Matthew rode beside me as we made our way back through Lancaster and on to Philadelphia. I spoke, more than once, but the words stuck, wanting to be free but finding the way too difficult. I forced myself to look at the young man whose life I had destroyed. Perhaps I was hoping to see grace. But my hard heart saw only myself as if reflected in a mirror. A wolf, and nothing more.

"I have been a fool," I spoke at last. "Oh, yes! I see that now. There is nothing to be gained in hoping for what might be when we know what is. And we are monsters. We will always be monsters."

Matthew smiled, not in pity, but in sympathy. He had spoken much of his doubts concerning a benevolent creator, so it would have been easy in that moment to be as the wagging tongues in Job and indulge in my angst, or point out the just payment for the lives I had stolen from others. He could have encouraged me to curse God and live. What more did I have to hope for? Instead, he rode on in silence, allowing grief its place in my heart. I knew then, whatever questions or doubts I might have, they were safe with Matthew.

"I wanted to live, but that has been robbed of me now that Beatrice is gone. I knew I should never have her. But I could exist knowing that she was safe and happy. And Gregory . . ." I shook my head, but it did nothing to shake the despair. "There is nothing left now."

"I know how you feel," was all Matthew said. His eyes were kind, his voice was gentle, and the bitterness left me as quickly as a flame is snuffed out of a candle.

"How did you do it? Forgive me. How are you here by my side when I did this to you?"

Matthew rode on, looking away, and I knew he was thinking.

"You know my father was a religious man. I can't say if I believe what he believed anymore, but I remember what he taught me." He sighed, "more than that, I remember what he showed me. He wasn't a good man all the time, but he wasn't a bad man either. He carried his own pain that he tried to wash away with ale. I was too young . . . well, no, I just didn't have any reason to understand yet, what makes a man . . . human. It's the wrong as much as the right that goes into a person." His eyes were far away for a moment and I waited for him to come back, for he always came back. He looked me full in the face and I could see tears forming. "I wish I could tell him I forgive him. I don't know that he would have ever asked for it, but I would say it if I could. And I would ask him to forgive me."

As we reached Philadelphia, I feared recognition from those who would remember me from my former life. We kept to the outskirts of town, only Mr. Baird and John venturing into the city to refill our stock of supplies while Matthew and I made camp in a secluded stretch of wood.

"It's a good thing you stayed here, Fenn. The news of the Chestertown attack revived the Staunton Slaughter gossip, and there is much speculation over whether Fenn Bancroft actually died," John said.

"For once, the gossips are on the right track."

"Yes, but let's not let them know it."

John rifled through his belongings, searching for a book to read by the fire and found the letter from Beatrice. The day he had received it, the news of her murder overshadowed all else, and he had forgotten that he had tucked it away in his satchel amongst the undelivered letter and the few possessions I had of worth. These he gave back to me, apologizing for not giving me the letter sooner. I did not even respond. I was so overcome, holding the last words I would ever read from my beloved.

The handwriting addressing me as Mr. Bancroft looked as though it was penned in duress and a splotch in the corner showed a tear had spread the ink before it dried. I hesitated a moment, wondering if I really wanted to know what she felt those last weeks, knowing I was a murderer. A monster. Even if it was a denunciation of all her love and devotion, still, I wanted to hear from her one last time.

Mr. Bancroft,

Fenn

I know not what to think. I have heard of "monstrous deeds," and this time your name is attached to them. At first I thought, surely there was some mistake or some other Mr. Bancroft. The description of your person, namely, the birthmark on your left cheek, only proved to me it was my love who was on trial . . . my love who admitted to . . . and the caravan massacre? . . . it is too much.

My father does not want me to have anything more to do with you, of course. He would likely burn this letter should he find it. But I feel I must write to you one last time, or I should never forgive myself for all that would remain unsaid.

I know you. At least, I thought I knew you. I cannot reconcile the man who did those horrible, wretched things with the man that I was prepared to spend my life with. Something must have happened to you in the wild . . . something wicked must hold sway over you.

Please, my heart . . . yes, you will have it, for it seems I cannot wrench it from you no matter how much I try to hate you or forget you. The love I had for you will not be murdered, not even by you.

Please, cast off the evil that has dominion over you. Repent and turn to the One who can forgive even this. It is never too late.

I believe I will never see you again on this earth, but I pray I will in the hereafter, knowing that no evil is insurmountable to He who is greater.

Farewell, Fenn Bancroft.

Beatrice

My heart was pounding and I gasped as a sob rose. To know that she believed I could not be the monster of my own accord, and that up to her death she still loved me, it was enough. More than enough, it was what I wanted to lift me out of the pit and set my feet firmly in my resolve to overcome this scourge. For her, I could go on. Whether here or in heaven, she was the cord that could keep me from losing my way completely. I folded the letter as tears dripped from the tip of my nose. I pinned it inside my coat, next to my heart, and it will stay there, always.

We planned our route to the Great Lakes, believing that we may still find the werewolf we sought there. All reports of wolf attacks prior to Gregory becoming one had been concentrated around the eastern side of Lake Erie and the southern side of Lake Ontario, an area controlled primarily by the French. Considering the climate of war that existed between the mother country and France, we were disinclined to approach a French fort, even on the terms of peaceful inquiry. We also risked a meeting with hostile natives, who wanted us out of the new world still more. In any case, we had to travel first on the Albany Post Road to the town of the same name. There, we would find our route west.

Approaching Albany following the Hudson River, I could see the high stone walls of the fort that sat atop a steep hill. Most of the city was concentrated within those walls, but wealthy merchants had settled outside the city limits and we passed large estates worked by black slaves, a sight which rather surprised me. Leaving the plantations of the southern colonies, I had expected we would not be witness to the same multitude of forced labor now that we were in the north. However, Albany had the largest slave population of anywhere in the northern colonies, and I saw why when we noted the amount of crops and goods produced for trade, namely wool, flaxen cloth, and even wampum. We entered the city and traveled the wide road that spanned between two places of worship: the Dutch church on the east end and the English church on the west. The town center, where the market met twice a week, was relatively quiet that evening, and we avoided any negative attention. The people of Albany were mainly Dutch and, though none of us knew the language, we smiled and nodded as we passed many snugly built houses where the inhabitants and their neighbors sat out on benches lining their street doors, men and women alike with children playing in the gardens, and we could not help but feel the warmth of neighborly affection. We continued on to a building near the stockade, which housed traders, mostly the native tribesmen who traveled in the fair summer months to barter with the merchants. We assumed the identity of tradesmen ourselves and found lodging with the natives, one of which knew enough English and Dutch to act as our interpreter and helped us settle in for the night.

A black servant offered us Albany beef, which was another name for the sturgeon that flooded the waters of the Hudson. Beer, bread, and fresh vegetables accompanied our meat, and we found it was a hearty meal which would fortify us for our journey ahead. As the night wore on, I watched as Dutch merchants met with the native traders and began negotiations. The natives were fond of beer but did not have the experience to know when to cease consumption. They would soon become drunk, and in their impaired mental state, the merchants would close the deal, cheating the natives out of much of the profit the furs should have brought them. I could tell by the expressions on the merchant's faces that they delighted in this trickery and wondered how often they used such schemes. But estates like the Schuyler Family Manse and the Vanderhuyden Palace, both of which we passed on our way through town, were examples of the abundant wealth in the Dutch community, and I gathered their prosperity came from shrewd business tactics as much as from hard work and frugality.

As I sat pondering these things, the door to the large front room of the trading house swung open and a large man with a look of panicked misgiving on his face made me forget all else as I felt the contents of my meal churn in my stomach at the sight of him. He saw us sitting by the enormous fireplace that had consumed wood incessantly to feed its hungry lodgers, and the relief that came over his entire frame was instantaneous.

"Oh, thank God Almighty! I feared the worst, but you're alright."

I said nothing. I had thought I would never have to face the man again. I certainly never expected to have to subdue the impulses of the wolf in the light of day. My hand clutched the letter from Beatrice in an effort to stifle the desire to kill. As if I awoke from a nightmare, I caught my breath and looked around the table to determine if anyone had noticed the moment my affliction surfaced. It appeared it surprised my companions as well to look upon the man, so no one had paid any attention to me. I opened my mouth to speak; I do not even know what it was I would say, when words stumbled out of his.

"It's after you! I've been trackin' that shadow that's been followin' me for so long, but now it's comin' for you all!" Gregory's frantic eyes were scanning each of us as if to know that we understood, and when his eyes met mine, his furrowed brow smoothed from fear to shame. The urgency never left him, but his voice softened as he addressed me.

"I wouldn't've come. I wouldn't've put my hateful face before you if I didn't believe you were in danger." He went on, speaking to all of us. "I left Chestertown, and meant to go west, like I said, and never come back. My future was taking me in the same direction, to the Great Wagon Road. But I stayed back so you all wouldn't have to know I was there and that's when I saw it, or her, whatever, following John. I fought with myself over what to do. Leave you all be and go my own way or keep following and find out what I could. I followed 'cause I wouldn't be able to live with myself if I left and somethin' happened to you all, not if I could've stopped it.

"Oh, but there might be two of 'em! At least, there was. I saw my tracker talkin' with a tall man, looked like they were fightin', and then the man took off on horseback west. I don't know what road he meant to take 'cause he just took off into the woods, but I haven't seen him since. But the other one—and now I'm sure it's got to be a woman—she kept on. When you all got here, she didn't go into the city. She's in the woods still, far as I know, probably watchin' for a way to strike, though this stockade may be enough to keep her out."

"You're sure it's the same person?" John asked.

"Wouldn't forget those eyes. They practically glow they're so blue."

"Did you see any other features?" John continued his questioning, concern lining his words.

"Whoever it was must be a native. I don't know any Pale-Faces that can turn into a ghost in the woods like the Injuns can. Tracking animals long as I have gave me an advantage to hear what others don't and notice things amiss that others wouldn't. I had all the clues but couldn't figure on what the thing was. Till I saw it looking at me, watching me, from a bush. Blended into the leaves, but those blue eyes . . . they weren't animals' eyes."

"A native woman with blue eyes?" I remembered John's

report of the woman in the ordinary who reminded him of the one in Staunton. The same woman that was at my hanging.

"I know, don't fit, does it?"

"I've seen her. Mr. Baird has too, if he remembers?" John looked at Mr. Baird to confirm.

"Aye! Now you mention it, I remember that young lass. The one who seemed to ken that Fenn was still alive?"

"What did she look like?" Gregory demanded.

John was almost wistful as he described her.

"She was beautiful, in an earthy sort of way. She was dressed like a lady, her skin and hair were clearly touched with native blood, and her eyes were bright blue."

"I have seen her as well. She led me to know that Mr. Baird was a student at William and Mary's when I was searching for a minister. And she was in the crowd at my execution." I added my account, controlling my tone and being careful to avoid Gregory's eye, for I could barely stand his presence. Even still, I could see Gregory's confusion was growing.

"She seems benevolent," John concluded, and I wondered if it had more to do with how her beauty made him feel than whether he truly believed it.

"There's something going on, especially now that I know she's not alone. She feels like a threat to me," Gregory answered.

"She's not. She was the one who helped me when I was attacked by Fenn. She bandaged my wounds and told me I would be ok," Matthew spoke up, and I could see the others were surprised, though I remembered Matthew telling me about the native who helped him. Aside from the few words she spoke into Mr. Baird's ear, she had no contact with anyone but Matthew. I wondered if his opinion of her was the most reliable. Yet, I acknowledged she must have known who we were and how we were all connected, and I shared my fear with the group.

"What if she is the wolf we are looking for?"

"I thought that too, for a moment, but now I don't think so. The one that got me was much taller." Gregory's eyes grew large, as if someone had stabbed him in the chest that very moment. "It was him! That man she was talkin' to in the woods! He's the one that did this to me." The shock of realization turned to anger. "He was right there, and I was too scared to do anything. What the hell do I have to be afraid of? What can he do to me if I can't die? Oh, what a coward I am! What a worthless waste of breath!"

I was inclined to let Gregory believe he was a coward, for in that moment it was all I held him to be and I clung to that opinion of him. However, my friends chose compassion and assured Gregory he had no way of knowing the man was our enemy. Even if he had suspected, he could not know for sure. Attacking a stranger in the woods on an assumption would have been foolish.

I continued in silence for the rest of the conversation, which comprised the others convincing Gregory to remain with us. His knowledge of the area and reputation as a trader known by the merchants in Albany would be beneficial for gathering information and supplies needed to continue west. I was forced to agree. It was wise to have someone in our party who knew the territory we would enter, as it was foreign to the rest of us. And I knew I would have to face the anger or it would destroy me. But Gregory required nothing of me and kept his distance as much as possible. Even in my bitterness, I could acknowledge that he would do nothing intending to hurt me, just as I had done nothing to intentionally hurt the victims of my affliction. It was so easy for me, once again, to justify my behavior as excusable while holding Gregory's mistakes beyond grace.

We were prepared to leave Albany and make our way to the Mohawk Trail that followed the river, also of the same name, when Colonel Bradstreet's army paused before the stoned fortress on its way to Fort Oswego.

"We should follow the soldiers, try to blend in with the army. To them, we'll be merchants on our way to trade with the natives at Oswego. To our shadow, we'll be part of a sea of bodies, hopefully lost in the rabble," Gregory urged. It was sound advice, but I felt compelled to challenge him every step of the way.

"Until the full moon. We cannot become the wolves amongst all those people. And we will need to bring our cages. What will they think of that?"

"We'll cover 'em with our supplies and pass 'em off as goods for trade. I guess we'll have to figure out the full moon when it comes to that."

Again, I had to concede that the plan was the best one available to us. The soldiers would be a shield from not only our particular enemy, but all others we may encounter along the way. The irony did not elude me that I would now march alongside the army I had so intentionally avoided. Instead of escaping the conflict, I was walking into the heart of it, for we would be entering the contested territory, the very front lines of the war, and werewolves would not be our only threat. Though the afflicted among us could not die, we had two mortal souls to consider, and try as we might to convince them to stay in Albany and leave us to our mission, they would not hear of it. Mr. Baird was intent on documenting all he could of our condition, and I believe John would not leave Mr. Baird.

The August full moon arrived as a welcome distraction from the drudgery of a long, slow march to the fort. While the army traveled by a flotilla of bateaux on the Mohawk River, we lost some of the human cover we had hoped to travel under. It did, however, make it easier for us to find seclusion when it came time for the beasts to emerge.

We set the cages while the non-afflicted built their fire, preparing for the watch that would keep them awake till nearly dawn. Guns were loaded and kept at the ready, the fire was stoked, and wood was piled nearby as a handy source to fuel the flames. We encouraged Mr. Baird and John to rest until just before the time of locking us wolf-men into our restraints. As the moon rose high in the night sky, its light casting a glow even into the thicker parts of the wood and throwing eerie shadows in the open spaces, we woke our guards and climbed into the gibbets. They were secured; the locks were checked, and I could sense all felt safe and ready to pass the night waiting while we passed off our human form for that of the wolf. The feeling was premature, and I noted how any time I felt at peace, it was sure to be disrupted by reality.

As Mr. Baird and Mr. Andrews remained near the fire, listening but avoiding the spectacle that, after once observing, they felt unnecessary to revisit, those of us with the affliction watched the moon as it unlocked the beast from its fleshly cage. We could not know from then on what would happen until we came to our humanity in the dawn light and our companions shared with us how their night had been spent.

Between the narratives of John and Mr. Baird, we learned that us wolf-men were quiet for a time, seeming to drift to sleep, before grunts, groaning, and, eventually, growls broke through the sounds of the night creatures as a grotesque chorus out of hell might interrupt the sweet voices of the heavenly beings.

Our friends attempted to bear the sounds of rattling metal and the angered howling that took prominence in their mind and forbade them from human-ly discourse. Mr. Baird, once again, noticed the silence coming from the cage that housed Matthew. He motioned for John to follow him, and reluctantly, the lawyer obeyed. They approached the cage that had been secured to a tree, Matthew having requested his to remain open to the night air; the other two sat in the wagons and were covered with tarps of animal skins. There, as John described poetically, 'the man of law and the man of God, beheld the creature of Hell' who sat still, arms hugging his knees to his chest, and eyes downcast and sullen. The creature that was Matthew heard the men approach and raised his head. This time, he did not flash with ravenous rage, but nodded to the men and resumed his posture as before. John looked at Mr. Baird in wonder, and they returned to the fire to discuss.

"He can control it," Mr. Baird explained to John, who noted he was so overcome by the spectacle that he had not even time to order his thoughts in any coherent form.

"How?"

"I dunna ken. But he's gettin' stronger over the beast."

"If only Gregory had the power to control his." While John told this part of the story, it seemed he had not considered how Gregory might feel in response to his comment. I felt embarrassment for Gregory, pity even, and my immediate impulse was to shelter him from shame. But the monster in me clung to anger, and I watched Gregory's eyes turn downcast, feeling justified to let him wallow in it.

My attention returned to the tale as the men went on. While they had watched us wolves, a twig in the woods snapped and they had started, looking in the noise's direction. It came from just beyond the cages, yet from the vantage point of the two at the fire, they feared it was the breach of one of the rapacious animals. Their rifles were already in their hands before a walking wolf emerged into the firelight. Those of us in our werewolf form grew even more restless at the presence of another creature, and it was said we howled and clawed at the bars, all but Matthew, who looked on the new monster with the fearful visage one would expect to see in a wounded dog awaiting a death blow. His ears were flat and his eyes darted from the creature to the men.

As the tall, almost stately-looking wolf slowly approached the cages, Mr. Baird noted the creature's maw was turned up in what he could only describe as a grin. It approached the wagon holding Gregory and pulled back the flap of skins that covered the cage. The beast inside erupted in rage and fear, crashing into the sides with all his might. The newcomer inspected the lock and appeared to be considering the best way to break it before the boom of a rifle snapped him out of his trance. John had fired and was frantically reloading, as fear had made him forget the other weapons loaded within reach. The wolf turned to the men at the fire, crouched on all fours, and leapt. Mr. Baird held his rifle up, took aim, and as the beast was in the air with not a limb touching the ground, lodged a bullet into its shoulder. The animal recoiled at the jolt and grabbed at the wound with his paw. Mr. Baird told how he quickly raised a second rifle and took aim when the wolf turned and fled, likely unwilling to incur more injury than necessary that night.

John admitted he shook as he stood to raise the rifle he had finally reloaded when Mr. Baird assured him the beast had escaped and, for the moment, they were safe.

"What if it comes back?" John had asked in a terrified whisper.

"I dunna think it will tonight, lad. That wound was a hard one and he'll likely want to eat afore dawn. I fear he may head for the soldiers' camp, where he can find a meal among the poor souls on the outskirts."

The men had no time to compose themselves before another figure stepped into the firelight, this time silent as a ghost. It was another wolf, but this one was slight, almost graceful, with a mournfulness on its face that took the men off guard. It put a paw up to Matthew's cage and, instead of trying to break the lock or wrench the bars open, it looked deep and long into his eyes. Mr. Baird noticed a look of recognition come across the wolf of Matthew as he hung his head. John, coming to himself and fearing that this new wolf may turn at any moment to attack, shot into the night sky. The small wolf started and turned its head to look at the men. The eyes caught the glint of the firelight and, while they reflected the red and gold of the blaze, the irises were clearly blue; a strong, vibrant, glowing blue. John said he could not move when he realized who the wolf was. And though Mr. Baird held his gun up and ready, he knew he would not shoot should the beast even come for him.

Instead, she retreated, eyes fastened on the men with the

guns, until her form blended in with the shadows like an apparition fading into the mist.

"It was her! My shadow!" Gregory exclaimed after the men finished the telling. We were sitting around the snuffed-out fire having our midday meal now that we all had recovered from the long, restless night.

"I know. She spoke to me." I knew Matthew could see through the eyes of the beast, but I had not known how much control his consciousness had.

"Spoke to you?" I asked. I admit, I was incredulous.

"Yes. Well, not in words. Her eyes told me she wanted to help me."

"Help you? How? In what way?" I knew myself to be growing louder, but somehow I could not stop. Matthew looked, for a moment, embarrassed or ashamed under my harsh inquisition. I recognized then that I felt threatened by the ghostly werewolf, not because she had stalked us, but because she had treated Matthew with kindness when I had failed him in every way. Of course, he would feel beholden to her. I eased back in my chair and gave Matthew space to answer.

"I'm not sure. I just know she isn't here to hurt us."

"You were terrified when you saw the other one, the first one that came and looked like he wanted to break Gregory out." John had noted that Gregory and I had reacted none differently to the two beasts. We raged all the same. But Matthew's wolf had cowered from one and seemed to want to embrace the other.

"He was different. Though he looked curious and slightly amused, there was a rage in him and I could sense he wanted to hurt someone."

"'Course he wants to hurt someone! He's been killin' people left and right for who knows how long. And she's his accomplice. Got to be. Why else would she be acquainted with him and followin' us?" Gregory spat.

"I don't know, but she could have hurt me in the woods when Fenn attacked and she didn't."

Gregory obviously did not like the idea of this shadow being benevolent. Neither did I, yet I knew it was not for the same reason. I was worried we were going to lose Matthew somehow, and it would be because of her.

We packed up and carried on our way west. Gregory said we would reach a portage place and likely catch up to Colonel Bradstreet's men there. He was not wrong as we approached the Great Carrying Place where the bateaux had been transferred from the Mohawk River to Wood Creek. A remnant of the army that had struck out from Albany was left at the Oneida Carry in order to lay the groundwork for refortification; the existing forts having been destroyed in '56. We came to the outlying camps and found a group digging graves for the bodies of three victims.

The soldiers looked haggard and worn, and we wondered if these were the casualties of battle. We soon discovered, however, that 'something like a wolf or rabid bear' had attacked the camp in the night and carried off three men before they noticed anything was amiss. The men said they had shot into the woods, but when the light of dawn illuminated the region, they could find no evidence of a wounded creature. Only three bodies, mangled and half eaten, were left behind.

"He knows what he's doing. He isn't trying to stop himself," Matthew whispered aside to us as the group of soldiers carried on with the interment. Yes, it was clear that this man was not like us.

"If that is the case, then he is evil beyond the darkness that emerges from him. He is not afflicted; he is equipped," I spat. His was a wickedness I was not accustomed to, even amidst all I had encountered in the many months I suffered against the beast inside me.

As we moved past the bodies carefully wrapped and awaiting burial, my eye caught a tag listing the name of one man inside: Lt. Ainsley. I thought of Gertrude and the irony that her husband would not die from battle but from a monster like me. Yet, I would have traded places with Mr. Ainsley then and there. For he had known love, he had known courage, and his friends would remember him as a hero.

"Oh, Lord," I whispered. How many of my friends would be marred by this affliction? "We must stop this," I said.

"How are we gonna do such a thing when we know he can't die?" I knew Gregory was right, but I hated him for asking.

"Mr. Baird, you said something about natural means. Do you think there could be another way to destroy the beast?" John was the only one not full of emotion as he questioned the scholar.

"Oh, all I ken is that whatever is to be done to stop this evil, it willnae come by the hands of mortal men."

"Well, we are not mortal men anymore," I said as I tightened the reins in my hands.

"Aye, and therein lies the hope."

17

We reached Fort Oswego by Wood Creek and the Onondaga River. Following the waterways by land along trails that had been beaten down by trappers and traders was not an easy road. There were few quality thoroughfares anywhere in the colonies, in truth. But the way improved when we reached a portage area of about forty yards where the boats of Bradstreet's men had been carried to bypass a waterfall.

Not long after the moderate cascade, we arrived at the fort; little more than a ruin. Before it was lost to the French, who torched it rather than let it become useful once more to the British, Fort Oswego had been a strong, stonework fortress. Now it was merely a pile of rubble, crumbled by cannon fire and overgrown by two years of disuse. The soldiers were not there to rebuild, but simply to assemble and await the command to cross Lake Ontario and attack Fort Frontenac. The question that faced us on the shore of the lake was whether to cross with the army and search for the werewolf amongst the soldiers at Frontenac or remain at Oswego and wait for the wolf-man to find us.

I was apprehensive about either choice. Staying meant being vulnerable to any enemy who might chance by. Perhaps even a surprise attack. Crossing with the soldiers meant taking part in their conflict, and I was still disinclined to being shot at, even if I could not die. I allowed the others to deliberate rather than share concerns that were merely self-preservative.

"He knows we're here. Maybe he'll come to us if we wait," Matthew spoke up.

"Unless he is wanted at the fort when the British attack," John added.

"How are we to know this man is even French? We only know he's tall; otherwise, we know nothing about him. But he knows us. I don't think he cares much if he falls out of rank, if he's even part of an army. He'll find us," Matthew spoke with full confidence. "Besides, we aren't soldiers. We'll just get in the way."

"How can ye be so sure he'll come?" Baird looked shrewdly at the young man, who was ordinarily quiet and sullen.

"It's what I would do."

We decided then we would remain at the ruins of Fort Oswego while Bradstreet's men crossed the lake in bateaux. These flat-bottomed boats had carried troops, cargo, and small cannon upstream on the Mohawk River from Albany by the manpower of many strong oarsmen. More boats were built until the entire army, numbering roughly three thousand men, could sail across Lake Ontario to Fort Frontenac. The soldiers had sustained an exhausting journey and many of them had perished, deserted, or been left behind to work on the fortifications at the Oneida Carry. I understood then why the call to serve was often made in desperation when so many men were lost without a fight.

We avoided the notice of anyone who might question our business by assuming the disguise of merchants waiting for a meeting with the native traders. In any case, half of the soldiers were sick and far too concerned with their own business to worry about anyone else's. We were left alone, disregarded by the soldiers, and completely unnoticed by the officers.

The troops crossed on the 25th of August. We watched the

bateaux disappear across the lake and then settled in to wait on a visitation from the source of our woe. We were not disappointed when, that evening before dusk, the silhouette of a stranger approached the camp we had called home for several days. He stood apart, watching us without uttering a word. I stood near as Mr. Baird whispered to Gregory, asking if the man looked like a native, for his sight was not what it used to be. Gregory assured him it was not a native and described the French livery, blue vest and breeches, white coat, and gold trimmed tricorn hat the stranger wore. Out of the woods behind him, a smaller form emerged, dressed in the brown woolen robe I remembered from the tavern in Williamsburg. Her hair, straight and cascading over her shoulders, once again framed her face. The appearance of the young woman took all of us off guard as most were unsure whether she was friend or foe, and it appeared the Frenchman noticed our distraction. He smiled to himself, and I could tell he refrained from looking behind him at the creature he knew captivated our attention.

I restrained myself from approaching the villain and administering judgment upon his angular visage. I wondered how Gregory maintained his reserve as he stood, arms crossed and eyes blazing, against a tree. It was one moment in which I would have forgotten my disdain for Gregory and cheered him on should he have attacked then and there. After enough time passed that we all began fidgeting, the stranger continued to approach and even bowed with an arrogance that was unsettling.

"Bonjour, gentleman. It is so good of you all to make such a long journey to meet wis me. Merci. Merci." He looked around at the group and met each man's icy glare with a smile and a nod.

"We have come for answers. We care nothing for meeting you beyond that," I spoke for all.

"Oi, such 'ostility. No matter. You are my guests. I will be 'ospitible. Please, 'ave a seat!"

He motioned for us to join him around the fire as if we had

entered his home and were being welcomed to his hearth. We would not decline. That was, after all, what we had come to do, so we took seats as we had each night leading to that one. The Frenchman flicked his lapels behind him and reposed on a log, straight-backed and dignified, looking down on Gregory and Matthew, who had found a patch of grass on the ground; the rest of us sitting hunched on a pile of rubble. Matthew looked towards the woman, perhaps waiting for her to join the parlay, but she remained standing in the shade of the wood like a statue of bronze. The Frenchman noticed Matthew's distraction.

"She is of no importance 'ere." I watched Matthew force himself to look away and focus on the Frenchman in front of him. "You will want to know who I am, I am sure. Oh, you may not care who I was, but you 'ave come to ask about what I am, and so I will tell you."

I leaned forward, hopeful that the interview would be more advantageous than I had previously expected. Perhaps we would not have to force any information from the man, but he would freely give us the aid we longed for.

"I am loup garou. Forgive me, ah . . . werewolf. But you already know zat. I am from France, true, but ze werewolf is not from France. It was a gift from a native of zis country. A medicine man."

"What kind of gift is that?" spat Gregory.

"Ah, my friend, you fight against ze spirit of Okwaho. When you embrace it, it is a gift."

I scoffed and began speaking, but the Frenchman cut me off.

"I know what you will say, mon ami. Okwaho is a murderer. And it is true, if you submit to ze sensibilities of your Christian religion. But what if it is liberation?" He likely noted the objection we all longed to make, but he ignored us and went on. "Yes, it is true, zere must be law. Man must restrain ze . . . carnal urges, if 'e is to 'ave civilization. But for us wis zis gift, ze Okwaho makes us more zan 'uman. Must a demigod submit to ze laws of mortals? Oh no, zat is ridiculous."

This logic created a murderer of the vilest nature. My gut churned as all the apprehension that had been calmed flooded back and turned to disgust. I watched the Frenchman's words move Matthew in apparent discomfort, and I wondered where his thoughts were leading him. If our conversations of the past were any indication, I worried he might find his evolving philosophy aligned with the monster's and be tempted to unleash the passions that burned within.

I turned to the villain, my heart pounding in fear, not only for Matthew, but for all of us, should the Frenchman succeed in convincing him to sink in this depravity. I stood, unable to still my nerves, and challenged him.

"A demigod is not above God himself. How will you answer Him who will require a reckoning for the evil you have committed?"

The Frenchman laughed at me. He waved his hand as if to shoo a gnat.

"What can 'e do to me? I do not belong to your Christian God. I do not answer to 'im. Ze gift comes from ze Iroquois. From Sawiskera."

"Have you been adopted by the Iroquois then?" John asked, no doubt curious about the relationship between this Frenchman and the federation, which was allied with the British.

"I 'ave lived among zem, yes. Before I was taken captive by ze Mohawk, one of ze Iroquois tribes, many years ago, I was Gaspard. I survived zeir ordeal and zey honored my bravery by making me one of zem and giving me ze honored title of Dodcon. It means 'little devil,'" he chuckled. "I studied under ze shaman and he gave me ze gift, but it was given wizout ze knowledge of ze counsel. I was punished, so I left zem. Zey fear what zey do not understand."

"Such is the way with all men, lad. But ye cannae blame the natives for their fear . . . and, I suspect, wantin' to fix what one of 'em had done."

"Fix? No." The Frenchman laughed. "No'sing can fix zis."

"Do you not know of a cure?" I asked, appalled by his cavalier attitude toward a power so evil and destructive.

"Cure? Why would I need a cure? Why do you need a cure? Zere is no'sing wrong wis you!"

"Of course there is something wrong with us! It is not right nor human for a man to tear apart another man and consume him!"

"Oh, sir, you forget zat zere are many tribes who feast on flesh."

"Those without Christianity, yes, but only because they do not know better. You, a Frenchman! You know better!"

"As I said, I do not submit to ze Christian God."

There was no use in continuing the conversation, futile as it was, and as the anger within me swelled, I felt I could be driven to lash out and put a bullet in the man's brain, knowing full well that it would do nothing to stop him. I sat and hung my head in resignation. John picked up the interrogation where I left off.

"There is a law that transcends religion. Do you not consider yourself bound to the universal law that all men everywhere uphold? It's not right to murder." I knew John was not a religious man, a deist at most, and it did not surprise me he approached the villain with reason, though I was skeptical it would be met with penitence. In his profession, John dealt with criminals of all kinds, and surely he could see this was a man ruled not by conscience, but by corruption.

The Frenchman considered for a moment how to answer.

"Mankind 'as chained itself to an idea zat it owes charity to its fellow man. Ze idea is perpetuated srough its progeny. But ze trus is observed in ze nature of animals. Zere is no murder in ze natural law. Only survival."

"You don't need to eat humans to survive. That argument assumes you have no other diet that is natural to you. An animal doesn't eat everything or anything it wants. It must eat what it was made to eat. Humans eat meat, yes, but not that of other humans. Just as animals do not eat the flesh of their own kind."

"Ah, there you are right, mon ami. I 'ave been stupid." I lifted my head to see if the monster might actually concede to the right. "But I am no longer 'uman. Ze loup garou was made to eat 'uman flesh."

The others scoffed while I sniggered at myself for my foolish optimism. There would be no repentance.

"Oh, but sink on it. Mankind 'as no predator. It is unchecked. It takes from ze land and destroys wisout restraint. Zere is no one to stop it. Zere will be no end to its rapacious rule over ze world. You look at ze werewolf as a monster. You do not see ze monster zat is ze 'uman."

The shame I felt for my naïvety turned to scorn directed at the monster, and I could hold my tongue no longer. "We were made in God's image. We were given dominion over the world. He is the one who keeps the balance. He is the one who requires atonement for the sin against his creation!"

"Where is zis atonement? What 'as ze 'uman done to repay what it 'as taken? Ze shaman 'as seen what will come of zis new world. Zat is why 'e gave me zis gift. Ze loup garou will be ze balance . . . and ze reckoning."

It was this proclamation that sealed all our lips. Not only was this man a murderer with no remorse, he believed he had been given a grave and monumental purpose as the hand of retribution for the earth. Not even the authority of heaven existed in his eyes. Men who believe themselves to be gods either build civilizations or destroy them.

"I see I 'ave given you all much to sink about. I will leave you for tonight. I 'ear ze cannon fire . . . I wish to see what will become of zis battle." He walked away but, as if a thought stayed him, he turned back and held a finger in the air as the sound of a cannon boomed. "War . . . ze time when men kill and do not call it murder." He smirked, "adieu."

John attempted to call back our visitor to continue our debate, but I knew it was finished. The fiend walked on as if he had no particular place to be and rejoined the woman, who followed him into the woods where they disappeared.

Gregory spoke up after expending some of his swelling aggression in hewing logs for the fire. "Well, this is hopeless. We can't reason with him and we can't kill him. He's pure evil, alright, and we are his offspring. God help us! What's left to do?"

"There's always hope, lad. We canna give up so soon as that."

I felt myself chuckle at Mr. Baird and wondered what had happened to my faith, but I spoke what felt true to me in that moment.

"I admit, I agree with Gregory." I nearly tasted bile in my mouth as I said the words. "I feel as though there is nothing left worth fighting for, worth living for. But seeing as I can find no hope in the grave, I wonder, what does that leave? We cannot stop this man, but I would as soon gnaw off my own legs as join him."

I looked to Matthew who sat just out of range of the firelight. As the breeze brought a gracious chill of evening air and the sun was setting on the lake, painting beautiful colors over the surface of the water, for a moment I forgot he was of the damned and saw only the boy as my apprentice who sat at my fire dreaming of his future. It had not been so long ago.

"I may end up joining him," he announced. Every man stopped what he was doing and stared. "I admit to you all, I can't help but see the logic in his reasoning. Mankind may well be a curse. Perhaps this gift, as he called it, is the cure."

"Oh, Matthew, you cannot mean that." I was pleading, but I also knew that he could very well mean it, or something like it. If he felt he had nothing to live for, it must have been tempting to think he could be given a purpose.

"I fear I do. I think I know why I can control the monster; why the Frenchman can control his. I stopped resisting, and I let myself become it. I still don't like the idea of killing. But perhaps that's because I still believe I'm human."

I knelt before my friend and took his hands in mine.

"You are human. I am human. Remember what you said. There is the right and the wrong that make a man, and in you there is much that is right." I searched his eyes, but I saw only pain, remorse, hopelessness. "Please, my dear friend, if I could take back what I have done to you, I would, you know I would."

Matthew gave no answer, but turned his head to the fire and watched the sparks fly upward. What more could I say that would keep him with us but to give him whatever hope I could.

"We must persevere. We will find someone else to help us! We will scour the earth for answers. Heaven knows we have the time."

"I just don't think I want to anymore," he answered, just above a whisper. I searched his eyes one last time and knew I had lost him.

I could hear the cannon shells in the distance and, in order to distract myself from the world around me that was falling apart, I wondered what would become of Colonel Bradstreet's men.

I awoke before the others and started a fire to prepare what scant breakfast our provisions could afford. Mr. Baird soon joined me, and we spoke in hushed tones so as not to rouse the rest of the camp.

"I am concerned for Matthew. If the beast inside has not stolen his soul already, I fear he will hand it over by his own volition."

"It's no the end till the end, lad. There's still time for Matthew, I believe." Mr. Baird remained optimistic, though I sensed deep down he feared as I did.

"That vile monster Gaspard has infected his mind."

"Ye ken as well as I, the lad's been thinking thataway for some time." Mr. Baird was right, but I wanted someone to blame and Gaspard was already the villain. Soon, John and

Gregory joined us, and we kept our voices low as we talked about what was next for us.

"Should we stay here and wait for that French villain to come back? I say we go look for the shaman and get answers from the source," Gregory suggested. He was accustomed to dealing with the natives. However, the rest of us were not. Fear, well founded or not, prevented us from consenting to Gregory's suggestion, and it was decided we would wait for an encore with the werewolf, who all but promised to return, before deciding what course to take.

The sun had risen considerably, and the air felt warm and sticky when I knew it was time to check on Matthew. The conversation of the night before had been disturbing, and perhaps Matthew felt shame or embarrassment for his honest feelings. I wanted to reassure him that his words had not repulsed me and he was safe. I peeled back the flap to Matthew's makeshift tent and found it empty. There was no sign of the few possessions he had brought with him except for his copy of *The Pilgrim's Progress*, left behind for me.

"He is gone," I announced as I returned to the others, carrying the book. I knew then I had expected the tent to be empty, for I was not surprised.

"So the lad has made good on his word, eh? I dearly hoped he'd see the right and fight the beast," Mr. Baird frowned.

"What are we to do?" I could feel myself floundering, my grip tightening on the book. Nothing was turning out the way I had hoped. "This is my fault. All of it. We never should have come. We should have gone west and forgotten our old lives."

"No, you're blaming the wrong man," Gregory spoke up. "I shouldn't've gone to Chestertown. And now the girls are gone . . ." He cleared his throat from the knot that stuck tight in it. "I shouldn't've brought you with me to Williamsburg. I took a chance so I wouldn't have to be alone, but alone is what we are and can ever be. If I had the courage to bear my burden, none of this would've happened."

I felt heat rise to my face and the monster in me fighting for control of my emotions. Yes, it was all his fault. Everything that had happened to me and Matthew could be traced back to that September day Gregory had arrived in Chestertown to attend the feast. My lips curled in a grimace and my fingers bore into the binding of the book with such strength that I wondered if I was leaving a lasting imprint. Gregory's face was turned away in shame, and I believed I could have leapt upon him, wolf or no, and buried my teeth into the vein that protruded from his neck and tear it from his throat. At that moment, I saw Mr. Baird watching me. His expression was of pity as he regarded the look of foulness in me that could not be blamed on the moon. My gaze turned down, the heat in my face transferred its source from anger to shame, and I felt my hand ease its grasp on the book.

"What's done is done, and there ain't nothin' ye can do about it now, lads. No sense in mullin' over the shoulda's when there's real life going on in front of us and we have to decide what to do now."

All was cut short when the Frenchman sauntered up to our group, seemingly out of nowhere. Matthew was not with him.

"Where is he?" I felt like a spitting cobra slinging venom, but I had no other words to fling.

"Your friend is fine. 'E will stay wis me now. Ze invitation stands for you as well."

"Like hell I'll join you!" Gregory growled through his clenched jaw.

"Ah, but, in a way, you already 'ave. You 'ave killed and you 'ave created. You are as much like me as is possible," he smirked.

The reminder that each werewolf present had passed on the disease was a leveling point for the Frenchman. Not one of us was above reproach.

"We do not choose to murder. We have done all we can to protect the lives of the innocent. The times when we have taken life, it was an accident, an oversight . . . a very grave mistake." I spoke the last words slowly, not making eye contact with anyone in particular, but clearly taking one last jab at Gregory. Anger and bitterness, like thieves, continued to sneak in, unrequested, to steal the peace the old me longed for. I could see that Gregory knew I meant the words for him, yet he kept his head high in the face of his enemy, not wanting to show weakness. The Frenchman's eyes keenly scanned the body language between the two of us. I could see he hoped to use the rift to his advantage.

"It is true. You lack ze stomach to embrace ze power you 'ave. But it does not mean you will not . . ." he paused, as if searching for a word then smiled when it came to him. ". . . grow into your new life. I 'ave been a bad fazer, I apologize. I should not 'ave left you to wander ze world wizout any guidance." His tone was coddling, but he approached us as if he was genuinely concerned about our well being; his arms spread in a welcoming gesture. "Let me raise you, my young cubs, into the wolves you are meant to become!"

Gregory turned to walk away, his posture calm and resolute. It was the opportunity the Frenchman would use to strike.

"If you had embraced ze gift, maybe you would not 'ave killed someone special?" Gregory stopped walking and stood still, his back facing the villain. I glared at the Frenchman, searching to discover where he was going to take us with his words.

"I am right? Of course I am right. Your friend Matsew 'as told me about 'is family. It is a shame 'e did not know better. But 'e was a young pup, how could 'e? But you . . . I sense you knew better, no?" Gregory turned with fire in his eyes, clenching fists that were no doubt tempted to tear the man apart.

"I loved her. And I will never forgive myself for what I done. But I will not become an animal. Giving in to the devil is the opposite of penance!"

The Frenchman looked back and forth between us. He must have read the despair in my countenance.

"You loved 'er," the Frenchman reiterated to Gregory, and

then turned to me. "And you? You loved 'er as well?" I looked away.

"I loved Mary as a sister. But Beatrice, she was my heart."

"'Zere were two? Two young girls. Friends," the Frenchman stated. His keen gaze searched our faces. When we gave him nothing, his eyes opened wide, feigning surprise. "Sisters?"

We would not offer the fiend any more information. I believed Matthew must have told him what Gregory had done. I was overcome by the tragedy that had robbed me of the only good that remained in the world. And I saw Gregory was enduring the same penetrating pain of loss as I. My gaze softened and I did not find it as difficult to look upon him. It was John who spoke for us.

"Yes, sisters. The beloveds of these men and their reason for carrying on. You have no right to grope into their loss, no doubt attempting to use it as a wedge between them. I don't see how you hope to win them to your side by reminding them that this affliction has cost them everything they ever loved, and that you were the one whose reckless depravity infested them with it." John spoke in the same tone I had observed him use while on the stand.

"You are correct, mon ami. I see zere is no more to discuss." He turned to Gregory and I, and though we stood apart, it was the first time since our beloved's deaths that I did not feel as though we stood opposed. Gaspard must have sensed that his attempt to divide, and John's words, had only reminded us of our mutual agony and, in turn, our mutual enemy.

"You will persist in your 'umanity when you could be gods? So be it. Only, I will 'ave you know, you 'ave me to sank for freeing you from ze ties zat kept you bound to zis life."

"What do you mean?" Gregory looked at the man with his brow furrowed and hands that would no longer be easy to control.

"'Ow do you sink you got out of your cage, Gregory?"

18

Gregory sprang for the rifle that sat inside the fold of his tent, loaded and ready, waiting for a threat. He took aim, and before the Frenchman could turn to make his escape, Gregory fired a shot into the man's chest. Gaspard fell to his knees and slumped to the ground with a groan.

My jaw hung open and I could not move as I looked upon the crumpled form, waiting. Moments later, the Frenchman coughed and red liquid spurted from his mouth. He turned to his side and spat out the half congealed blood that had clogged his throat. As he positioned himself in a sitting posture, he chuckled. The laughter caused him to cough up more blood, and he put up his arm in a gesture that let us know he would recover and just required a moment to compose himself.

"Damn it! Damn you!" Gregory raged, and turned the rifle into a cudgel, taking a swing at the easy target. The butt met with the temple of the monster and the sound of skull cracking was like that of an axe splitting wood. Blood squirted up from the head wound and the body slumped once again, this time on its side. I watched the red fluid pulse from his skill and flow down the side of his face and neck until it joined up with the blood from his heart. Together, they formed a pool beneath him.

John stood frozen; he could not tear his eyes away from the carnage he was likely unaccustomed to.

"It is useless, lad, dunna waste yer time tenderizing this sack of meat. He'll just stand up and laugh at ye." Mr. Baird pulled Gregory away from the still form of the Frenchman just before he prepared to take another swing.

"An axe! Give me an axe!" Gregory wailed.

"Leave it be, son. Come, put down the gun. Come." He led Gregory to the shore of the lake not far away and motioned for him to cool his hand, which had burned when he grabbed the smoking muzzle of the rifle. Gregory clearly had not noticed the pain.

The Frenchman, in one inhuman motion, dragged his body up again. Finally, John looked away as the wounded man cracked his neck and took the kerchief from his coat pocket to staunch the blood that flowed still from the jagged fissure in his skull.

"Are you finished? I may be immortal, but I still feel pain." He could rise and stand before them again, the wound in his chest already stitching itself closed and his head no longer bleeding. I knew to expect his recovery, but it shocked me even still to see Gaspard already standing before us as if nothing more than a paper cut had momentarily required his attention.

"I 'ave been stabbed and 'acked. Scalped and burned. Zer is nosing you can do to me zat will kill me. You know zis. What can death do to death?"

"What if we remove your head from your shoulders?" I asked in derision.

The Frenchman only chuckled, and returned to the wood.

I turned to join Gregory, who had washed the blood from his arms and clothes.

"Gregory," I said his name and found it was not as hard as I imagined it would be. I hesitated to put my arm around his shoulder, fearing the thoughts I had harbored against him would take over at the touch, but my mind was clear of malice as I stared across the lake at cannon smoke rising from Fort Frontenac.

The weight, the awful heaviness of grief, felt slightly lighter as I released my friend from a debt of guilt he could never pay. Gregory was visibly lighter as well as he stood taller. A quick sob shook his shoulders, and he nodded at my unspoken forgiveness.

The next day, Bradstreet's men recrossed the lake to the ruins of Fort Oswego, victorious aboard commandeered French ships. I watched the flames lick the sky from the inferno they left behind as Frontenac was set ablaze, along with all the goods that could not be plundered. The soldiers eagerly hauled ashore cannon, guns, furs, and provisions that must have cost the French army dearly, and they had a raucous celebration that night before the camp finally quieted, resting in peace after three days of conflict. We felt a similar calm after the tumult of our interview with the werewolf and the loss of Matthew. But the burden of responsibility felt heavier than any of us could bear, and so we tried our best to assure one another that Matthew would return to us, as he always had.

We wondered if Gaspard would follow his countrymen in their retreat to Montreal, however uninterested he seemed in the war beyond the spectacle of bloodshed. There were other French forts in the region, which he might abide in for the time being, though it would be more difficult for him to keep Matthew, an Englishman, out of the notice of the French and those tribes which were allied with them. He could not freely mix among the English in Albany, either. So where would that leave the Frenchman, now that he had an Englishman in tow? Perhaps he had found shelter somewhere secluded in the lakes region where he meant to bide his time until the next full moon, when he would either hunt or build his pack. Now he had Matthew, he might feel emboldened to choose more hearty young men to leave behind mortality for damnation on earth. We mulled over these thoughts and others, remaining at Oswego long after Bradstreet's army had carried on down the Mohawk River back to the Oneida Carry.

It was quiet in the wilderness, away from the bustle of the large towns and cities, outside of the rumble of Conestogas on the Great Wagon Road. Far enough from civilization that the only mortals who crossed one's path were the natives who blended in with the forest and left scarce evidence of their presence. Game was plentiful and the climate surrounding the lake was a welcome break from the stuffy woods we had passed through or the open fields we had crossed while the heat of the sun blazed down on our backs. The ruins had become a refuge for us, and as we soaked in the landscape's tranquility we were content with no plan or direction for some time.

Days before the September full moon, Gregory and I examined the gibbet cages and discussed our intent for the next transformation. We would strive to gain control of the beast, not by becoming one with it, but by no longer fighting its presence. We resigned to give it space to exist while hopeful that we could reach past it to find consciousness. The idea of sharing a body with the monster was abhorrent to me, especially considering the struggle I had endured while in my right mind to keep its dark longings at bay, but I knew it was the only hope we had of controlling the weapon before Gaspard could reel us into his service. Gregory, on the other hand, strengthened his arms by splitting wood, as if he relished the possibility of using the curse against his creator.

On the night of the September full moon, we were locked in our gibbets while the preacher and the lawyer sat vigil, waiting to see if we could master the beasts. I opened my eyes the next morning to see John waiting anxiously. We had barely dressed before he accosted us.

"What was it like? Do you believe you could maintain it?" He asked, his eyes wide with excitement instead of his former disgust. Mr. Baird offered us each a cup of coffee. I accepted, eager for something comforting after the terrors I had endured, and spoke first.

"It was awful. I felt as though I had put on a skin that attached itself to my person like a leech. I wanted to crawl out of the thing, but it was me. I felt the evil desire for murder; the longing was stronger than anything I have ever felt . . . even for a woman." I blushed at the confession, but I knew not how to describe the feeling so that others could comprehend it.

"I'd have to agree there. It was a hunger I've never felt before, sure enough. But then my self was there too, refusing to give in. I wasn't fighting the monster; it was there, but I was tellin' it, 'no, not today,' and it was listening."

"Fascinating!" Mr. Baird exclaimed as he scribbled notes into his account and motioned for us to continue. I described the feeling of drowning as I gave in to the monster. Instead of fading to black, I held on to consciousness by submitting to the wave of power that washed over me. At first, I was in subjection to the werewolf. It had control, and it wanted flesh.

Gregory interrupted, "Yeah! But like I said, I told it no. I felt confused, but it wasn't me that was confused, it was the wolf. The animal obeyed, like a dog with its tail between its legs, but then it fell to like it was just a matter of course."

"Yes, I felt something similar. It was not so much a command on my part, but I asserted my human self and refused to be pushed aside. The feeling was almost a tug of war at first, and then yielding, as if I had pulled it to a line it would not cross," I added.

"You both cowered in the light and held your ears. Do you recall why?" John asked.

"I felt overwhelming shame once the beast yielded. I knew myself, but I also knew the monster, and the record of its iniquities passed before my eyes. I could hear the screams, and I clasped my ears to drown out the noise. It was deafening."

"Perhaps the creature was taunting you?"

"More like enticing. I felt more longing with each image, with every squeal. Like building up courage before a fight."

"Or guzzling a pint before doing something stupid," Gregory chimed in.

"It's a wonder you could resist it. I have all the more pity for Matthew," John stated, and I agreed, thinking of the conversation in which Matthew had alluded to his struggle against despair. Matthew had killed his own family. Did he relive that night and hear their screams while the monster tempted him to kill again?

"Yes, perhaps that is why he considers himself no better than Gaspard. Shame is a powerful hindrance to right thinking." Matthew could forgive his father and he could forgive me, but not himself, and perhaps that was why Gaspard was able to take him from us. It could only be supposed what he subjected Matthew to in the time of his absence. Though he had chosen his fate, we worried Gaspard would coerce him into paths that were beyond his comprehension. He was, after all, still rather a boy; not quite a man.

Eventually there was a silence that threatened nervous conversation, but we were all spent, having labored through the night. The sun was high and bright when we each retired to rest and found ourselves asleep before we could account for our heads reaching the pillows.

Since the full moon had passed, John volunteered to take leave of our group, this time to return to the Oneida Carry to gain intelligence; namely, had there been another attack and where? We wanted to know where Gaspard and his small troop might be. It did not take long for John to gather information, which he shared with us on returning from his errand.

"The men building the new forts were aflutter with conversation concerning an attack suffered by a regiment camped furthest from the fort. They supposed the enemy was a hostile tribe, perhaps in retribution for the fall of Fort Frontenac. Ordinarily, I would accept the account as given. However, certain details that floated about led me to ask specific questions, which seemed strange to the men hammering away.

"For example: 'Where were the victims found? Were they left in parts or were they whole? Were they scalped? Were there any wounded survivors who had no business being alive?' and so on. The answers came from several sources, all ready to chime in with what they heard.

'They were scattered about. A few were still in their beds, but those who must have heard the attack had time to get their guns before they were slaughtered,' one soldier informed me.

'There were some that were merely killed, but some, oh, some of 'em were hacked to pieces and made a mess of. Those savages!' a comrade added.

'None was scalped, far as the men that found 'em could tell. They figure the survivors chased the savages off before they had a chance, though the ones left alive weren't in no condition to tell what they did nor saw. Only said they was attacked and couldn't see who done it. They was left for dead and woulda, had they not been strong highland stock.'

'Where are the survivors now? The men?' I asked the group before me. Some men were terrified, rightfully so, but some seemed intrigued by the events they couldn't account for.

'Oh, they stayed to bury their dead brothers-in-arms. Though no one's seen them since. We assume they've sought revenge, and either been taken at last, or still searching the wilds for the reds responsible.'

"I left the men to their work, but I believed the attack was not by the natives, though they have been known to massacre whole settlements in the cloak of night. The account didn't line up with what I've heard of the natives' ways. Too many of the victims died in their beds. Only a few made it out of their tents with weapons to meet their foe. The natives are known to make a war cry before attacking. They would have relished in the chaos of a surprise, but announced, onslaught. Killing the victims in their beds would bring no honor to a brave. Those hired by France would have squandered their rewards if they left the scalps on their victim's heads. They also burn the tents, homes, and forts they conquer. They wouldn't leave anything standing to be used by another group of Pale-Faced invaders. There was not one sign that the camp had been torched. I would have loved to seek out the survivors—two large, burly men, from what I was told—and question them more completely about the events of the night. But knowing Gaspard had likely made two more monsters and was building an army made it imperative that I return to warn you.

"I found myself forced to spend a night in the woods near Oneida Lake on my way back to Fort Oswego. The moon was a waning crescent, a thumbnail hanging in the sky. I didn't fear for my life from the wolves, but I remained diligent. There are, after all, other beasts that roam these thick, primeval looking wilds. I kept my fire well fed through the night and retired to my tent that was positioned within the glow. Soon after I had drifted to sleep, a noise in the darkness roused me. It was not the sound of snuffing, as of a bear looking for scraps, nor was it the sound of small critters rustling in last autumn's leaf litter. It was the low, whispered sound of men's voices; a sound far more terrifying when one is alone outside the land of law.

"Peeking from behind the flap of my tent door, I could just make out the forms of two men. They were outside the range of the fire, but enough light penetrated the darkness to outline their forms against the backdrop of black. I couldn't tell for sure who the men were, but I soon found out when one of them, the taller, statelier looking one, convulsed and writhed upon the ground. The other stood watching, seemingly unaffected by the sight of a soul in torturous pain. I was tempted to offer aid to the men when the sufferer abruptly ended his torment and stood once again, this time hunched and snarling, his mouth elongated into a snout, his legs bending in the wrong direction, and the nails at the ends of his fingers forming curled claws. I knew then who they were and hastily grabbed my gun, which sat nearby in the tent. It was loaded and ready, as I knew by then not to trust anyone or anything.

"The wolf approached slowly, with all the assurance of one who knows where his next meal will come from, but then stopped and returned to the withering, writhing state he had assumed moments before. The change wouldn't stick, and he returned to the form of a man. His companion looked on without emotion. This appeared to be something he had witnessed before and would likely witness again. When the man on the ground regained his composure, he beckoned to the other man, whom I knew to be Matthew, to attempt his own transformation. Matthew looked hesitant to comply, but then began a charade of moans and gesticulations before sighing and, in apparent exhaustion, crumpling to the ground. A third form, with elegant, compassionate movements, came to Matthew's side and helped him to his feet. The Frenchman swore and then attempted to regain his gentlemanly airs while grappling at shreds of fabric that had been torn from his uniform. I didn't know whether to shoot or to remain silent and feign sleep. If the Frenchman knew I saw him, it would likely be over for me; whether from the hands of a werewolf or a man, it would not change the outcome. I wondered if the three even knew whose tent they had discovered in the woods or had just happened upon their foe by chance.

"I waited to learn what the party would do before making a move. Matthew looked tired and bored. The woman appeared patient or apathetic. Gaspard looked angry, but clearly undeterred. I believe he'll make another attempt, and another, to break free from the confines of the full moon. If he learns to change at will, there'll be no hope for mankind.

"The wolves in human skin left the fireside and disappeared into the woods. I sighed in relief at the departure, but my stomach would not be persuaded to relax. There were hours left before sunrise would make it safe enough to finish my journey back to Fort Oswego. Sleep evaded me as I pondered what this new revelation would mean for everyone."

As John told us what he had discovered, I was crouched by the lake, attempting to shave my overgrown stubble. I had only completed the right side by the time he was done, for I could not bring myself to worry about my scruff in light of his intelligence.

"Turnin' at will? What if he learns to change during the day? We'll have no chance then, none!" Gregory said as he paced, running his hands through his hair.

My razor slipped, cutting my chin, and I threw it down in exasperation. I was frustrated beyond the knick in my skin, for it seemed every move we made would be forced upon us.

"Then it must be this full moon. We cannot wait any longer to be ready. He is evolving, it would seem, and we will not be able to keep up with him before long," I concluded.

"But what can we do? We don't even know if we can stop him." Gregory stopped pacing and hauled a log to the bank so he could sit.

"I do not know. Trap him? Cage him until we can discover a way to cure him, or kill him."

I offered my ideas, but Gregory scoffed at the mention of keeping Gaspard alive. Nevertheless, I knew it was probable we could do no more than detain him. Still, we had to try to keep him from killing, or worse, turning more victims into weapons. "Even with Matthew and the woman, we may be evenly matched when considering your strength and size."

"What about the soldiers he has turned?" John asked. The sound of his voice startled me, so intent was I in our dilemma. It reminded me that Gregory and I were not alone. "If Gaspard has his new pups with him, you are sorely outnumbered."

"They won't know what they are till the full moon. Maybe they'll reject the Frenchman's schemes—if he gets to them," Gregory reasoned.

"And then what? They will be werewolves like us, but without knowing it, and will kill with abandon. No, it would be best if Gaspard finds them. If we are successful in our endeavor to dispatch the Frenchman and win Matthew back to our side, we will not have the added burden of hunting down two men who will likely wreak havoc in the meantime," I reasoned as I attempted to return to my task at hand. "If nothing else, we must do our best to save Matthew. When he is no longer under the fiend's spell, perhaps he will come back to reason." I was not prepared to count my faultless friend an enemy, no matter whose side he was on.

Gregory rose and went back to pacing. I knew he wanted to meet his foe directly, but it was still a fortnight before the next moon. We could only hope that Gaspard would not perfect his ability to turn at will before we had our chance. He stopped in his pacing and turned to me while I performed the blade stroke that removed the last of the hair from my cheek.

"What if we try to trap him as a man? Why wait for the full moon? If we can cage him now, we'll have him at our mercy come the next moon."

"I have thought of that. But then we will be at his mercy, searching the wilderness for him. We do not know if he is armed; we could walk into an ambush." There were many ways in which the plan could fail, yet our options were few. "If we can harness this power, together we may subdue him. Otherwise, I do not know what upper hand we have in our human flesh."

Gregory threw up his hands. "We've got to try. I can't sit here another two weeks waitin' and hopin' that by the time the moon comes, we'll be fit to stand against a monster who's had the time to hone his skills. I'm a good shot. I can't kill him, but I can bring him down long enough for us to bag him."

I nodded and rinsed my face in the cool lake water. "Alright. But we may only have one opportunity to catch him. After that, I am sure he will not let us try a second time."

"They could be far from here by now," John reminded us. It was Mr. Baird who responded this time.

"Aye, but he don't mean to leave these two alone. If he cannae draw them to his side, he will remove them from his path. I dunna think he will go far."

19

We packed our camp in the morning, leaving behind all that was obsolete for the road we were entering upon. Gregory led the tracking expedition, enthusiastically searching the landscape for footprints and other physical information, giving him the opportunity to use his talents once more. He found that tracking men was easier than tracking deer, but the real challenge would come with trapping them. The wagon was a cumbersome, yet necessary, addition, but it prevented any opportunity for an ambush, so we assumed the guise of travelers rather than hunters. We took the same path we had forged along the rivers, passed the new forts as men worked hastily to erect them, and carried on along the Mohawk Trail until we found a secluded area where we might remain hidden from mortals happening by. The horses were glad to rest and sauntered off to the bank of the Mohawk River for refreshment. We waited, hoping to be visited by our prey so we could execute our plan in a posture that assured us the upper hand.

The new moon, hidden from the light of the sun, was invisible in the inky blackness of night. We kept the fire bright while Gregory slinked off into the shadows, silent as a native. His task was to keep watch around the perimeter of the camp and ours was to be ready should he subdue our target.

Our vigil proved fruitful when we heard snapping twigs and the nervous stamping of the horses. I strained to listen closely to the sound, noting the direction it came from. A few yards away, I could hear footsteps and grunts. I judged by the amount of noise that there was more than one person lurking in the wood around our campsite, and when I heard a thud, followed by a groan and the sound of something heavy falling to the ground, I knew it must be Gaspard and at least one of his vassals. My heart pounded and my breath quickened as I waited in anticipation.

The cage sat ready as John, Mr. Baird, and I, with weapons and ropes, moved as quietly as possible toward the commotion. The steady sickening sound of guttural grunts and stifled roars rent the still night air. We crouched, trembling, behind a thicket, and I searched with unseeing eyes for the source of the noise, but the utter blackness of the night left me floundering. John must have found a heading for he whispered, "Follow me," and groped around for Mr. Baird and I. A violent cry stopped us, and I felt a cold chill rise up my spine, fearing that the man had become the wolf. Instead of howls, a gun blast resounded, seeming all the louder for not being able to see, and I could hear a body fall and the muffled cries of alarm.

"I got him! Come on!" Gregory's voice rang clear. John moved quickly while Mr. Baird and I struggled to keep up, following the sound of crackling leaves and breaking twigs. Before we reached Gaspard, I could hear him groaning as if he was trying to get up. Another shot cracked, so loud I nearly fell to the ground in fright, and as Gregory spoke again, I realized we were right behind him.

"Grab him and get him to the cage. I'll get Matthew," he shouted, and I heard him take off toward the sound of a runner in the woods.

"Don't shoot if you can help it!" I called after him. John and Mr. Baird were already upon the unconscious body of our foe, but it would not remain so for long. I joined them; the three of us trussing him with knots of every kind. The two soldiers were at hand, one knocked to the ground and moaning, the other immobile and stunned, likely by fear of becoming the next victim.

As we led all three captives to our camp, I could faintly hear splashing from the creek.

"Matthew! Stop! I won't hurt you!" Gregory shouted, and I hoped he would remain true to his word.

We secured Gaspard in his cage before he had time to struggle much against his capture. The other two captives we tied to trees at the furthest reach of the fire's glow. Mr. Baird worked to remove the gags from the mouths of the two soldiers and helped them to drink some ale.

"I'm sorry, friends, but we canna let ye go jus yet. Get ye some rest and we'll sort this out in the mornin'." He made them as comfortable as possible, and the men, being highlanders as well, resigned themselves to the care of a fellow countryman.

Gregory returned shortly to the fireside, his clothes wet and dripping, but he had nothing to show for his swim in the creek.

"He got away," he groaned as he sat on a log.

"What about the woman?"

"Never saw her. Never heard her either. Either she wasn't with 'em or she's a ghost."

I frowned and looked to John and Mr. Baird, who both seemed concerned, but their concern could not overpower their exhaustion. There was nothing left that night but to lay aside our worries and rest before the new day dawned fresh troubles of its own.

The morning light brought on frenzied mumblings concerning our captives. I took it upon myself to explain the situation to the hogtied victims, revealing the truth of their encounter and what would become of them. It did not surprise me to be laughed at and scorned, foul language and spittle accentuating the ridicule.

"Give them time to let it settle. Maybe they will be smarter than us and believe it before it's proved to them," Gregory remarked as he took a sip of his coffee.

"I doubt it. Who could believe such a thing and own it for oneself? It would be far easier to believe your neighbor is a monster out of the pages of a fairy tale than to accept that you have been taken over by a demon from hell."

A chuckle came from the cage holding our French captive.

"It is no demon, mes amis. You are still 'olding on to ze lies of ze church."

"Oh, put a damper on it, you bastard, 'fore I put a bullet down your gullet."

"Oh contraire, I am no bastard. My mozer was 'appily married to my fazer; zat is, until she died in childbirs."

"So you've been a murderer since you were born, eh?"

"Quit provoking him, friend. It gives you no credit to mince words with this mongrel," I said.

"Mongrel . . . zis is a word for dog, no? Ha-ha! I am 'appy to be in ze company of many mongrels." The Frenchman raised his arms as far as he was able in his gibbet to exalt over the pack of wolves he had propagated.

"Son of a bitch," Gregory mumbled under his breath while trading his cup for a gun and lifting it to silence his mocker. The Frenchman laughed all the more at Gregory's insult.

"Stop, Gregory! Please, it will only make a mess and accomplish nothing of purpose."

"No, but I'd feel better shutting that trap of his, that's for sure." He threw down the weapon and retreated to the creek to cool off, for the morning was a sultry one for October and we were all sweating enough without the help of anger boiling our blood.

"What now?" I looked to Mr. Baird, who was quickly

becoming the authority on werewolves for all the research and field notes he had accumulated.

"Well, lad, ye ken he cannae be killed in the natural way. 'Tis a shame the next full moon is no' for a fortnight. Seems we are to be stuck with 'em till then."

"And then what?"

"Then ye see what can be done when yer in yer beastly form."

We were not fortunate enough to hold on to our captives for two more weeks. Each night that the moon grew, so did the power of the Frenchman over his gift. Mr. Baird calculated the length of time the wolf was able to stay in his werewolf form until he was mastering the transformation long enough to attack the gibbet with gusto. I became anxious about the welfare of the non-afflicted. I urged them to retreat to Albany before it was too late. If Gaspard were to escape, they would have no hope of leaving the woods as citizens of the living. Finally, the men relented, admitting they had already been contemplating how to leave us now that the conditions were far too volatile for them to remain. They knew they could contribute nothing of value in a confrontation, and would only be distractions for us who would be compelled to protect them. They left not a moment too soon, for three nights later, Gaspard worked the lock of his gibbet and freed himself before Gregory lodged a succession of bullets into his back.

I could feel the heat from the day still radiating off the hard ground of our camp that night, and the fire, though necessary, made the atmosphere nearly unbearable. The creek afforded some respite as its cooler waters brought a refreshing chill to the breezes that passed over it, but we were still uncomfortable and slept outside our tents rather than contribute our body heat and sweat to the sultriness of the air. I listened with little concern to the guttural sounds of Gaspard as he once again practiced his transformations on demand. He had changed back and forth, holding the form longer each time before allowing himself to fall back into his human state. It was like exercise for him, and he was building up his beastly muscles. After one such transformation, I noticed an eerie silence. I heard no more of the huffing or straining that frequently flowed from the werewolf. The only sound, aside from the crackling of the fire, was the croaking of the night-heron mingled with the belches of bullfrogs. Eventually, I heard what I thought to be a creak as a rusty hinge would make, and a muffled thump, but when I lifted my head to inspect the noise, I saw both gibbets closed and quiet, separated by the tree where the men were still tied and too terrified by the nightly emergence of the monster to attempt escape. I resumed my posture of sleep and would have drifted off, had the fire of a rifle just over my head not violently roused me. Another shot and another as Gregory picked up each loaded piece, took aim, and pulled. I leaped to my feet to discover what had caused Gregory to fire, and while I surveyed the scene, I noticed the trail of blood that ran from the tree to the gibbet. The man inside was not Gaspard, but in his place was a soldier he had birthed into his pack, knocked unconscious and securely locked in the cage. I ran to the gibbet to check on the man inside. The soldier was just coming to after a head injury, and I wondered how I had not noticed the noise or the scene Gaspard had left behind.

I watched as the human form of Gaspard lay as if dead while Gregory rushed to incarcerate him. But the reflex of the monster took over and, before Gregory could finish shoving the body into the empty cage, Gaspard was the werewolf and lunged at his attacker, grabbing hold of Gregory's arm and nearly severing it from his elbow. Gregory screamed and fell back writhing as his human form gave way to canines and claws!

My jaw hung open as I watched Gregory become the wolf ahead of the full moon and I felt my heart skip a beat in anticipation, expecting the moment of our victory to be upon us. But my mouth suddenly went dry and all my swelling excitement caught as a lump in my throat when I saw that Gregory's arm did not recover as it would have done by any other means of violence. Instead, Gregory, now completely transformed, gnawed off the useless appendage and the human arm was cast off into the fire. The lump threatened to break forth as a sob, for I knew then what we all secretly surmised but had, as yet, no evidence of—only a werewolf could kill a werewolf.

The Frenchman beheld his match. Gregory was handicapped in the loss of his arm, but he more than made up for it in the prominence of his stature. He was the largest man of them, save one of the soldiers bound to the tree, who rivaled him for girth. The Frenchman was of a delicate disposition. He was tall but slender and his muscle mass proved wanting against the barrel chested trapper. Gregory towered over his foe and snarled, the pain in his arm no doubt giving him fuel for his rage. Gaspard was still half lodged in the gibbet, but struggled to free himself as the wolf was waning. A gunshot drew Gregory's focus from his prey, and Gaspard tore from the cage, leaping into the thick flora surrounding the camp. A second bullet hit its mark, and I found Gregory sprawled on the ground in front of the gibbet, his head bleeding but quickly mending while the wound from his arm continued to paint the ground red beneath him. He was melting back into humanity as I tied a strip of my shirt round his arm to quit the flow of blood. While Gregory was still unconscious, I grabbed a flaming brand from the fire and scorched the wound to stop the bleeding. The new violence to his torn flesh awoke Gregory, and he wailed in agony.

"Forget me, man! Go after him!" he said as soon as he could speak again.

"Like this?" I gestured at my ineffectual human form. "No, it will have to wait for another night. He is far flown from here."

"Oh, but that traitor, Matthew, he likely won't be far!" Gregory snarled as he sat up, holding his stunted arm in his remaining hand.

"How can you be sure it was him? Just as likely it was the woman."

"'Cause she uses a bow and arrow."

I shook my head and looked off into the woods. So Matthew was truly on the mad-man's side. It was a painful truth, but I acknowledged I had no reason to believe it was not so.

"Come, we need to wrap that wound."

Gregory came to himself and looked down at the stump. "Oh, God! He bit off my arm!" The loss came upon him like a lightning bolt, and he recoiled as if struck.

"You will live to seek revenge," I assured him.

Gregory attempted to stand, but tottered. "I'll live, but I'll never shoot again. Oh, the bastard! The damned son of a . . ." Before he could curse the man a second time, he fell back to the ground, unconscious.

To my surprise, there were no further attacks before the full moon. The two soldiers, who were as yet unwilling to admit their own affliction, remained captives of the camp and, after the hysterics of Gaspard's escape, became belligerent and attempted escapes of their own. It fell to Gregory, as he nursed his wound, to see that the men failed, while I hunted and spied out the surrounding areas looking for clues of the whereabouts of our enemies. No sign of another living soul could be found, but I wondered if the men were truly gone or if I just made a poor scout.

The full moon came upon us quicker than Gregory's wound could heal, even with the rude use of fire to close it. He was not an easy patient and would not rest his arm as it required. I knew it would likely reopen when he turned again, giving us an immediate disadvantage in a fight. However, nothing could persuade Gregory to remain immobile; he insisted on training his left arm to do what came naturally to his right.

A thick veil of clouds hid the moon; still, I could feel my

body preparing for the change that would overtake me involuntarily. I did not resist but readied myself, as well as I knew how, to meet our foe, whom we expected would come upon us that night. We locked the two infant werewolves in the gibbets. There was no use for them in battle; they would likely just run off to find prey elsewhere. And if Gaspard controlled them, we would be doomed.

I felt the wave of desire come over me before my body lurched to the ground and convulsed. I paid attention this time, as much as I was able, to the change I underwent, primarily so that I could relay to Mr. Baird the physical transformation in detail. The thoughts I had of my scholarly friend sunk from benevolent to ones filled with ravenous hunger, and I recoiled at the notions that flirted with my psyche. Instead of Mr. Baird, I focused on the elongation of my limbs, the cracking of my legs as they bent backwards, and the nails that seemed to leap out of my fingers as if they were retractable and had always been there. My jaw jutted forward as the canine teeth came to a point. There was pain in the process, yet I would not allow myself to writhe senseless in it. I felt through it to each change, noting in what order they came and how the parts of my body seemed to move into position. Nothing grew out of nowhere—it was all me, only stretched and pulled until I took on the shape of a wolf.

I looked over to where Gregory had been and saw he had also transformed and stood licking the wound on his arm which, as I had surmised, was split where his skin had stretched. Inside the cages, the soldiers were undergoing transformations of their own, but unlike us more seasoned werewolves, screams turned to shrieking howls and rage-filled longing drove them to batter the cages in hysteria.

I could feel the torment between my human mind and the instincts of the monster. I forced myself to ignore the memories of kills, the taste of flesh and warm blood, the sounds of screaming women and crying children. I honed my attention on one thought and one aim only: the termination of the author of my nightmare.

We could hear running feet before we saw them. I had smelled the enemy even before I heard him. We braced ourselves for the onslaught, readying to claw and gnash our way to victory. Matthew appeared out of the thick woods just as the clouds parted and light from the moon illuminated him. He was one of the smallest wolves, tall but scrawny, larger only than the woman, but he was agile and quick. He leapt at Gregory, sinking his teeth into the broad shoulder of my ally. The wolf in me, ravenous and raging, moved toward Matthew to attack and devour, but the human in me saw what I was about to do and stopped, wanting nothing less than to hurt the young man I cared for. I regained control of the weapon, but still had to draw Matthew off of Gregory. I knew Gaspard was close behind and would likely go for Gregory as well, hoping they could easily reduce their opponents to one. My claws found purchase on Matthew's back and ripped him off Gregory, who was losing ground under the relentless attack of the young wolf.

I threw Matthew and stood in front of Gregory in time for the lunge from Gaspard. He was not as hasty as his protégé and took to sparring instead. We locked eyes, claws at the ready, and moved in a circle, looking for the best opportunity to strike. Gaspard was advancing forward as he moved, pushing me closer to the fire. I caught a glimpse of Gregory over Gaspard's shoulder. He was embroiled in a rematch with Matthew, holding him by the throat with his one good arm, keeping him pinned to the ground. Matthew struggled and slashed with his claws, meeting flesh more often than not, but Gregory bore each slashing swipe and remained intent on strangling the boy to death.

I took the opportunity to leap at Gaspard, driving him backwards and into Gregory. When their bodies met, Gaspard tripped and fell over Gregory's back, landing on his own. I lodged my claws into the shoulders of my foe and howled for Gregory to come to my aid. Gregory was in a rage, and though the skirmish had knocked him sideways off Matthew, he quickly regained his posture of dominance and went again for the throat, this time with his teeth. A quick blow from Matthew landed across Gregory's face, cutting his cheek and nearly losing him an eye. He recoiled enough that Matthew was able to scramble out from under Gregory's girth and retreated to the woods. Gregory wiped away the blood that ran down the side of his face and moved to join me, but it was too late. Gaspard threw me and I landed dangerously close to the fire, singeing my coat.

The French wolf used the brief moments that Gregory and I were both occupied with our injuries to attack the cages that held his berserker cubs and set one of them free. The new wolf immediately dove for Gregory, who had just realized where his foe had gone, and toppled him over. It was the one who matched Gregory for size, but he had the upper hand, for unlike my friend, he was not missing one of his. I discovered the intent of Gaspard and attacked before he could release the other wolf.

None of the fighting monsters saw Matthew reappear from the woods and open the other cage. In moments, six wolves were clawing, biting, and howling, leaving a scene of grotesque shadows dancing across the backdrop of trees.

The smaller of the newborn wolves approached me in a frenzy of teeth and claws. As I lashed out in the heat of the battle, my claw hit an artery and left the wolf clutching at his throat. A grin of pleasure formed on my maw, but when I saw what I had done, I recovered quickly from my trance and tried to staunch the flow, but there was nothing I could do. Moments later, he slumped to the ground, dead.

Gaspard and Matthew were overpowering Gregory when I returned to the fray. The other new wolf, unaware of whose side he was on and to whom he owed allegiance, bit into Gaspard's leg. The alpha wolf howled and turned on his creation. I watched as Gaspard released the hold he had on Gregory and took the new wolf's head in his claws. He was greater in stature than Gaspard, but the soldier was not in control of the beast. He whimpered as any captured dog would. Another wolf, small and slim, but fierce, sprang into the firelight and dove at Gaspard. With one swift movement, Gaspard batted at the female and sent her flying into the fire. She rolled out of it, howling and whimpering, frantic to put out the flames that scorched her fur. Gaspard returned to the fledgling who had bitten him, and I heard a cracking, snapping sound as he crushed the wolf's skull with his bare hands. The animal slinked to the ground, returning to his human form before lying still. I expected Gaspard to recommence his attack on Gregory, but before Gregory could brace himself, I watched Matthew leap in front of him, not to attack him, but to defend him from Gaspard. The wolf and his protégé met in a violent collision. Gaspard looked confused, but also angered as he met Matthew's attack with blows and bites of his own.

From behind, the female wolf leapt at Gaspard and clung to his back, tearing at his shoulder. The Frenchman reached behind him, dug his claws into the woman's ribs and threw her over his head. She remained still where she landed. Matthew roared, and I watched as all the sullenness left him for rage. He tore into Gaspard's chest, slashing and scrambling to get his teeth near his foe. Gregory and I saw the opportunity and joined Matthew, one on each side of the fiend. Outmatched, exhausted, and overpowered, Gaspard cowered on his haunches as if he would submit to vengeance or plead for mercy. But it was a ruse. He slunk down only so he could spring upon Matthew, catching him off guard. He pinned the boy to the ground and landed a blow to his gut. I saw the wound, and a howl left my chest as the wolf called out to the moon to be merciful, yet I knew it would be fatal.

Before we could seek revenge, the villain tore from the circle of bodies we had created and took off for the woods. Gregory and I chased after him, the light of the moon playing with the shadows in the wood so that thickets became crouched monsters and branches clawed arms, until I was so turned about by the landscape before me that I left the chase to Gregory and returned to Matthew.

Dawn lit the horizon. As my mind shed the turmoil of the battle, my body shed the wolf and I returned as a man to find Matthew lying near the fire, clutching at his abdomen. Though I knew I had not dealt this wound, it felt the same as the day I had attacked my dear friend and I sobbed. I looked away from the carnage and held Matthew's head as he lay dying.

"I'm sorry," he spoke in a whispery gurgle as blood spilled over his lips. I caught my breath and wiped away the tears that clouded my vision.

"No, friend, do not waste words on apologies. You have always been forgiven by me." As he tried to speak again, I could see that the blood was choking him. I lifted him up higher into my arms and attempted to clear the thick fluid from his mouth.

"I saw the evil . . . too late . . ." he managed.

"It matters not when. Remember the thief on the cross." All I could give him, yet again, was hope in the face of darkness and despair. He was leaving me and it was all I could do.

Matthew gasped with a sharp pain that then eased to a numb peacefulness. His eyes looked around at the fire, the dawn, the cold and fading moon. A gentle fall breeze passed over his face, bringing relief from the stifling heat of flame. His gaze returned to meet mine, and his face glowed as it reflected the fire beside him.

"The Celestial City," he whispered.

"Yes, friend. Paradise." I controlled my heaving sobs long enough to smooth the hair from his face.

A smile passed over Matthew's lips, ever so briefly, before the death rattle released the last of the breath from his lungs and he lay limp.

20

In the early light of dawn, the sound of the shovel overturning the mossy dirt near the creek bed mixed with the soft sobs that escaped my chest as I dug. The body of my friend lay peacefully by two others, awaiting his final resting place. Gregory stood by the fire, which had long ceased to glow, nursing the wound to his shoulder. A bandaged but breathing woman lay close by, sleeping fitfully.

It was clear Gregory could not relax as he paced about the small clearing. The enemy had escaped. The war was not over. I was exhausted from the long, agonizing night and, though my body did not show it, I was no less frustrated than Gregory looked. Nothing of the tension I had felt approaching our confrontation with the enemy had left me. Instead, I felt a growing rage and longing for revenge. Only the death of Beatrice could compare to the visceral hatred I felt. Yet, I believed myself to be all the more responsible for Matthew, for I was all he had left in the world, and I had failed him.

"We gotta get her to a barber or physician. I've done what I can for those wounds, but they're beyond bandages," Gregory said as he ran his hand through his hair.

"Perhaps we should just leave her to fate." My jaw was

clenched and my fists wanted to beat the body that lay before me. The idea frightened me for a moment, but after all, I had just returned from burying Matthew, and the last task I wanted was to care for his murderer's accomplice.

"Fenn, you saw as well as I did that she came to our aid. And I have more reason than you to think her a villain, seeing as she hunted me all that time, but I think we owe it to Matthew to try. He seemed to care for her."

I took a deep breath and conceded, "I know you are right." She had, after all, fought alongside us and suffered greatly for it. "We should leave at once. Can you manage?"

"I admit, I'm battered more than I've been in a long time. These wounds will have to heal the old-fashioned way. But I can ride."

The road seemed all the harder for the injuries we sustained. Though my burns were not as extensive as the woman's, I had deep gashes and bite wounds that were not closing, and Gregory's arm, after reopening the wound, was slowly seeping through the bandages we wrapped it in. We traveled slowly, and the woman slept almost peacefully, though the jarring motion of the wagon at times roused her and she would cry out in pain before losing consciousness once again. The burns covered half of her torso and the fire had licked one side of her face. In addition, she had suffered multiple puncture wounds from Gaspard's claws, which miraculously, as far as Gregory could tell, had not reached any vital organs. Even minor wounds carried the risk of putrefaction, and we believed she could die from shock.

Even more than our wounds, we traveled in the abject despondency of those who have utterly failed. However, it was not shame that I carried with me. It was rage. It was bloodlust. It was loathing. I recoiled more than once at the thoughts that flooded my waking moments. I feared Gaspard had succeeded in more than defeating us in battle; he had made me into a monster.

We returned to Albany to find our friends waiting for us at

the same lodgings we had used over a month before. They could tell by our expressions that we were far from victorious. John's face betrayed concern as he looked between Gregory and me, noting someone was missing.

"The villain escaped, but not before he killed Matthew," I answered the question John had yet to ask.

"I am very sorry to hear that." He paused and dropped his head. Not one of us was ready to dwell on the loss. It was fresher than the flesh wounds and would take longer to heal. When the silence nearly became heavier than words, he turned his attention to the woman and said, "What will you do with her?"

Mr. Baird knew of common herbs that were useful for burns, which he made into a poultice and was busy applying to the woman's wounds.

"Ask her what she wants. I don't know why she was with that devil. All I know is she helped us," was Gregory's gracious answer.

"Or maybe she was just leading us right where they wanted us." I had enough compassion to save her life, but it did not take away my suspicion or scorn.

"Maybe so. But I'll be the first to let her prove she ain't a threat. Besides, we're gonna have to face that bastard again. We might need her."

The reminder that we would likely endure another night like the one that had cost us so much already brought my blood to boil and I felt my face flush in hot anger.

"You alright, Fenn?" Gregory asked.

"Yes," I lied. What good would it do to admit that I was losing control of the man, even when the monster was safely hidden away? I wondered in that moment if Matthew had been right and the wolf was just our hearts in the flesh.

The mysterious blue eyed woman lifted her lids a week later to find Mr. Baird reading at her bedside as I sat in a corner, waiting. It was the first time she had come to consciousness when the pain had not driven her back to oblivion. A physician had been to see her and tended to her wounds. He noted many old scars that littered her torso, and I wondered how many times she had laid abed recovering as she was now.

"Hmmhm . . . wh . . . where am I?" Her voice was faint and scratchy, but once she was able to clear her throat, her words came out in discern-able noises. Mr. Baird put down his book and turned to call my attention, but I was already up and moving toward the invalid. As I approached the other side of the bed, I wanted to smile in reassurance, but found my face would not comply.

"Please, do not strain yourself," I managed.

"Where am I?" the lady repeated. This time, her voice was clearer and stronger.

"A room we have rented in Albany. I have had a physician treat your wounds properly, and he has assured us you will recover," I answered, struggling to veil my bitterness.

The woman closed her eyes and swallowed hard. She began to rise, but I would not allow her to exert herself. Instead, I helped her drink before restoring her to the pillow. I knew we were unlikely to get any information out of her if I continued to be hostile, so I cleared my throat and forced a smile.

"Can you tell us your name?" I asked.

"Talise."

Her eyes were wide and reminded me so of Beatrice that I found it difficult to hide my discomfort, which manifested as contempt.

"Well, I believe you already know our names, but for the sake of formal introductions, my name is Fenn, and this is Mr. Baird. Gregory and John are away at the moment, but I will have them greet you when they return. For now, I will leave you to rest."

"Wait," she said as she grabbed my hand. I cringed at the touch, but turned back to look her in the eye.

"Did you kill him?" she asked, her voice betraying trepidation.

"The Frenchman? No, no, we did not." I thought she sighed with relief, but then her eyes grew wide with terror.

"He cannot find me! He cannot know I'm alive." I stepped away, surprised by her sudden outburst.

"Then you should thank Gregory for bringing you here. I would have left you by that creek." She did not appear to be shocked by my answer, but I certainly was. I looked at Mr. Baird, feeling as if I owed him an apology for my sudden change in character, but he only smiled in compassion.

"Where is Matthew?" Talise asked, ignoring my statement.

I could not conceal the flash of anger that swept across my face, but I turned back to her and answered, "Gaspard killed him. I buried his body by the creek."

Her eyes fluttered. I could not be certain if sorrow or sleep came to claim her, but a tear slid down her cheek and the lids remained closed. I excused myself, fearful that I could no longer contain my rage, and left her with Mr. Baird.

That night I prayed, for the first time in many months, and asked only for patience. My real enemy was Gaspard, and if Talise could bring us to him or assist us in ridding him from the face of the earth, then it would behoove me to control the urge to unleash my revenge upon her.

It was Gregory who was beside her when she next opened her eyes. I watched, once again waiting across the room, as Gregory introduced himself. "Hello there, miss. Fenn tells me your name is Talise. I'm Gregory. Though you should know that, since you were following me all over this new world." Gregory grew fierce, and I suspected the temptation to interrogate her was almost too strong to quell, but he steadied himself and smirked at the invalid, whom I judged to be around the same age. She simply nodded as John stepped in, the most awkward of us all.

"John Andrews, lawyer, at your service, ma'am."

"I hardly think she needs your services, John. The law's not after her, far as I know," Gregory said, his smile growing more cheerful.

"Forgive me, I just meant to introduce myself."

Gregory laughed and slapped John on the back. I envied Gregory for his lightheartedness, and yet I found myself simultaneously annoyed that he was not full of the same contempt and anger that had consumed me. What had I become?

Instead of attempting to get information out of the woman, Gregory left the room. John looked to the door as if he would excuse himself, decided better of it, and sat beside her. "I'm sorry. I didn't mean to introduce myself so formally. You can call me John."

Talise said nothing. She had not spoken since asking me the result of the battle the day before, and seemed to have no intention of speaking more unless someone asked her a question. It was likely her strength would not return for a fortnight, and I wondered if she would ever tell us what I assumed we all longed to know.

"We are very interested in hearing your story. Mr. Baird and I have taken this journey, not only for the sake of friendship, but also for the knowledge we have accumulated concerning this affliction. We are hardly the most qualified for the study, but we are sympathetic, so I hope you will not be afraid to share; when you are ready, that is."

She could not possibly trust us yet, and if it had been left to me, she would have been right not to, but she swallowed and answered John. "Perhaps I will tell you . . . something. But not today."

John nodded his head and smiled before he excused himself to leave her in peace.

Nearly three weeks had passed since the battle with Gaspard before Talise was well enough to tell her story. It started out in many disjointed pieces, focusing on the role she played with each one of us.

She had known of Gregory soon after he was attacked. According to Talise, Gaspard had been growing careless with his hunts. The night Gregory became a wolf, the Frenchman had followed the group of men, treating the attack as a game of cat and mouse until, as dawn was approaching, he knew he would run out of time if he did not hasten. He thought he had killed each one before he began feasting, but Gregory was still alive, his wound deadly, but the kind that kills slowly and painfully. When Gaspard was interrupted by the natives, he fled without checking to make sure Gregory was gone. He never intended to create another wolf. At the time, he had wanted all the glory for himself. To be the sole hand of reckoning for all mankind. The one and only god.

"But what about you? Are you not like us?" I asked.

"Yes, and no. But that is for another time. In any case, he interpreted the gift as a weapon for vengeance, and I was not involved in his work . . . until Gregory."

Talise had followed Gregory, not to hunt him as he had believed, but to observe him. She looked for the signs that he was ready to wield control over the beast, but they never came. On the other hand, Gaspard had found that he and the animal were one on his very first moon.

"Cause he's evil!" Gregory scoffed.

"Perhaps. I think it was because he knew when he was made what he was made to be. There was no war inside between the man and the gift. He simply embraced it," Talise explained.

I fought the urge to scoff as well at the insinuation that this affliction could be considered a gift. But for the sake of hearing the rest of the story, I simply averted my eyes so she would not see the anger in them.

She then shared how she had been involved on the night I was made. It was she, not the werewolf, who had released him from his cage. I watched Gregory's fists tighten as he listened to her describe that night. Scenes of shredded flesh and blood involuntarily invaded my mind, and I could not focus on what Talise was saying. I took a draught of beer, hoping to calm my nerves so I could hear her story and not the memory of my screams. It was becoming more difficult to silence the wolf in me —and his memories.

"I thought I could lure you to follow me. I thought I could teach you to control it. It was foolish of me, I know. You were too wild. When you lunged at me, I ran, and instead of following me, you went for Fenn."

She had heard the gunshot and a howl and hoped I had come out unscathed. But when she returned to the campsite later and found me lying on the ground, bleeding out the last of my life, she knew I would become one of them. She stayed with me from then on, to see if I would have better control, and helped me find Mr. Baird.

"Why did you never reveal yourself? You could have explained things to us. We could have made wiser choices!" My voice grew louder with each sentence, and I nearly rose from my seat to confront her.

"It was forbidden. Gaspard would have killed me."

"You did all that for him."

"Yes. I had to." She did not elaborate on her peculiar relationship with Gaspard. "I returned to him then. He would have come for me if I hadn't. I feared what he would do. We heard about the attack on the Wagon Road and that was when he knew Gregory had made another wolf. He punished me for not telling him about you." She would not meet anyone's gaze, perhaps avoiding the pity she would find there. We understood, then, the scars that covered her torso. Her body told the story before she did.

She then explained what had happened when I escaped the cellar. She had not helped me, but she was there. She said she had tried to stop the monster that I became, but I was larger, stronger, and full of animal passion; there was nothing she could do. Once I reached Matthew, she hoped I would kill him and it would end there. But Matthew had shot me and I fled, unable to finish what I had started.

"Why didn't you end it for him instead of letting him be cursed?" Gregory asked, clearly agitated as his leg bounced while he sat. I was frustrated as well by all the opportunities this woman had squandered to spare us from what we had become.

"I considered it. I wanted to. But I couldn't." She stopped and I thought she would cry, but no tear escaped her eye, and she composed herself to continue. "I wanted to find someone who could be like me, who wasn't him." I knew she meant Gaspard, and I imagined the depth of loneliness one would feel being the only one of a kind or tethered to another who was evil. The man in me that had grown so quiet fought to be heard, and for the first time, I felt compassion for Talise. After composing herself, she went on.

"I cared for Matthew. I almost told him, whispering in his ear when he was in and out of consciousness, dying in my arms, that he was given a gift and must learn to control it. But the words would not come, and I feared Gaspard though he was hundreds of miles away. I heard you coming, so I left him by the road. Eventually you left. I didn't know if you would come back. But I knew he would awaken, and I didn't want him to be alone, so I brought him to my tent, bandaged him, and told him he was safe."

With three wolves to care for, she tried to watch us all, but though she could travel quickly and quietly through the woods, she could not be there for each of us. Even so, she was present the day I was arrested and Matthew was shot. She had tried to help. The arrow had been hers, but she feared what the men of law would do to her if they found her, so she fled. She wanted to reveal herself to Matthew, but she could feel that Gaspard was near.

"He was there in time for Fenn's trial, and he found me and made me stay with him. We watched the execution."

"I saw you in the crowd," I said, remembering her unfeeling face watching me die.

"Yes. I knew you would come back to life, but it was best if the world thought you dead. It is almost impossible to live among mortals when you are no longer one. I was able to get away from Gaspard long enough to tell Mr. Baird you needed him, and I left you in good hands. In any case, Gaspard wanted to find Gregory."

It was at that point in her story we all acknowledged we could bear no more that day. I, for one, could not stand to hear of what had actually happened to Beatrice and Mary. It was too much. I asked her to stop, and she nodded, left the fireside where we had all been enraptured in her tale, and bid us goodnight.

The next evening, we gathered once again. This time, Gregory filled in the pieces of his story that were previously unknown to all of us, likely encouraged by Talise's candid narrative. After his execution, he explained, he had come to consciousness on a riverbank, having been carried only a short distance from the spot on the Wagon Road where his body had been tossed. He was closer to Big Lick, but would not chance a meeting with those of the caravan who believed him to be dead. So he made his way, shivering and recovering repeatedly from frostbite, through the mountainous terrain until he reached a homestead where it appeared the family was absent and borrowed a set of clothes and a horse.

"Come to think of it, I never did pay them back for what I took. I'm afraid we may not make it back that way." I smiled at Gregory's sense of honor, reminded of the simple goodness of his heart, even amidst the circumstances we all found ourselves in. It was then I realized I had not truly smiled in weeks. Besides amusement, I was relieved that Gregory no longer ignited the flames of malice in me he once did, for it would exhaust me carrying any more than I was already.

Gregory went on to describe how he had been aimless for a time, concerned with what he would do to contain the beast when the next full moon arrived, now that he was without his wagon. He spent the first in the mountains, and to his knowledge, no human life was lost that night. He considered using an old bear trap upon himself on the next moon, yet he could not be sure the beast would not gnaw his own foot off to be free. A deserted shack, somewhere in Ohio Country, that had likely been erected as a stopping point along a route used by troops earlier in the war, served as a refuge, and he remained there for the winter months, living off what he could hunt and using the few items that had been abandoned to construct a new cage. It withstood the torments of the beast, but he knew it could not hold together for long. And so, in the spring, he took the pelts he had collected through the winter and traded them for the work of a blacksmith in Philadelphia, who built a new cage to his specifications. It proved to be stronger and more reliable than his last. From that time on, he had worked odd jobs to earn a horse and wagon.

"I planned to find a way west, over the mountains. I'd come to enjoy the simple, solitary life, so I had no reason to stay near civilization. I also knew, even around all them people, that I was bein' followed again. My time to leave had come. It was July, and I knew I only had a few days before the full moon, but my cage worked so well the months before that I thought it was safe. So I did the most foolish thing I've ever done and I went to go see Mary one last time."

Gregory would not go on. The details of those days had been shared with John, and through him, the rest of us knew. I did not believe I could bear to dwell on it again. Even so, Talise began where Gregory left off, and curiosity got the better of my apprehension, so I sat to hear the parts that Gregory would only remember when he took the form of the wolf and saw it all play before his mind's eye.

"We left immediately after the execution to find Gregory. Gaspard had decided he wanted a pack. He no longer wanted to be the only wolf bringing retribution. He wanted his pups, as he called you all, to join him. We knew Matthew was learning to control his wolf. Gaspard said it was because he had no one left to love, and therefore, it would be easier for him to throw off his humanity. But you, Fenn and Gregory, you were tethered to the mortal life because of your love for the sisters. He wanted me to kill them, and then find Gregory and convert him to the mission. When we reached Chestertown, I made excuses and put it off as long as I could, but he grew angrier and more impatient. He threatened me, and I was about to give in, when he saw Gregory sulking about the estate and decided we would wait for the full moon, and then he would kill them and let Gregory believe he had done it."

I watched as Gregory quickly lifted his bowed head, the glint of hope in his eyes, and searched Talise's face. I looked as well, waiting for her to admit it had been Gaspard, and not Gregory, who cut down those perfect creatures we loved. She saw the yearning in our faces and her response was a sorrowful no, spoken without words. Gregory slowly let his head fall once more.

"How could you have transformed before the full moon?" John asked, perhaps the only one at that moment who was concerned with the other details of her story.

"Because I am not bound by the moon the way the others are." She did not elaborate, and I assumed she had mastered the skill Gaspard had been practicing. "That night . . . Gregory, that night I tried to save them. I tried to keep you from them. Gaspard saw you cage yourself, and he was furious. He decided it would be you that would sever your tie to mortality. He couldn't control you, but he could lead you, and he did. He led you right to the house on the river and would have led you through the front door, but he saw them walking in the moonlight. I tried to lure you elsewhere, but you had seen them too. You lunged after them, and I was about to get in your way, but Gaspard, he noticed what I wanted to do and he . . . I was afraid. I ran. I would not watch." Her eyes were not dry now, though her face remained as stoic as ever.

Curiosity could hold me no longer, and I felt burning in my throat and pressure in my head until I would let the heaving sobs free. I saw Gregory fighting his own emotions, his jaw clenched and his face like a stone. Only his eyes glistened with the tears that wanted to fall but could not. I excused myself and left the room, yet I could still hear Gregory growl out words as he sniffed back the liquid that likely escaped his nose.

"Go on!"

There was a pause, and then I heard Talise cautiously resume her tale. "Gaspard left you. I didn't want you to have more blood on your hands, so I found you, wandering the river's edge, looking for someone, anyone. You saw me and you chased me. I brought you back to the woods where your cage was hidden, and you were suddenly calm. I wondered if you had control, but I could see the wolf was all there was in your eyes. I lured you back into your cage with the rabbit. I didn't know how to use the lock, so I jammed it back in and stayed close by to make sure you wouldn't leave again. We waited, Gaspard and I, to see what you would do. He wanted me to approach you, but then John was there. When John left to join the others without you, Gaspard made me follow them. He told me to make it obvious because he knew you would then follow me. He wanted you with them. He wanted you all to find him together. He was waiting for you to come."

"I don't understand why you stayed with that monster. If you coulda killed him, why didn't you?"

I rejoined the group, wanting to see her face when she answered him. It seemed every tragedy could have been prevented had Talise killed Gaspard long before he had a chance to make more werewolves.

She stared into the fire for a moment, and then answered, not turning her head to meet anyone's gaze. "I will tell you my story now."

As if we were all boys again and mother had called us to story time, we settled in and waited in impatient anticipation for the tale we had been hoping for all along: the history of this mysterious creature who had enraptured each one of us in our own way.

21

"I was born with the wolf.
 Some of the Iroquois are given gifts from our gods. For many, it is a certain skill which comes naturally to the warrior, or a talented craftsman embroidering with wampum like no other. But I was born with the ability to shape-shift; to become a wolf.

I didn't know I had the gift until I was a little girl and I came across a lone young wolf in the woods. It was ravenous, for it had been a desolate winter, and I was terrified. I closed my eyes. I remember wishing I could have the power to overcome the beast who wanted to eat me. And then, I could feel something changing. I didn't know if it was the air around me or the ground beneath me, but I opened my eyes to see the wolf cower and whimper. Imagining I would see an even greater threat behind me, I hesitated to look around. But there was nothing there, and I realized it was me the wolf was afraid of. I looked at my hands and they were claws. When I felt my face, there was a snout and long, sharp teeth. The wolf fled in one direction and I in the other, right to my tribe. I ran to my mother, and she backed away from me, but I pleaded with my eyes for her to see me, and she did. She calmed me. I thought hard again that I wanted to be myself, and I felt my body fade back into the little girl.

The tribe was proud to have a daughter of the Okwaho. My mother was from the wolf clan, descended from another shape-shifter, and so I was seen as a sign of blessing upon the clan.

But my father did not see it that way. He was a Pale-Face from England, who had married my mother, a Ganiengehaka, or as you would say, a Mohawk, and joined the tribe, living with her family in their longhouse. My father believed my gift to be the work of a demon. He wanted to take me to a reverend, but my mother refused. He would not look at me anymore, and I wondered if he was right. They fought and fought over me until my father could bear it no longer and he left the tribe. I tried to go with him, but he forced me back. I never saw his eyes again except in the reflection of my own.

My mother loved my father dearly, and I knew she, too, found it hard to look at me and see a reminder of her beloved. Eventually, she gave in to her grief and she was gone. I was an orphan among the Mohawk. They cared for me, but I never felt I truly belonged. I was a creature torn between three worlds: the Mohawk, the white man, and the wolf. So when my mother died, I lost control. The tribe questioned whether I was truly a blessing. Some believed I was a curse; that the spirits had judged the union between my father and mother and the result was me. I feared I would be turned out when I was old enough to be considered a woman. But I was still a child and still a daughter of a Mohawk, and so they kept me, however regrettably.

And then Gaspard came.

He was not yet a man, but more than a boy, and he had a fierce fire in him. His father and sister had been slaughtered during a raid and he was taken prisoner. But he showed such great courage, intelligence, and charisma that the tribe embraced him, adopted him, and he, in turn, embraced the Mohawk. Our friendship blossomed out of our shared duality: orphans and outsiders. And he was not afraid of me. He knew what I was, but he never showed the fear or apprehension in my presence that had become normal for the others. I helped him learn our language and he told me more about the world of the white man; the world of my father. Over the years, we grew to love each other.

I remember when I first realized that Gaspard held my heart. The woods of the mountains are a hauntingly beautiful escape. The forest canopy and overgrowth shaded the light of day, and it felt like I was walking into a living cave. Especially after the rain, when the bark was dark brown, and the leaves stood out in a verdant green. Gaspard loved to hunt; I was drawn to the flora. On this occasion, he was looking for elk and I was looking for a small, purple herb that we use for healing. It grows best in the open, out of the dense enclosure of the woods, so I wandered from where Gaspard was tracking to a place I had found the herb before.

A small lake, enclosed by mountainous ravines and age-old trees, was bordered by a grassy field where wildflowers grow in abundance. I began searching for the purple flowers amongst the other late-blooming varieties when I realized I was being watched. I had unknowingly ventured near a catamount and her young, who were drinking from the clear, cool lake. I froze, knowing if I ran, she would chase me down, and if I shouted for Gaspard, she would lunge. Her three cubs, large, but still showing spots, were so close I could hear them sniffing my scent. The mother looked in my eyes, and I knew, no matter what I did, she was preparing to attack. I had not turned into the wolf in years, hoping the tribe would forget that I was different, but then I had to. The transformation was complete by the time she leaped at me, and I could see the fear in her eyes when a wolf met her instead of a weak human. Even amid the struggle, I didn't want to kill her. She was strong and beautiful, and her cubs were more important to her than her own life. I was able to throw her far enough from me to escape into the thick, dark forest, but not without the evidence of the catamount's claws on my body.

I was still in the wolf form, too wounded to relax back into humanity, so I tried to hide before Gaspard could find me that way. But it was too late. He had seen my transformation, and he rushed to where I was, curled on the ground, whimpering and clutching my side where the injury was most painful. He held my wolf head in his lap and stroked it, believing I was dying, while his tears dripped onto my fur. I looked up at him and saw nothing of the fear and revulsion I expected; instead, his eyes held awe and adoration mixed with grief and pain. I knew I would survive, and in that moment, I let go of the battle within myself to hide away. I reached to him as the wolf, and slowly my form returned to the woman; I was naked, but I felt no shame. He removed his shirt and draped it over me with tenderness and compassion, and we stayed like that in the stillness of the afternoon, in the sanctuary of the woodland bower, simply holding one another.

You have only seen Gaspard, the monster. But I knew Gaspard when he was a man.

From then on, we were young lovers, and though we were both of the wolf clan and marriage within clans was usually discouraged, we approached the counsel for consent, nonetheless. They were hesitant to allow it, not only for that reason but also because they remembered what had resulted from my mother's marriage to a Pale-Face. But Gaspard could persuade others in a way that they not only agreed with him, but believed it had been their own idea. The counsel consented, and our marriage ceremony preparations were immediately underway.

Over the years leading up to that point, Gaspard had been enamored with the shaman and learned all he could from him. He was deeply spiritual and was drawn to the religion of our tribe. The earth spoke to him; the trees held spirits he knew by name; the animals were his kinsman. Since the shaman trusted him, one day, a day just before we were to be wed, he told Gaspard of a vision he had: our world was coming to an end.

The white men would drive the Iroquois from their homes and their hunting grounds. Their greed for land and resources would bring desolation to the spirit of the woods. It would not end until the white men had covered the entire continent, as far as the setting sun. Gaspard knew it was true. It was inevitable. He begged the shaman to give him a weapon, something so great and powerful that it would drive all the white men away. No weapon made by human hands could do this, but the shaman knew he could give Gaspard a gift that would make him the weapon. Gaspard didn't hesitate. He accepted the gift, though it came from Sawiskera, the evil son of Sky Woman, who should never be trusted. It was the first time Gaspard kept a secret from me.

The day of our wedding was beautiful. The wedding wheel was hung at the entrance of the longhouse where our ceremony was held. Gaspard had on a beautiful deerskin coat, breeches, and the moccasins I made for him. I wore a pale deerskin dress with intricate embroidery and fringe. The elders stood behind the bench where we sat while Gaspard's adoptive mother and my aunt sat on either side. We both felt the grief that our birth mothers were not there to share in our joy.

We promised each other many things that day, things we held to at first, but I didn't think it would end like this. That we would fall so far from that love we had while we lived among my people.

The council made speeches; we exchanged ceremonial baskets; the wampum was passed, and the celebration began. I had never felt more welcome and celebrated since my mother was alive than I did that day. The entire tribe was filled with joy over our marriage. That night, we entered my ancestor's longhouse where we would live together as husband and wife. When he drew me into his arms, when our flesh became one, I felt complete. Gaspard entered me and I consumed him.

But all the joy and peace of that union was short-lived. Only a few weeks later, on the night of our first full moon as man and wife, Gaspard became a wolf.

He had enough control of the beast to keep it from attacking our people, but he killed a dog and consumed parts of it before escaping into the woods, hunting until dawn. We could hear his howls while the tribe gathered weapons and stood watch in case he returned. I was confused and terrified. I feared for Gaspard, but I also feared what would become of us. Already my people were convinced that I had given him the wolf when we laid together; that I spread my curse like a disease. For then, no one believed it was anything but a curse. The counsel regretted giving consent to our union, to any union with me, and they discussed what was to be done with Gaspard, should he return.

He came back that dawn, naked and exhausted, with slick, sticky blood coating his hands and face. I ran to him and covered him. I pushed aside the men that wanted to take him from me and brought him into our home to clean and clothe him. He acted just as confused as we all were and accepted the notion that I had made him like myself. I met with the counsel and defended him. If I could control it, I argued, then so could he. He had not attacked a single person, and though he craved flesh in his wolf form, he chose to only eat the flesh of animals. I promised to help him keep it under control. The counsel agreed on the condition that neither of us ever let the wolf form out again. And for the next four weeks, it was a promise we kept. But it was not one Gaspard could keep forever. By the next full moon, he had burst forth from our longhouse and escaped again to the woods to feast until dawn. It was clear that he was not like me.

When he returned, the counsel told us to gather our possessions and leave. That was when Gaspard told them the truth. The shaman was brought forth, and he confessed to giving Gaspard a gift to use against the Pale-Faces. The counsel was enraged. They had never consented to such a dangerous gift, and demanded that the shaman remove it. But he could not. Once a gift was given, it could not be taken back. The counsel was forced to relent and allow us to stay, but we were to build our own house. We couldn't live any longer with my aunt's family and were pushed to the outskirts of the village. Every day that I moved among the people, I felt their scorn. All the welcome and community I had known on our wedding day evaporated into suspicion and rejection. We were an island unto ourselves. And even though I had Gaspard, I never felt more alone, because he had lied to me.

Shortly after that disgrace was brought upon us, I knew I was with child. I had always imagined what I would feel when I knew that a life was growing inside of me. That all the elements of the heavens and earth were forming together in my womb to bring forth the miracle of a human being. But I could feel none of the giddy anticipation that I imagined. I only felt fear, apprehension, even, I am ashamed to say, disgust. What would come forth? Would it be a person or something else?

We carried on with our quiet lives. Slowly, my heart mended toward Gaspard. Slowly, I looked forward to the baby we had made. The full moon was the only reminder that we were not normal.

In those early months he returned scared, shivering, almost frail. I held him in the dawn light as he recovered. Sometimes I cried, quietly, for the frightened child trapped in the man's body. Sometimes for the future that would never be ours. But mostly because, in those moments, he was the most tender, the most vulnerable, the most like the Gaspard that I had fallen in love with in the woods when I was laid bare and vulnerable before him. But as the man became more like the wolf, he changed.

The changes were slight at first. Simply becoming easily irritated. Sometimes lashing out for no apparent reason. He was becoming almost cruel in ways that I had never known before. And he was eager to use the gift for its purpose. He wanted to go where the Pale-Faces were plentiful. I asked him what he wanted to do if he got near them, and he answered, 'Terrify them.' I didn't know until much later, when we finally entered the world of the Pale-Faces, that he had traveled on the nights of the moon to the closest settlements he could find, killed the livestock, destroyed the crops, and burned the houses to the ground.

22

"Our child was born, and she was perfect. She had many of the features of Gaspard, his long nose and sharp, pointed chin, but she had my eyes. I hung a dreamcatcher where she slept, hoping it would catch not only the evil dreams, but any inhuman desires, and prayed to the spirits that she would not be like us. She grew up like a normal child, and I watched as Gaspard came back. His anger and angst slipped away and was replaced by love for his daughter. He was a doting father, far more involved in the daily life of our home than most of the men in our village, who viewed the raising and caring of children, daughters especially, to lie completely in the hands of the women. But Gaspard wanted to be present for everything. He would hunt and provide for us, yet when he returned he would ask if our little Fayette, or Fay as he sometimes called her, had done anything new that day. She truly was like a little creature from the fairytales my father told me when I was small. I fell asleep to those tales again, this time told by Gaspard to our little Fay. He seemed to let go of the idea that prompted the gift's bestowal. He no longer traveled far on the nights of the full moon and discussions of the plague of the white man ceased to be. Fayette brought Gaspard back to me.

On a gloomy, downcast day when Fayette was just a young child, not quite six, I left her outside my family's longhouse with other children who were playing with cornhusk dolls. My aunt was ill, so I brought her a stew I had cooked with healing herbs. As I sat with my aunt, helping her eat, I heard a low growl. There were dogs and some tamed wolves in our village, but this growl sounded odd, like a mix between a catamount's high-pitched wail and the gruff gargle of a wolf. Then, children were screaming. I rushed out of the longhouse to see a small wolf tearing apart a little girl. The child's throat had been torn open, her face was mangled beyond recognition, and the wolf had torn into her stomach.

'Where is Fayette?' I had yelled, fearing the child being eaten by this wolf was my little girl.

I screamed and lunged at the creature and, as I did so, I felt I had turned. I tore the wolf from the body of the girl and prepared to attack again when I saw its blue eyes, confused and terrified, looking back at me.

At that moment, I knew where Fayette was.

Before I could do anything to stop him, a warrior, in one swift motion, lodged a tomahawk in her ribs, piercing her heart. We returned to our human form together as I held her in my arms. My baby, my sweet little fairy, was dead.

I found out later that the little girl had taken Fay's corn husk doll and wouldn't give it back. Fayette was a mix of both of us. She could change when she wanted like me, but the bloodlust, the craving for flesh, that was from her father. In one brief bout of uncontrolled rage, two precious little girls were gone.

Gaspard returned from hunting. I still remember his smile as he approached our little home carrying a buck over his shoulders. It was the last time I ever saw him happy. He looked around for little Fay, who always ran with outstretched arms to meet her papa. My eyes told him all he needed to know, and he fell under the weight of the deer, screams of rage and despair leaving his chest, until I believed the grief would tear his heart and I would lose them both that day.

He sat sullen and disconnected from the world as I explained what had happened. He asked me who the warrior was that had killed her. I feared telling him because I saw murder in his eyes, but he turned on me with such fierceness that I feared what he would do if I didn't tell him. He did nothing that day. Or the next. Or the next. For days and days he sat in our home, refusing to eat, sleeping only when his will to remain awake was weaker than his body's needs.

The tribe buried both the girls in the ceremonial tradition. The counsel had compassion on Fayette, knowing it was out of her control, and did not allow her victim's family to seek revenge on ours. I had grown numb watching Gaspard sink deeper into a void that I couldn't follow him into. I finally understood how my mother felt, knowing she would never see my father again, and I longed to die and escape life without Fay.

Gaspard was freed from his stupor on the night of the full moon. I heard him transform, as I had dozens of times, and expected him to vanish into the woods, and perhaps this time, never return. Instead, I heard screaming in the village, and I knew why. Gaspard had killed the warrior who threw the tomahawk. All the warriors of our tribe grabbed weapons and hunted him down. I was amazed that they caught him, but I wonder now if he had let them so there would be an end to his miserable life. They didn't wait for permission from the counsel. Every warrior hacked and hewed at him, and I watched him die over and over. He would come to life and howl and rage, and they would strike him down again. Nothing could kill him. By dawn he had returned to the form of a man, and I was sure that would be the end, that he would finally be at rest in the sleep of death. But no matter how many times they tried and how many ways they devised, he would not die.

I screamed for it to be enough. I pleaded with them to let him go; let us go. They relented and stood aside. His mangled, broken body healed rapidly, and I helped him back to our home, where we gathered all we could carry and fled. At first we went east, deeper into the mountain forests that had been my sanctuary, but Gaspard's mind had fractured in the loss of Fayette and he could never be content with our love or life again.

We traveled along the Saint Lawrence River west to the Great Lakes and attempted to assimilate into the colonies of the French. We remained by the French forts, Gaspard sometimes masquerading as a soldier, other times a trapper, but always we lived on the cusp of civilization, never truly belonging anywhere. I depended on him for everything. For two years we lived in this limbo, while Gaspard devised his ultimate plan. He would learn to change at will, as I could, and he would begin by terrorizing the settlements closest to the lakes, moving further east as the people eventually fled the wilderness. He stirred up fear with his full moon attacks, but it wasn't enough; the white men kept coming.

My job in his scheme was to collect information. Being swift and slight, I could move quickly while blending in with the forest. Gaspard, for all his wit and guile, was too cumbersome to go undetected amongst our neighbors. He called me his fantome. I existed like a ghost to the world, including Gaspard. He never saw me anymore. His vacant eyes were always looking into a future I didn't exist in. I tried to bring him back to me. I tried so many times, but I had become nothing to him. I was only useful for two things.

Those times of hostility against my flesh, when Gaspard would have me, I imagined the moor my father had described to me. The wide open, treeless landscape that looked like the sea on a stormy day. A creek running through and the heather, the purple carpet of wildflowers, that stretched to the horizon. I had only ever known the dense and endless woods cut by rivers and lakes, but I thought if I could picture the sky full of rolling clouds at dusk, when the sunset cast a purple glow, it was almost as if the moor came alive. When my body couldn't escape, I went there in my mind. I still loved Gaspard, but the man who had me was not him.

Gaspard became even more reckless. He no longer followed his own rules or plans, but feasted on any human form he came across, except children. It was the only way I knew Gaspard was still inside the monster. His love for Fayette kept him from striking down the young girls and boys that must have reminded him of her.

When he accidentally made Gregory, he was angry. As I told you, he never wanted to share his deity with another being, even me. However, when he saw what multiple monsters could do, it was as if a new passion for his mission took hold of him. He relished the idea that it was possible to pass on the gift; that he could create an army. I have already explained to you what happened those months after Gregory was turned. Between Gaspard and I, there was enmity. I didn't want to feel alone anymore, but I also knew that creating more creatures like him would be disastrous. I never shared Gaspard's disdain for the colonizers. How could we possibly know what the future would bring? I had seen peace between the tribes and the white men, and this country was big enough for all of us. Gaspard would not hear of it. I reminded him he didn't belong here either. 'Who better to drive out the white men than one of their own? I know how they think,' was his response. He asked things of me I was not willing to do, and that was when he began to threaten me.

Until then, he had borne my presence with indifference, unless he wanted to use me. But when I tried to reason with him, when I finally stood up to him, I learned why I had lost him in the first place. He blamed me for Fayette's death.

I had fought the guilt that came naturally to me. Had I been with her, I would have seen the change, and I could have calmed her or taken her away before she attacked. If I had known it was her, I wouldn't have thrown her off the other girl, and the warrior would not have killed her. If I had attacked the warrior before he could touch her with his blade, she would still be here. The accusations weren't foreign to me; I had been living with them since the day I let her die. But I had yet to hear them from Gaspard. He spoke to me as if I disgusted him. I knew, without a doubt, that he hated me. And then he told me a truth that I hadn't even acknowledged, that I never thought would be a weapon used so singularly against me since it was a fact for all mankind. He knew I could die.

Fayette had been killed with one blade stroke. She was not immortal as Gaspard appeared to be. For so long, the resentment had grown that I had passed on mortality to her when she could have lived forever with him. He told me that day that if I didn't obey, he would kill me.

At first, I welcomed the idea. What did the world have to offer me now that my child was gone and my husband reviled me? I tried to run away, yet he found me. I waited for him to strike, but he knew what I was doing, so he tortured me instead. You can't imagine what it is to be treated in that way by someone you loved so completely. It is a betrayal worse than if he had just killed me. I knew he still could, but as long as I was content with dying, he would keep me alive. I had no choice from then on but to obey his every command, knowing what came if I didn't.

To this day, I still wonder, how did it come to this? How could someone who was kind and compassionate, gentle and adoring, become a hateful, vengeful villain? I lived with the werewolf . . . but this new man—he was the monster.

My only comfort came with Matthew. He was sad and lonely. We had both lost everything. In that way, we were a solace to each other. While Gaspard raged every night, trying to become the wolf, Matthew and I waited in silence together. During the day, when Gaspard made us travel for food or information, we spoke of what our lives were before. We shared stories of the ones we had lost. We laughed and cried together, and for the first time, I could grieve.

Matthew said he couldn't let go of the guilt. He talked about the faith of his family and the promise of his religion, but he said he didn't believe that it was available to him anymore. He also shared how much he hated being pitted against his friends, but he wanted to believe that there was a purpose for the monster. Gaspard's plan gave him something to exist for. I had to tread carefully with what I said to Matthew. If Gaspard knew I tried to dissuade him from following along, he would hurt me. So I simply asked questions, hoping he would find, through the answers, that this was not the road for him. But he had already made up his mind and acknowledged what it meant to use the wolf as a weapon. His heart was broken. He saw nothing good left in the world.

There was no hope that anything would change. I watched for months as Gaspard spiraled out of control, and his yearning for destruction only increased with each new wolf created. I knew it would never end until the world was overrun with wolves, and then what would be left? I would have no place in that world. But I believed death would elude you all. That you would fight, and tear, and bite, and devour, but that come morning, you would all still be alive, and then Gaspard would have won. I knew he would never stop destroying every person you loved until there was nothing left for you but to become like him.

I watched the battle from the trees, waiting for the violence to end so I could have my only friend return to me. I watched as Fenn lashed at one of the new wolves and it didn't get back up. His human form lay still. I realized then: maybe Gaspard could be killed.

I don't know how to describe fully all the varied emotions that overcame me with that knowledge. At first I was relieved. There could be an end to all of it, and I could be free. But then I felt fear. Fear that he would win and kill the only opponents capable of subduing him. And then fear that he would die, and I would lose him irrevocably, forever. Even after all the pain, I still loved the Gaspard I knew so many years ago. That man was gone, I acknowledged, but even so, there was the smallest bit of hope that I could have him back, as long as he existed. As the battle wore on and it seemed that Gaspard would win, I knew I must not let him. I chose to let him go for good in order to stop his madness from spreading. He grabbed the other new wolf, and I had no more doubts. I lunged at him, and, perhaps for a moment, I thought he would hold back from hurting me. It was foolish to imagine him capable of mercy, but I hoped. And then he threw me into the fire. He was willing to kill anyone who was in his way. He would kill me. I attacked again. Before he tore me from his back, I felt my bite tear through his neck. After I landed on the ground, I believed I was going to die. I saw Matthew come to his senses; his heart had not turned hard and black like he claimed it was. I watched as he fought with you against Gaspard until I could no longer remain conscious and let myself slide away."

23

No one spoke when Talise finished her story. The weight of her words mixed with the smoke in the air, and I felt a heaviness descend upon us all.

"I know you will try again and I want to help you," she concluded.

I was not expecting her to so easily volunteer, especially as she was still weak from the injuries that were barely healed. I looked around the room to see how the others had reacted. Gregory betrayed a smirk on the corner of his lip. John spoke up.

"You shouldn't do that, Talise. You've risked enough already. Another trial like the one you've been through will be fatal."

"I did not say I would fight him. But I can find him." She took a deep breath and spoke in dismay, "He's still my husband."

I struggled to understand how she could feel anything but contempt for the man who had caused so much harm to all of us. I had heard of women so devoted that they would stand by their husbands in the very shadow of the gallows. After all, is that not what I had hoped Beatrice would do for me? Yet I also knew that Gaspard was in a class far beyond that of a common rogue, even beyond some of the most foul murderers. I watched the tear as it trailed down Talise's cheek and I knew I should have felt compassion. But I only wanted revenge.

All told, it was enough for me that Talise would help us find him, and I was as eager for action as Gregory had ever been.

Talise bid us goodnight. I could see exhaustion burdening her body and her feet carried her slowly to bed. While she slept, the rest of us digested the narrative.

"It's a shame what happened to the Frenchman. Can't say I feel anything for him, though. We lost people too, and we didn't leave our humanity behind," Gregory said as he stood by the fire holding a cup of ale.

"But we did not lose a child. I cannot assume I would remember what is right and good if a tragedy such as that came upon me." I was relieved that grace was winning out against the monster, and I clung to empathy as one clings to the mast in a storm. I was feeling as if I could easily be swept away.

"No, I can't say I know I wouldn't become like him. But it seems he took it too far, hurtin' Talise like that. Wasn't her fault. You can't pick what you pass on." I knew Gregory well enough, though he may have doubted it himself, to say he would not have become like Gaspard. He had made awful mistakes, but he was not a monster, and I believed he never could become one.

I noticed John sitting quietly in the corner, his hand massaging his brow, as was his habit when the wheels in his head were turning.

"You are thinking of something, Mr. Andrews." John looked up at me and left the far-away to join our conversation.

"Yes, I was considering how a court would try Gaspard's case should he ever stand trial. I shouldn't wonder if I would volunteer to defend him."

Gregory had just taken a sip of his drink and nearly spit it across the room. He swallowed before asking, "Defend that monster! Why?"

"Well, a man can only suffer so much before his mind can't handle any more. Gaspard lost his beloved daughter and then, after avenging her death, he was brutally attacked for hours for it. He may have recovered, but there is no question he felt a relentless pain and agony that no man on earth has ever sustained. He had lost everything, and the one person who should have brought succor to his wounds . . . well, his mind made her an enemy, too. What did he have left but to curse the world, curse God, and go on cursing till the end of time? Can you imagine carrying that pain with no recourse to bear up under it, no faith to give you strength, no friend or lover to share the burden? It would be hell on earth.

"I don't wonder that he has become the wolf in every way. Does it excuse what he's done? Never. I wouldn't even argue for mercy. But I would want the chance to argue that a man can only bear so much. If we aren't careful, we will make monsters out of men."

I scoffed. "Even so, he has embraced evil. He has delighted in it. And you will not have the opportunity to defend him because he will be dead." All the beneficence I had felt faded as I imagined Gaspard getting away with what he had done. The list of offenses had grown to an unimaginable ledger of atrocities.

John rose from the chair and stood alongside Gregory and I. "You're right. He may have been made, in more ways than one, into the monster, but he's still responsible." He smiled and awoke Mr. Baird, who had fallen asleep in his chair. The two left Gregory and me by the fire as they retired.

"Are we really gonna let Talise get involved in this again? She can die," Gregory spoke when he was sure no one else was about.

"So can we."

"You know it's not the same."

"No. But we have one opportunity, only one night. She can ensure that it is not wasted."

"I don't know, Fenn. Seems like more than we should ask of her."

"We did not ask."

Gregory nodded his head. I knew it was not the chivalrous

thing to do, involving Talise in our affairs, yet they were hers as much as ours. More so. We were invited into her battle, and I was more than willing to join.

As the full moon was approaching, we decided to leave the next day, back on the Mohawk Trail, hopeful that Gaspard had not traveled far or fled across the ocean. Talise was confident he would do no such thing. He coveted his power over her and would see it as a concession of defeat. I was weary of it all, but the flame of vengeance burned brightly and fueled my desire to carry on, no matter how tiresome.

With our belongings packed and our horses saddled, it was time to bid farewell to our faithful friends, who had carried a burden that was never theirs for far too long.

"I hope we meet again someday, my friends, though under better circumstances," I said as I offered my hand to John.

"It has been an adventure and I'm not sorry for having it!" he said as he shook it. "And please, be careful." His glance seemed to move involuntarily to Talise, as if admonishing me to protect her. I already felt the burden, and though I was beset with waves of turmoil, I knew I must regard her as an ally.

"Take care of yerselves, lads!" Mr. Baird added. "And let us know soon as you've overcome yer enemy. I'll hold ye up in me prayers." Mr. Baird winked and heaved himself into the saddle of his horse.

From Albany, the mortals took the road leading south while us wolves charted our course west. We took the same route to the Great Lakes that we had traveled with Colonel Bradstreet's army. This time it was quiet, and I noticed more of the natural beauty of the wilds now that thousands of soldiers were not invading the peace with their clamor. I hoped that the tranquility would be a balm for my restless soul, but the quiet would not remain as a flock of birds arrived, replacing the soldiers squabbling with their own. There were thousands, perhaps millions, roosting in the trees as we continued our way toward the Great Lakes.

"French call 'em 'passager' birds cause they just keep passin' by. They don't stay anywhere long but to nest, and then they move on, one big flock of 'em, to the next spot." Gregory was fairly yelling in order for me to hear him; the sound of the birds was deafening. Between those that were cooing, and those that were in flight, still arriving to take up what space might be left on the already crowded branches, there was no end to the noise.

"Hunted 'em a few years ago. All we had to do was shoot and we'd hit a dozen of 'em."

"I believe it!" I yelled. To my left, a large branch snapped at the weight of the birds, and the squawks and shrieks that rose from the angry horde as they sought a new place to light were almost more than I could bear. The ground under the trees was covered in dung so that nothing was left to be seen of grass or flowers that might have grown. I knew we had passed the place of our battle, but I could not decipher it from any other as it was now covered in refuse.

"How much farther, Talise?" I said, masking my impatience with the fact that I was forced to yell to be heard. We had followed her, trusting in a sense we could not access and hoping we had not been foolish. We were wide open to ambush.

"He is not far, but we must keep moving. We will reach the end of the birds and that is where we will wait," she declared, her confidence not permitting any dissension.

We traveled miles before we reached the end of the outskirts of the flock. As we steered our horses through the muck, some birds took flight, and others followed, until it seemed the horde was ready to move on once more. They darted through the trees and followed one after the other so that it appeared an undulating serpent was flying through the forest. Gregory pulled out his gun. Shooting with his left hand was still difficult for him, but as the blast sounded, a gap opened up in the sky snake and several birds fell to the ground while the rest adjusted their course. Gregory laughed heartily and motioned for my gun, but I would not hand it over. Once again, I envied his jollity, but I had need to shoot something, anything, to rid myself of the niggling craving for violence that would not let me rest. I raised the weapon, and another blast rang out, parting the flock for a moment before they filled back in, as if they were drops of water drawn together by an irresistible attraction. The thud of birds hitting the ground was like heavy rain after leaving a swollen cloud. We gathered up the catch from those two blasts and were satisfied to have a handful for each of us to dine on that night.

As the forest grew quiet once more, Talise stopped her horse and dismounted without a word. We followed suit, unloading the few belongings we had maintained over our many months of nomadic living. We had abandoned the cages in Albany, believing we had already displayed the ability to restrain the monster within, and I hoped the battle I had been waging in my mind was not an omen of something evil mounting inside of me, something that would not be so easily pushed aside.

The full moon would be the following night, so we established as comfortable a camp as possible and composed ourselves to wait.

"How do you know he'll come to us?" Gregory asked after we had consumed the roasted pigeons.

"He has been tracking us for miles," Talise said as she cleaned her knife.

Gregory looked around at the woods, confusion and disappointment written on his face. "I didn't catch that!"

"No, you wouldn't. But I know him. I know his smell. I know his breath. Once we were past the birds, it was as if the essence of him rushed upon me and I knew it all in a moment."

"What if he attacks tonight?" I asked. If he could hold the form of the wolf, he could dispatch all three of us with little effort.

"You still don't understand him, even after all I've told you.

This is more than just putting aside a nuisance. He has to win, and he can't win without a fight."

I was hesitant to rest on her assurance. The only thought keeping me from abandoning all cares and letting the monster have his way was knowing that if he won, if we let him, then Beatrice, Mary, and Matthew would have died for nothing. Nothing more than the whims of a madman.

We spent the following day in anticipation. We all tried to rest as well as we were able, knowing what the night would bring, but Gregory could not sit, his nerves driving him to pace or hew away at whatever bit of dead wood he could find. And I wrestled with thoughts, feelings, impulses that I had never known before. I wondered if the others could see the mania in my eyes. I questioned if they were truly on my side. What was happening to me? I forced myself to relive the night Matthew died with reason as my guide. Something had broken in my psyche that night, and I knew not where, when, or how it had happened. But the evil was leaking its way into my human self, and I was terrified. I resolved to defeat the villain and prayed it would be enough to silence the monster within.

"What's on your mind, Fenn? I saw you mullin' about in your head there," Gregory asked as I sat staring off into the dense wood that I thought must carry on for miles and miles.

"Nothing worth mentioning. Do not trouble yourself about me, friend. I will be alright."

Gregory slapped me on the shoulder and went about his puttering angst while Talise worked diligently, as she had been all that day, weaving rushes into what I assumed to be a rope of some sort. I knew that musing any longer would drive me further and deeper into the black hole in my soul, so I approached her instead.

"What is that for?"

"As far as I know, the wolf cannot climb a tree."

"You mean to hide away?"

"I must. He will look for me first, and he will kill me if he finds me."

I looked around the area we had made for our camp, and there was a large tree with thick branches. A notch about fifty feet in the air looked to be the perfect spot for a body to sit snuggly and watch whatever chanced to happen below. She saw where my eyes had turned.

"Yes, there."

"And the rope is so you do not fall?"

"Yes. And so I don't jump." I could see she may have been fighting her own demons since our battle with Gaspard, and I smiled in compassion, for I knew the thoughts well.

As night fell, Talise climbed into the tree, and I watched as she secured herself with the rope into the notch. She looked small and innocent as she hugged her knees to her chest and laid her head upon them.

Gregory had worn away his anxiety in hours of fretting, and he merely sat by the fire, waiting. I looked about the woods, reflecting on how different this meeting felt to the one before. Then, we were two against five. Not only were the odds against us, but we had never fought another werewolf before, yet we were full of hope, courage, and we were naïve.

The night of our second battle, I felt we were about to face the devil himself. My palms were clammy and my stomach rolled in anxious knots. I felt my breath quickening, and the short, stunted intakes made me dizzy. I bent and clasped my knees as my vision blurred, and I saw lights that were not there.

"Whoa, come on, sit down, now." Gregory was at my side, leading me to a log that had served as a chair.

"I do not know what has come over me. I have never felt this way before."

"Looks like yer having a shock, there. Close your eyes and breathe deep." I listened to my friend and gripped his hand to steady myself. He was like a rock in a stormy sea, and I clung to him while the waves tossed over me. When the feeling passed and I no longer feared that my heart would explode, I reached for the ale that Gregory held before me.

"I can't say it'll be alright. I can't say we'll win this time. But, seeing as we're all that's left, we just gotta work together. I'm here for you. You're here for me, right."

I nodded and breathed deeply one last time before I tested my legs and felt that, though weak at first, they were strong enough to hold me up. I looked at the moon, and it was nearly time. For once, I welcomed the transformation with anticipation, for I knew that when the wolf came over me, all feelings of human inadequacy and weakness would flee before the raw power and wrath of the beast.

I felt the change as it came, but there were moments, perhaps even stretches of time, where all was black and I fought for consciousness.

Gaspard was upon us shortly after we turned, and the frenzied storm of slashes and gnashing teeth commenced before darkness came over me.

I found the light. I do not know how long I had been in the dark, but when my eyes adjusted to what was before me, I saw Gregory on the ground, holding me back with his one arm. When I realized I was attacking him, I recoiled. I turned about and saw that Gaspard was rising from the ground nearby, his eyes flashing fire, fierce and menacing, as he lunged at me. I forced my mind to stay present, to refuse the beast inside that was clawing at my mind for a turn. I lunged at Gaspard, and our bodies met in a tangle of arms, legs, and snouts. My teeth found purchase on flesh, and I tore with all my might until I felt shredding to my arm like hot metal being dragged across and into it. I let go of the grip I had with my jaw and watched while Gregory recovered from my attack and flew upon Gaspard's back. The villain reached and writhed, attempting to rip his attacker from him. He would have failed had it not been for Gregory's missing arm. But soon Gregory lost hold and fell while Gaspard turned and leapt upon him. The black rose again, my vision blurred, and I grabbed my head as a rushing came over me that threatened to bring me to the ground.

"Fenn! Stay! Stay for Matthew! Stay for Beatrice!" The woman shouted over the din of growls and howls. Talise was watching over us. I remembered why I was there and who was before me. I remembered I was not the animal. I was not the monster. And I would not let the beast in.

I felt my feet planted firmly in the ground as my legs bent, and leapt with a force that I do not think I will ever muster again. I tore Gaspard from Gregory and our bodies flew through the air, landing with a hard thud on the earth by the fire. I reached for a log that stuck out and jammed the flaming end into my enemy's eye. He shrieked and howled before my teeth shredded into his face and neck, tearing away flesh.

The warm blood filled my mouth and flowed down my throat until I once again felt the power of the darkness invade my mind, and I let go of my hold over the beast. It was too strong.

I do not know how long I was in the grip of the Frenchman before Gregory threw him off me, but I came to myself to see Gaspard scramble to his feet and flee for the woods. We both gave chase until he reached the river, where he fell to the ground and struggled to crawl, his hand clutching his neck. I could hear him laughing while spitting up what I assumed to be blood, as his human form replaced that of the monster and he slid into the water. His body floated over the glistening river until slowly it sank away.

We returned as men to the fire and found Talise there. Her eyes glistened with tears, though I could see a peacefulness in them that had not been there before. Gregory and I were both covered in blood, sweat, and mud, the only clothing fit for a werewolf, but she held us both in turn. All the fight in me was spent. All the rage had been consumed. And in her arms, my body fell limp.

24

Talise left us the following morning. There was nothing left to say or do. Nothing left for her in the Great Lakes or in the world of the white man. She would return to the Mohawk, she said. We watched as she rode into the thick of the woods, where the morning dew evaporated into clouds of fog. She became a fantome, and she was gone.

Gregory and I had no plan for what would come after our trial. We knew we were still werewolves. Defeating our maker had not lifted his curse. What was worse, I knew that my hold over the monster was tenuous. Until I could be sure that I had mastered the beast, I could not remain in civilization.

"I've always wanted to go west," Gregory said, as if he knew what I was thinking.

"Well, we are already halfway there."

We did not need to debate it. We packed up what little had been our camp and loaded it into the saddlebags, continuing our way west along the Mohawk Trail.

The construction of the forts had not stalled, and there was a substantial stockade by the time we reached the Oneida Carry Place. We did not stop, even to visit the grave of my friend Mr. Ainsley, not wanting to waste daylight hours, until we reached the site of the old Fort Oswego. An abandoned bateau sat close to where our camp had been in August, and we were gratified in the good fortune of a boat of our own to carry us through the waterways of the Great Lakes. It was large enough to carry ourselves and our horses, and so we rowed across Lake Ontario until we reached the Niagara River.

I marveled at how my trials had built an endurance in me I had not known before as I kept pace with Gregory. How different one's circumstances may be in a year's time, in a dozen moons. I had time to reflect on all that had passed and what change it had brought. Disastrous change. And we were left with our grief, forced to live forever with it.

What was there worth living for, anyway? I looked at Gregory and wondered if he had asked himself the same dreadful question. We were now the only ones, besides Talise, who could put an end to each other's cursed existence, yet could we do it, even if we wanted to? I felt we were beyond the despair that would lead us to such a desperate conclusion. Though Beatrice was gone from this world, there was always that still small voice of hope that told me, by God's grace, I may yet see her again. And I had friendship, a companion who understood, and that was no small thing. Yet before us lay, as far as we knew, a half-life that would not end until the earth ceased to exist.

How does one comprehend endless days? Endless griefs. Endless longings.

My mind muddled over such things as the oar clapped the water in rhythmic regularity. Eventually, the water of the river grew too turbulent to fight against, so we found a place to bring our boat ashore and made a portage over land until we could reach a calmer portion of Lake Erie. We spent hours traversing the rocky gorge that followed the river's course, our horses maneuvering better than ourselves, when we came upon a waterfall so great I marveled at the wonder of nature before us. It was vast and turned in several directions, carving half moon shapes into the landscape, so that I could not behold all of it in one view, even at a distance. As we passed close to the thundering waterfalls that dumped their liquid cargo a hundred feet onto battered boulders, I watched as the waters churned up a milky foam rising in a veil of mist. Apart from the blue mountains of the backcountry, it was one of the most beautiful landscapes I had ever seen. It was a moment of grace, and I thanked its maker for the privilege to behold it.

Thus was the sum of our expedition, following rivers and tributaries, carrying when necessary, and sailing on Lake Erie, Lake Huron, and Lake Michigan, all of which felt like oceans. We rowed along the Illinois River until we reached the 'great river,' Mississippi. Passing French forts and settlements along the way, Gregory proved invaluable in keeping us out of the hands of our country's enemy. We posed as trappers, though the unlicensed kind they called 'coureur de bois,' a title Gregory balked at, but it was enough to remain unmolested.

Traveling down the Mississippi was the least tiresome part of our journey, for we followed the current as it carried us on and on over the muddy waters. Gregory knew of a trading post that became our destination. It was French, as everything was in that part of the new world, but he knew it was not hostile. It was far enough away from the front lines of the war and the rest of society that he believed it would suit our purpose, which was to recuse ourselves from the world and all who knew we existed.

Gregory remembered the description he had been given, years hence, by a fellow trapper of where to find the mouth of the Cumberland, the river on which the post rested. Upon reaching this tributary, we were forced once again to fight against the current until we reached the French Lick where a trader named Charleville had, decades before, set up a post to barter furs for manufactured goods.

"If it isn't already a working post, I'll make it one," Gregory boasted. He delighted in the idea of hunting the plentiful game that flocked to the salt lick and trading the furs for any comforts we could desire. We spent the next few weeks building our small cottage before the chill of winter days set in.

Gregory, of course, grew well acquainted with the French, both those from the north in Canada and the south in New Orleans, who traveled up and down the Mississippi and its tributaries. We learned a bit of their language; enough, at least, to carry on living as neighbors.

Letters arrived through these traders from Mr. Baird and John. Mr. Baird had, since we parted ways, been ordained and began serving in a new church near Staunton. John's law practice thrived with the influx of population in Williamsburg, and he hinted at a budding courtship, though he seemed pessimistic it would lead to anything substantial. The law was still his first love, so he claimed.

Though we were exiles from the world we knew, we had become part of another, and I no longer felt as though we were outcasts. We found we could still subdue the beast within, though at times I felt the tingling in my mind as the monster petitioned for its time under the moon. But there was no more malice in me to give it purchase and, apart from seasons of apathy bordering on despair, I could quiet the turmoil in me to a peaceful hum.

Our existence would be a modest one, but we were safe, and so was the world we left behind. As the new year, 1759, approached, I reflected on the contrast of the future I had hoped for versus the one that was given to me. Nothing about what lay ahead was what I had planned when I built my castle in the sky.

But as I cannot change what has befallen us, I must be content to live at peace, come what may.

EPILOGUE

In the summer of 1764, Gregory and I received information that upset the trajectory of our otherwise quiet lives.

The French we traded with did not concern themselves with the war their country had been fighting against ours for seven years, and neither had we. So when news reached our tiny outpost that the British had won the war a year hence, and a treaty had been signed granting all the land east of the Mississippi to the mother country, we took it as an afterthought; it was inconsequential to our lives. Even the proclamation forbidding settlement west of the mountains phased us not, for we knew it would hardly be enforced in our quiet neck of the woods. But what got our attention was the chatter among the traders of wolf attacks that were terrorizing a small village in France.

I would have ignored the information. Wolf attacks were common in Europe, but as the Frenchman described what he had heard from a relative who lived in the Gevaudan, I feared it was more than a natural wolf. The animal was targeting humans; killing and partially devouring them.

"Could just be coincidence. Don't see how any of it points to a werewolf," Gregory concluded when we returned from our dealings with the French to our log house on the river. I could not push aside the attacks, thinking only of how greatly they resembled our own experience, though I had tried for years to forget.

"It could be ordinary wolves, yes, but what if not? We might be the only ones who know how to kill the beast, if it is a werewolf, and we might be the only ones who can."

Gregory sighed. I knew the idea of returning to the world, France no less, and hunting a werewolf was not what he had in mind. He had enjoyed our carefree life in the wilderness, as it had been year after year, so his hesitation did not surprise me.

"I wager John and Mr. Baird have heard of this and are already collecting information. I believe there may be more to this story than merely a rogue wolf harassing a village. Maybe it is time to leave the wild and make an overdue visit to our friends in civilization," I argued. Gregory's brow furrowed as his eyes bored into mine, likely trying to determine if I was serious. When he still did not answer, I prodded again. "What say you, then? Should we venture to find out if there is something to this story?"

"Oh, why not? Let's go visit old Baird and Andrews. Whether there is anything to this, it would be nice to talk to other humans again, besides the French who we can barely understand. And I'm gettin' tired of looking at your ugly face. No offense," Gregory smirked.

With that, it was decided. We would leave our woodland refuge and return to the haunts of men, this time in pursuit of the beast of the Gevaudan.

AUTHOR'S NOTE

While this is primarily a tale of gothic horror, it is also set in a time and place in history. Writing historical fiction is an ambitious task. Not only must one create an engaging narrative, but one should also attempt to depict the setting and characters with a certain level of accuracy. It is a difficult balance to portray history accurately while also being sensitive of our modern understanding.

The 1750's of Colonial America was a world in which European colonizers and Native American tribes collided in a war over land and resources. My story has characters of various nationalities including British, French, Scots-Irish and Native American. These people had ideas about the 'other' which do not reflect our day and age, or my personal opinions and beliefs, yet in order to create a narrative based in a time in history, it is necessary to depict the characters with authenticity, being careful not to perpetuate those behaviors as acceptable.

Colonialism has become an iconic era in American history, fleshed out by holiday traditions and pop culture references. In the hopes of immersing my readers in the time, I spent hours studying the America of the French and Indian War, and while it is nowhere near a perfect depiction of the time or the people who lived in it, I attempted to remain as faithful to the truth as my research allowed.

ACKNOWLEDGMENTS

I could not have published this book without the unwavering support of my husband, Kyle. Being a creative himself, he understands the commitment it requires to take a project from idea to fruition. His encouragement and practical help are why this book is in your hands.

Next to my husband, my editor, Amy DeBoer, was indispensable. This novel has benefited from her understanding of story, her wealth of literary knowledge and her close reading skills, and would not be what it is without her.

And many thanks to my dear friends who spent their valuable time reading Lycan and giving me the courage to put it out into the world.

ABOUT THE AUTHOR

Originally from Buffalo, NY, D.L. Prohaska lives in a creative household with her husband, two children and a beloved cat in Nashville, TN. She received her BA and MA in English from Buffalo State College and uses her degrees primarily to educate her children. When she's not teaching, she spends her time reading, writing, and collecting books.

Made in United States
North Haven, CT
11 October 2023